THE COMPLETE CABALISTIC CASES OF SEMI DUAL, THE OCCULT DETECTOR, VOLUME 2: 1912–13

THE COMPLETE CABALISTIC CASES OF

SEMI DUAL

THE OCCULT DETECTOR, VOLUME 2: 1912–13

J.U. GIESY AND
JUNIUS B. SMITH

INTRODUCTION BY
GARYN ROBERTS, PH.D

ALTUS PRESS
2016

© 2016 Steeger Properties, LLC, under license to Altus Press • First Edition—2016

EDITED AND DESIGNED BY
Matthew Moring

ASSOCIATE EDITOR
Ray Riethmeier

PUBLISHING HISTORY
"Introduction" appears here for the first time. Copyright © 2016 Garyn Roberts. All
  Rights Reserved.
"The Purple Light" originally appeared in the October 5, 12, and 19, 1912 issues of
  The Cavalier magazine (Vol. 20, No. 4–Vol. 21, No. 2). Copyright © 1912 by The
  Frank A. Munsey Company.
"The Master Mind" originally appeared in the January 25, 1913 issue of *The Cavalier*
  magazine (Vol. 25, No. 1). Copyright © 1913 by The Frank A. Munsey
  Company.
"Rubies of Doom" originally appeared in the July 5 and 12, 1913 issues of *The
  Cavalier* magazine (Vol. 30, Nos. 3 & 4). Copyright © 1913 by The Frank A.
  Munsey Company.
"About the Author: Dr. J.U. Giesy" originally appeared in the February 14, 1931
  issue of *Argosy* magazine (Vol. 218, No. 6). Copyright © 1931 by The Frank A.
  Munsey Company. Copyright renewed © 1958 and assigned to Steeger
  Properties, LLC. All rights reserved.
"About the Author: Junius B. Smith" originally appeared in the February 21, 1931
  issue of *Argosy* magazine (Vol. 219, No. 1). Copyright © 1931 by The Frank A.
  Munsey Company. Copyright renewed © 1958 and assigned to Steeger
  Properties, LLC. All rights reserved.

THANKS TO
Everard P. Digges LaTouche

ISBN
978-1-61827-236-2

Visit *altuspress.com* for more books like this.
Printed in the United States of America.

TABLE OF CONTENTS

INTRODUCTION

GARYN ROBERTS, PH.D.

THE SECOND VOLUME of *The Complete Cabalistic Cases of Semi Dual, The Occult Detector* is in your hands! Subsequent introductions and volumes are already underway. The excitement is building in the series, and hardcore fans and scholars (including one whose initials are "Rick Lai") have politely encouraged.

As we further pursue the adventures of J.U. Giesy and Junius B. Smith's Occult Detector, and the historical and literary context that explains those adventures, hearty acknowledgement is made to Terence E. Hanley and his impressive, detailed and very accurate on-line *Tellers of Weird Tales* (tellersofweirdtales. blogspot.com/2013/04/ju-giesy-1877-1877-1947.html). Other acknowledgments are found at the end of this introduction. More will follow in future volumes.

MORE HISTORICAL CONTEXT
FOR 1912 AND 1913

AMIDST all the world news of 1912 and 1913, baseball seemed to permeate most every aspect of life during this era. Feats of pitching and hitting, and unique plays on the field (including types and sorts of double and triple plays) captured many people's attentions. This time frame is remembered for the founding and early days of the Boy Scouts of America and the Girl Scouts of America. And, of course, the tragedy of the

H.M.S. *Titanic* is recounted and continued in very pointed and emotionally charged detail.

Silent film (with historic origins back to the 1890s) is coming into its own, and on June 8, 1912, Carl Laemmle incorporates Universal Pictures. On September 23, Mack Sennet presents the first Keystone Cops short. This film is entitled *Cohen Collects a Debt*. December 23, just in time for Christmas, the "Keystone Cops" film, *Hoffmeyer's Legacy,* debuts. Others followed, including *The Bangville Police* (April 24, 1913). (Sometimes "Keystone Cops" was spelled "Keystone Kops.")

On October 26, the Woolwich Tunnel under the Thames River opened. With this opening the Scientific Romances of Jules Verne, H.G. Wells, Edward Page Mitchell and others became reality.

February 19, 1913, the first prize was included in a Cracker Jack Box. Frederick William Rueckheim first presented the popcorn confection that would eventually become commercially marketed as "Cracker Jack" at the Columbian Exposition of the 1893 World's Fair (in Chicago).

Other famous personalities of the era included Jim Thorpe, Pablo Picasso, George Bernard Shaw, Charlie Chaplin, John D. Rockefeller, Woodrow Wilson, Mahatma Gandhi, and lots of baseball players.

Racial references are found throughout the history of popular fiction. Sometimes, in the historical context of any given era, these references are considered acceptable—sometimes, they even *are* acceptable, then and now. Sometimes, however, these references were and are *never* acceptable. Lots of complex considerations regarding history, generalizations, categorizations, intent, "truths," "fallacies," and "mythology" are in play.

Spring 2015 there is a prolific television advertisement for lawn-care products. The spokesman for these products is a detailed, carefully constructed stereotype—he is a rather short, medium-sized young man—maybe 25 years of age—who has beautiful, bright reddish-orange hair, and who speaks in a very lyrical Irish/Scottish brogue. His name is "Scottie," and he shills for Scots Lawn Products. Probably, very few people object to the very stereotypic nature of "Scottie" the mascot. Yet, who knows what future generations will think about our now, present-day culturally specific Scottie?

Early adventures of Semi Dual in 1912 and '13 make occasional racial references to "Japs," Germans, Jews, and others. These very likely served as popular story conventions that helped readers relate to the worlds created by Giesy and Smith. Most writers and readers of 1912 and '13 probably did not give much thought to these references.

Today—and thankfully and appropriately so—we are much more sensitive to such stereotypes—broad generalizations and categorizations—and perhaps just a little more intellectual and fair about these portrayals. Let's hope.

So, racial references and stereotypes are part of Semi Dual stories. These adventures also feature some then contemporary views of gender rôles, and other demographic characterizations such as occupation, age, education, social class and so on. One hundred years later, we appreciate these portrayals for what they were and were not. The biggest stereotype of the long-running Semi Dual saga is, of course, the title character himself. As we read further into the collected Semi Dual series, we learn more about the mysterious and stereotypic central character.

MORE ON THE AUTHORS

THANKS to pulp magazine and genre fiction scholars Terence E. Hanley and Robert Weinberg, and other sources, more details are falling into place regarding the lives and careers of J.U. Giesy and Junius B. Smith.

J(ohn) U(lrich) Giesy was born near Chillicothe, Ross County, Ohio (August 6, 1877) and died in Salt Lake City, Utah (September 8, 1947). His was both a physician and a successful and prolific author. As a contributor to pulp magazine fiction, Giesy wrote for, among a number of others, *All-Story, Argosy, Adventure, The Cavalier, Romance, Snappy Stories, Street & Smith's Love Story Magazine, Top-Notch*, and *Weird Tales*.

In 1914, Giesy had his four-part serial, "All for His Country," published. In 1915, this serial was published as a hardcover novel. The circumstances, content and public reception of this novel will be discussed in the third volume of Semi Dual stories assembled by Altus Press. The Semi Dual stories reprinted in that next volume are contemporary with Giesy's serial and novel, *All for His Country*.

Some of J.U. Giesy's best-remembered single-authored stories are part of the following three series:

White Kate:
"The Blue Bomb" *(The Cavalier,* November 8, 15 and 22, 1913), 3-part serial
"House of the Hawk" *(All-Story Weekly,* June 12, 19, 26, and July 3, 1915), 4-part serial

Professor Zapt:
"Indegestible [sic] Dog Biscuits" *(All-Story Weekly,* July 3, 1915), 1-shot[1]
"Zapt's Repulsive Paste" *(All-Story Weekly,* November 29, 1919), 1-shot
"Blind Man's Bluff" *(All-Story Weekly,* January 24, 1920), 1-shot
"The Wicked Flea" *(Weird Tales,* October 1925), 1-shot

Jason Croft:
"Palos of the Dog Star Pack" *(All-Story Weekly,* July 13 to August 10, 1918), 5-part serial
"The Mouthpiece of Zitu" *(All-Story Weekly,* July 5 to August 2, 1919), 5-part serial
"Jason, Son of Jason" *(All-Story Weekly,* April 16 to May 21, 1921), 6-part serial

---

1 NOTE: *The writer of this intro/essay has not seen the table of contents page for* All-Story Weekly, *July 3, 1915, but all indications are that Giesy's fourth and last installment of the White Kate serial "House of the Hawk" appeared in the same issue as Giesy's one-shot Professor Zapt tale, "Indegestible Dog Biscuits."*

There were many more, and these will be explored in future introductions to the Altus Press Semi Dual volumes. To get details regarding publication appearance exact (as we know, information on the internet, no matter how well intended, needs to be checked and cross-checked for accuracy), copies or facsimile images of the once prolific, now obscure original Munsey *All-Story* pulps—and other pulps of the era—need to be consulted.

Junius B(ailey) Smith (1883 to 1945) was born in Salt Lake City when Utah was still a territory, not yet a state. His grandfather was a brother of Joseph Smith, the founder of the Mormonism. Junius was an attorney by trade. He supplemented his income by writing for the pulps. Most often this writing was done in collaboration with J.U. Giesy, and, as Giesy's co-author, Smith was prolific.

On several occasions, Junius B. Smith published work as a single author. *The Cavalier* included the author's "A Study in Somnolism" in its November 2, 1912 issue. This appeared a couple of issues after the conclusion of Smith and Giesy's fourth Semi Dual serial, "The Purple Light" (reprinted in this volume).

Street & Smith publishers' legendary, uneven, relatively short-lived, yet fun *The Thrill Book* featured Junius B. Smith's "Unexpected" in its September 1, 1919 issue.

Junius B. Smith had three pieces printed in *Weird Tales*. "The Man Who Dared to Know" appeared in the April 1924 issue; "An Arc of Direction" is found in the June 1925 installment of "The Unique Magazine." *Weird Tales'* August 25, 1925 issue printed a letter from Smith.

REVIEW OF THE FIRST THREE STORIES

"The Occult Detector" (*The Cavalier*, February 17 and 24, March 2, 1912)—3-part serial

A brief tangent:

Rex Stout was born December 1, 1886 in Noblesville, Indiana. He died October 27, 1975. Stout began professionally selling his stories to the early pulp magazines about 1910. This early work was often published in Munsey magazines—some of the very same magazines where J.U. Giesy and Junius B. Smith were first published at roughly the same time. By 1912, when Giesy and Smith's Semi Dual debuted and began a prolific first year, Rex Stout had to have been aware of his contemporaries in the Munsey pulps, and he probably was specifically aware of the prolific Giesy and Smith. Some of Stout's earliest stories have been collected in a variety and sundry places. Some have not, and some are believed lost.

Of course, despite a range of very readable stories before, during and since, Rex Stout is best remembered for his Nero Wolfe Mystery series. The Nero Wolfe series (1934 to 1975) is legendary, and great fun. Interestingly, when the first Wolfe story appeared in 1934—the novel, *Fer-De-Lance*—the Hard-Boiled/Private Eye/Gumshoe Detective had been developed and made archetype in Captain Joseph T. Shaw's editorial work for *(The) Black Mask* in the 1920s. Of course, the Classical/Locked-Room/Armchair Detective story had been around for decades by that time. Tales of Stout's Wolfe were the epitome of both then very different, seemingly contradictory Mystery formulas. The title character, the physical and intellectual behemoth, Nero Wolfe (the Classical Detective) was accompanied by his gumshoe partner, Archie Goodwin (the Private Investigator). (Probably only coincidentally, there is a character named "Archie" in early Semi Dual stories.)

Wolfe and Goodwin's exploits are often set in and characterized by Nero Wolfe's Brownstone building—from where Wolfe rarely travels—and all that building's features, neatly detailed and referenced by Stout. Among these details is the roof garden, replete with Wolfe's collection of the world's most exotic orchids. These prove an eccentric avocation and obsession for a man who himself is eccentric and obsessive, and these plants figure in more than one of the Nero Wolfe stories. Details regarding Wolfe's Brownstone home continue to unfold with the advent of ensuing Nero Wolfe mysteries.

Now, let's go back more than 20 years to the publication debut of Semi Dual in "The Occult Detector." Rex Stout's contemporaries of the early 1910s, Giesy and Smith, introduce us readers to Semi Dual by, in part, describing the psychic detective's home. The authors describe newspaperman Glace's first encounter with Semi Dual. Glace takes an express elevator to the 20th floor of the Urania, and climbs further staircases upward. Glace was later given the first name "Gordon."

Glace asks, "Mr. Dual, if your mission is to help others, why do you remove yourself so completely from their midst?" The newspaperman continues, "This manner of dwelling which you possess—this taking of a roof for a home. I admit it is charming, the garden alone is wonderful." (vol. 1, p. 8) Semi Dual's responses are detailed and powerful, and are found early in the first serial. We begin to learn of the 20th floor of the Urania Building (sometimes "Tower"). As the Semi Dual saga moves forward, we readers increasingly learn more about the psychic detective's home. The first serial concludes with a Classical Mystery ending, with the detective hero detailing the specifics of the crime and revealing the ultimate perpetrator.

"The Significance of the High 'D'" *(The Cavalier,* March 9, 16 and 23, 1912)—3-part serial

The first installment of the second Semi Dual serial follows right after the first serial ends. In fact, it begins in the very next issue of *The Cavalier.* In the beginning of "The Significance of the High 'D'" we find the physician and title character engaged in some scientific experiments. The origin and mysterious nature of Semi Dual begins to become clearer, the second adventure of "The Occult Detector" immediately pulls us in. Newspaperman Glace is waiting at the Police Station as a man named "Sheldon" is brought in as a prisoner. Setting, strong characterizations and well-written dialogue really help develop the mystery.

The "Newspaperman as Detective" plot motif—very popular in pulp magazine Detective Fiction of the first half of the 20th Century—works well here. A significant percentage of pulp magazine writers either worked, or had worked, as newspaper reporters. (For example, one of the most famous scribes of Detective Fiction with newspaper experience was *The Shadow's* Walter B. Gibson. There were many others.) This situation provided pulp authors with a way of life they could incorporate into their storylines. And, among other things, the early multi-part Semi Dual stories read as full-length Mystery novels. The invention of each of these stories, of course, is the title character and his often-unorthodox methods of detection. At the end of "The Significance of the High 'D'" there is foreshadowing suggesting that Newspaperman Glace may increasingly, in up-coming adventures, become better titled "Detective Glace."

"The Wistaria Scarf" *(The Cavalier,* June 1, 8 and 15, 1912)— 3-part serial

A very effective story continuity is found at the beginning of the third Semi Dual serial. The Sheldon Family—central to "The Sign of the High 'D'"—is referenced, and is continued as part of the larger, ongoing story. This third serial further details Semi Dual and recurring supporting characters. The result is that the reader is further invested in a Dickensian soap opera, of sorts. With this story, J.U. Giesy and Junius B. Smith provide a sort of cosmopolitan quality (via Persia, Russia and Germany) for the title character and his story. We are also taken to Semi Dual's ancestral palace and heritage.

If you do own and have not read Altus Press' *The Complete Cabalistic Cases of Semi Dual, The Occult Detector, Volume 1,* you need to get this immediately.

ABOUT THE COVER ILLUSTRATION
FOR VOLUME ONE

The cover illustration for the first volume of Altus Press' *The Complete Cabalistic Adventures of Semi Dual, The Occult Detector* is based upon a painting by P.J. Monahan. P(atrick) J(ohn Sullivan) Monahan was born January 4, 1882 in Des Moines, Iowa. He died less than 50 years later on November 1, 1931 in Woodcliff Lake, New Jersey. Yet his beautiful and prolific cover art for many, many pulp magazines, and a diverse range of other places, belies his relatively short lifespan. We can be thankful that some excellent and detailed scholarship related to the life and works of Monahan has been produced throughout the decades following his passing. Chief among this scholarship is a two-part feature done for *ERBzine* (volumes 1671 and 1672: www.erbzine.com/mag16/1671.html), an online source entitled *Pulp Artists* (www.pulpartists.com/Monahan.html), and work by one of the world's greatest authorities on pulp magazine art—my good friend, David Saunders.

Monahan's paintings graced the covers of some of the giants of pulp magazine history. The artist's résumé includes work for *All-Story, Amazing, Argosy, Blue Book, Cavalier, Fantastic Adventures, Red Book, Thrilling Adventure Stories,* and other periodicals from the Frank Munsey, Hugo Gernsback, and Street & Smith stables. Perhaps his best remembered pulp magazine cover art was that which illustrated Edgar Rice Burroughs' creations and storylines.

P.J. Monahan provided cover art for non-pulp magazine projects, as well. His artistry appeared on the covers of "slick" magazines such as *Cosmopolitan, The Ladies' Home Journal, Liberty, Pearson's Magazine,* and others. It appeared in books and catalogues. Monahan provided the cover and eight interiors for his friend's—Jack London's (1876–1916)— first edition episodic adventure novel, *Smoke Bellow* (published by the Century Company in 1912). The artist's work appeared on movie posters, a range of other posters, and more. We are left to wonder, "What would P.J. Monahan done if he had had 20 or 30 more years?"

All of this is to provide a little bit of context and explanation for the cover for Altus Press' *Semi Dual*, volume one. That cover illustration comes from *The Cavalier*, dated Saturday, December 20, 1913. It illustrates the one-shot Semi Dual adventure, "The Ghost of a Name." Now, here is the thing. When the first *Semi Dual* serial was published by Munsey in 1912, there was no cover art that illustrated the stories, much less the title character. This was a common situation. Consider the first several installments of Street & Smith's *The Shadow*. It was months before an image of the Shadow appeared on his magazine's cover—that image was still to be finalized. So, Altus Press' selection of P.J. Monahan's image of the psychic detective for the first collection is not only well chosen, it is excellent. As the series moves along, the Occult Detector is regularly depicted on the covers of the pulps in which he appears. Subsequent Altus Press Semi Dual volumes will reproduce those images.

A PREVIEW OF STORIES FOUR, FIVE AND SIX

"The Purple Light" *(The Cavalier,* October 5, 12 and 19, 1912) 3-part serial

J.U. Giesy and Junius B. Smith neatly carry forward the continuity of the cabalistic cases of their occult detector in "The Purple Light." The author's latest installment references Glace's first encounter with Semi Dual, and the fruit juice elixir. It also reminds the reader already familiar with Dual of, or introduces the new reader to, the unique nature of Semi Dual's elaborate abode on top of Urania Tower. Once again, the home of Rex Stout's Nero Wolfe—introduced two decades after the first mention of the Urania Tower—comes to mind. Giesy and Smith write:

[Semi Dual] dwelt on the roof of one of the largest office buildings, in the tower of which he had fitted up sumptuous quarters. Here he had made himself a wonderful garden of flowers, potted shrubs, and climbing vines, the whole roofed in winter by a curved dome of glass and steel. Thus he dwelt apart from man, yet in touch with his every activity. To me [Glace] Semi Dual seemed to be rather incarnated mind than man in the ordinary sense.

More on this fourth serial, and serials five and six, in Altus Press' Semi Dual, Volume 3. In "The Purple Light," Giesy and Smith increasingly attempt to tie the metaphysical, psychological and more speculative sciences with tangible "hard sciences." (As was the case in volume one, as the introducer of this volume, I do not want to spoil storylines and give away secrets before readers complete the stories of Semi Dual for themselves.)

"The Master Mind" *(The Cavalier,* January 25, 1913) 1-shot

The Sheldon family is back, as is Gordon Glace, and the bank provides, as it has in the past, the opening setting. Interestingly, Chapter Two is entitled "Golden Nasturtiums." Rex Stout titled one of his Nero Wolfe books *Black Orchids* (1942). (The title novella, originally published in *The American Magazine* in 1941, is one of two Stout mysteries collected in that book.)

"Rubies of Doom" *(The Cavalier,* July 5 and 12, 1913) 2-part serial

On a steamboat from New Orleans destined for St. Louis and points west, Gordon Glace, his new wife, Connie, and Semi Dual, the Occult Detector make an odd trio. In Old Wild West fashion, a crooked card game starts the conflict on the steamer. Glace, Connie and Dual witness the altercation. As a sort of an aside, Glace explains that he is no longer a reporter on the

Record. He is now the senior partner of the private inquiry bureau, "Glace and Bryce." The bureau is located on the 7th floor of the Urania Building. (Remember that Semi Dual lives on the 20th floor of the same building.)

Back on the steamboat the situation is rather strange—even for those already familiar with the relationship between Gordon Glace and Semi Dual—because the young couple on honeymoon bring Glace's friend and accomplice, Psychological Physician Semi Dual, with them. The trio continues their travels reminiscent of Mark Twain in real history and in fiction. Chapter Two is entitled "Innocence [not "Innocents"] Abroad." Certainly the reference here was not lost on readers of 1912. Mark Twain (pseudonym for Samuel Clemens) had died just two years earlier in 1910.

Interestingly, the unlikeable card sharp at the beginning of "Rubies of Doom" is named "Isaac Swartzberg." Were J.U. Giesy and Junius B. Smith reflecting, in stereotype, animosity for German types that would be outright villains a few years later in The Great War (later deemed "World War I")?

One thing is certain—Giesy and Smith worked very well together as co-authors, and had a unique ability to plot and interweave storylines. The ongoing adventures of Semi Dual continued to build and increase (in a good way) in complexity.

BY NOW, readers who bought in from the start with the first installment of "The Occult Detector" serial were assuredly hooked and wanted more. New readers could "jump in" at any point and not be lost. However, without doubt, those new readers wanted to find those previous Semi Dual adventures and looked forward to those upcoming. As do we, in Altus Press' third volume of *The Complete Cabalistic Cases of Semi Dual, The Occult Detector, Volume 3!*

Future introductions for the Semi Dual reprints will feature all kinds of "neat" details and considerations including more historical, cultural and literary context for each subsequent story, more biography of authors J.U. Giesy and Junius B. Smith;

further consideration of the Munsey, Street & Smith, and other pulps that were part of the authors' world; and details regarding publication history. We will also consider how Giesy and Smith may have been influenced by a range of other authors (some from the pulps, some before that era), and how Giesy and Smith may have influenced other writers. More information will be gleaned from Terence E. Hanley's work, and other newly discovered sources. And a detailed (maybe even annotated) Works Cited page/Bibliography of material about J.U. Giesy and Junius B. Smith, Semi Dual, and related relevant topics will be presented. This pulp archaeology, pioneered by scholars including Gene Christie and John Locke, is underway and continuing.

If you, our valued reader, have any suggestions or information for consideration for upcoming introductions to the Altus Press Semi Dual series, please contact garynroberts@yahoo.com. These are appreciated and will be appropriately cited.

In the meantime, a few important acknowledgements cannot wait. Sincere thanks for unique information, collegiality and friendship are extended to Terence Hanley and Rick Lai. Thanks for the good information, Terence, and thanks for the good questions and insight, Rick. Thanks to John Locke and Gene Christie (who have already done some groundbreaking research on the late 19th and early 20th century Munsey pulps), and that stalwart Walker Martin, too. Sincere appreciation is also extended to Virginia Woods Roberts, one helluva public library director, accomplished researcher, and partner. Thank you to the Minocqua Public Library (WI) and the Rhinelander Public Library (WI)—ports in a storm during my geographical moving.

IV

THE PURPLE LIGHT

CHAPTER I

SUICIDE OR MURDER?

Note: Purple light being the highest in the spectrum is regarded by occultists as the highest auric color—that given off by the purest and most highly developed souls. Being of very intense vibratory rate, its effect is to stimulate mental activity in certain directions. On a material nature, its effect would not be wholly agreeable.

IT WAS PICKING up a medical magazine in a street car which sent me to Semi Dual that night. I suppose some doctor must have dropped it on the seat. I was on my way to the *Record* office, and chanced to see the book where it lay. I picked it up and idly turned its pages, and then all at once I stopped, as a title caught my eye: "Use of Fruit Juices in Typhoid."

I read the article, and as I read I grinned. So the profession was coming around to an agreement with Dual. I remembered the peculiar beverage with which he had refreshed me on my first visit. He had told me it was a mixture of preserved juices of fruits.

Natural association of ideas made me think it would be a pleasure to show him this article. I looked at my watch. I still had time; I had been out on an assignment which might take one or five hours, according to circumstance. I decided that I would call upon my friend.

To you who have followed the adventures of Semi Dual, this will convey all that is necessary. But for the benefit of those who are not acquainted with the wonderful intelligence which we knew as the "occult detector," let me state he was a man of remarkable mental attainments, who applied his knowledge of what is commonly called esoteric philosophy to the straightening out of the kinks and tangles of mortal mundane life. Many people would have called him a mystic; in reality he was an exponent of the higher universal laws, which few of us recognize, let alone use.

He dwelt on the roof of one of our largest office buildings, in the tower of which he had fitted up sumptuous quarters. Here he had made himself a wonderful garden of flowers, potted shrubs, and climbing vines, the whole roofed in winter by a curved dome of glass and steel. Thus he dwelt apart from man, yet in touch with his every activity. To me Semi Dual seemed to be rather incarnated mind than man in the ordinary sense.

I left the car at the next corner and turned toward the Urania Building, where Semi had his unusual abode. I was glad of the chance of a few minutes with him. Since the affair of the Wistaria Scarf I had not seen much of the man, save at long intervals. It had been a hard, hot season, with little spare time for me. I looked up to the dark heights of the building.

Passing into the marble corridor, I waited beside the bronze grill of the shaft for a car. It came, and I went up to the top floor, turned up the great staircase, which led to Dual's domain, and was soon treading my way across the prismatic surface of the illuminated annunciator plate, sniffing the odor of cool growing things from the plants and flowers of the garden, which Semi kept ever green. The chimes of the annunciator bells broke on the night soft and low, and a moment later Semi's own voice, itself bell-like, reached my ear:

"This way, friend Glace."

I turned aside at the sound and saw him at some distance, reclining upon a bench beneath a small flowering shrub. There was a small, shaded reading-lamp affixed to one end of the bench or couch. The concentrated light from this struck down upon his face and the book which now lay in his lap. I say lap, because he was clad in a flowing robe of peculiar texture and purest white color, save for a purple edging on collar, hem, and cuffs, which enveloped him from head to heels.

As I approached he looked up and smiled, then swung his feet to the floor.

"There is something in the rhythm of Persian poetry which accords with the night and the moon," he remarked, *apropos* of the book in his lap. "And the light of interest is in your eyes."

I drew up a small footstool, got out my magazine, and explained.

Semi Dual put out a hand and took the pamphlet, glancing over the indicated page. He handed it back with another smile.

"Little by little the children of men shall learn the truth," said he.

"I thought it would interest you," I suggested.

"It does," said Semi Dual. "Any advance of man interests me, my friend."

"Also," I went on, "while I do not fancy that I'm getting typhoid, still—"

"Prevention is a good thing," smiled Semi. "Henri has several bottles on ice. Wait."

He put out a hand and pressed some unseen button, and presently Henri appeared coming down the path with a tray in his hands.

"I have things rather convenient here," Dual observed in answer to my unspoken question. "I can get anything I want by pressing the button in the back of the bench a certain number of times."

Henri approached, and in a few minutes I sat with a glass of the delicious beverage in my hand, the ice in the tall crystal tinkling musically against the sides. Dual sipped at his own glass slowly.

"It's a good while since you have favored me," he accused.

"I've been busy, Dual—on the go."

"You will be again," said Semi Dual, holding his glass up to the moon.

"Of course. In the newspaper game one expects to be."

"To-night, I think," my friend went on. "There's violence of some sort in the air. I can often sense such things."

"And it affects me?" I questioned, remembering that other time when he had told me that I was to be sent on a case, the first time we had ever met.

"Indirectly," said Dual. "Suppose we find out." He set down his glass, reached up, and switched off the light above his head.

So for a time we sat in silence, Dual lying relaxed against the back of the seat, eyes closed, seeming hardly to breathe; myself, sitting rigidly erect, with my eyes on the face of my strange companion, marveling how he got his results, which seemed to be infallibly correct.

The roof was shrouded in dusk, save for the faint light of a moon which flitted back of some black clouds. There was an electric something in the air which accorded well with Dual's statement that violence was abroad. Gradually I became aware of a peculiar sensation tickling its way up my spine and of a marked contraction of my scalp. The whole situation was beginning to get badly on my nerves when, without warning, Semi suddenly came back to life, and, straightening, rose to his feet.

"I was right," he announced. "Come! You must go to the tower and call your office on my wire. Unless I mistake, Smithson wants you badly, and there is no time to lose."

"What's—" I began, but Semi shook his head and moved off.

I followed meekly, as he walked with rapid strides to the tower and led me across the reception-room to his office. He went immediately to his desk, opened a door in one end, and dragged out a phone, which he handed to me.

I lifted the receiver from the hook. In a moment I had the *Record* office and asked for Smithson himself.

"Hello! What—" came his voice to my ear.

"Glace," I threw back.

"Thank the Lord!" cried Smithson. "I've been wishing you were here."

"What's up?" I interrupted.

"Plenty," snapped my city editor. "There's a murder or suicide at the Virginia Apartments—middle-aged woman, name of Matilda Greenig. I sent Grant down; but you get on the case as soon as you can. Where are you now?"

"At the Urania, but I'm off," I returned, as I jambed the receiver back on the hook and set down the phone.

"You sure were right," I told Dual as I turned for the door. "It's violence, all right, and I'll be busy I expect. Maybe I'll see you pretty soon again."

"You will," smiled Semi. "One moment. Did you get the name of the deceased?" There was a twinkle in his eye.

Once more he was at his trick of reading my thoughts, and I grinned as I turned away. "It was—" I began, and then paused deliberately.

"Thanks," said my friend, still smiling, "I merely wanted to concentrate your mind on the name, Gordon. You had better hurry along. Mrs. Matilda Greenig may prove an interesting case.

His ability was uncanny. I turned away without a word and hurried forth into the darkness of the roof.

I lost no time in getting to the Virginia. It was an up-to-date pile of apartments, located some little way from the center of town, near a small park. Well-to-do people dwelled there, and a rather exclusive atmosphere was maintained. In view of the fact that I was getting a late start and could expect to find the detectives and police already on the field, I took a taxi and was whirled to the scene of the tragedy as fast as the chauffeur would consent to go.

At the Virginia I dismissed my driver and, turning to the chauffeur of the motor patrol which was standing at the curb, I asked him the number of the apartment I was to seek.

He knew me well and replied promptly: "Ground floor, front."

As I pushed into the entrance-hall, the sound of heavy voices came from behind the door on my right. Without waiting I tried the door of the suite on that side, found it unlocked, and in a moment had entered the apartment.

The room where I stood was a sort of parlor. Back of this was a dining-room from which opened a number of doors. One of these was open, and I could see the backs of several men as I crossed toward it from the front. On reaching the doorway I could look into a fairly large bedroom and size up the condition of affairs.

Several policemen and detectives, an inspector, and a few newspapermen, Grant among them, first caught my eye. My next glance fell upon the figure of a girl in a nurse's uniform, sitting upon a chair near an open window, through which fanned a slight breeze. What attracted my attention mainly was a look of unmistakable horror graven upon the woman's face. The next moment Grant caught sight of me and beckoned me to approach. I crossed the floor and shouldered my way among the men.

On the bed in one corner of the room was stretched the body of a woman of perhaps fifty-five, to judge by appearances. She had been a frail little woman, and sickness seemed to have wasted her greatly of late. Her face was sunken, and her hands shriveled almost into claws. But the thing which drew and held my eyes with a morbid fascination was a dark splotch on the white sheets—a splotch which came from under her arm and dwindled into an irregular triangle as it crept to the edge of the bed and over its side to widen again upon the floor. I knew that splotch was blood. In making it, the frail life of the little woman had been used. It began to look to me as if, after all, this was a case of suicide.

Grant started to whisper in my ear. "They found a knife—one the nurse says was the woman's own penknife—on the bed beside her other hand, the right one. It was open, and the little blade was blood-stained, as were the fingers of that hand. It looks like she did it herself, Glace."

I nodded. "How long have you been here?" I asked.

"Not over five minutes," he answered. "Smithson must have found you almost as soon as I left."

"What are they waiting for?" I inquired, struck by the inactivity of all in the room.

"For the doctor," said Grant. "They've sent for her own physician, or rather the nurse did before I arrived."

Dean, of the *Dispatch*, pushed his way to my side. "Hello," he greeted. "I guess the old girl did for herself while the nurse was out. I've been talking to the girl, and she says she went for a walk, and found things like this when she got back. What do you think?"

I shook my head. I had been looking at the quiet, refined face of the figure on the bed. Somehow it seemed hard to connect it with any preconceived notions of self-murder, for even in death it was strong. I edged in closer and spoke to Bryce, the inspector, who stood near the bed: "Found anything besides the knife?"

He glanced up, and made a negative sign. "Nothing, Glace. At present we're waiting for a doctor and the coroner, who have been sent for, before making any systematic search."

I nodded, and leaned still closer to the bed and the thin, pale face. Now I could see the red in the dark splotch on the sheet, in the middle of which lay the slender arm of the woman. Back in the corner of the room the air from the open window was scarcely felt because of the clustering figures, and as I bent over the quiet body it seemed that I sensed a difference—a subtle something in the atmosphere.

Bending even closer, I scanned her face, and all at once I noticed what seemed a slight unnaturalness in the color of the skin about the tip of the nose and the lips. I motioned the inspector to my side and pointed. "Looks like it had been almost blistered," I said.

Bryce stooped low and scrutinized the skin carefully. "That's right," he admitted, with interest. "Now, what do you suppose could have done that?"

I did not offer any attempted explanation; but as we leaned above the bed it seemed to me that I again sensed the difference in the air of that part of the room. I sniffed slightly. "Notice anything in the air—any odor?" I questioned Bryce.

He shook his head. "Don't get it," he replied.

I was standing nearer the head of the bed than he, and we were both leaning forward with our hands on the edge. Now as we straightened there came a little thud, as though some light object had dropped to the floor.

Stooping, I glanced under the edge of the bed. Almost at once a small glass vial caught my eye. It was the size supposed to hold two ounces, and lay in full sight upon the rug, where it had evidently just fallen from above. I got down and fished it out.

All at once the strange, illusive odor grew stronger, became recognizable. Instinctively I raised the open end to my nose.

Then I was sure what it was.

The bottle had held chloroform!

CHAPTER II

INCRIMINATING ADMISSIONS

AS LUCK WOULD have it, I had picked the thing up by the neck; though I confess I did not think of that at the time. Still holding it, I turned and thrust it under Bryce's nose.

His eyes widened in surprise, and after his first involuntary start he sniffed excitedly at the narrow neck. Then he lifted his head and looked me full in the eye.

"It was under the bed," I explained. "It must have slipped down back of the mattress and so been overlooked. It was loosened when we took our hands off the edge, and I heard it drop."

Bryce's eyes narrowed, and he nodded comprehension as he turned to the rest of the men, who were pushing forward, attracted by our actions.

"It's murder, all right," he announced with conviction. Back of the semicircle of men I distinctly heard the sound of a gasp from the nurse. A moment later there was a ring at the bell.

A dark man with black imperial entered the room carrying a small black bag. He was followed by the nurse who had answered his ring.

During the interruption caused by his arrival I was seized by an impulse, and acted upon it at once. Every one was inspecting the man as he entered, and I was unobserved. I slipped the bottle into my pocket, where I hoped that it might be allowed to remain. All of a sudden I had conceived the idea of taking it with me to Semi Dual.

The doctor, as he proved to be, came rapidly across to the bed, set down his bag, and bent above the body of the woman. After a perfunctory examination he raised his head.

"She is quite dead," he announced, and, ignoring every one else, turned to the nurse. "Miss Riley, just when did you discover Mrs. Greenig as she is?"

"About ten or fifteen minutes before I got you on the phone, doctor," said the girl, who had remained standing at one side.

"Are you this woman's physician?" Bryce cut in.

"I am. I am Dr. Herman," the dark man replied crisply. "The nurse just called me here by telephone."

Again there came a ring at the bell. Miss Riley went once more to the front, and shortly afterward the coroner appeared.

In a few brief questions he caught up the thread of events; then, addressing the physician, he asked: "Just what, doctor, do you think of the affair?"

"Apparently it is suicide," replied the physician quickly. "Mrs. Greenig bled to death from a cut in the arm just below the bend of the elbow. A vein was opened there. She could easily have done it herself, and the fingers of her right hand are stained with blood."

"Was a weapon found?" the coroner inquired.

"We found a small penknife," said Bryce. "The nurse here says it belonged to the dead woman. Here it is." He extended a small knife with an open, blood-soiled blade.

The coroner received it, turned it about, inspected it carefully; and then, turning to the nurse, who was again on her chair, he began to question her.

"Does this knife belong to the deceased?"

"It does," replied the girl.

"You are sure of that? Be careful, my girl."

"Yes, sir, I am sure. I have seen her use it to sharpen pencils."

"How long have you been nursing here?"

"Some six weeks—ever since Mrs. Greenig has needed a nurse."

"What is your name?"

"Gertrude Riley. I am a trained nurse."

"Where were you to-night when this affair occurred?"

"I suppose I was up in the little park just beyond here. Every evening at this time I have been in the habit of going out for a breath of air. I did so to-night as usual. When I returned Mrs. Greenig was—as you see her." She hesitated slightly over the last words.

"How long were you gone?"

"I left at nine-thirty. It was not quite eleven when I returned."

"Was the door locked when you returned—the front door?"

"Yes. I locked it as I went out and found it so when I came back."

"Doctor," said the coroner, turning to Herman, "what was the matter with Mrs. Greenig?"

"She had typhoid," the physician replied.

"She'd been pretty sick?"

"Yes; at one time we believed her death inevitable."

"Had she been delirious—in any way deranged mentally?"

"At the height of her disease. Not recently."

"Miss Riley"—the official addressed the girl again—"did you meet any one, speak to any one, in the park?"

"No."

"Had Mrs. Greenig been mentally depressed of late?"

"Oh, no! Quite recently she has been very anxious to get well."

"You say recently. Was she formerly depressed?"

"When she first took sick she had just had some trouble with a relative," said the girl. "She felt very badly about that, but a few days ago it was all made up. Since the reconciliation she was anxious to recover, in order that she might see to changing her will."

I think we all pricked up our ears at that.

"Her will?" questioned the coroner. "How is that?"

Dr. Herman interrupted at this point. "Pardon me," said he. "Mrs. Greenig had a bit of trouble with a nephew, of whose manner of life she did not approve. Lately, however, they had come to a better understanding, and she intended making him her chief beneficiary in a new document."

The coroner nodded, turned, and engaged Bryce in conversation for a moment or two. At the end of that time the inspector and he apparently arrived at a mutual understanding, and he again addressed the nurse.

"Miss Riley, there is a janitor in the building, is there not?"

"Yes," said the girl. "He lives directly under this room."

The coroner signed to Bryce, who immediately despatched one of his men to bring the janitor up.

"Did you always lock the door when you went out, Miss Riley?" the coroner resumed.

"Oh, yes; always."

"With your own key, or with Mrs. Greenig's?"

"With my own. Mrs. Greenig gave me a pass-key. She also had one on a key-ring with her other keys."

"Have you your key now?"

"Yes; it is in my purse."

"Where are Mrs. Greenig's keys?"

"As a rule, since she has been sick, they have lain on the dresser over there." Miss Riley indicated the article of furniture by a wave of her hand.

The coroner crossed the room, and presently picked up a bunch or keys. "Are these the ones?" he inquired.

"Yes, I think so."

"Show me the key to the front door," he requested as he advanced to her side.

The woman took the keys and glanced hurriedly through them. A second time she ran them over more slowly, then lifted startled eyes to the man's face.

"It isn't here now," she said.

"But you have yours?"

"Yes. I used it in getting in."

The patrolman now came back accompanied by the janitor, and the coroner turned his attention to him. The man gave his name as Henry Clay, and proved to be of African descent.

Questioned as to the events of the night, he said that he had retired about half after nine. About ten, he thought it was, he had been awakened by a scream. He had listened carefully, and, hearing nothing more, had again gone to sleep, and remained so until the patrol arrived.

Under further questioning as to whether he had heard any other noise in the flat above his room, he admitted that he had heard the sound of voices, but had supposed that it was Mrs. Greenig talking to her nurse, who, he pointed out, was possessed of a voice of low timbre. This was a fact which I had myself observed.

Asked about the key arrangement, he stated that all apartments in the building were furnished with two keys to the front door. Beyond this his information was practically valueless, and he was excused.

While the coroner had been conducting, his examination of the negro several of the police had questioned the other inmates of that part of the building in which Mrs. Greenig had lived.

Across the hall one woman was found who admitted that she had heard a single scream at about ten o'clock. She had been sitting in her own bedroom, which adjoined that of the deceased, and had risen, and gone to her front door to listen for any further outcry. She said she thought the scream had come from the room of the sick woman next door. She had heard nothing more. The flat immediately above that occupied by the dead woman was empty at the time.

The whole result of the investigation seemed to be that both the janitor and a tenant had heard a single scream some time around ten o'clock, and that the janitor believed he had heard voices in the flat immediately afterward. The coroner at once took up his questioning of the nurse again.

"Miss Riley, when you returned and discovered that Mrs. Greenig was dead, did you notice whether the blinds on her bedroom windows were up or down?"

"They were drawn. I had pulled them down before I went out."

"Was the window where you are now sitting up or down?"

"I left it up. Mrs. Greenig asked me to do so, as it was a hot night. I merely drew down the shade, and the window was still raised when I returned."

"So that some one could have got in or out that way?"

"I suppose they might."

"When you discovered that Mrs. Greenig was dead what did you do?"

"I first called for Dr. Herman, but I failed to get an answer. Then I called the police station and told them of the affair. Then I kept trying to get Dr. Herman, and finally succeeded. He said he had just come in from a call and was retiring, but that he would dress and come over at once."

"Was that before or after the police arrived?"

"Just afterward."

"Then you did not notify any one in the house?"

"No, sir, I did not."

"Didn't even call the janitor?"

"No."

"Why not?"

"I was greatly excited, and I was busy trying to get the doctor and calling the police. I had become very fond of my patient, and was dreadfully shocked. I suppose I didn't think of it."

"Did you meet any one when you came back to the flat—in the hall or on the steps?"

"No."

"You don't know of any one who would have been likely to wish Mrs. Greenig dead?"

"No, sir, I do not."

"Now about this will Mrs. Greenig intended to make—what was her nephew's name?"

"Mr. Richard Martin. He was her brother's child. While she was ill he called a number of times, and they had several long talks together since she has been recovering. Only to-day she told me that she intended changing her present will, so as to give the bulk of her property to him."

"Do you know anything about the will or the trouble between Mrs. Greenig and her nephew?"

"Oh, yes; Mrs. Greenig talked freely to me at times. Mr. Martin had been living extravagantly, and his aunt did not approve. When she thought she was going to die she was still nursing her pique at his refusal to follow her wishes, and she changed her will so as to cut him off with a small allowance."

"Did you witness the making of that will?"

"Oh, no," said the girl quickly, in evident misunderstanding of his meaning. "Dr. Herman and the janitor were asked to witness it."

Herman gave a nervous cough, and I glanced his way. It seemed to me that he was endeavoring earnestly to catch the girl's eye. If that was his purpose, it failed. She sat quietly with her gaze fixed steadily upon the coroner's face, and seemed only intent upon answering his questions to the best of her ability.

"Why was the janitor—a negro—called in rather than you?" the official demanded almost at once.

For the first time the woman appeared uneasy under his searching questions. She flushed slightly, and hesitated the least bit before making any reply.

"I suppose because under this will I was the chief beneficiary," she said at length.

One could have heard a pin drop in the ensuing quiet. I don't think there was any one in the room who did not show surprise. The physician scowled fiercely and began to stroke his beard. The coroner and Bryce looked their triumph. Dean, at my elbow, whistled softly and began to make frantic notes in his book. As for myself, I looked at the girl, sitting quietly in her chair, and wondered what further thoughts lurked under her crown of brown hair, back of her Irish-blue eyes. She was slender, willowy, pink and white, with a pure, soft skin—withal very dainty in her crisp uniform. Could it be possible that she was really a murderess?

The coroner's voice brought me back from speculation. "So that in event of Mrs. Greenig's death you would have come in for a nice sum?"

"Why—why—I suppose so," said the woman slowly. "I'm sure I didn't think of it like that, though."

"Just how Mid Mrs. Greenig come to make you the recipient of her wealth in the first place?"

"She had no other relatives, and she had grown fond of me, I think."

"As her nurse, you could see that she was going to get well?"

"Oh, yes! We talked it over lots of times, and we were both very glad. Only yesterday we planned out how her new will was to read."

"You were her confidante, then—knew nearly all her plans?"

"Yes."

"When was the new will to be executed?"

"To-morrow if she was strong enough. She asked Dr. Herman about it to-day."

"Is that correct?" the coroner turned to Herman to ask.

The physician merely bowed. I noticed that his lips were pressed into a thin, hard line under his black mustache.

"Miss Riley, how much would you have inherited under the last will?" the coroner continued.

"You mean the last one made?" The girl was palpably growing nervous, though she still answered readily enough.

"Yes."

"I think it was seventy-five thousand, to be exact," said the girl with an effort, plainly embarrassed.

"That's all," said the coroner, with a glance at Bryce.

The inspector immediately approached the woman, and laid a hand upon her shoulder.

"Gertrude Riley, I arrest you for the murder of Matilda Greenig, and warn you that anything you may say will be used as evidence against you."

The warning was needless, for without a word the girl sank unconscious into his arms.

CHAPTER III

THE MARK ON THE BOTTLE

GERTRUDE RILEY, STILL unconscious, was carried to the patrol, accompanied by Dr. Herman. The coroner left, saying he would send for the body of the dead woman. Bryce and a detective, Dean and myself remained.

I phoned Smithson from the apartment, and told him the main details, adding that I had sent Grant to the station to look after that end and later bring the story to the office, while I remained on the scene.

"You say the girl fainted when arrested, and is now at the station?" asked Smithson.

I admitted that that was correct.

"Then what are you sticking around there for now?" he wanted to know.

"I'm waiting to see what a search of the room may show," I explained rather lamely. I didn't like to admit that, because Semi Dual had predicted that I would be busy, I could not feel that the mere arrest of the nurse would settle the case. Yet that was the real cause of my act. Afterward Dean said he stayed because I did.

Smithson grunted and hung up his phone.

I followed suit; and then Dean took the phone and had a chat with the office of the *Dispatch*.

Meanwhile the two officers were ransacking the room, but they failed to find anything suspicious in the least. From front to back there was nothing disturbed. The rear door was locked with a spring-lock, which might indicate a possible exit for any one who had entered and done the deed; yet from act to motive the case was apparently clear against the nurse. I could see that both the detective and Bryce regarded their arrest as quite the proper solution to the affair.

On the face of things they were right. In no particular could the girl sustain her claims that she had been absent at the time when the murder was done. The only possible things in her favor were the missing key from the ring of the deceased and the janitor's positive assertion that there had been two such keys. One was found in the purse of the nurse, which had been taken by the police. The other was still missing after our search was done.

Then there were the peculiar half-burned spots on the skin of the victim's face. It really looked as though the girl, seeing herself threatened with the loss of what she had come to regard as her own, had used chloroform to overcome her patient, and then slashed her arm with the knife.

"By the way," said Bryce on a sudden, "where is that bottle you found, Glace?"

I was cornered, and all at once I remembered that Dual had always told me to trust to the truth at such times.

"I've got it," I replied.

Bryce grinned. "Come across," he suggested. "It's an exhibit in the case."

I shook my head, and returned his grin.

"To-morrow," I answered. "Be a sport, Bryce, and let me keep it to-night. I've got a theory about that bottle which I want to test."

"Don't tell me you think we're in wrong," the inspector laughed.

"I don't know what I believe just yet," I confessed. "Here"— I got the bottle out—"make some sort of a mark on the thing for identification and trust me till morning. Only hold it by the neck."

I caught the eyes of the detective and saw he was aware of the vague idea I had formed. He nodded to Bryce. "All right, inspector," he assented. "Let Glace have it till morning. He'll come across with what he finds out. Let him grab off a scoop for himself if he can."

I readily agreed to that.

Still grinning, Bryce scratched a mark on the bottom of the bottle with a diamond he wore, and handed the vial back to me.

"There you are, my amateur sleuth," he remarked lightly, and we all rose to depart.

Dean started straight for the office of the *Dispatch* to write up his story, after begging me to let him in on what he called the "bottle mystery." He even offered a bribe of a late supper at a rathskeller of which we knew, but for once I was not to be tempted in any such way. Finally he gave it up and went off in disgust. When he was gone, I assured myself that I still had the bottle, then I set out for the Urania and Semi Dual.

I had to walk up the twenty flights, but I think I made it in record time. I wanted to get to my peculiar friend and see what he had to say. I remembered that other time, when he had played ducks and drakes with a bunch of circumstantial evidence a long time ago. Then, as now, I had visited him at night and climbed twenty flights of stairs in order to make the call.

The moon had come clear of the clouds. When I stepped out on the Urania's roof all the place was flooded by a clear, white light. To me, walking toward the door of the tower, it seemed almost an augury—a promise of the triumph of light over darkness.

I paused and lifted my face to the heavens and took a long breath of the cool, damp air. What was up there, in the purple ether? What was all this struggle of life and death? What poor blind mortals we all were.

Anyway, Dual knew far more of the secret than I. I was on his threshold. Why should I delay? I turned and found him standing in the tower door.

He took me into the inner room, waved me to a chair and, seating himself at his desk, picked up a sheet of paper upon which he had evidently been at work when I arrived. Then he gave me a surprise.

"The woman was murdered," he announced.

"That's what the police say," I stammered. "At first, though, it looked like suicide."

"It was no suicide," said Semi Dual. "My calculations show that she had at this time a positive death-point, preceded by a threatened one. In the positive case, death would result from murder; and did."

"I don't see how you do it," I confessed.

"Astrology," said Semi Dual. "If I have a person's name, I can set a figure of their life."

"I thought you did it from the stars," I began.

"In view of the fact that every letter has an astrological value, one can do it from a name also," returned Dual.

"But Matilda is sometimes spelled with an 'h,'" said I. "How did you know?"

"That," smiled Semi, "was easily determined by setting up the calculation. In this case the 'h' would have produced a figure which would have precluded the person's death at this time. Do you see?"

"So that while I was gone, you learned the facts of the case right here in this room?"

"Precisely, my friend."

"Would the figure you have set up give a description of the woman herself?"

Dual smiled. "She was past middle age; about fifty-five or six; slight of build, and of refined appearance. In earlier life one would have described her as of medium complexion, though now she is probably slightly faded, as she has had a long illness. She—"

"You might have been in the room itself, from the way you talk," I burst out. His demonstrations never ceased to amaze me.

Dual nodded. "This is only re-proving proven science," he continued. "We are wasting time in such discussion. Briefly, the woman was murdered somewhere near ten o'clock, by some one she completely trusted, and some one who felt sure that suspicion would never rest on him."

I sat up in my chair. "Him?" I cried.

"Naturally," said Semi. "The murderer was a man."

"But, good Heavens, Dual! Every circumstance points another way. Before I left, the police arrested the woman's nurse. She's at the station now."

Dual smiled at my excitement.

"Though she is, she is innocent, nonetheless, Gordon," he said calmly. "Of that I am sure. The stars never lie, and if a mistake occurs in a reading, it is we who mistake. This murder was done by a man."

"But she practically convicted herself."

"In what way?" asked Dual.

"By her answers to the coroner," I explained.

"A very strong argument in her favor," said my friend. "Having nothing to conceal, she spoke freely. That has often happened before. Yet in the end, the truth will prevail."

"Then what is to be done?" I questioned.

"Prove her innocence," replied my friend. Suddenly his face softened, and took on a new light. "Once upon a time I told you that I lived to help others—to smooth out the path for other feet. If I can help one wrongly accused or suspected, or protect the helpless, surely I have spent my time in a good cause and not lived in vain."

His voice sank and ceased, and for a moment he sat staring silently before him.

Then again his words rang out like a clarion call: "Glace, that girl is as innocent of this crime as you are; now what shall we do?"

"Prove her innocence!" I cried.

Dual smiled. "We *will* prove her innocence," said he.

He lay back in his chair. "Tell me everything you saw or heard while you were gone," he directed. "Omit nothing—but by now you know what I mean when I say that—proceed."

I did know. He wanted everything down to the least detail. He had an uncanny way of picking up a thread of a clue from some little thing, which the average man would deem of small importance, and following it to a startling denouement. Therefore I began to detail very carefully every incident of the night, while he lay wrapped in his long white robe, listening in silence to my words. The strong olive face was as immobile as a graven figure; he neither moved nor spoke in all the tale; yet from time to time I could feel his eyes upon me and knew that they were alive with the activities of his wonderful brain.

When I had finished, he sat forward and held out his hand. "Now let me see the evidence you have brought with you," he began.

I grinned as I drew the bottle from my pocket and set it on the desk. I had purposely failed to tell him that I had brought it, although mentioning that I had found the thing. Yet he asked for it as coolly as if I had spoken of nothing else from the start. Like a kid caught secreting some forbidden article, I grinned and gave up.

Dual picked it up and held it to the light. Then he set it down and went to a cabinet, from which he brought a small box. He opened this on the desk, exposing to view a grayish powder. With this he dusted the sides of the bottle, shook off the surplus, glanced at me, and smiled.

"Our assassin is possessed of an oily skin," he remarked in his quiet way. "He has left his autograph on the bottle. See?"

He held it toward me, and I could see the fine lines of a thumb-print etched in the gray powder on the glass.

"I hoped for that. That's why I brought the bottle," I said.

"It was well thought of," declared Dual. "We have here our first material clue—the sort which will stand with the police.

In support of my statements, notice that this print is large for that of a woman. The girl did not hold this bottle—so much is plain already. We must make a photograph of this thumb-mark."

I explained that I had promised to return the bottle in the morning without fail.

Dual nodded. "We can use a flash-light," he decided, and began preparing for the work.

While he moved about, he took up the matter of the missing key. "The murderer made two mistakes," he announced. "Probably he is an amateur in practical crime. First, he took away the key; secondly, he overlooked the bottle when he left. He should have reversed that order, and he might feel safer a great deal. In writing your story, allow me to suggest that you make the most of the fact that the key has been missed.

"Having a guilty conscience, it may be possible that the murderer will seek to return it or dispose of it in some way, which will give us another clue to his identity—one that can be used as evidence. Criminals practically always make some such mistake, if one knows how to read the trail aright. Now if you will assist me, we will take the picture."

He had arranged the bottle on a table in front of a piece of black cloth. Against the dark background the gray lines on the glass stood out plainly. Now he gave me the flash-powder and its holder and showed me how to set it off. He then took up his camera, focused it to his satisfaction, and gave me the word.

A blinding light flashed and left me blinking in the darkness which followed. But I had heard the click of the shutter, and dimly I perceived Semi Dual smiling as he reached out and took the apparatus from my hands.

"That should be a perfect negative," he remarked. "Now we will put the bottle in a box and you can take it back to your friend, the inspector, with the thumb-print in plain sight."

I sat down and pressed my hands to my eyes. "And to-morrow?" I questioned. "What shall I do? Where do I begin?"

Semi Dual smiled as he seated himself. "Begin to get legal proof," said he. "Already the murderer is pretty plainly indicated, I think, but we must have proof which will be accepted by the court. Your task will be to collect that.

"Take this bottle, for instance. The criminal's mark is on the glass. There is no label; therefore the criminal did not buy it at a drug-store, or he changed bottles afterward, or he soaked the label off.

"The police already suspect the nurse of having done the deed. We, however, know she is innocent, as we know it was the work of a man. We have now to prove beyond doubt that it was a man, and *that* he actually did the thing. To-morrow go and see Miss Riley and get her story. Get also a sample of her writing.

"Hunt up this nephew and see what sort of a man he is. Find out what he has to say, and how he says it. Get a sample of his writing if you can. Also see the doctor, and do the same with him. Play up the key story and watch for its return.

"If you can't get a sample of the doctor's writing any other way, find out where the prescriptions were filled for Mrs. Greenig. Go to the drug-store and borrow one of the filled blanks which he sent in. With what you bring me to-morrow— or to-day rather, I shall hope to be able to give you the murderer's name."

His words filled me with confidence, and I put myself unreservedly in his hands. All my preconceived ideas of the case I cast aside. In their place I set up a picture of a blue-eyed girl being carried unconscious from a room of horror in a burly patrolman's arms, and now doubtless suffering mental agonies in a cell. In part, at least, it was to be my privilege to help free her. I rose from my chair and picked up my hat.

"I'll get all the evidence I can," I assured Semi, and turned to the door.

"You will succeed," said my friend, with utter seriousness. "To help the innocent is a privilege indeed."

I arrived at the *Record* office shortly before two o'clock. Smithson was just starting home. "That's once the department got quick action," said he.

"Meaning the Greenig case?" I answered. "The girl's arrest is all bunk."

My city editor eyed me closely for a moment, then: "Didn't you send Grant in with a story that the nurse had been arrested as the murderess?" he inquired. "What are you trying to pull on me now?"

"A beat, if it comes the way I think," I replied.

"What's the answer, son?"

"Come on back while I write the story, and I'll show you," I responded. "We've got to get this in the late edition at least."

He followed me back, and I wrote my story against time, tossing each page to Smithson as I took if off the machine.

When it was done there was a light of interested speculation in his eyes.

"Who do you suppose has the key? Who could have left the bottle with its telltale thumb-mark?"

CHAPTER IV

A SUCCESSFUL INTERVIEW

"**HERE'S BRYCE'S BOTTLE**," I said to my friend Desk-Sergeant Harrington the next morning, as I handed a small package tied securely across the rail to him.

Dan took it with a grin and tossed it on the end of his desk. "Did you find the criminal's photograph blown in the glass?" he inquired.

"No, but I found his autograph on the side," I retorted. "You see if Bryce don't jump when he examines the thing."

Dan eyed me for a moment; then: "What do ye mane?" he asked. "Bryce told me to take care of the thing. What's ut about?"

"There's the thumb-print of the murderer of the woman who was killed last night at the Virginia on that bottle," said I.

"The girl's?" Harrington evinced sudden interest.

"Not so, Daniel—the man's," I replied. "Any new developments in the case?"

"Wait a bit," said Harrington.

"What are ye gettin' at? Are ye goin' to pick some more flaws with our arrest of the girl? Who's runnin' the department—the *Record* or us?"

"Then something has happened," I grinned back. "You must have read my story. What are you so touchy about, and where's Bryce?"

"He's out," growled Dan, then he chuckled. "Oh, well, Gordon, 'twixt you ah' me an' the cell-house door, I'm thinkin' Bryce himself has some doubts about the girl's havin' croaked the old dame. There was an intelligent voter in here this morning telling us as how he saw a man sneakin' up the alley back of the Virginia at a quarter to eleven last night. Said the chap had his coat-collar turned up around his face an' his hat pulled down, an' was in a hurry to get out of sight."

"My compliments to the intelligent voter," said I.

Dan shook his head. "You're an impertinent young feller, Glace," he opined. "Still, it's tough on this kid if she didn't do the job. They tell me she's takin' it hard; didn't sleep at all last night; didn't make no fuss either; just sat there starin' at the wall; an' the matron was tellin' one of th' boys that she only drunk a cup of coffee this mornin'. I'd have to feel pretty bad to pass up my breakfast, I'm thinkin'. So you got the bug that it's a man's job, too?"

"Did you read the *Record* this morning?" I asked.

"Uh-huh," grunted Harrington. "You beat 'em all if you're right."

"If," I jeered. "Say, Dan, I'm not only going to find fault with your pinch in this case; I'm going to tear it all to pieces pretty soon."

"Uh-huh," said Harrington again. "Wasn't it justified?"

"Sure! Bryce had to do it. The girl forced his hand herself. By the way, I want to see her, if I may."

"Oh!" growled the sergeant, somewhat mollified. "Then you wasn't meanin' nuthin, only you was goin' to help us find the right man?"

"What else? I've done it before. Do I see the girl?" I laughed.

"Well, I dunno," he began slowly.

"Double the smokes for you and your brother," I wheedled, reverting to our old gag, by which Dan always got two cigars out of me—one for a relative who was purely mythical.

Harrington grinned.

"Bribin' an officer now. Gee! Ain't you fierce! Oh, well, I dunno as it kin do any harm—only I don't believe she'll talk to you. All the same, I'll send you back and you kin see. She's a nice-lookin' kid. Honest, Glace, betwixt us two, I hope you're right."

I rummaged my pockets and found three cigars, which I handed to the sergeant, with the promise of the other one later on. Dan called a man, and I followed him back to the women's section of the jail, and was turned over to the matron herself, who conducted me down the long corridor of small rooms to the door of a cell.

As we paused the figure of a woman was plainly visible, sitting upon the edge of the cot, hands clasped in lap, eyes cast down. In response to the matron's tap on the bars the woman raised her head, and on the instant I was gazing into Gertrude Riley's blue eyes.

"Here's a gentleman to see you, dearie," said the matron in a surprisingly soft tone of voice, as she began unlocking the door, that I might step inside. "She's no' like the others here," she added to me with meaning, and immediately afterward turned and hurried away.

Evidently the girl had found a friend in the matron; who sensed the difference between the nurse and the other female inmates. Suddenly I found myself feeling glad of that. I entered the cell, and remained standing until the girl herself motioned me to a seat.

She looked a wreck in the light reflected from the white-washed walls. Her face was drawn and haggard; and there were dark circles under her eyes, which looked very large. I noticed that she kept twisting her fingers together, locking and unlocking them in a nervous manner, even while I was introducing myself.

I sat down on a little stool.

"Miss Riley," I began, "I am Mr. Glace of the *Record*—"That was as far as I got.

"Oh, dear!" gasped the girl. "Won't you please go away again? I can't bear to talk of this to any one."

"But, Miss Riley," I protested, "we want to get at the truth—to help you if we can."

"The truth is—that I didn't do it," she burst out with sudden vehemence. "Oh, how can they think—"

"But we don't," I interrupted. "We know that you are innocent."

It was a good thing I meant it, or I could not have endured the sweep of her eyes. They were wild, sleepless, soul-tortured; and yet at my words hope flickered faintly in their depths.

"You know I am innocent," she whispered in a moment. "Then you have found out who did it? Is that what you mean?"

"Well—not exactly," I confessed, and I hated to do it. "We want you to tell us all about the matter, so we can try and find the man who really did do the thing."

She sank back on the cot from which she had half risen, and the hope in her eyes died away.

"Only that," she said softly. "Oh, I hoped you knew! Was it a trick?"

"It was no trick," I answered, "and it is true that we do not believe you guilty—we on the paper, I mean. Won't you help us prove ourselves right?"

"What can I do, Mr. Glace?"

"Answer my questions. Tell me all you know."

"East night I answered everything they asked me, and they arrested me after I had told the truth," said the girl. "Only at the last did I suspect what they meant to do. Then, after making me tell everything, they warned me that anything I said would be used against me. I would like to talk to someone, but I am almost afraid to speak, lest they twist my words into something more to my discredit. What is a girl to do?"

"Yet, since we are trying to prove the truth of all you did say and are championing your case, don't you think you ought to give us any information which you have to help us in the work we are trying to do?" I replied.

For a moment she made no answer. Plainly she was trying to reach a determination. At last: "Very well," she assented. She began to twist her hands together again.

"Was there anything disgraceful in the actions of Mrs. Greenig's nephew which caused her to change her will?" I began.

"No, I think not; only Mr. Martin was wasteful of money," said Miss Riley. "He was not inclined to work. His aunt had always been too liberal with him, and he had never learned the responsibility of earning money. When she wanted him to settle down and apply himself to some useful object in life he did not wish to. At least that is what she told me."

"Then what made her change her mind?"

"While she was sick Mr. Martin came to see her often, and was very nice. Finally he told her that he had taken a position, or rather that he had arranged to do so the first of the month, and admitted that he felt she had been right all along. He told her that he had given up his expensive apartments and broken with his fast friends.

"If you know anything about women, Mr. Glace, you will see how that might affect his aunt. We are more or less all romanticists, always hoping that some one we like will be true to his better self. Anyway, it was after that that Mrs. Greenig changed her mind about him."

"Well," I questioned, "what did she say to you about changing her will after making the other one in your favor? You said that you had discussed the matter, I think."

"She asked me if I cared," said the girl, "and I told her no; that it was her money to do with as she pleased, and that I hoped that she would feel no hesitation in making any change she desired. I pointed out to her that Mr. Martin was, after all, her own flesh and blood, and I a comparative stranger. I really meant that, too, Mr. Glace. I never felt right about the other will from the very first; but at the time she made it she was very weak, and we had to humor her in everything."

I nodded. "You say Dr. Herman knew of the will in your favor?"

"Yes, he witnessed the drawing of the will."

"Do you know the doctor well, Miss Riley?"

To my surprise she flushed slightly, and in her next words took my breath away.

"Quite well, Mr. Glace; we were to have been married quite soon."

That was a decided surprise. No wonder Herman had looked strange during the events of the night before, and gone to the jail with the girl. I almost felt a sort of pity for the chap. It must have been pretty rough to see the girl he expected to marry in such a position. As soon as I could find words to do so I apologized.

"I beg your pardon, Miss Riley. I'm sorry I got on private grounds, so to speak, but I couldn't possibly know."

"Of course not, Mr. Glace," said the girl.

"Have you relatives, Miss Riley?"

"No, Mr. Glace, I am an only child, and an orphan. To-day I thank God that it is so." She rose from her seat and began nervously pacing the floor.

"You mustn't feel like that," I tried to reassure her. "This will all come right, you know."

"The disgrace of the thing can never come right," she cried out, and paused with compressed lips.

I sought to switch from so painful a theme. "When you returned to the apartment last evening and discovered Mrs. Greenig's body, you didn't see any evidences of any one having been in the flat, did you?"

"Not that I can recall, or that impressed me," said the girl. "Mr. Glace, I was terrified—horrified. I couldn't seem to believe it true at first. Just before I left, Mrs. Greenig had been laughing and talking to me, and seemed so happy at her rapidly returning strength.

"I spoke to her, called her by name, tried to find the least sign of a heart-beat. Then when I realized that I had been absent when her need of me was greatest, and had come back too late, I did what I thought best—called the doctor and the police."

"I believe you said last night that the doctor did not answer at first?"

"No, he did not. I called him four times in all. The last time was after the police arrived. He said he had been out on a call and had just come in, and started to undress."

"And how long would that have been after you first discovered that Mrs. Greenig was dead?"

"Ten or fifteen minutes, I suppose, Mr. Glace."

"Pardon me if I seem impertinent, or to open up a personal matter," I said with some hesitation, "but have you known the doctor long?"

"About a year," she replied frankly enough. "I have nursed several cases for him."

"Did Mrs. Greenig know you were engaged to marry Dr. Herman, Miss Riley?"

"I think not. I am sure I never told her about it."

"How far from the Virginia does Dr. Herman live?" I inquired.

"About four blocks, at 960 Madison Street," said the nurse.

"I believe he came here with you last night?"

"Oh, yes! He not only came with me, but remained until I was quiet and told him to go. It helped me to bear the ordeal a great deal better, I am sure."

"Have you heard from him yet to-day? I know it seems as if I was prying, but I have an object in asking, please believe."

"He was here early this morning." The girl smiled quietly as she answered. "He promised to come last night."

My line of questioning was arriving nowhere. I made another change: "By the way, Miss Riley, do you know where Mr. Martin is living now?"

"His address is a cheap hotel—the Cécile—on River Street," said the nurse. "I heard him tell his aunt the other day. He laughed at the time, and said the accommodations were not quite up to the standard of the Glenn Arms, where he was staying before."

"Did he know that his aunt contemplated reinstating him in her will?"

Miss Riley half smiled. "Mr. Glace," said she, "I can now see where you newspapermen get your reputation. You want to know about everything, it seems. To answer your question, Mrs. Greenig was a peculiar woman in some ways. She talked freely to me, but not to every one.

"I happen to know that she never told Mr. Richard that he had been cut off in her will. All he knew was that his liberal allowance had been cut down to next to nothing. So far as I know, he still thought himself his aunt's heir.

"That was one thing I didn't like about the affair—I always felt guilty when he was around. I heard a good deal of what they said from time to time, and he impressed me as a very nice young man, only careless of money and how it was spent. I was glad when Mrs. Greenig decided to reinstate him as her heir.

"She told him that she wanted him to get into some sort of work, and learn the worth of a dollar—and he would just laugh.

She intimated that his so-called friends were in reality leeches on his good nature and pocket-book—and again he laughed at her. She gave him a chance to find out the truth by letting him shift for himself.

"If he didn't try to brace up and make a man of himself, she intended to let him go; but I know she was very happy when he really showed his intention of getting out and providing for himself. Even in the will she made in my favor I was to give him a certain amount every quarter as long as I lived."

Here, at last, was something important. I felt a sense of elation as I listened to the words of the nurse. At last I seemed on the track of something. I decided to press forward along that line.

"But he really didn't know that he was cut off?" I repeated. "You are sure of that? It may be important, I think."

"I don't think he did," said the girl.

"Did he seem angry with his aunt at any time—speak angrily in any of the conversations you heard?"

"Oh no; he was always the perfect gentleman in every way," responded Miss Riley. "He impressed one as being just a good-natured boy."

"Did you hear him mention what he was going to do after the first?" I asked.

"He said he was going to work in a wholesale drug-house. A day or two ago he mentioned that he had spent a whole day there, getting acquainted with what his duties would be."

"Would he have had an opportunity to handle any drugs at that time, do you think?"

Miss Riley's expression became one of surprised interrogation. "I really don't know, Mr. Glace," she said quickly. "Why?"

"There wasn't any chloroform used by the physician at any time during Mrs. Greenig's illness, was there?" I asked.

"No," she replied with positive emphasis, "there was not." No sooner had she spoken than I could see that she was endeavoring to repress a growing excitement. "Was that what had been in the bottle you found, Mr. Glace? Was that why the inspector decided that it was murder instead of suicide?" she questioned me in turn.

"Yes," I told her, "Mrs. Greenig was chloroformed before she was killed."

"Then it must have been planned!" she said with a gasp. "The murderer came with his mind made up—prepared. Oh!"

"That is what we think at present, Miss Riley. Furthermore, he left his thumb-print on the glass of the bottle. We have at least found out that much." The woman clenched her hands with a sudden impulsive gesture, seated herself, and sat rigidly upright on the edge of the cot. Suddenly a shudder ran through her frame.

"It is too horrible—what your questions and statements seem to lead to—too awful!" she cried in protest. "I can't believe it—any more than I can believe that I did it myself. I feel sure that Mr. Martin is not the type of man who would do such a thing as that."

"Then there's the key," I continued, without commenting on her outburst. "Somebody took the other key, Miss Riley. To have done this, that somebody must have been in the room before the murder was committed. When did you see the key last?"

"I don't remember," she responded slowly. "Recently I have always used the one I had in my purse."

A tap at the door interrupted our conversation. We both turned to see the matron, her arms full of flowers, and a smile on her face.

"Some one's been sendin' you posies, Miss Riley," she began gladly. "Sure they are beauties. I'll be gettin' you a pail to put them in."

Gertrude Riley sprang up with a cry of pleasure and ran to the grated door to take the flowers into her own arms, raise them, and bury her face in their mass of color. For a long moment she stood so—a slender figure against the bars of the cell—her eyes closed, her bosom rising and falling as she drank of the flowers' perfume.

Presently she raised her head and smiled upon me out of tear-dimmed eyes, as she began hunting for a card. She found it after a bit of fumbling, and held it out to me.

"From Dr. Herman," she said softly. "Oh, isn't it dear of him to think!" Again she smiled, and quite without reserve wiped her eyes. "That's the first tear I've been able to shed," she remarked, with a little laugh that caught in her throat; "and like all women, I've wanted to cry awfully, only somehow I wasn't able to."

I was mighty glad the chap had sent those flowers, and I felt sure he would feel well repaid if he could see the pleasure and help they gave.

"I know how you feel," I nodded. "Once when I was a kid they shut me up in a dark room for being a 'bad boy,' and I yelled myself hoarse—then I wanted to cry and I couldn't; I'd used up my voice."

This time Miss Riley's laugh did not catch in her throat.

I decided that I had gained about all I could for the present. There was only one thing more to do. "Miss Riley," I resumed, "I am going to see this Mr. Martin after I leave here. Would you consider it too much if I asked you, who know him, to write a line to him, requesting him to give me an interview? Sometimes it is hard to get people to accord a hearing to one of us chaps."

To one who knew, it was a thin excuse, but then Miss Riley didn't know. "If you think it will do any good, I will do so gladly," she said at once. Since the coming of the flowers she seemed quite cheered up. It is funny what a little thing sometimes makes or mars our attitude toward affairs.

I handed her a pad and pencil, and she wrote for a few moments.

"Will that do?" she asked presently, handing me the following:

Mr. Richard Martin,

Dear Sir:—This will introduce Mr. Glace, who is working in my behalf. Will you kindly help him in any way you can? Believe me, I am deeply grieved over this dreadful happening that has robbed us both—you of a sterling relative, and me of a very dear friend.

Sincerely yours,
Gertrude Riley.

"Very nicely," I assured her as I finished reading.

I rose to my feet and made my adieus. "Thank you for the interview, Miss Riley," I said. "Keep up your courage, and I am positive that everything will be cleared up before very long. I shall let you know of anything important, you may be assured. I shall now go to Mr. Martin at once."

"It is I who should thank you, Mr. Glace," she returned. "Your call has given me fresh courage and enabled me to hope that all will turn out as you say. I shall be very glad to see you at any time."

We clasped hands, and I noticed that she took mine like a man, I mean firmly, with a spirit back of the form. There was nothing half-way in the grip of her fingers. It felt sincere.

I turned toward the barred door, and just then the matron returned with a pail of water.

As she let me out I said: "Don't bother with me. Give first aid to the flowers on a morning like this. I can find my way out."

I left the two women—matron and prisoner—thrusting the long stems of roses into the depths of a tin pail, and started back for the office of the station. I was full of my success in the first part of my task. I had learned several things, and I had a whole note written by the girl.

CHAPTER V

THE MISSING KEY

WITH THE ASSISTANCE of the turnkey I got out of jail and went to the office, where Harrington was smoking one of my cigars. It lacked a few minutes of twelve. I decided to go over to River Street and see if I could find Mr. Richard Martin. But as events turned out, I was destined never to make the trip.

I had started toward the door when a man, coming in from the street, caused me to step aside. Having done so, I tarried yet longer because of what I saw as he pushed by.

The fellow was evidently in a hurry, for he was breathing rapidly. More: he was pale, and under plainly visible excitement. His face had a tense, drawn look, as I glimpsed it when he hurried past. To all appearances he was a man on the right side of thirty, clad in a suit of fashionable cut—now stained and spotted with dust, as were also his shoes. He had the look of a person who had walked for miles without especially heeding where he went. I noticed that he was dark-skinned, with a high-bred, sensitive face and a square jaw and chin.

Without looking to right or left, he advanced to the sergeant's desk, and his first words caused me to retrace my steps.

"I am Mr. Richard Martin," he addressed Harrington. "It was my aunt, Mrs. Greenig, who was murdered last night at the Virginia. I saw by the papers this morning that there had been an arrest made, and also that the key to the flat is missing. Now what brings me here, in part at least, is this: While I was reading the account in the paper, a letter was delivered to my hotel, and upon opening it I found this."

He withdrew a hand from the pocket of his coat and held up an envelope, which he proceeded to invert above Harrington's desk. With a little thud, *there fell out a key!*

"I have every reason," the man went on, without noticing my start of surprise or Dan's suspicious scowl, "to believe that this is the missing key to my aunt's apartment. Who sent it I do not know—haven't an idea, even; but I do know that whoever had it knew my address, and evidently my old one as well.

"You can see they mailed it to me wrapped in a sheet of Glenn Arms paper, and used one of the hotel's envelopes. I thought that it might prove an important clue, and so lost no time in bringing it here."

"It sure ought to," observed Dan with meaning, as he picked up the key and turned it over in his hand. Then he reached out for the envelope, and began subjecting it to equally close scrutiny.

I slipped up to the desk and stood by Martin's side while Dan was examining the things.

There was no doubt but that the envelope was one of the regular stock supplied to the Glenn Arms writing-room—it bore the hotel name and crest. The address was typewritten: "Mr. Richard Martin, Hotel Cécile, River Street, City." The postmark, that of the general office, at 7 A.M. of the present day. Inside was a single blank sheet of the hotel paper, faintly marked by the key, about which it had been folded.

Harrington tossed it aside and silently eyed the man.

"What makes you think this is the key?" he asked at length. "Do you know how your aunt's key looked?"

"No," said Martin, avoiding the trap in the question. "I drew the conclusion from the fact that a key was alleged to be missing, and that this one was mailed to me, her nearest relative."

"We kin find out in a minute," remarked the sergeant, as he slid from his chair and walked to the station safe, which he proceeded to unlock. "The nurse, who was brought in last night, had the other key, an' we got it here. If this one of yours matches, why, I guess it's the one we want."

He came back with a small flat key in his hand, such as are used in modern patent locks, and laid it down on the desk. It was tagged, numbered, and dated, in order to be identified without doubt. Dan picked up the key Martin had brought and laid it alongside of the one from the safe. They matched exactly; and without more ado, he began to write out a ticket for the second key.

Martin stood silently watching him, leaning against the grating of the desk. I turned my attention again to the sheet of paper and the envelope, and that was how I discovered something we all had overlooked.

Heretofore, we had given all our attention to the outside of the envelope and the key-marked side of the single sheet. Now I turned the letter over, and had to choke back a cry of delight. Whoever had wrapped up the key in the paper had pressed the sheet firmly down about it, with the result that, over the middle section of the folded page there was—the distinct print of a thumb!

On the instant, as the possible significance seized my brain, I turned to Martin with a question fairly bursting from my lips and asked:

"Do your hands perspire freely?"

He gave me a glance of quick surprise. "I don't think so; but what if they do?"

"Nothing at present," I parried, and took out my copy-pad to begin making notes.

Martin gave me a second stare of perplexity, then, apparently deciding that my interruption was not worthy of comment, turned back to Dan, who was now tying his tag of identification to the second key.

"By the way, sergeant," said he, "there's another matter I want to go into while I'm here. You mentioned the arrest of my aunt's nurse on the suspicion of having been directly responsible for her death. Now, that's absurd, you know. I've seen that girl enough to know that she'd never do anything like that. I should like to arrange for her release."

"There'd be a bit of red tape about that," observed Dan, with a grin.

"But it can be arranged, can it not?" Martin inquired.

"You'd have to see the chief," said Harrington, as he picked up the two keys. I noticed his left hand slip along the desk and press a button under its edge.

"Well, I can do that," agreed Martin. "Where is he, please?"

"He ain't here now," said Dan, with his eyes on the door.

Two officers entered the office quietly just then, and took seats back of where Martin and I stood, after exchanging a swift glance with the sergeant. Apparently, Martin did not notice; but it began to look to me as though he would have more difficulty in leaving the station than he had experienced in getting in. Things seemed to be promising something of interest.

Dan left his chair, and started for the safe with the keys. Half-way, he paused and glanced back at Martin. "What you got on for the next hour?" he asked.

"Nothing in particular," responded Martin. "Of course, I expect to arrange for my aunt's funeral."

"Then," suggested the sergeant, "suppose you stick around a bit. Inspector Bryce and Detective Johnson are handlin' this case. When they come in you kin talk this girl biz over with them."

Martin nodded, drew a case from his pocket, and extracted a cigarette, which he lit.

Meanwhile temptation seized me, and I fell. Dan was at the safe putting away the keys. Martin was staring out at the street. I laid my copy-pad down on the broad top of the rail in front of Dan's disk, and apparently went on with my notes.

In reality I slipped the folded sheet with the thumb-marks between the leaves of copy-paper. When I laid the envelope back on the sergeant's desk it was utterly empty; and I dared to hope he might overlook the fact. As it turned out, he did, for fate came to my aid.

I had gone into the reporters' room to get a camera—which we kept cached there—for it had occurred to me that I might as well snap a picture of the envelope for the *Record*, and I was just returning when Inspector Bryce and Detective Johnson, who had been with him the night before, came in at the front door.

Both men were plainly laboring under excitement, and seemed somewhat taken aback when they saw Martin standing at the desk. Bryce gave him one glance, and then came directly across to where he stood.

"I've been looking for you, Martin," he said shortly. "What have you done with your aunt's key?"

For a moment Martin gave him back glance for glance; then: "I've just brought it in," he replied. "But how—"

"I've just come from your hotel," Bryce cut in shortly. "Didn't you tell the clerk something about having had it sent you in the mail?"

"I did," said Martin. "I thought, under the circumstances, that it was better to mention it to some one before bringing it over here. So he told you about it, eh?"

"Uh-huh! You didn't explain to him where you were up to one o'clock this morning, though, did you?" snapped Bryce.

"What are you driving at, inspector?" said Martin, throwing away his cigarette. "My being out last night had nothing whatever to do with the key."

"Maybe," remarked the inspector. "I've been looking for you all morning, though. Come over to the chief's office. I want to have a talk with you."

Martin's face assumed a troubled expression as he turned away with the official. I hastily took my snap of the envelope and trailed along. Nobody objected to my presence, so I took a seat at one side, and kept my ears open to the talk which went on.

"Where'd you go last night, anyway?" began Bryce, after they had all taken seats.

"I went for a walk," replied Martin readily enough.

"Everybody seems to have been walkin' last night," sneered the inspector. "It seems the nurse went out for an airin', too."

"Nevertheless, that is a correct answer to your question," said Martin with some heat.

"Maybe you walked in the same direction as the nurse?" suggested the inspector. "Still, if you was sore at anybody, I would have thought it would have been at her. It was her cut you out."

"Cut me out?" repeated Martin. "Say, inspector, I don't know what you're talking about, you know. Cut me out of what?"

"Drop it!" commanded Bryce on the instant. "That won't work here. Cut you out of your aunt's coin, of course."

"She did not!" flashed Martin. "I tell you, inspector, there's a mistake somewhere. You'll have to explain, I fear."

"There's a mistake, all right; but you're makin' it," growled Bryce.

"In what way?"

"In thinkin' you can play innocent," said Bryce. On the word, he leaned forward and stared Martin full in the face. "In tryin' to run in a stall like your not knowin' that the Riley woman had got your aunt to make a will in her favor, leaving you out."

"Good Lord!" exclaimed Martin. "Say, I think you're mistaken. Just what do you mean?"

"Didn't you say you'd read the papers?" snarled Bryce.

"Well, not all of them," Martin admitted. "You see, the key came just after I had glanced over the first few lines."

"So you still thought you was your aunt's heir?"

"I certainly did." Martin spoke in the tone of a man who was laboring under an entirely unexpected shock of information.

Bryce and the detective exchanged glances. "What made you leave the Glenn Arms?" the inspector asked.

"Lack of money," responded Martin shortly. "My aunt cut my allowance. She told me of that when she did it, but she certainly never even intimated that she intended cutting me quite off."

"An' what made you stay out till one this mornin', an' come in all over dust?" Bryce came back to his original question again.

"I stayed out because I wasn't ready to come in. I came in all over dust, because it was dusty where I went," snapped Martin with growing impatience. "I'm still all over dust, for that matter, because I hurried over here with the key without stopping to brush up."

"There's no use in gettin' hot," cautioned Bryce. "What made you pick out last night for takin' your walk?"

"I wasn't feeling well," said Martin more quietly. "I had expected to get a bit of money from a chap who owed it to me, and he turned me down, I had been banking on it pretty heavily, and not getting it jolted me a bit.

"I had the blues and I went out to walk off the fit. That is a habit of mine. To hear you talk, one would think you suspected that I knew my aunt was to be murdered last night."

"I don't know as you're far off in that," observed Bryce.

Martin turned pale. "My God, man! You can't be serious," he gasped.

"I ain't jokin' either," said the inspector. "You've just admitted you was hard up—that your aunt had cut down on your pocket money; but that you still thought you was her heir an' would get all of hers when she was gone. Your hotel says you was out from nine to one. Your aunt got hers between ten and eleven.

"You come back lookin' like the deuce, from all we can find out—an' this mornin' you come here with this story about the key bein' sent to you in the mail.

"It is my opinion that you did the job, come off with the key, discovered it after you had made your getaway, and thought it would be a smart trick to mail it to yourself at your new hotel, and then threw dust in our eyes by playin' the interested citizen and bringin' it in.

"So you uses an envelope of the Glenn Arms, where you uster stop, an' slips the thing into a mail-box. It wasn't such a bad scheme if it wasn't for the other facts in the case."

Martin seemed to me to sway where he sat. He opened his lips as if to speak, and closed them again without a sound. Presently, after what seemed a long time, he said hoarsely: "And you think I would do that?"

"I ain't sayin' exactly all I think, Mr. Martin," hedged Bryce, "but I think maybe you'd better stick around here for a little bit until we can find out what you did do last night."

"Then, inspector, I suppose I am under arrest?"

"I reckon that's about it," said Bryce. He rose and motioned to Johnson. The two men retired to a corner of the room and entered into a low-toned argument.

Martin sat up in his chair, and suddenly he laughed shortly. "It's a nice thing to get, when you were trying to do only what you thought best," he began. "I wish I'd let you hunt for the infernal key by yourselves."

Neither Bryce nor Johnson paid any attention to his outburst, and after a moment, I rose and went over to his side and introduced myself. I explained that I had intended calling upon him, and showed Miss Riley's note. He evinced some little interest in that, and was going to keep it, until I insisted upon his giving it back.

"I think I can use it in her interests," said I.

"I don't believe for a minute that that girl did it, Glace, any more than I did," he remarked as he relinquished the note. "I saw her several times at my aunt's. She's a fine little woman, and it's too bad these dunderheads have arrested her."

Suddenly he smiled. "I fancy you'll think me a silly ass, but it's a fact—she had more to do with my resolving to try to take a brace and make good than Aunt Matilda's cutting down on me did. I know it sounds mushy, but honestly, I was rather fond of that girl. I never told her, of course—but I thought I might— if I ever did make good."

"Then you didn't know she was engaged to Dr. Herman?" I asked.

He looked at me in palpable surprise. I could see that he was actually shocked.

"I don't seem to have known much of anything, old chap," he exclaimed. "Why, last night, while I was plowing along a country road, I was wondering how long it would take me, at one hundred and fifty per, to get into a position to speak to the girl—and here she was already engaged—and I never dreamed of the thing." Again he laughed, then sighed, reached into his pocket and drew out a cigar.

"And now they're trying to make a murderer out of me. I ought to have thrown the darned key into the river and let them all go hang. But—no, I don't mean that either—better me than Miss Gertrude, and surely they can't hold us both, can they, Glace?"

"Only for a limited time, on suspicion," I replied.

"Was that right about my aunt's having left her money to Gertrude Riley?" he asked.

"I believe so, Martin," I told him. "That is what she said herself."

"I don't blame her," declared Martin, puffing on his cigar. "I've been a rather worthless sort of expense to her for years. If she'd told me, I wouldn't have kicked. And last night Gertrude told them that, and so they supposed that she had killed her patient to get the money. I saw as much as that in the head-lines this morning, and thought they must be crazy, but now I see what they meant.

"I only had time to glance at the first lines of the story before that blessed key showed up. Say"—he shot a quick glance at me—"honest, Glace, you don't think I did the thing?"

"I should hope not," I replied.

Martin smiled ruefully. "Of course, I was a fool to ask you that, old chap. Well, I suppose I'll have to stand it if fate has decided to give me a wallop or two."

"Who could have sent you the key, do you imagine?" I suggested.

"I don't, and I can't imagine," said Martin with a frown.

"If I thought I could help you, would you be willing to do something I might ask," I went on.

"Would a hungry man—eat?" retorted Martin with a grin.

"Then give me your signature." I thrust a piece of paper and a pencil into his hands.

"My signature!" repeated Martin. "But, Good Lord! How can that help my case?"

"Never mind," I retorted. "If you're innocent it can't hurt you, and I may be able to make it do you some good. Take a chance."

He wrote for a moment, then handed the paper to me. "It's a funny business," he remarked, "but there's my moniker. What are you going to do with it, if one may ask? Are you collecting autographs of potential as well as convicted criminals?"

"I'm going to use it to find out whether you did the job or some one else," I informed him, and rose.

"If you can do it from that, I'm as good as cleared," he said with an attempt at lightness. "If you had a sample of my aunt's handwriting I suppose you could tell for sure if she was murdered or committed suicide?"

"Possibly," I agreed.

"Here's a note she wrote," he informed me, taking an envelope from his coat and handing it to me. I took it with great readiness and felt that luck was with me.

"And now, as one good turn deserves another," said Martin, "do something for me."

"Yours to command," said I.

He drew some currency from his pocket and handed me a bill.

"Send the little girl some flowers for me," he requested, and flushed slightly as he spoke.

I promised, rose, and crossed to where Bryce and Johnson still talked.

"I gave Dan your bottle," I told him. "Better look at it before you go any further. I think it will interest you."

He nodded and went on with his conversation. I left the room and went straight to the *Record* office, where I left the plate I had made of the envelope to be developed in the art-room. Then I went out to get a bite of lunch, and send Gertrude Riley Martin's bouquet.

CHAPTER VI

ANOTHER THUMB-MARK

BY THE TIME I had obtained my lunch and gone back to the office for a print of the plate I made at the station, it was between two and three o'clock. I decided that if I was to see Dr. Herman I had better be about it; so I caught a car to that part of town where Miss Riley had said he lived.

I found 960 Madison Street to be a small brick dwelling, in the front window of which I could see the doctor's gilt-lettered sign, while above a side door on the porch swung another with the word "office" printed below.

I turned in the gate, went up the path, and rang the bell on the indicated door. A moment later the doctor himself responded, and asked me to walk in.

The room, which had once been of good size, had been cut in two by a partition, so as to divide it into a waiting-room and a consulting office beyond.

It was to the farther apartment that Herman led me, and waved me to a chair before seating himself at a desk upon which was a typewriter with a sheet of paper on the roll. Other close-ly-written sheets lay at one side of the machine, and I imagined that he had been actively at work when I rang.

I introduced myself briefly, stating my name and occupation, and adding that I had come in the hope of being accorded a personal interview, which I could write up for the *Record*. As I finished speaking the physician frowned.

"Really, Mr. Glace, there is little to be said of the case. I think I saw you at the apartments last night, did I not? Then doubtless you saw as much as I."

"Of the general details, yes. But that isn't the point, doctor," I returned. "I am sent here to get a professional statement from you. Naturally, I want to make good with my editor."

I began to fear that my last call was going to be the difficult one of the three. The doctor was palpably indisposed to discuss the affair, and I wondered how I was going to get a sample of his writing if I couldn't even make him talk.

"But of what good is all that?"

"Did you see the *Record* this morning?" I asked.

"Yes, I read it," he responded indifferently.

"Then you know our theory of the case—that it was done by some one other than the nurse."

"It was," said the doctor with conviction. "Miss Riley is a very estimable young woman. I have every confidence in her. I am positive that she is totally innocent of any wrong. I regard her arrest as a blunder of the authorities."

"In the light of her statements, which you yourself heard, they could, however, scarcely do otherwise, doctor, you must admit."

"Miss Riley, unfortunately for herself, told the whole truth," said the man. "Her story seemed sincere to me."

"Then her story about walking to the little park is in your judgment correct?" I coaxed him on.

"Perfectly. I know positively that she was in the habit of going out in the evenings for a little rest and exercise. She had been very attentive to her patient, and had felt the effects upon her own condition. Recently I myself had advised that she have an hour or two off each evening. That is, since Mrs. Greenig's recovery was assured.

"On several occasions she told me that she spent her time in the park, where it was dark and cool, and Mrs. Greenig confirmed the same statements as well. Unfortunately, however, she could not substantiate the fact last night."

"Then her statements about the wills were correct as well?"

I seemed to have got him started at last.

"Absolutely correct, Mr. Glace. The girl felt her innocence, and, having nothing to conceal, spoke without reservation, never suspecting that she was being entrapped into what looked like incriminating replies. At one time I tried to catch her eye and warn her by a glance, because I feared where her frankness might lead with the police."

"How about this nephew of Mrs. Greenig's, Dr. Herman?" I questioned.

The doctor took some time before he replied. He seemed to be making up his mind just how much to say.

"He's a good deal of a rake, I imagine," he said at length; "what people are accustomed to call a man about town. I do not know that he is naturally vicious; but he has lived from his aunt's bounty for years, until she grew tired of his course and cut him off with the proverbial shilling, as I understand."

"Did you know that he had been arrested shortly after noon to-day on suspicion of knowing too much about the case?" I asked. I saw that I could keep him talking if I could only keep up his interest.

"No. Is that so?" he exclaimed, with a sudden accession of awakened attention. "I had, of course, no way of knowing," he added in the next breath, as though he regretted the startled excitement of his first reply.

"Yes, he had the missing door-key to the flat," I informed him. "Said it had been sent him anonymously in this morning's mail."

"Rather far-fetched, don't you think?" said the doctor after an interval of thought.

"The police think that he mailed it to himself," I added.

"I fear I would be inclined to the same view," said Herman.

"Now as to the actual cause of death, doctor"—I returned to my original theme—"just how would you advise me to say in my story that Mrs. Greenig was killed?"

"She died of hemorrhage, of course, Mr. Glace."

"Yes, I know; but can't we get it a bit more technical than that?"

"How?"

"Well, couldn't we describe which vessel, vein, or artery, or whatever it was that was cut?"

I had suddenly conceived of a way to get what I was after, and I decided to push it to a successful end. Dual had told me to get a sample of this man's writing. Personally I couldn't see at the time what possible bearing the chirography of the dead woman's physician could have; but, knowing Dual as I did, I knew equally well that he had a reason for everything he said—a reason which, as a rule, I couldn't see until long afterward. Therefore, I was determined to get what he wanted and trust the results to him.

Herman smiled again. "Of course, one could say that the median basilic vein was the one opened, and that death was the result of hemorrhage from that," he admitted; "but I hardly see that it would add any particular interest to a newspaper account. Not one person in fifty would know where the vessel was."

I began to write it down, then I paused. "Let's see—median ba-ba— How do you spell the thing, anyway?"

"B-a-s-i-l-i-c," he replied.

"B-a-s-c," I began, and then laughed. I handed my pad over to him with a smile, which I tried to make childlike and bland. "Write it down for me, doctor, so I'll be sure to have it right."

Without further comment he took the pad and wrote the words plainly below the notes I had made, then passed it back to me.

"There, Mr. Glace," he remarked. "Outside the profession they won't know what you are talking about, but at least your editor should be satisfied."

"Thank you, doctor," I said as I took the page and put it carefully away in my pocket-folder. "I suppose the median basilic is the vein just below the bend of the elbow on the inner surface of the forearm, the one which was cut?"

"Naturally—the one which was cut, Mr. Glace."

"How long in your opinion would it take a woman to bleed to death from that sort of a cut?" I next asked.

"It would depend upon several things," said the debtor rather nervously, I thought.

He glanced openly at the typewriter and back to me. It grew upon me that he desired to terminate the interview, and was endeavoring to give me a tacit hint. I didn't take it, as I wasn't yet through.

"In the first place," he went on after a slight pause, "all that would be necessary to induce death would be for enough blood to escape so that the heart would not have sufficient remaining upon which to contract.

"When hemorrhage reaches that stage death results—even though a great deal of blood still remains in the vessels themselves. In a woman already weakened by a protracted illness it would not take very long; thirty minutes at most, perhaps."

"So that if the cut was made about ten o'clock the murderer would have had time to satisfy himself that his work was complete and escape by a quarter to eleven—am I right?"

For a moment I fancied that he had not followed my question; then, just as I was about to repeat it, he answered: "You are perfectly right, Mr. Glace."

"That should cover the ground I was to ask about," I said, "but there is a question which I should like to ask you on my own behalf. Is it true that you were engaged to marry the nurse?"

Herman sat forward in his chair, as though thrown up by a spring, and stared at me for as much as a minute before he made any reply. During the time his face paled slightly, and he seemed to be struggling with some inner emotion.

Presently, however, he spoke. "Mr. Glace, I consider any such question as that a rank impertinence. Is there no single detail of a man's private business which you fellows consider sufficiently personal to be left alone? It's getting to a pass where the press has altogether too much liberty.

"My personal feelings for Miss Riley do not, so far as I can see, concern the reading public in any way. So far as the rest of this interview is concerned, I have tried to give you what you asked, although I thought it a waste of valuable time; but this is a different thing, and I shall reply to your question by simply stating that it is no business of yours."

Personally I really agreed with the man. As a reporter I was satisfied that I had verified Miss Riley's statements made to me at the jail.

"The reason I asked was because Miss Riley so stated to me this morning," I made explanation, "and I naturally desired to verify it with you."

Suddenly the doctor smiled. "Then surely as a gentleman I may not question the lady's word," said he.

"Was it while she was nursing Mrs. Greenig that you became engaged?" I asked.

Herman looked for a moment as though he were tempted to hurl the typewriter at my head, but evidently decided that violence would do no good.

"I told you that I didn't care to discuss the matter," he said shortly, "and, as I have work to do, and you are evidently minded to pursue your unpleasant line of questioning, I would suggest that we call this interview at an end; I am sorry to seem rude, but I will not tolerate any more prying into my affairs."

I rose and picked up my hat. "Did you ever use fruit juices in the treatment of typhoid?" I inquired.

The doctor shot me a puzzled glance. Apparently he didn't see the reason for my abrupt change of front. "Yes," he replied sullenly, "I have."

"On Mrs. Greenig's case?"

"Yes. I believe that they were responsible for her change from a condition apparently predicating certain death to one promising a complete recovery. Why?"

"Only that I have been reading an article on the subject in the last twenty-four hours," I answered, "and that I have a friend who advocated such things to me quite a while ago before I had ever seen anything in print to that effect. I naturally felt an interest in the matter when I read the article, as it coincided with his views, and I thought I'd like to know what you thought."

"Is your friend a physician?"

"Not in the sense you mean," I responded. "He is a scientist, however, of remarkable ability, to my way of thinking at least."

"I should like to meet him," said Herman. "Where does he live?"

"Here in the city I am sure he, too, would enjoy meeting you. I shall mention the matter of our talk to him when I see him. Let me thank you, doctor, for the interview and apologize for what you quite naturally deemed my impertinence. We newspapermen have to do lots of things as reporters which we would never think of doing as individual citizens."

I thought of the folded sheet of paper which I had purloined at the station, and I felt that I had spoken the truth in what I had said.

The doctor rose and offered me his hand. "Suppose we forget all that, Glace," he said. "Naturally, you can appreciate that I feel a bit touchy over the affair with the girl whom I expected to marry resting under such a suspicion as is placed upon Miss Riley just now. Her arrest came upon me as a totally unexpected complication of the matter, and I have been deeply worried ever since."

"But she'll be cleared of that," I returned.

"I sincerely hope so," said Herman. "It's a dreadful situation for her to find herself in through no fault of hers. Yes, at any cost the girl must be cleared."

I noticed that he spoke with a sudden fire, which at the time I couldn't understand. He seemed to be a person who fluctuated between rapidly changing moods.

"Her mere accusation will not affect your attitude toward her, will it?" I suggested.

"That will depend upon her," he responded. "I shall marry her if she will consent, if that's what you mean."

A car was coming along the street, so I said good afternoon and went down to intercept it. After I was aboard I sank into a seat and gave myself up to a little thought. I had surely had a busy day, but in the end I had obtained all Dual had asked me to get.

I wondered what Semi had been at while I was working on the task he had set for me. All at once I smiled. Semi and I were like body and mind when we worked on a case. Like the mind—he sat enthroned in his strange abode and directed the activities which brought in the details for him to piece together into the perfect whole. Like the body—I ran hither and yon at his behest and did his bidding, and fetched and carried, marveling at the results he got out of the things I did.

I got out the sheet of paper on which the doctor had written the name of the vein, and opened it out to see what his writing looked like and to wonder how Dual read the souls of men from the writing of their hands. For a moment I didn't know whether to laugh or swear.

I have already mentioned that Dr. Herman had been using a typewriter when I entered his office, and that we began our talk immediately. Then, when I asked him to write the name of the blood-vessel, he had taken the pad and held it in his hand as he wrote.

Well, as a result of those seemingly trivial facts I had got more than I hoped for, or had any right to expect, for, besides the written words on the page, there was the carbon-smudged imprint of a thumb! Doubtless the doctor had been arranging his ribbon on the machine, got some of the stuff on his hands, and failed to wash it off. This was the result. It seemed to be my day for getting thumb-prints, all right. I chuckled as I thought that this at least would surprise Dual.

CHAPTER VII

A NOTE TO THE DOCTOR

I DROPPED OFF the car at the office of the *Record,* and went up-stairs to pound off the story of Martin's arrest. I rather expected that Smithson would have some characteristic sarcasm on tap for me about my absence, and I was not far wrong.

When I carried my copy to his desk, he took it in silence and glanced over the first page before he looked up.

"Why is it," he snorted, "that every time you get out on a big assignment, you leave this office in the dark until you get good and ready to report?"

I was tired after a hard, hot day, so I dropped into a chair. "Now don't go to howling until the finish," I said, grinning. "I haven't been here because there were better places to be."

Smithson tapped the copy I had just turned in. "This is all rehash," he declared with positive emphasis. "Every evening sheet will have it spread across the front page. I thought you were making a roar last night that we were in for a scoop?"

"Did you ever know me to make a crack like that and not come across with the stuff?" I inquired. It seemed to me that he ought to know that I meant what I said, by this time.

Smithson grinned. No, son," said he, "I never did. But your methods get on my nerves. A city editor likes to know a little bit about how the work on his sheet is being done; while you insist upon playing it alone."

I made myself a cigarette and got it to going nicely; and then I got to my feet.

"Where are you going now?" said Smithson suspiciously.

"I am now going to get the real murderer's name," I announced as I started for the door. "After I get it, you'll have your scoop."

"Go to the devil!" said Smithson.

Instead, I went to Semi Dual. Henri met me when I got to the Urania, and, motioning me to follow, led me back through the inner room to a part of the place I had never visited before, up a short flight of steps and down a passage lined with potted plants.

As I advanced I became aware of the soft sound of running water, and pretty soon we came out into a vaulted dome of green glass; and I halted in amazement.

The room was nearly circular, and in the center was a pool some fifty feet across, which danced and shimmered and sparkled in the cool, subdued light. About the sides were potted shrubs, and flowering vines climbed up a trellis inside the transparent walls. The twitter of flitting birds came down to my ears from the vaulted dome.

In the pool was a rocky little island, from the side of which gushed a stream of water, which cascaded into the pool below in a rippling, tinkling flood.

The place was cool and delicious, after the heat of the outer July day. It was quiet and restful with its yellow-green light and its shimmering water. I drew in a great breath of delight.

At first I did not see a sign of Dual anywhere. Then there came a splash, an agitation of the water in the pool; and Semi's body darted slanting around the island and shot across toward where I stood enjoying the unexpectedness of it all.

Dual shook the water from his head and smiled into my face. *"Bonan vesperon, mia amika,"* said he in Esperanto, then in English: "How do you like my new swimming pool?"

"Good evening, yourself," I responded. "It looks great, and very much as though it was cool."

"It is," laughed Dual. "Come on in; the water's fine."

"I'd like to, all right," I admitted, "but I guess I hadn't better go swimming to-day. I've got a lot of things to show you and a lot to tell."

"Time enough for that afterward," said Dual. "Henri will take your clothes. You look shot and tired. A bath will do you good and prepare you for what we have before us to-night."

The temptation was too great to be resisted. I slipped out of my clothing, and, tossing it to Henri took a header into the clear, green water of the pool.

It was delightful, and as I splashed about in the cool liquid, I laughed in pure enjoyment of the rest I felt.

"Great, isn't it?" said Semi. "I thought I'd surprise you when you came."

"It reminds me of another bath you once gave me in Teheran," I said, rolling over on my back, and paddling my hands in the cooling flood.

"There is one innovation which makes it very different from the other," said Semi. "Wait."

In a long, sweeping stroke, he slid to one side of the pool, and apparently pressed a button in the rim of the bath. Instantly gentle little needles of sensation played over my skin. In surprise I turned over and stood up, and, as my feet touched the floor, the sensation grew. I lifted first one foot, then the other. Dual was grinning like a boy.

"Turn it off," I begged, still dancing. "Plain water suits me best."

The current died, and Semi swam over to me.

"All the same it will do you good," he remarked. "I've had men working on this all summer. It was finished a week ago.

Only at the last did I think about arranging it so as to charge the pool with a weak current of electricity.

"I took a good deal of time in planning out the entire arrangement, and then I had to persuade the building people to let me go ahead; but it's worth all the effort to be able to enjoy it every day. I have it so arranged that I can heat the water in winter, so that I have a year-round plunge-bath.

"Any time you wish, come up and take a swim. Henri will let you in, if I am busy. Now, if you are ready—I see Henri has brought in a robe for you—we'll slip into the things and get to work finishing up your case."

We climbed out of the pool, and Semi led me back to the room where we always sat and talked.

Henri turned off somewhere on the way, and by the time Semi had offered me a cigarette, a little table slid noiselessly in through the wall, with its burden of cakes, fruits, and Dual's peculiar blend of fruit juice nectar.

As we lunched, Semi asked for my story of the day, which I began at once, after requesting that Henri bring my coat, which contained the various samples of writing.

Dual nodded and went on eating a peach. I hesitated in my tale.

"Go on," he directed, and then smiled. "Oh, I called Henri, friend Glace. I've been educating him to come when I wish it, and he is growing quite proficient. See; he is approaching now."

The servant came in, and Semi told him to get my things.

I shook a bewildered head, and he laughed. "Why wonder? I call you to me from a far greater distance," he reminded. "Why think it so wonderful that I can summon my own man?"

"It was its unexpectedness," I said in explanation, "though by now I ought to be used to that up here. It seems to me everything partakes of the same quality. Even this food is different. A very little seems to satisfy. I've meant to ask you about that."

"It's because it is alive," said Dual. He held up his peach. "The atomic corpuscles of this bit of fruit are still in a state of vibration; the cell life of the peach is still intact. As a result, a little of it satisfies the body's needs far better than the half-dead food of the modern markets. But get on with your report."

I told him everything which had occurred, and at the end I got out the specimens of handwriting and the thumb-marked sheet of paper which had been folded about the key.

Semi took them, rose to press a button, which caused the table to vanish through the wall, and walked over to the desk, where he spread the various papers out in front of him. As on former occasions, he had recourse to his powerful magnifying glass.

The afternoon sun streamed in through the window and fell about him as he sat at the great desk, poring over the pages, to all appearances oblivious to all else.

The whimsical idea woke in my brain that the light hovered in a sort of halo about the noble head of the man. At least it brought out with cameolike distinctness his splendid features as he bent forward above the samples of different writing and the finger-marks which I had brought, scanning them through the powerful glass.

At that moment I felt a great admiration and love for Semi Dual. He lived apart from the world, yet, because of his love for mankind, devoted all his abilities to helping those in trouble, and to searching out the true causes of criminal acts without asking a price for his work.

True, one may argue that he had everything necessary for his needs. That is true. Yet I could name many who had far more, and still devoted their time and wealth to the furtherance of purely selfish ends.

As I sat and watched his keen face it dawned upon me more strongly than ever that it was my rare privilege to sit in the presence of a true superman and call him my friend.

Semi rose and crossed to a cabinet, from which he took the plates of the thumb-print on the bottle, and as he reseated himself he smiled at me.

There was approbation in that smile, and I felt its glow steal through me like the warmth of wine. Semi could always say more in a glance than I could in words. I imagined that I could now understand what made men willing to follow a beloved leader to death. I sat up, and waited anxiously while he continued his examination, now and then making a mark or a note on a sheet of blank paper, again peering through the glass at some peculiarity of the writing.

The strangeness of it all came over me in a flood. Somewhere out in the sunshine, or hiding, perhaps, or already under arrest, was the man who had taken life last night. Perhaps he was torn by fear; perhaps he fancied himself safe, and walked boldly about. But, no matter what his frame of mind might be, it would not change the result.

While he gloated in confidence or suffered in fear and remorse, here sat a man—fashioned even as was he—with a glass and a pencil and some pieces of paper, who, by and by, was going to put out his finger and say: "Behold the man!"—and it would be true.

Was Semi Dual really Destiny? The idea was whimsical, yet I did not smile. At least, he was an unimpassioned force, working for the ends of immutable justice, with my bits of written paper and his own wonderful brain as the tools. The lines of his own countryman, Omar, came into my mind, and I whispered them softly to myself. Dual took the very words out of my mouth, as it were.

" 'The moving finger writes, and, having writ, moves on'—and writes again," said he, pushing back the several specimens of chirography and turning to me with a smile. "Gordon—you have done a good day's work. In these little samples of writing the fingers of four souls have writ their messages to the world, and told the story of a crime."

"Then you know?" I cried.

"I have proof," Dual corrected. "Myself, I was certain last night. Now I am ready to support my claims to the world of material men, who must always have 'proof.'"

"But you know who murdered the woman last night, Dual?"

Dual smiled again at my excitement. "I know," he replied.

"Then your astrological calculations must have told you," I cried.

"They did," said Semi Dual.

"So that you could recognize him even then?"

"Shall I describe the real criminal to you?" my friend volunteered.

"Go on," I begged him. "I shall never understand it; but it is wonderful."

"He is a man of medium build, very dark complexion, bearded, quick temper, selfish to a degree, a materialist, fond of money and unscrupulous as to how he gets it, so long as he does. Yet, he occupies a position of great trust, and few people know the real man behind a suave and smiling mask. What does that convey to your mind, friend Glace?"

"It suggests an almost unbelievable possibility!" I exclaimed.

Dual smiled a little sadly, I thought. "There is nothing unbelievable of human frailty," said he, and turned again to his desk.

He drew a sheet of paper to him and wrote rapidly a few lines, selected an envelope, and enclosed what he had written, sealed it and wrote an address. As he finished Henri appeared.

Dual handed him the note, and told him to deliver it to the written address, and to be sure to bring back an answer when he returned. Then, as the man left the room, he swung back to me.

"I have sent the murderer an invitation to call upon me tonight," he explained. "When he arrives I shall prove to you that all I have said is correct. In the mean time let me outline to you a bit of what your work has resulted in revealing. After that we will prepare to receive the guilty man when he arrives."

"And you think he will come?" I queried. It seemed unlikely to me that any man in his senses would walk into the trap.

But Semi only smiled once again. "He will come," he assured. "Now draw a chair over here by the desk. From the amount of doubt-waves you generate, you should have been named Thomas, my friend."

In abashed silence I drew my chair up beside Semi Dual.

CHAPTER VIII

WHAT THE HANDWRITING TOLD

"TO BEGIN WITH," said Semi, as he spread before him the several pieces of paper, "let us take up each sample of chirography and see what story the 'moving finger' told.

"First, here is the note which Mrs. Greenig wrote to her nephew, and he handed to you. This is the writing of a person prostrated by illness. Note its wavy lines, the unevenness of the letters. Yet, on the whole, it denotes a person of mental strength, and its lines slant slightly upward across the page. The writer was convalescent from her malady, though, of course, we already know that. But there was no thought in her mind of suicide. The handwriting of a person contemplating self-murder always slants downward across the page. We may therefore cast this specimen aside.

"Secondly, here is a strong yet delicate chirography. There is nothing in it to indicate crime. The person who wrote it is lovable in most ways, and inclined to be generous. Such an individual would be apt to give the other fellow the benefit of the doubt in trying to judge him, and to show mercy so far as a sense of justice would allow. Suffering or pain would always appeal to this individual, at least in the concrete example. In hunting for one criminal we may eliminate this person, adding that the writer has evidently a high regard for the truth."

"All of which supports your prior deductions concerning the nurse," said I.

"Exactly," said Semi Dual. "I only gave you the reading of her note in order to show how everything points to her innocence."

He picked up another piece of paper and held it in his hand. "Here we have another type of writing altogether. If you will look at it closely you will notice that in some ways it resembles two others which I have explained to you in the past.

"In the first place, observe that the last letter in the first name is a bit higher than most people make it. In the second place, the loop of the capital beginning the first name is made very large compared to the other letters in the signature. Also the second letter of the first word is not joined to the capital, which indicates that the writer removed his pencil from the sheet after making the first letter, and then wrote the rest of the word.

"There is a slight difference in the height of the three loops of the 'M,' the last loop being the highest of the three. Again, while the small letters are the same size to the end of the word and cannot be said to taper, the pressure on the pencil was lightened as each one was written, so that the end of the word appears lighter in color than the beginning.

"This holds good in the surname as well as in the first; and you will notice that the top of each 'a' in both the words is broken—that is, the loop of the 'a' is not quite closed. The writer's pencil did not go up quite far enough to join the loop to the upright, thus leaving the break.

"Now a person who writes that sort of a hand is apt to be of a more or less peculiar personality. He will be a person who is generous, but frequently in the wrong direction. He will be proud, with a good, strong self-respect; he may even be a little given to boasting in a mild way, more from a desire to make people pay attention to him than from any genuine or inherent egotism.

"Under natural conditions he will not be a person liable to criminal impulses, and if he commits a crime, it will be one of impulse rather than of deliberate intent, and will be followed by the most bitter remorse. In the main he will be an individual of high ideals, but with a lack of perseverance in following out his purposes. He will be apt to waste his time and squander his money, unless he very carefully watches himself. For designing persons he will be an easy mark. Yet with a proper impulse and motive he can control all this.

"His main weakness, in fact, is a poor power of control in his individual habits, which really hurt no one but himself—this is indicated by the form of the letter 'M.' He will be apt to have fits of great elation, and equal depression. Such a person needs the help of a companion who is cool-headed and sympathetic. So much for him how.

"In the fourth specimen of writing we now find a very different type displayed. The writing is primarily heavy to an unusual degree, as you can easily notice, and each word diminishes in size from the first letter to the last, but in size, observe, not in the pressure on the pencil, which is even throughout.

"Persons who write such a hand are almost certain to be exceedingly selfish, unless there is some other redeeming characteristic in their writing; and I do not find it here. Such people are usually materialists in the most pronounced sense. They make good scientists because of that tendency.

"Again, you will notice, there is a slight break—visible only under the microscope or a powerful glass—in the bottom of the letter 'a.' If there were other looped letters in the name here written, they would doubtless show similar breaks. In other words, by a strange coincidence, we have the exact reverse condition of the formation of the 'a' in this signature from the one we examined last.

"Such breaks in a letter are not apt to indicate a latent criminality of impulse, and in a naturally selfish and material person they are dangerous, to say the least. Such writers are apt to be very easily tempted where money is at stake.

"I wish that he had written some word containing a 't,' in order that I might have seen how he would have crossed it. Reasoning, however, from the words here shown, we may deduce that it would only confirm my belief showing indications of a personality which would not shrink from committing murder to gain a wholly selfish end."

"But, Dual," I cried in excitement, "that is the signature of a man whose mission in life is to save life!"

"Do men always live up to their missions?" my friend inquired in his calm way.

"But he was the woman's own physician!"

"Well—go on," said Dual.

"Well, look what it involves."

"Does that alter the true reading of the facts?" said Semi slowly. "The moving finger writes. We may read, if we wish, what it has written, Gordon, either of good or bad, of joy or sorrow; but when it has once written, nothing can alter that immutable record. That is the law of all life."

"I looked at it with the eyes of the average man, I suppose," I began. "Not all of us can be Semi Duals."

"My friend," Dual took me up, "in a way it grieves me that you should always feel that I am criticizing when I explain. That is the wrong attitude to hold, Gordon. All men, if they wish, may be Semi Duals—you—every one. Semi Dual is only a soul which has seen much, lived much, suffered much, and thereby, please God, learned a little of the truth.

"To you and all men he desires only to be the mouthpiece of that truth in so much as you care to hear. And remember this: You can say nothing to offend me, unless you wish, my brother, and I know you well enough to know that you do not—wish."

"Heaven forbid!" I cried, abashed at the ever-fresh wonder of each new glimpse into the man's soul. "Sometimes, I fancy, I grow confused at the way you calmly turn the light into places where light has never been, and show up the ghastly relics of so-called respectable souls."

Dual smiled slightly. His smiles seemed to be but facial ripples set up by the thoughts which agitated his mind.

"Each of us has his own little burial-ground of mistakes and disgraces, Gordon. Confucius said that there is no disgrace in falling. The disgrace lies in not getting up again. Shall I go on with my lecture of proof?"

"Is there yet further proof of the man's rascality?"

"Much more," said Dual. "The strongest part. The part which will convict. See here." He drew across to him the plate from the thumb-print on the bottle, the folded paper I had stolen at the station, and the paper on which Dr. Herman had written the name of the vein.

"We are reasonably sure that the finger-marks on the bottle are those of the real criminal, so we will pass that by now," continued Dual. "Now, on the paper you got at the station there are two different finger-marks—"

"Two!" I exclaimed.

"Two," repeated Semi Dual. "One quite plain, and the others so faint that only the glass brings them out with any distinctness at all. Furthermore, your picture of the envelope which contained the key is fortunately a very good negative and shows the picture of yet another print. It corresponds to the second one on the paper, so far as I can see, only it is more distinct—such, in fact, as a person with not overclean hands might make in holding an envelope while tearing it across one end."

"And that is the way it was opened," I threw in.

"The picture shows that," smiled Semi.

"And the thumb-marks are those—" I began in excited surmise.

"Of Martin," Dual completed the remark.

"Then, if they don't match those on the bottle, that will be enough to free the chap right away," I followed up the thought.

"If you were to telephone to Inspector Bryce no doubt he would tell you as much by now. They have doubtless made Martin give them a thumb-print after seeing the bottle you took back," said Dual.

"The real interest in all this," he continued, "is that the plainer mark on the paper corresponds line for line with that taken from the bottle last night. This would indicate that the murderer had that piece of paper in his hands at some time."

"But why did he send the key to Martin?" I cried.

"Primarily to get rid of it, of course," Dual answered. "Secondly, to cast suspicion on Martin if he was foolish enough to return it. You, yourself, saw that it accomplished just this."

"But look how easily you read through the thing," I began, and stopped at the quizzical expression in Dual's eyes.

"The person in question did not expect me to be called into the case, my dear Gordon, nor could he," said Semi Dual. "His materialistic mind would never consider a mystic as a possible element in the affair. Consequently you are taking a wrong hypothesis."

He tossed the folded sheet aside and picked up the one with the carbon-smudged print, which I had brought from my last interview.

"Here," he continued, "is the last link which completes the chain and binds our criminal fast in the eyes of the law. By an irony of fate, he gave it to you himself. This print of a thumb, which you yourself witnessed in the making, corresponds to that on the folded paper and that on the bottle of last night.

"There is no court of law which will refuse such evidence, and I am now safe in making the charges which last night would have sounded ridiculous, unless backed by some such support. Now let us put all these things in a safe place, and get ready for our visitor when he comes. Suppose we go up to the observatory a bit."

I rose and followed him up the spiral stairs to the room at the top, where he had his great telescope and all his other instruments of scientific purpose. He led me to one end of the apartment and paused before a large and very complicated machine.

So far as I could see, it consisted of a bewildering mass of great diaphragms and a series of tubes and pipes, wheels and springs and wires. Its purpose did not dawn upon me at the moment; not, in fact, until Semi Dual himself explained.

"This," said he, "is the universalion, the machine which plays the harmony of etheric vibration, and is operated by the same force whose rhythmic measures it gives forth. You heard its music, on that night before Mrs. Parton started for Europe on her eventful trip."

"I remember," I answered. "It is a frightfully complicated-looking device. How does it work?"

Dual smiled. He stepped close to the mechanism and ran a loving hand over its several parts.

"In the main," said he, "it consists of a series of diaphragms for receiving the vibrations of the interplanetary ether, as scientists call it, or pranic vibration or force, as we transcendentalists have named it for ourselves. These it conducts to reproducing magnets, weakly charged with electricity.

"These magnets in turn affect a series of small vibrators, which magnify and intensify the received waves and conduct them to the sounders of a series of pipes, something like those of an organ, as you can see. These sounders are built very much after the principle of the reproducer of a phonograph.

"There is a tube for every note of the musical scale and every tone of the human voice. These are used for ordinary organ or reed effects and for speaking parts. Another part of the machine will, by a modification of the idea, give the effect of stringed instruments of all sorts.

"If the machine is merely switched on as it is, it will give off a sound which is the component of all the vibrations of the planetary ether. This is what you have already heard it play. If, however, a record be inserted in the holder, the ordinary vibrations will be so broken up as to reproduce the melody desired; and in that way any selection, instrumental or vocal, can be played, for any natural sound reproduced with lifelike fidelity.

"A series of buttons control the machine from any place where a transmitter is installed, and an automatic feeder will remove and insert new records in the machine in any order in which they may be arranged in a carrier device, so that I can enjoy a concert at any time by simply pressing the proper button on the switch."

"It's a remarkable piece of work," I declared. Actually I felt almost in awe of the thing. Once more I marveled at the brain of the man which had evolved this wonderful mechanism.

"But what is its purpose in to-night's work?" I inquired of Dual, who was busy inserting a series of small, numbered disks in what I judged was the feeding carrier of the machine.

"I made some new records this afternoon," said Semi, "which I intend exhibiting to our expected caller. They should put him into a proper mental condition for doing what I intend compelling him to do."

I sat down on a chair and watched him in silent wonder. Always he was springing something new. One never knew what to expect with Semi Dual. Therein, in part, lay his grip on one—his ability never to pall on a friend.

For a few minutes Semi worked about the universalion, as he called it, then moved toward the stairs, and we again descended to the inner room, where he immediately began changing the globes on his electrics from plain glass to a violet-tinted shade.

When he had quite finished he turned on the lights and pulled down the blinds. The effect was indescribably beautiful at first, but became in a moment strangely unnatural. To me in my chair it seemed that I was bathed in a sea of intense purple light, and at the same moment I became aware of the odor of violets, subtle and sweet.

"In Heaven's name, what now?" I gasped.

"Purple light—the test of the light," said Semi, again smiling. "It is trying to one of a material mind. In the great esoteric or occult brotherhoods, Gordon, a great many tests are applied to the candidate desiring admission. One of these is the test of 'the purple light.' He who cannot stand; this test is not eligible to the higher brotherhood, the inner circle, as it were."

I shook my head. Dual was standing very straight, with face partly lifted to the glow of violet rays from above. I felt awed and strangely thrilled by the sight. Almost he looked like some great priest in his white-and-purple robe.

"It's too deep for me, I'm afraid," I managed to say at length.

Dual seemed to come back from an abstraction with a start. "Every individual soul throws off vibratory emanations which correspond to varying degrees of the light spectrum," he said slowly, "and can be perceived by the trained soul as various colored lights. Such personal color atmospheres are known as auras. They are the personal atmosphere of every soul.

"Even those who cannot sense them as light may be affected by them. To a great measure they explain the instinctive likes and dislikes which occur between men and women, and are felt, but not understood. If a man of low qualities, hence of low vibration and poor auric color, be placed in an atmosphere of the higher sort, he will be rendered uncomfortable in proportion to the difference in his own and the other atmosphere. Suppose a pure materialist, a man with a red aura—a murderer, with his mind full of his crime—were plunged into a purple light, which is at the opposite extreme of the scale, the sufferings of that man would be excruciating indeed."

"And you intend using its effect on the murderer to-night?" I exclaimed. "Now I see. But what of the odor of violets?"

"The odor is harmonious, helps to complete the effect—the violet is a symbol of purity, as is the violet light. The effect is simply produced by a container of scent set under an indrawing ventilator in the wall. I think that our stage arrangements may now be called complete, so all we have to do is to wait." He switched off the lights and raised the blind, and once more the summer twilight filled the room.

Dual seated himself at his desk and lit a cigarette. "A bit of material indulgence will not hurt me, as I am to be exposed to violet rays for some time. Better have a cocktail or a brandy and soda, Glace. It will stimulate your vibratory rate temporarily and bring you nearer up to the key."

I nodded, and he rang for Henri. To me it seemed that he was deliberately courting the material now. Yet when Henri came he ordered a brandy and soda, which I had mentally decided to ask for, and then smiled at my quizzical stare.

"Force of habit," said Semi Dual.

"Do you know," I observed as I sipped my brandy and soda, "that Martin told me to-day that he was in love with the nurse, and that it was that more than anything which made him decide to go to work?"

"His handwriting would indicate a more or less romantic tendency," said Semi Dual. "However, she ought to make him a good mate. She has well-defined qualities which he lacks, and would have a good balancing effect on his impulsive qualities. All the cynics in the world to the contrary, the most successful men are those who have had some good woman to climb upward beside them, hand in hand."

"The only trouble will be that the girl inherits Mrs. Greenig's wealth, and that will hold Martin off," I opined.

"The girl will attend to that unless I am mistaken," said Semi, grinning at the end of his cigarette. "I rather fancy that girl will refuse to have anything to do with the money. Now, you had better get into your street clothes to receive our visitor."

I hastened to don my own garments, and then returned to my seat. Dual seemed to have fallen into a reverie of some sort, so I sat and gazed out into the deepening twilight, and thought my own thoughts.

By and by the great clock in the corner struck eight times. Dual rose and drew the blinds and switched on the lights, at the same time starting the spiral ventilator to revolving, then returned to his seat.

Under the violet-purple light his face looked strange, pallid, ghastly, unnatural. I suppose my own looked the same. The lights in the room were so arranged that the bulbs themselves did not show, being set in hanging baskets and oriental lanterns, which threw their radiance upward, so that the effect was of light streaming from the ceiling in a purple flood. Only the golden apple in Dual's life-sized bronze Venus glowed faintly yellow.

I found myself breathing more rapidly than was my wont. The atmosphere of the place was getting on my nerves already. Dual looked at me and smiled. Suddenly the chimes of the annunciator rang out. Steps sounded in the other room. Henri appeared at the door and bowed.

"*Monsieur* has arrived," he announced and stood aside.

A figure appeared behind him, and a moment later Dr. Heinrich Herman entered the room.

CHAPTER IX

UNDER THE PURPLE LIGHT

DUAL ROSE AND greeted his guest with the greatest courtesy and offered him a chair.

"It is always a pleasure to me to meet a brother scientist," he remarked. "My friend Glace, whom you have already met, tells me that we entertain kindred views on the use of fruit juices in the treatment and prevention of disease."

The doctor took a chair and glanced about the room. I fancied he did not seem entirely at ease. He swept the apartment with a curious eye and glanced up to the source of the peculiar purple light, then turned back to his host.

"Yes, yes, just so," he replied, as though but slightly interested in the subject. Again his eyes began sweeping the room.

"You are noticing my lighting arrangement and the color of the light, no doubt," said Semi, taking his chair.

"Yes," admitted the doctor, with more animation. "It is most peculiar."

"I have found that it has a stimulating effect upon mental activity," explained Dual. "One can think more rapidly and with more certain effect in such a light. It is almost an artificial moonlight in its effects, and stimulates the higher faculties and ideals."

"Rather risky, however, is it not? Sort of burning your candle at both ends? I have heard that the moon makes lunatics, and I know that purple light has recently been proven destructive to germ life," said Herman, more at his ease.

"Yes, if continued for long at a time," returned Dual. "The fact is, I am rather trying an experiment than making a steady use of the light. I thought I would let you test its effects with me to-night, if you don't mind, and see if it would affect you as it does me—" he paused, and then added:—"in the interests of truth. By the way, let me give you a sample of my preparation of fruit juices."

He rang for Henri, and ordered a glass of the beverage. Presently it was served, and Semi kept up a running fire of comment and theory on its use.

Herman took the single glass from the server and raised it to his lips. I noticed that neither Dual nor I received a glass, though the fact did not seem to impress Herman in the least. I smiled grimly to myself. The Oriental in Semi would not allow him to drink with the victim he had trapped, even though in all justice the man deserved what he was to get.

Suddenly Dual turned to his desk. "Let us have some music while you drink," he suggested. "To appreciate the juice rightly it must be sipped and its bouquet tasted slowly, like that of old wine." His finger crept under the edge of the desk for an instant, and in a moment the notes of the "Spring Song" filled the room.

The doctor looked his surprise. He glanced about the room with a sudden nervous twist of his head. Evidently he had not noticed Dual's finger, and could not place the source of the rich notes which pulsed and throbbed through the air from no visible instrument. In a moment, however, he smiled.

"Very clever indeed. Phonograph?" he inquired at length.

Semi shook his head. "An invention of my own. It can reproduce any natural sound and speak as well as play. Here is something which should interest you, I think." Again his finger, shielded by his body from the other's observation, slid under the edge of the desk. In a last faint chord the harmony died and a voice floated through the room in spoken words.

"The oath of Hippocrates!" it cried in announcement, paused an instant, and then went sonorously on: "I swear by Apollo, the physician, by Hygeia, by Panacea, and by all the gods and goddesses, calling them to witness that, according to my ability and judgment, I will in every particular keep this my oath and covenant. I will use that regimen which, according to my ability and judgment, shall be for the welfare of the sick, and I will refrain from that which shall be baneful and injurious. If any shall ask me for a drug to produce death, I will not give it, nor will I suggest such counsel.

"With purity and holiness will I watch closely my life and my art. Into whatsoever houses I enter I will go to aid the sick, abstaining from every voluntary act of injustice and corruption or licentiousness. Whatever in the life of men I shall see or hear in my practise, or without my practise, which should not be made public this will I hold in silence, believing such things should not be spoken.

"While I keep this my oath inviolate and unbroken, may it be granted to me to enjoy life and my art, forever honored by all men; but should I by transgression violate it, be mine the reverse."

The speaking died, and for an instant silence fell over the room. Then, without warning there came laughter, wild, shrill, like the mirth of fiends. I started in my chair. Herman, who had been sitting with bowed head, listening to the solemn words of the medical oath, half sprang from his seat and stared about the apartment. The horrible sounds of laughter without soul tore the air into palpitating shreds and died slowly into a silence, which left me trembling with the recollection of what had gone before.

As the diabolical laughter died Herman sank back into his chair, and Dual's finger slipped from beneath the desk.

The hand of the physician was visibly shaking as he put it out and took up his glass. His face was pale, and his voice not quite steady as he tried to speak in a casual tone.

"Very clever, indeed, Mr. Dual; but wasn't that a rather odd ending to tack on to the physician's oath?"

"That is as one may look at it," rejoined Dual. "Personally, while admiring the oath in itself, and even the spirit back of the words, I have thought that in this day, when the dollar is all which counts with so many men, it should be called the oath of hypocrites, rather than of Hippocrates. The laughter does sound a bit awful, however—almost like the gloating of all the elementals over the fall of a human soul. So might fiends laugh in an orthodox hell."

Herman half raised his glass, then set it down. For the first time I noticed an expression of suspicion in his close-set eyes. He was plainly nervous under the glance of Dual.

"What did you mean by that?" he rasped out in the accent of overstrained nerves.

"By what?" returned Dual calmly. "My dear doctor, I fear the thing has upset you—er—got on your nerves. Suppose we go back to the music for a time?"

Yet, when again the strains of the Universalion filled the room, it was not the choice I would have deliberately made myself; for, though grand, and played with wonderful expression and effect, it was the "Dead March" from "Saul."

In solemn harmony the music went on to the last grand chord, and hard on the end came again a speaking voice: "And the Lord said unto Cain: Where is Abel, thy brother? and he said: I know not. Am I my brother's keeper? And He said: What hast thou done? The voice of thy brother's blood crieth unto me from the ground, and now art thou accursed from the earth, which hath opened her mouth to receive thy brother's blood, from thy hand."

The glass fell from Herman's hand and rang in a splintering shower on the floor. With a spring he came out of the chair and took one quick stride toward where Semi Dual sat.

"What is the meaning of this buffoonery?" he cried in a shrill voice of excitement, which he strove to make strong. "What is your object in this trickery of lights and music-boxes? Speak, you smiling devil! Speak, or by all the fiends in perdition, I'll pull the truth out of you! What are you, anyway? Is this a chamber of the third degree? Why did you send me that note, telling me you had something to tell me which would prove of value? Don't sit there smiling! Answer me! Answer me—you!" His hand darted to the pocket of his coat, and reappeared with a weapon in its grasp.

I started from my chair, but only to sink back again. The eyes of my friend were staring steadily full into those of the man who threatened him with the raised gun. Once myself I had endured that piercing, penetrating, paralyzing glance of Dual, and I knew that now he was safe. Also I knew why the man who stood between us wavered as he stood and seemed suddenly stricken powerless.

For a long minute he stood there, a figure of arrested motion. Then, very slowly, his arm extended until Semi Dual's fingers closed about the revolver and deflected its barrel. With equal slowness, like the movements of an automaton, a thing deprived of any personal volition, the gripping fingers released the weapon's butt, and the extended arm dropped back to the man's side.

Dual tossed the gun upon his desk and waved the other to his chair, toward which he retreated slowly step by step, finally sinking into it and passing a bewildered, groping hand across his eyes.

"You have asked me a question which I shall answer," Semi Dual began speaking. "If I err in details, you shall be at liberty to interrupt. I brought you here for that purpose to-night—to tell you my story—and worded my note so as to be sure that you would come. The story I wish to tell you is the story of your crime. Although, as a physician, you keep up a good appearance, you are really financially embarrassed, as I know from having your rating looked up.

"When you took the case of Mrs. Matilda Greenig, you did it as you would any other case—for the purpose of getting her well. Unfortunately for all concerned, she was rich. When she thought, and you thought, that she was going to die, she made a will. As she was at least temporarily estranged from her nephew, she made it in favor of her nurse. You witnessed the will, and it gave you an idea, which you attempted to follow out.

"You made love to and finally proposed to the nurse, and she accepted. You cared nothing for her as a woman, but you fancied that, when Mrs. Greenig died, your wife would be rich. Feeling so sure of her death, you tried an experiment upon her with the juices of fresh fruits. That was your first mistake.

"Mrs. Greenig took a change for the better, and continued to gain. Your position was now embarrassing. Then Mrs. Greenig mentioned a reconciliation with her only relative. You made a desperate plan to prevent the miscarriage of your scheme.

"You were frequently at your patient's apartment, and you managed to slip her key from her ring. You arranged it so that, at a time when few persons were around, the nurse would be out of the way. You went to Mrs. Greenig's room and overpowered her with chloroform before she could do more than utter a single scream. When she was under the influence of the anesthetic you took her own penknife and opened a vein in her left arm, and dabbled her other hand in the blood, and laid the knife beside her on the bed.

"You intended that they should think it suicide—you even so pronounced it yourself, when the nurse called you back there that night—and they might have done so but for some mistakes which you made. First, you pressed the chloroform so closely over her mouth and nose that you burned the skin on her face. Secondly, you were evidently so disturbed that you forgot the bottle which had contained the chloroform. Thirdly, you took away the key.

"When you discovered the latter you went to the hotel where her nephew had been stopping formerly, got paper and envelope, and mailed the key to the nephew at his new address. Then you thought that if he returned it suspicion would light on him and that you were safe.

"Your plan looked as if it might work out. Martin took the key back and was arrested on suspicion, but your second error overcame your last act. The bottle was found. It contained a thumb-print, which we presumed was from the murderer's hand. On the paper which you folded about the key was a thumb-print which corresponded to that on the bottle. On a piece of paper which you wrote upon for Glace this afternoon you left a third carbon smudge of your thumb, which matched the other two.

"By all of this you stand convicted as a murderer. By the way, what were you writing this afternoon? Might it be that, fearing the nurse would be convicted, and so unable to inherit under the law, you meant to make a confession and run for it, hoping later to come in for a part of her money? Have you anything you wish to say?"

During the time Dual was speaking the physician had sunk gradually lower and lower in his chair. Now he straightened by an effort and sat rigidly erect.

"No," he replied slowly, "I really have little to say. You're deductions are clever and, unfortunately, correct. It seems almost an irony of fate, however, to think that the reason why I had that carbon on my thumb to-day was actually because I was at work writing out a full confession.

"In only one detail are you wrong, Dual. I had made up my mind—not from the motive you suggest, but from my regard for the girl, which was genuine—that if she could be freed in no other way, I would leave town and mail the confession back. I was not willing to let her pay the price of my crime. I had not fallen quite that low, even yet, Dual.

"Even if I had meant what you suggest, I knew Miss Riley too well ever to hope that she would in any way compound with a confessed murderer. Now, if you wish, you can send an officer to my office. He will find the confession in my desk. You see, I place myself utterly in your hands. I have played—and lost."

He bent forward and suddenly covered his face.

"I knew," said Semi, "that you meant to confess. I am glad to know that the act was prompted by a better motive than I gave you credit for." He reached to the little door in his desk and drew out his telephone.

"Glace," he addressed me, "will you call headquarters and tell them that Dr. Herman has just confessed. Ask them to send a man to his office to get his written confession out of his desk, and to send the patrol to the door of the Urania for the man himself."

I rose and went to the desk, and did as he asked.

Semi reached out and rang Henri's call. When it was answered he again turned to me. "Will you help Henri escort Dr. Herman below?" he suggested, and leaned wearily back in his chair.

Henri and I took each an arm of the figure slouched in the chair and assisted the man to his feet. Without a word or a sign, we walked with him to the door and left the room.

He came with us like one in a daze. Behind us the chimes sounded faintly as we passed down the stairs. Not once did he speak as we took him down to the street, nor even when we surrendered him to the wondering officers of the law.

When he was gone, Henri and I turned back the way we had come, and I don't remember that either of us spoke as we went up in the elevator.

I found Semi Dual still sitting as I had left him, his head resting upon one hand. The purple light still flooded the room.

I crossed to the desk and took up the phone. I called the *Record*, and Smithson himself answered the ring. "Smithson," said I, "Dr. Herman has just confessed to having killed Mrs. Greenig, and is now on his way to the jail."

My editor's voice came back in excited question, but I cut him short.

"Listen," I protested. "I haven't time to get down and write this for the extra. Herman is on his way to the jail now. In his office he left a written confession, which the police have sent for, and will get in a few minutes. Phone Davidson to grab it at the station as soon as it comes in. Martin and the nurse will be released at once, of course. I'll be down in a hurry to write up the story for the regular edition, but this will be enough for your scoop."

"'By. Get a wiggle on you, son," said Smithson. "You're a revolutionary in journalism, but I like your work."

I hung up the receiver and turned again to my friend.

"Things like this almost shake one's faith in human nature," I remarked.

Dual raised his head and smiled a slow smile. "No," he responded, "there is some good lurking in every soul. Did you ever see a production of 'Chantecler,' friend Glace?"

I really couldn't see the connection, but I merely shook my head.

"It's a very beautiful allegory," said Semi Dual. "There are some exquisite passages in its lines. One in particular applies to your remark. True faith, either in man or God, never dies. Wait; perhaps I can let you hear that particular part before you go." He pressed a button and Henri appeared.

"Go up-stairs," Semi directed, "and insert record 2009 in the universalion."

The man turned away.

"Even in this poor soul who just left to learn a bitter lesson there was good," continued Dual. "It showed in his determination to free the girl by his confession. You will find such anomalies in all the records of human life. They are the star-points of light in the night of sin."

The sound of a bubbling bird-song filled the room, swelled and thrilled and died.

"The buhl-buhl bird," said Semi Dual. "The Persian nightingale."

Hard on his words came the sound of a shot, and a voice cried: "The nightingale is dead!"

For a space nothing was heard—all was silent, then again came the glad triumph of the song, ringing out in seeming defiance of death. Again it sank into silence, and the voice came sweet and clear: "There must always be a nightingale in the forest—and in the soul; a faith which lives, no matter how oft 'tis slain."

"That is your answer," said Semi Dual.

I looked at the clear, strong face of my friend, and a lump rose in my throat. Without a word I put out my hand and clasped his. Then, still in silence, I passed out to the sweet warm dusk of the roof.

V

THE MASTER MIND

CHAPTER I

IMPOSSIBLE. AND YET—

IT WAS A gusty, windy day in December, with a fine drive of snow in the air, which had already whitened the pavements, when I dropped into the station and nodded to Sergeant Harrington.

Dan's signal phone rang as I slipped off my coat, and he reached for the receiver even as he answered my nod. A moment later he threw it back on the hook with a bang, and spoke to me: "Wait a minute, Glace. If you beat it out the back, you can catch the wagon. There's the divil to pay up to the Merchants' Bank."

His hand went out and pressed a button which signaled the patrol garage, and another which summoned an inspector and several other officers from an adjoining room.

They came on the jump. I struggled back into my coat.

Dan bawled the address, and we turned away in a bunch to the rear, where the motor was already throbbing at the door. Without ceremony we swarmed in. There were Bryce, the inspector; Johnson, a detective, and a roundsman whom Bryce directed to come along. Also there was myself. Bryce recognized me with a grin. "Who let you in on this?" he wanted to know.

"Dan said I might as well come along," I answered as we skidded around a corner, and the chauffeur opened up the car. "If you don't want me, stop, and I'll get out."

"Haven't time," grinned the inspector, his eyes twinkling. "You and Dan rather stand in—don't you, Glace?"

"Why not?" I challenged. "Doesn't the *Record* handle you fellows right?"

"Oh, I'm not objectin', son," said the inspector. "Gad, Jerry will have us in the ditch if he does that again!"

We had lurched about a corner in a manner to make us all cling to the seat and hold our breaths until the car straightened out again.

"What's wrong at the Merchants'?" I asked when I was sure we were still on four wheels.

"I guess you heard as much as I did," returned Bryce; "but at this rate we ought to find out pretty soon. Let's see; Mulcally is on that beat right now." He turned and glanced out of the front of the patrol. "There's a crowd on the pavement in front of the bank, at any rate, an' I can see Mulcally's helmet among 'em. Here we are."

The patrol shot up to the curb and stopped with a slide. We all piled out, and I got my first chance to size matters up: A great limousine car stood in front of the side door of the bank, which had two entrances, opening upon two streets. It was manifestly the private car of somebody of wealth, for it was of the latest model and luxurious in every part. Between it and the door of the bank was a crowd, collected as such gatherings always will collect when something unusual happens; and on the curb, standing so as to half face the crowd and half guard the limousine, was Officer Mulcally, holding a disheveled and hatless youth.

The arrival of the patrol caused some little widening out of the close-pressed mass of the morbidly curious, and Bryce, Johnson, and the roundsman pushed their way rapidly to Mulcally's side. I followed along.

"What's wrong here, Mulcally?" began Bryce as soon as he was within speaking distance of the patrolman. At his words the prisoner raised his face, and my heart stopped. For a moment I think I lost some of the conversation which occurred immediately about me, for the face of the man—white, drawn, and horror-stricken—was that of Connie's brother, Billy Baird.

He was standing with his wrist linked to that of the burly Mulcally by a chain of handcuff, his clothing awry and torn as though from a struggle. His hat lay battered and dented upon the foot-board of the limousine, and his dark-reddish hair was tousled and mussed until it hung in crooked tendrils over his deathly white brow. For just a moment his eyes met mine, and both terror and appeal looked out of them.

Mulcally's voice brought me back to the realization that I was probably missing something most important. Controlling myself and my emotions as best I could, I motioned Billy to keep still, and tried to hear what the officer was saying to Bryce.

"And so"—I caught up the thread of his statement—"jist as I come around the corner, sor, I sees this felly standin' with wan foot on the step of the autymobile here. I comes down, an' jist as I was passin' I looked at him agin, 'cause I thought it was funny he'd keep standin' there like that in the storm. Then I sees there is another felly in the autymobile, an' I walks over. Well, this here felly didn't pay no attention till I was most to him; then he turns around, an' I see his face was awfully white an' funny, an' I notices that he has a spanner in his hand.

" 'Oh, hello, officer!' says he. 'Somebody's killed the shoofer!'

"Course, sor, I got pretty busy at that, an' I looks in the auty. There was that felly who's there yet, layin' back, propped up in a seat, wid the whole side of his head caved in. I makes this felly give me the spanner, an' sure enough it had blood and some hair stuck on it. Well, the shoofer was still warm an' bleedin', an' I reckon I saw the whole business, only this felly didn't know I was lookin' when he struck him wid the spanner. I jist put the cuff on him and telyphoned for the wagon, an' that's all. There can't be no mistake, 'cause I seen the whole thing."

Billy broke the silence which followed. "It's a lie!" he cried wildly. "He never saw me do it, because I didn't do it, and I don't know who did. I tell you I didn't do it. You ask Glace, here, if I'd do a thing like that! He'll tell you. Why, I can prove it myself. I was on my way to the branch of the Fourth National over on Grant and Market, and I had stopped to deliver a package for President Carlton at this bank. I was so rattled I never thought to tell the policeman here, but they'll tell you inside that I was delivering the package when this man was killed."

Bryce turned to me. "Do you know him, Glace?" he inquired.

I nodded. "He's Will Baird from the Fourth National, all right," I hastened to assure him. "I've known him for years. He never did this thing, Bryce."

"I tell you I saw him," Mulcally cut in. "He was bendin' over this shoofer wid the spanner in his mitt when I seen him."

"I'd just found him, and the spanner was on the seat beside him, when I found he was dead. I picked it up," protested Billy. "I tell you I was in the bank. I'd just come out."

"You can tell all that in court," Bryce checked him. "What were you goin' to the branch bank for?"

"I was taking a transfer of funds to them from the main bank," Billy replied somewhat more quietly.

"Where is it now? In the cab?" asked Bryce.

"I suppose so. I was so shocked when I saw Sardon was dead that I never gave the money a thought."

"Suppose you look, Potter," suggested Bryce to the roundsman, who had accompanied us from the station; and the man climbed into the car beside the body of the chauffeur and carefully searched for the package which Billy had said he was taking to the branch bank. In a moment he emerged with a cynical grin on his face.

" 'Tain't there, sir," he declared.

The officers exchanged glances then. "How much was there in this package?" Bryce asked Baird.

"Fifty thousand dollars," Billy responded promptly enough.

"What was it in?"

"In a heavy pigskin grip, double-locked with padlocks. Sardon had stepped into the car to guard it while I went into the bank here to deliver the other package."

"You didn't see any such grip as that, did you, Mulcally?" the inspector asked.

"Nuthin' at all, sor. If it was here, it went away before I looked into the car."

"Let me see the spanner," said Bryce.

He took it in his hand, and turned it over. One end was stained with blood, which was congealing in the cold air, and stuck to it by the same blood were some short brown hairs. Bryce nodded and stepped over to the limousine which he entered, with Johnson at his heels.

The crowd began to press in closer to Mulcally and his prisoner, muttering. Bryce paused long enough to order Potter to clear the street. As he was turning back I asked him if I might come, too, and he assented with a nod.

Inside the car we three gave our attention to the body. It was that of a slightly built, foreign-looking fellow, apparently French, as his name would indicate. He was dressed in a dark, bottle-green livery with goggles and gauntlets, and a green cap which now lay on the floor of the car. His feet were encased in puttees of leather, and some snow still clung to the soles. Down the left side of his face some blood had trickled from the wound where the spanner had crushed in his temple. Bryce now laid the spanner over this spot and nodded to Johnson. The hair on the spanner, like that on Sardon's head, was short and brown. A moment later the detective pointed to the man's throat, upon which were some marks which looked greatly like finger-prints.

"Whoever killed him choked him, and then beat his head in," said Johnson. "Looks like the kid might have done it while some pal of his made a sneak with the bag. What you think, Bryce?"

"Looks like a safe bet now," the inspector replied.

While they talked I had been nosing about the car, and had found the half-burned butt of a cigarette. I showed it to Bryce.

"See if he has any more on him," I suggested, nodding to the dead chauffeur.

The officers set to work searching his clothes. They found several cigars, but no cigarettes, tobacco, or papers for making them.

"Somebody probably left it in the car and it wasn't swept out," said Bryce at the end of the examination. "Does your friend smoke cigarettes?" He jerked his arm toward Billy.

I shook my head. Just at the time I couldn't speak, for while they had been hunting through Sardon's clothing I had picked up the man's right hand, which was still encased in its gauntlet, and discovered that which interested me far more than any cigarette: The gloves had fastened with a patent catch, and caught in the lowest fastening of the one I held was a little tuft of dark-reddish hair.

My heart came up into my throat, and I glanced out of the window to where Billy was still standing beside the patrolman. As far as I could see, the hair in the catch of the gauntlet and that on Billy's head was of the same shade.

Suddenly I felt strangely sick. I knew that for months Billy had been grouching about his inability to make more money. I had known of others in his position who had yielded to a sudden mad temptation. Could Connie's brother have—I refused to allow even myself to complete the question. Believe it I would not! There remained but one thing to do. Very slowly and carefully, with my eyes on Bryce and Johnson, who were now preparing to leave the limousine, I slipped down my hand and drew out the little mass of hairs from the catch, intending to take them away.

For once fate was unkind to me as it seemed. Bryce saw my move, and just as I was congratulating myself on my own deftness his voice exploded all my confidence:

"I'll take whatever that is, Glace."

Caught in the act, my face showed my guilt. Bryce put out his hand and rather meekly I surrendered the few hairs into his palm. He glanced at me, and then out of the window and smiled dryly: "Where did you get them?" he asked.

"Caught on the fastening of Sardon's gauntlet," I told him. "But if you're thinking they're Baird's hairs I'll bet money you're wrong."

Bryce fastened me with a keen glance. "You seem to be a pretty good friend of his," he remarked, poking the hairs on his palm. "Now, these look like a mighty good match to me. What do you know about the youngster, Glace?"

In that moment I decided to follow Dual's plan and tell the truth. I looked the inspector straight in the eye. "He's my future brother-in-law," I answered slowly.

Bryce whistled softly. "I don't wonder you're hard hit," he said after a moment. "Deuce take it, it's too bad! So that's why you were trying to cover up the hairs?"

"See here," I begged, "there's enough there for both of us. Split them with me, Bryce! I wasn't trying to frustrate justice as you think, but I knew how it would look. I knew you'd consider it as additional evidence against Billy, while I believe they came from a different head. I wanted them as a possible clue, and I tried to get 'em. Well, give me a couple and keep the rest. I'd like to clear the boy if I can."

I suppose I seemed like a sentimental fool to Bryce, who now seemed fully satisfied of Billy's guilt, for he smiled in a rather tolerant fashion at my request, then gravely handed me two hairs. "There's a couple, just to show you I recognize your feelin's," he remarked, handing them over. "Wrap 'em up, an' we'll be gettin' out."

I wrapped those two hairs up in a bit of copy-paper as tenderly and as carefully as though each one had been an article precious beyond price, and stowed them away in a pocket-folder I carried. Bryce also wrapped his and put them away, and we all left the limousine.

The inspector spoke to Mulcally: "You made a good pinch, all right, Denny. We just found some red hair caught on Sardon's gauntlet which matches your man's thatch. We may as well be putting him in the wagon now, I guess. And, by the way—whose limousine is this, anyway?"

"It belongs to President Carlton of our bank," Billy put in.

"Sardon was Carlton's own chauffeur?"

"Yes."

"All right," directed Bryce. "Take 'im away!"

But Baird vigorously protested at this. "I told you I was in this bank when Sardon was killed," he reasserted. "Aren't you at least going to give me a chance to prove that to you?"

Bryce and Johnson paused and whispered together. "We may as well see what the stall is," Johnson finally decided in a low voice. "Just wait a minute, Denny, an' we'll settle the matter right now."

As though his words had been a signal, the revolving door in the storm entrance of the bank turned out a uniformed messenger, who ran down the steps glancing from Johnson to Bryce. "Which of you officers is in charge here?" he asked as he reached the street.

"I am at present," said Bryce.

"Then I was to ask you to step inside a minute, sir. Our cashier wants to see you before you go away."

"Lead me to him," assented the inspector, and turned to Mulcally. "May as well bring your man inside, Denny, till we see what they want."

We all passed up the steps and entered the bank. I took the occasion to walk at Billy's side, and he turned his troubled eyes to me at once. "My God, Gordon, what am I going to do?" he whispered. "This is awful! You know I didn't do it, don't you? And yet they seem to have the goods on me, too. What will Connie think? Oh, I wish to God they'd killed me instead of Sardon! This will queer me at the bank and send me to jail at least. What am I going to do?"

"Keep cool and don't talk so much," I told him. "I know you didn't do it, old man, and Connie won't give it a moment's belief. We'll work it out, all right. Now, brace up!"

I tried to speak with confidence and inspire him with some of the same feeling as we entered the bank. The trouble was I didn't see myself just where everything was leading. If only I could have had a few minutes' talk with my friend, Semi Dual— Of only one thing did I feel certain, and that was that Billy could not have done the foul deed of which he now stood suspected. Yet I knew that, against Mulcally's sworn word that he had caught him in the act, his chances of vindication would be slight.

Meanwhile, the page had led us across the general banking floor to a room at one side, whose door was lettered with the one word "Cashier," and was now tapping upon that door.

A voice bade us enter, and a moment later we were within the room.

A gray-haired man in pince-nez glasses, with a keen yet kindly face, half rose, as we entered, and fixed his eyes upon Baird.

"What is the meaning of all this, Billy?" he asked.

"I'm under arrest, sir," said Billy. "When I left here, after giving you that package, I found Mr. Carlton's chauffeur dead in his car, and the bank's bag of money gone. I was examining Sardon to be sure he was dead when I was arrested, Mr. Grier."

"Our patrolman found him hanging over the chauffeur with a bloody spanner in his hand," explained Bryce. "He was insisting that he was in the bank when the man was killed, and demanding that we bring him inside for you to verify his statement when your messenger came out after us. Now, let me ask you if this young fellow—Baird—brought you a package this morning, like he says he did?"

"He certainly did," responded Grier, and I felt my heart leap at his words. "It was concerning that that I wanted to see you, inspector."

"What about it?" asked Bryce.

If my heart had leaped before, it fell to the very depths now as the cashier replied: "That is the peculiar thing. It purported to be a bundle of valuable securities, according to Baird, who said he had been instructed to deliver it to me in person. Naturally, as soon as he had gone, I opened it, and discovered that it contained nothing but strips of blank paper, folded into document size."

Bryce sat down in a chair and regarded the cashier of the Merchants' Bank for a long minute, placing his hands together so that the pointed finger-tips aimed straight to the official. "You've known this lad for some time?" he spoke at last.

"Certainly. For some years."

"So that he had the full confidence both of his employers and you?"

"Naturally. He often acted as messenger, and handled funds between the banks."

Bryce nodded. "It's all deucedly clever," he announced. "This chap, Baird, and his pal, whoever he was, decided to make a haul. They fixed it so as to make it appear that he had an alibi. He come in here an' left the chauffeur on guard; then he goes out, quietly croaked the chauffeur, and his pal ducked with the swag. They counted on its appearing that it was the work of a gang, and that Baird had really discovered the chauffeur was dead when he went out again. The trouble was, Mulcally here pinched him with the spanner in his hand just after he'd done for the chauffeur. Mr. Grier, your package was this fellow's alibi, that's all."

"But that seems clumsy to me, and certain of question," objected Grier.

"Most likely they'd have claimed that the package was sent out from the Fourth National after Baird was in the car, and trusted that, to support their claim, it was the work of a gang," said Bryce, with a smile.

"That's just what happened!" cried Baird.

Bryce continued to smile at the cashier. "You see, sir. He's going to try and stick it out along the original lines. We learn about what to expect in our work."

Grier shook his head sadly. "I admit it looks bad, inspector, but I hate to think of anything like that of Baird."

"Fifty thousand looks like a lot to a boy," said Bryce.

There came a tap on the door. Then it swung slowly open. "I beg your pardon," came a voice which thrilled me, "but I was looking for Mr. Gordon Glace."

The next moment Semi Dual stepped into the room.

CHAPTER II

GOLDEN NASTURTIUMS

I SPRANG TO my feet and hastened to his side. "Dual!" I cried softly. "Thank Heaven you're here! I've been wishing for you."

"For something over a half-hour," said Semi, glancing at the clock. "That is why I am here."

I gazed at him in amazement. "You mean—" I stammered.

"That I knew you were in some trouble, my friend. Therefore, I came to you. That should not surprise you now, Glace."

The other occupants of the room were gazing at us in silent question, and yet I felt that I must speak more fully to Dual. "Come outside a moment," I said.

Semi swept the room with his keen gray eyes for an instant, then turned with me through the door. I found seats for us in the general banking room, briefly told him all I had learned, and gave him the little paper with the two hairs, and also the stub of the cigarette.

He accepted them with a smile, and put them away. "Go back into the room and keep your ears open," he advised as he rose. "I'll be about when needed; if not here, at least at the

Fourth National Bank. I know Cashier Sheldon fairly well, you may recall. If they take Baird back there before taking him to the station, as I think they will, I will accompany them."

He walked slowly in the direction of the side entrance and disappeared through the revolving door. I hurried back to the cashier's room.

Just as I entered, Bryce turned to Mulcally. "Take your man out to the wagon," he directed. "We'll come along in a minute now." Then, as the patrolman led Billy out, he swung back to Grier. "I think, sir, that the quicker we break this fellow down the quicker the bank he's looted will get back the money. It may even be possible that he had some accomplice from the bank itself. I am going to take him back to the Fourth National and sift every statement he has made straight down to the truth. But looks to me like an open and shut case from first to last. Johnson, let's be goin'! Good morning, Mr. Grier."

We went out to the street again, where Potter was guarding the limousine, with Sardon's body still in it, and Bryce stepped to the curb. "Can you run that wagon, Potter?" he asked.

"I ought to," said Potter. "I used to be on the motor squad, you know, Bryce."

"Well, then, take the body to the morgue and bring the car back to the side entrance of the Fourth National," Bryce ordered, and turned away to the patrol, where Mulcally and Billy sat. "You can go back on your beat, Denny, an' I'll speak about you to the captain," he said as he climbed to a seat. "I'm takin' your man with me for a while."

I had been looking about for Semi, but he was nowhere to be seen. I decided that he had gone on to the other bank, and that I would find him there when we arrived. As a matter of fact, he had done exactly that and was talking to Dick Sheldon, the assistant cashier, when we arrived.

Bryce's first move was to telephone to the station for a couple of men to guard the bank's entrances and issue an order against any of the employees being allowed to leave, until his investigations had been made.

It was while we were waiting for him to do this that the door of the president's office opened and a very pretty young girl, with brown hair and a slender, graceful figure, came out with some papers in her hands.

Johnson and Baird, the latter with a pair of ordinary handcuffs about his wrists, were sitting upon a bench inside the railing of Sheldon's quarters when she passed. Bryce was still at the phone on Sheldon's desk. Sheldon and Dual were standing a little to one side, still conversing, so that the woman had an unobstructed view of Baird.

Suddenly she uttered a little scream. The papers fluttered from her hands and scattered over the tiles. Her dark eyes opened wide with sudden horror and she literally flung herself through the swing-door in the railing, and rushed to Billy's side. "Billy!" she cried, apparently oblivious of all others. "Oh, Billy, what happened? What went wrong?"

I saw Bryce straighten slightly as he sat at the phone, and caught the quick glance he threw at the girl. Johnson, too, pricked up his ears.

Baird tried to meet the situation. "Nothing much, I hope, Noriene," he replied to the girl's frantic inquiry. "These chaps here think I killed Sardon and stole the bank's money, and I can't make them believe that I didn't, as yet."

The girl turned to Johnson in a fury.

"But Billy wouldn't do that!" she cried. "President Carlton trusts him implicitly. Why, that was why he sent him to-day. You know I'm the president's stenographer, and I knew all about this transfer and that Billy was to be sent with it. It's perfectly ridiculous to say he would steal, let alone kill. You men ought to be ashamed!" She swung on Dick Sheldon. "Mr. Sheldon, make them let Billy go!"

Sheldon interrupted anything more she might have said. "Miss O'Niel, you must control yourself. None of us in the bank really believe that Billy is guilty; but it is a very terrible affair, and at present circumstances seem, to some extent, to implicate Baird. But every one knows how untrustworthy circumstantial evidence often is. Do not be anxious! Now, as we are just about to begin investigating the matter, you must really leave us alone for the present. I say again that I think everything will come out all right in the end."

Both Billy and Miss O'Niel threw him a grateful glance. Billy and I both knew that Dick Sheldon had good cause to say that circumstantial evidence was apt to be uncertain. There had been a time when, save for Semi Dual, who now stood leaning against the railing, he himself might have been sent to a felon's cell.

As for the girl, she appreciated his avowal of his belief in Billy's innocence. She dropped her hand to his shoulder. "Never mind, Billy, boy," she comforted. "If they send you to jail, I'll come to see you every day and bring you flowers." She turned to leave the railed enclosure when Bryce arrested her by a word.

He had turned from the phone and now addressed her direct: "You say you're Carlton's stenographer and knew all about this transfer of cash yesterday?"

"Yes, sir, I am; I did."

"I suppose you tipped it off to Baird, eh?" snapped Bryce.

"No, sir, I did not."

"All right, run along," Bryce directed with a thin-lipped smile under his black mustache.

The girl's eyes flashed for an instant, then she went out and began to gather up her papers from the floor.

Bryce rose. "Well, let's get at this business," he began, and Sheldon led us toward the president's room.

In the Fourth National the officers' quarters occupied one side toward the front. First, at the extreme front, was the room of President Carlton, overlooking the street. Back of that and communicating with it was the room of the cashier, and next, back of that, the railed-in space in which Sheldon had his desk.

Between that and the cages of the various tellers was the entrance to the safety deposit-vaults.

Sheldon now led the two officers, Baird, Dual, and I directly through the room of the cashier into that of the president, where Mr. Carlton sat, a short, fleshy individual, with black hair, eyes and mustache. He was a man of large holdings and always immaculate of dress. He was chewing somewhat nervously upon a cigar when we came in, and immediately fastened his eyes upon Baird's face. I was glad to see that Billy held his own head high, and gave him back glance for glance.

"Be seated, gentlemen," the president greeted our advent; and, continuing, spoke directly to the boy: "Baird, I want you to understand that we are trying to handle this thing fairly. You have the confidence of the officers of the bank. That is why I selected you for our messenger this morning. Still, we have just lost a great sum of money and I personally have sustained the death of a trusted servant. We have to get to the bottom of the affair. I want you now to begin and tell us, slowly and carefully, everything which happened from the time you took the grip from my office until you found Sardon dead. Begin, my boy."

"One moment," interrupted Bryce, glancing at Semi. "Is this gentleman to remain?"

Instantly Sheldon was on his feet. "At my request," he began as he rose. "I have a good reason, which you, Mr. Carlton, will understand if I recall to your mind the affair in which I myself was once implicated."

Carlton's eyes lighted for a moment. "The gentleman will remain," he told Bryce. "Now, Billy, go on."

"I took the bag," began Baird, "and went out to the car. One of the vault-guards went with me to the machine. I got in, and we were just starting away when I heard some one calling my name. I looked out and asked Sardon to stop. A boy, whom I did not know, but wearing the uniform of our messengers, ran up and handed me a parcel, which he said you desired me to deliver, in person, to Mr. Grier, of the Merchants' Bank, before going to our branch."

"Impossible," ejaculated Carlton. "Gentlemen, I did not send any such parcel or word. There is some mistake here. I did not know anything of Baird's movements after he left here, until we heard of his arrest."

"There's no mistake about his having left a package with Grier," said Bryce, crossing his legs with a smile. "Only it was full of blank paper. In my opinion that was part of his scheme—a stall for an alibi."

"Well, no such parcel came from this bank," Carlton asserted.

"I wouldn't be too sure of that," Bryce told him, grinning.

"What do you mean?"

"Nothing—yet. Let Baird go ahead."

"The boy said it was a package of valuable securities," Billy resumed, "and that I was to stop at the Merchants' and let Sardon guard the bag for our bank while I was delivering it. We made the run to the Merchants' and I delivered the package to Mr. Grier."

"Hold on," the inspector checked him. "Can you tell us what time all this occurred?"

"Yes, sir. I left here at twenty minutes to ten, so as to get to the branch before opening. I remember looking at the clock at the Merchants' when I went in, and it was a quarter to ten. I had to wait to see Mr. Grier, who was busy, and it was ten minutes to ten when I went into his room. I know I was afraid I might be late if I had to wait too long. I was in Mr. Grier's room just a minute, and, when I came out, I started to leave by the side door, and lost about a minute there—"

"How?" snapped Bryce.

"They have revolving-doors there, and there was a man going out ahead of me. I was in a hurry and threw myself against the door hard, and it hit him in the heels. He lost his balance and stumbled to his knees and threw up his hands against the glass panel to steady himself. Of course, I stopped and waited until he got up, and he was so long about it I was afraid he was hurt. When we got outside I apologized to him, but he walked off without a word."

"Could you see the limousine from within the door?" Carlton asked.

"No, sir; not from where I stood," said Billy. "Sardon had stopped a little beyond the entrance. I went down and started to get into the car. Sardon was sitting on the seat, and I thought it funny he made no move to get out. I spoke to him, and then I looked at him closer, and I saw the blood on his face. I backed out of the car and looked around. Then I caught sight of the spanner on the seat beside him, and I leaned back into the car and picked it up. I was looking at it when the patrolman came up. I told him Sardon was dead, and he looked at the spanner and arrested me. It wasn't until after the other officers came that I thought of the bag or knew it was gone."

"And so it was just seven minutes from the time you went into the bank until you found out that Sardon was dead?" said Bryce.

"Yes, sir; just about."

"And you want us to believe that in that time somebody attacked and killed him and carried off the money? Pretty quick work, son!"

"Why, you say I killed him after I came out!" flashed Baird.

"Never mind what I say," Bryce retorted. "Explain if you can how he came to have some of your hair stuck in the catch of his glove?"

Billy turned pale. "He didn't!" he cried. "How could he have had?"

"Just supposin'," said Bryce slowly, "that you grabbed him and choked him, and that he threw up his hands to fight you off, and one of the catches on one of his gauntlets caught a bit of your hair and pulled it out before you mashed his head with the spanner? See here!" He took out his paper of hair, and, unwrapping it, held the hair up against Billy's. It matched, in color at least.

"My God!" gasped Carlton as he grasped the meaning. "Inspector, did you really find that on Sardon's glove?"

"Exactly, Mr. Carlton. Now, get this right. We ain't pickin' on the youngster for nothin'. But when a cop sees a man with a bloody iron standin' over another who has just been killed with that sort of a thing, an' then finds some of the first man's hair pulled out of his head, an' stickin' to the other fellow's glove, it looks sort of suspicious to us."

"Of course—of course, inspector—but Baird—he's been with us for years!"

"Them's sometimes the worst kind, Mr. Carlton," remarked the officer sagely. "Now, I figure that this was all doped out between Baird an' some one else. Course he had a pal, an' most likely some one to help him in the bank, too. Most likely the fellow who slipped him the package was his pal, an', after he was sure everything was all right, he grabs a taxi and beats it to the Merchants'. Then when Baird comes out they croaks Sardon, an' the pal beats it with the grip. Bein' in uniform, nobody would notice him, except to spot him for a bank-messenger. Baird was goin' to pretend to discover Sardon, an' after the row blew over they'd cut the swag. All they'd need to work it was to find out just when the transfer was to be made in advance, and I think I know how that was done."

He seemed to have it all pretty well figured out, I had to admit, and I wondered how it struck Semi Dual. I glanced at my friend. He was sitting slouched down in his chair, fiddling with his little swagger cane. So far he had said no word; just sat and listened while the others talked, but as my eyes fell upon him he turned his toward mine. I caught a faint glimpse of them under drooping lids, and they were intensely bright. I knew then that, back of his seeming boredom, his wonderful brain was awake and on guard.

"It was this way, I reckon," Bryce was running on. "Maybe Baird has a girl he's sweet on, or who's stuck on him, workin' here in the bank. Maybe you know something about it, sir?"

"I believe," said Carlton slowly, "that he and Miss O'Niel have been going about a good deal."

"She's your stenographer, isn't she?" inquired Bryce.

"Yes."

"She knew of this transfer as early as yesterday?"

Carlton nodded in silence. "I told her myself," he said at length.

"Let's see what she has to say," suggested the officer.

Baird came to his feet in a bound. "Curse you, Bryce!" he cried in a treble of excitement and strained nerves. "You leave her out of this. She never told me a—"

I dragged him down myself and told him to be still. Carlton pressed his stenographer call and we sat and waited until the girl came in.

"Sit down, Miss O'Niel," Bryce directed. "I think you admitted that you knew of this affair last night?"

"Yes," she responded, her eyes searching Baird's face.

"But you didn't tell Baird?"

"I've already answered that once to-day, I think."

"Did you know his pal—the fellow who helped pull off the deal?"

"Mr. Carlton," she appealed to the president, "I am no criminal."

"If you didn't tell Baird, maybe you signaled to somebody else," the inspector persisted.

"I told no one, nor signaled to any one," she flashed.

"That's all," said Bryce. And again he smiled.

The girl rose and now again I noticed Dual. He had risen and moved over to the front window, where there was a typewriter desk, upon one end of which was a small bowl full of deep golden nasturtiums. As the girl turned to leave the room, he looked her full in the face and smiled. For just an instant she half drew back, then responded to his look with a faint smile of her own. "Do you like flowers?" said Semi Dual.

"Very much," she answered. "These were a surprise."

"Then they *are* yours?"

"Oh, yes. I found them on my desk this morning, but I think I know who sent them." I saw her eyes turn Billy's way.

"Rather hard to get—nasturtiums—in winter," said Semi Dual.

"They're a favorite of mine—" she began, when Bryce interrupted:

"Sheldon, is this a flower carnival or a police investigation?"

Dual threw up his head and met the inspector's eyes for an instant. It was like the contemptuous gaze of a great, noble dog at a snapping cur. Slowly at first and then in a flood, the blood rushed into the officer's face. Then very courteously, Dual led the girl to the door, opened it for her and resumed his seat without speaking.

Bryce cleared his throat. "Is there another girl working here with whom this kid is chummy," he asked Carlton. "She was lyin' just now or I'm a goat! She shied at most everything I asked!"

"I believe she and Miss Golding are rather friendly," said Carlton. "Shall I call Miss Golding in?"

"Better," decided Bryce.

"Will you call her, Sheldon," Carlton requested. "She's our cashier's stenographer," he explained to Bryce.

Sheldon rose and left the room, to return after a moment with the girl. To this day I don't know in what category to place her. She was of the "show-girl" type, to put it in a word. Rather tall for a woman and built in voluptuous lines. Her walk was a sort of stealthy glide rather than a walk, with an undulation of the hips with each step. Her face was beautiful, I had to admit, but in a sophisticated way; her eyes yellow—I am sure that is the best word—and I felt positive that her great mass of light hair was bleached. Some way, she came into the room, she reminded me of a soft, tawny cat with long, hard claws. She advanced to a chair and sank into it with a sort of languid grace.

"Miss Golding," began Bryce, "we want to know if you have any reason to believe that Mr. Baird and Miss O'Niel are anything more than friends—sweethearts, say?"

"I should think they were. Everybody knows that," said the girl.

"Engaged? Do you know?"

"Well," said Miss Golding with a smile. "I've heard them talkin' of gettin' married."

"Soon?"

"Not hardly. Billy thought he was too hard up. I heard him grouchin' about it more than once."

"What did he say?"

"Say, I don't like to answer that," objected the woman, "because I think most likely he only meant it as a joke."

"Meant what?" demanded Bryce sharply. "If you know anything it's your duty to put us wise."

"Well, I did hear him tell Noriene once that if they ever got married he guessed he'd have to steal enough to set up housekeeping on."

"And when was that?"

"Oh, about two weeks ago, I think."

Bryce looked at Johnson and then at Carlton with a triumphant smile, then turned to Baird. "Did you say that?" he snarled.

"I was only joking. Miss Golding knows that," said Billy in a hoarse voice.

"Miss Golding," the inspector resumed, "did you know anything about this transfer which was to be made?"

"Goodness, no! I'm sure I never heard a word."

"Do you think that if Miss O'Niel knew about it she might have told Baird?"

"She might, of course, if she knew about it," replied Miss Golding, with a simper. "We women are all more or less fools with the men we like, an' they was out together last night."

"How do you know that?" Bryce asked instantly.

"Why, they was on the street and I just happened to see them. They was standin' in front of a window looking at—"

"Nasturtiums," said Semi Dual.

"What!" Miss Golding's voice rose high and shrill.

"An unusual flower in the winter and a favorite of Miss O'Niel's." Dual rose and crossed to the bowl upon the typewriter desk by the window and stood looking down at them, delicately fingering their petals. "See, she has some on her table now." He raised his head and looked directly into the woman's yellow eyes, turned away, and stared straight out of the window across the street. Then without warning he turned back to the room, resting his hips upon the desk beside which he stood.

I could see that Bryce resented this second interruption, although he endured it with such grace as he could muster.

"Well, what was they lookin' at?" he resumed with a frown.

"Nasturtiums—er—er—I mean flowers—in a florist's window." Miss Golding seemed suddenly very ill at ease.

Bryce turned to Carlton. "I guess that's enough," said he. "By the way, I told a man of ours to bring your car back here after takin' Sardon to the morgue. We'll finish our work somewhere's else"—with a scowl directed at Semi, who was again fingering the flowers in a thoughtful way. "For the present we'll hold Baird on a charge of murder and take the O'Niel girl for complicity."

I opened my mouth to protest, when Dual spoke for the third time: "By Jove! That might even have been a *sign* between them."

Bryce swung in sudden irritation. "What are you talking about?" he snapped. "There might have been a sign of what, between who?"

"Nasturtiums," said Semi.

"Them flowers?" grinned Bryce. "A sign, of what?"

"Oh," returned Semi, looking at him at last, "why, of *love*."

Bryce snorted: "If you'll bring Baird along," he addressed Johnson, "I'll go out and get the girl."

Meanwhile, I was watching the Golding woman and Dual. She was sitting straight up in her chair, staring fixedly at him, and very pale. Semi was holding her with his merciless gaze once more. As I watched he smiled slightly, put down a hand and picked one of the flowers from the bowl on the desk and drew it into his buttonhole.

CHAPTER III

A CONFERENCE AND A PHOTOGRAPH

I WENT WITH them when they led Billy out and put both him and the now white-faced Noriene O'Niel into the patrol. I wanted to keep the boy company as long as I could. At the last I gripped his hand and urged him again to be as brave as he could and not to talk to any one until I saw him again.

Bryce waited until I was done saying good-by. "I'm sorry for this, Glace," he told me as he swung up into the "wagon," "but you can see how it is."

"I'm giving you credit for thinking you're right," I answered, "only I bet you're dead wrong. Good-by, Billy. You'll come through all right!"

The patrol hummed away down the snow-whitened street, and I turned from watching it to find Semi Dual standing on the curb twirling his light stick and still wearing the nasturtium in his buttonhole. I stepped to his side and he greeted me with a smile.

"Quick work for you now, Gordon," he said. "Follow those two to the station and get an interview out of them both. Find out everything you possibly can. Also get samples of their hand-writing and some of Baird's hair. I think you told me you kept a camera at the station? Well, here—" he drew a small package from his coat pocket. "After your interviews at the jail go to the morgue, dust this powder on the finger-marks on Sardon's throat and take a photograph. And don't waste time! As soon as you have done these things come to the Urania. And, by the way, tell Miss O'Niel that those flowers on her table did not come from her sweetheart, Baird."

"And you think Billy is innocent—" I began.

Dual cut me short: "Gordon, do you think that I have ever worked to frustrate justice or protect the guilty? Would I have answered your mental cry for help unless I could justify my course? When you see your *fiancée*, Baird's sister, tell her that I say she need not worry and have taken up the case. Now, waste no more time!" He held up his stick at a passing taxi and was whirled away.

For the first time in the past two hours my own heart seemed to beat with renewed hope as I thought over the words of my peculiar friend. Unconsciously from the first, I had wished for his presence. I knew, now, that the subconscious yearning had been there from the first, and that he had answered my call. He had said I should not be surprised, and I had to admit that if he could call me to him by his telepathic force, as he often did, it was not singular that he had sensed my own cry for help, and even been able to place the time when I had begun to wish for him.

And, because I was his friend, he had come. Truly the word friend was not one to be used lightly with Semi Dual. To him it stood for all it should imply. I quickened my step in search for a telephone-booth. Once more we were working together. Semi Dual—my general—was commanding and had set me a task. I threw back my shoulders and drew in a deep breath of the snow-laden air. Once more I felt confidence thrill me and resolved to prove worthy of the faith imposed in me by Connie and Billy and Semi Dual.

I entered a drug-store and stepped into a sound-proof booth. First, I called up Connie and told her the unhappy news. I would rather have gone to her with it, but didn't have time, and I knew she herself would put Billy's interests first. As it was, I broke it to her as gently as I could and told her that Dual was already working in Billy's behalf. She took it very well and promised to meet me at the station as soon as she could dress and come down. Then I told her about the O'Niel girl and she cried out afresh over that.

"She's a dear thing, Gordon," she ended; "and I think almost as much of her as Billy does. I'll dress and come right over. They'll let me see Billy, I suppose?"

"I'll attend to that," I promised, and hung up the phone.

Then I called Smithson on the wire, and presently his voice snapped back at me: "Well?"

"Smithson," I told him, "this is Glace. Say, Smithson, I can't handle this bank story which has just broke. You'll have to turn it over to somebody else."

"You've got to handle it," he declared quickly. "You were on the ground, as I know, and have all the facts. What's the matter with you, Glace? You ought to know you can't lay down like that. I want those facts and I want 'em quick!"

"I'll give you the facts right now," I retorted, "but I won't write the story! I can't do it! Smithson, listen: This Baird, who is suspected, is my girl, Connie's, brother. I've tried to be a good man for you folks up there, but I'm human after all, and I can't write that stuff."

"The devil!" said Smithson. "Well, give *me* the facts! Quick now! Go ahead!"

I told him all I knew, and he jotted it down, pausing now and then to ask for some detail. "All right," he snapped at the end, "I'll see that it's handled. Now see here; is the kid guilty?"

"He is not," I asserted with all the conviction I could put into my voice.

"Sure?" demanded the old man.

"I'll write up that end of the story if you'll let me," I offered.

"That's enough," grunted Smithson. "Take a day off if you need it. Good-by, and good luck."

I left the booth, went to the station, and walked straight across to Harrington's desk. Connie had not yet arrived.

"I've got to see Baird right away, Dan," I began as soon as I was close enough to make my remarks audible to him alone. "This is the very deuce of a fix I'm in, because the boy is the brother of the girl I am going to marry. She's coming down here pretty soon, and I want you to pass us both in so she can see her brother, and Miss O'Niel, who is a friend of hers. The thing's been an awful shock to her."

Dan nodded. For once he did not indulge in any facetious by-play about my request for privileges. "I'll fix it as soon as she gets here," he promised. "I'm sorry for both of ye, Glace. Th' bhye's got himself an' th' girl in bad. Most loike that's his sister comin' in the door now."

I turned and saw Connie just entering the station, and hurried to meet her as she paused and looked uncertainly around.

Her face lighted the least trifle as she saw me coming, and she advanced toward me, so that we met in the middle of the floor. She took my hand without a word, and I could feel hers quiver in my own. "Have they brought Billy here yet?" she asked in a half whisper at last.

I nodded. "We're going right in to see him," I told her, and glanced at Dan.

He motioned to an officer, and jerked his head toward the jail at the rear. The policeman rose, and came out from behind the railing, signing me to follow him back to the corridor door. Drawing Connie's hand through my arm, I led her with me, following the man to the barred entrance, where he tapped on the grating and told a warder to take us to Billy's cell.

The great door swung inward, and we passed, and it closed behind us with a clang like the stroke of doom. Connie caught her breath audibly at the sound, and pressed closer to my side. "And they've brought Billy here," she whispered. "Oh, Gordon, help me to be brave and tell me what to do."

"Just keep cool and tell Billy that everything will come out all right. He needs encouragement more than anything now," I coached her, as the warder led us down the whitewashed corridor of cells. Half timidly she glanced to right and left as we walked, her eyes darting into the little rooms where crouched the trapped members of the race. I saw her nostrils quiver, and her hand tightened on my arm.

Our guide had paused by a door, which he now unlocked. "Somebody to see you, young feller," he said not unkindly to the man within, and motioned us to enter the cell.

"Be brave," I whispered to Connie, and led her to the door.

Baird had sat up on his cot, and turned his eyes toward our voices. His face was still haggard and worried, but lighted at the sight of us.

In a moment Connie was at his side, her arms about him, drawing his head to her breast. "Oh, Billy, Billy brother," she murmured. "Don't take it so hard, boy. It will all come out all right. Gordon is going to help us, and his wonderful friend, Mr. Dual. Don't worry, Billy. Everything will end all right."

Billy rose well to the occasion. "I'm trying not to, Con," he assured her. "Of course a chap hates a thing like this, but I've been thinking and I'm going to keep cool. If only it wasn't for Noriene, I believe I could keep from worrying at all. But it's awful to think what I've brought on that little girl. It's an awful thing for a girl like her to be shut up in a place like this. I don't mind it so much for myself, but, when I think of her, I feel as if I could tear down this place. And of course I hate to bring disgrace on you, Con dear."

"Nonsense," said Connie. "As you didn't do it, there is no disgrace, and it will all be cleared up before long, and I'll come to see you every day."

"I want you to see Noriene, too," requested the boy.

"Of course I will," Connie assured him, and then I stepped in.

"Pull a couple of hairs out of your head, and give them to me, and write your 'John Hancock' on this sheet of paper," I directed shoving a copy pad into his hand.

"What for?" said Billy, then in a different tone. "Oh, I guess I see." He took the pad and scrawled his name, then jerked some hairs from his head and handed them to me. "I suppose Dual wants them, don't he?" he said, smiling, as I took them.

I nodded. "You remember what Dual did for Sheldon on that forgery case, Billy? Well, he's at work now for you, and he told me to tell Connie that everything would come out right. Now, all you've got to do is to wait. I suppose you don't know anything more about the case than you told at the bank?"

Billy shook his head. "Not a thing," he replied. "Or wait—of course. I may be mistaken, but if I'm right, I've seen the chap who played the part of messenger, and gave me the phoney message and the package, talking to the Golding girl several nights ago."

That looked important, and I hastened to follow it up. "Are you sure of that, Billy?" I asked.

"I couldn't swear to it," he answered slowly, "but I think it was the same chap. He came across the street from the taxi-stand, several nights ago, and met her, just as we were both leaving the bank."

"And that's all you can add?"

"Everything, Gordon," said Billy. "It's up to you and Semi Dual."

I tapped on the door for the warder. "I'm going over and see Miss O'Niel," I explained to Connie and Billy. "I want to see her alone for a few minutes. I'll be back here when I get through over there."

"Give her my love," said Billy as I turned away.

The warder came and let me out, and I explained to him that I wanted to see Miss O'Niel, and would come back for Connie.

He nodded and closed the door. Then, as we moved away, he jerked his head back toward the cell. "He looks like a nice feller," he remarked, as I handed him a couple of cigars. "This working in a bank must be the very devil to make him go off his dip an' do a thing like that."

"Keep it under your hat," I boasted, "but he didn't do it at all!"

The fellow grinned. "If you prove that, Bryce will have three kinds of a fit. He's gettin' bouquets now for his lightning pinch."

"They'll wither and fade," I predicted, as I turned off toward the woman's section of the jail, leaving the warder smelling a cigar and shaking his head.

I found the matron, and got her to take me to Miss O'Niel's cell. She recognized me instantly. "You're the newspaperman what come to see the little nurse once on a time, aren't you?" she smiled.

I nodded.

"I hope you can do the same for this little body ye did for the other one," she went on. "This girl is no criminal, mind ye, young man. I've been here for a good many years, and I'm a woman. I kin tell by lookin' in their eyes, and the sound of the voices of them. Always look in a woman's eyes, says I—ye kin tell her soul by her eyes. Well, come along."

She led me down the row of cells to the one where Noriene O'Niel sat upon her narrow cot. Her eyes showed the marks of recent tears, and a haunted look besides, as she turned them toward me. At that moment she reminded me forcibly of a wild rabbit I once caught in a trap as a boy. It seemed to me that she looked at me with the same soft appeal of brown eyes as that little creature of the wild which had fallen into my snare. I had let the rabbit go and remembered its eyes all the years. Now I felt my heart swell with the hope that I might be instrumental in freeing this greater soul.

She started to rise, but I motioned her to be still. "Miss O'Niel," I began. "I want to ask you some questions, not as a reporter, but as a friend of yourself and Baird, in whose interests I am working on this case."

"How is Billy? Have you seen him?" she asked at once.

"He is well enough," I assured her, "and raving because you are here. You see he blames himself for your arrest."

The girl smiled softly. As I hoped, she cuddled the thought of Billy's interest to her heart. "The foolish boy! How could he help it?" she cried.

"He couldn't, of course," I responded. "Anyway, he asked me to give you his love, just before I left him to come here. Now we must get down to business, as I have to hurry back to my friend Dual, whom you saw at the bank to-day."

"The gentleman who spoke to me about the flowers?" Miss O'Niel questioned at once.

"The same, Miss O'Niel."

"Oh, I like him!" she exclaimed quickly, and I smiled. Dual always had that effect upon good women. The other sort avoided him, I had found. They seemed to sense an unassailable personality about the man.

"He is working to prove both yourself and Billy innocent," I resumed.

"Is he a detective?" she inquired.

"The greatest in the world, and he is working for us. Now: Have you recently had any reason to believe that any one in the bank could be getting information about the transfers of the bank's moneys?"

"I never even thought of such a thing," she replied.

"Was there any correspondence about this particular transfer of to-day?"

"Nothing," she said, "except a brief note from Mr. Carlton, which was sent yesterday, by messenger, to the branch, stating that the currency would be forwarded to-day before opening."

"Who wrote that note. Miss O'Niel?"

"I did, Mr. Glace."

"Directly on the machine, or from notes?"

"From notes."

"Which you probably took down in your stenographer's book?"

"Yes."

"Why was a note written? Why did not Mr. Carlton use the phone?"

"Mr. Carlton hardly ever used the phone in regard to money transfers, Mr. Glace. He knows that operators sometimes listen in."

"Where are your note-books kept, Miss O'Niel?"

"Why, in my desk," said the girl in some surprise.

"Then, to any one who could read shorthand, the message to the branch might have been easily available?" I suggested.

"Why, I suppose so; if they saw my book before I locked my desk for the night. You don't think—"

"One never can tell," I replied to her half-question. "Now, think carefully, Miss O'Niel. Did any one, say yesterday, disturb anything about your desk, after the note was written to the bank?"

She knit her brows in an effort at concentration. "I don't recall anything of the sort," she decided after an interval; "unless— Why, I do remember now, that, just before I went home, last night, I had been out of Mr. Carlton's office. He had gone home, and I stepped out to wash my hands, and left my dictation pad on the leaf of my desk. When I came back, it was on the floor, but I never gave it any thought. I supposed it had just fallen down, and picked it up and put it away. You don't suppose—"

"At what time do you usually leave the bank. Miss O'Niel?" I next asked.

"At about five o'clock."

"Does Miss Golding quit at the same time?"

"She did last night. We went out together."

"Miss O'Niel, do you know whether or not Miss Golding has any gentleman friend who is in the habit of meeting her after she leaves the bank?"

"Her brother meets her sometimes, Mr. Glace."

"Then she has relatives?"

"Only her brother. She tells me they are orphans. I know her only through our both working at the bank, and what she has told me of herself."

"Miss O'Niel," I began on a new line of questions, "I am going to be what you may perhaps deem impertinent, but I want you to believe that all I say or ask is for a good reason: What made you think that the flowers on your table were from Baird?"

Noriene O'Niel opened her eyes in surprise: "Why, because he often brought me flowers for my table," she replied.

"Were you out with him last night, and did you stop at a florist's and look at the flowers in the window?"

"That's queer, Mr. Glace," said she. "How did you know we did that?"

"Maybe I'll tell you sometime," I replied smiling. "Then you did do that?"

"Why, yes."

"But Billy didn't buy you any nasturtiums then—last night?"

"No. That's why I felt so sure they were from him. They had them in the window last night at the florist's."

"What shop was that?" I questioned.

"Hudson's, just a block from the bank."

"Miss O'Niel," I said as she paused after answering my question, "before I came down here, my friend, Semi Dual, asked me to tell you that those flowers did not come from Mr. Baird."

"Not from Billy!" cried the girl. "Why, where did they come from, then?"

"I don't know," I admitted, and I confess I felt strangely puzzled as I recalled the scene in the bank that morning. Dimly,

I saw, even so early, that Dual had picked up something we all had overlooked. Suddenly I felt a sense of elation, and a desire to chuckle. Already he was upon the trail. What might he not have discovered while I was here at the station? "I don't know." I repeated, "but I'll wager my friend Dual, does. And that reminds me: I was to get you to write your signature on a bit of paper for him."

"Of course I will if it will help any," she assented. "Oh, Mr. Glace, isn't he the man who helped Mr. Sheldon out of his trouble sometime ago? He must be wonderful!"

"He is that," I agreed with enthusiasm and handed her my copy pad. "Just write your full name on that, please."

She took the pad and pencil and wrote "Noriene Malley O'Niel" and handed the pad back to me:

"I feel awfully relieved," said she. "He used handwriting in clearing up that case, didn't he? Now I shall just feel sure that everything will be cleared up and I shall sit here and pray for his success."

I took the pad and rose. "I am sure that your prayers will be answered," I told her. "I have never known Dual to fail on a case yet. In fact, he has to feel sure that the party he works for is innocent before he will interfere, and he has a habit of working awfully fast."

The matron let me out and I went back to get Connie and to ask Billy a question which had come into my mind.

"About this man whom you tripped up at the Merchants'," I began, after Connie had said good-by—"what was he like? Describe him as nearly as you can."

"He was a tall chap," said Billy. "I should judge something over six feet, and when he did get up he stood very straight. I couldn't see much of him except that he wore a long gray over-coat with a close-fitting back and a gray cap. Even when I apologized for my awkwardness he never looked at me and yet I'm almost sure he was light-complexioned and had a little mustache. There was one thing I did notice, though," he went on. "When he was down on his knees with his hands up against the glass of the door, trying to get up, I saw that he was wearing what looked like an immense ruby set in a ring on the little finger of his left hand."

"No more now, Billy," I answered. "I saw Noriene and she's all right. She's a game little girl and says this mix-up isn't any of your fault. Cheer up now and we'll get you out of this in no time at all!"

Connie insisted on going to see Noriene; and, after getting it fixed for her to have a half-hour with the girl, I promised to call her up that evening and let her know the latest news. Then I left the station and set off for the morgue. It was half past one and I deemed haste essential, so I took a taxi and was soon put down at the door of the gloomy house of the dead.

I had little trouble there, for I was rather well known in most such places through my connection with the *Record*. Newspapermen are pretty much free-lances in the pursuit of their calling.

I got an attendant whom I knew and we went back to where the body of Sardon lay upon one of the glass slabs. There I blew some of the powder Dual had given me upon the marks on his neck and a moment later had my photograph of them.

We covered the poor fellow up and I went back to my cab and told the driver to take me to the Urania. I had covered the first part of my assignment and now I was going to report to Semi Dual.

CHAPTER IV

BLIND OBEDIENCE

THE TAXI SET me down at the Urania at a few minutes after two and I made haste to catch an express just leaving for the top floor. I made it, thanks to the starter, who knew me through my frequent visits and was kind enough to hold the cage until I could slip in.

A spirit of impatience drove me now; and I was conscious of resentment that the cage was required to make each of its scheduled stops. However, we reached the twentieth floor in due time and I got out and turned up the great flight of marble stairs which led to Dual's quarters on the roof. I took them two at a time.

Then, despite my hurry and the drive of my anxiety for my friends, I paused at the top.

Outside it was snowing. Here all was soft moist warmth and the scent of blossoms. Under the great dome of curved glass Dual's winter-garden was in bloom, its plants and shrubs filling all the place with the odor of some vast conservatory, through which flitted chirping birds. The light of the outside filtered in through the greenish-yellow glass, giving almost the effect of a weak sunshine, pervading the place, and the tinkle of the little fountain in the midst of the garden came softly to the ear.

It was peaceful, beautiful, serene, and, as always, cast its strange spell of rest and soothing over my tingling nerves. It was like a quiet oasis from which the mad war and strife of life, the world, the elements themselves, was shut out; a temple of harmony not to be profaned by any disharmonizing influence. For one moment I paused and drank in its sedative atmosphere. While I stood the last flake of snow melted from my clothing. It was hard to realize that only the sheets of green-yellow glass were between me and the wintry forces, which now howled outside, as though trying to storm this citadel of tranquility.

I drew another deep breath and stepped upon the inlaid electric annunciator plate in the floor and I thought of the words which its curiously set glasses spelled out:

> Pause and consider, oh, stranger. For he who cometh against me with evil intent shall live to rue it until the uttermost part of his debt shall have been paid; yet he who cometh in peace and with a pure heart shall surely find that which he seeks.

Many a time since I had first read these words had I trod across their caution to the insincere and the evil-minded, but never, I believe, had I come with a more wholly clean desire to see the innocent cleared from suspicion than to-day. "Shall surely find that which he seeks." I wondered if I should.

The clear notes of the chime broke out on the air as I crossed to the path and went on up to the tower and, as their mellow notes beat softly about me, I felt myself chiding my momentary questioning of the future. Surely by now I, of all men, should know that I *should* find!

The door of the tower stood ajar, but no soft-footed Henri answered the chime of the bells. I pushed tentatively against it and it swung inward so that I stepped into the room. Across from me was the door of that inner room in which I had seen Dual unravel the tangled skeins of other lives in the past. I approached it and found it, too, upon the latch. Again I pushed it before me and looked into the room. Then very softly I entered and made my way to a chair and sank into it.

Semi Dual, clad in the loose robe he wore when at home, lay stretched at full length upon a couch, his eyes closed, his hands folded upon his breast. Not by a movement or a sign did he appear to be aware of my presence. Save for the slight rise and fall of his chest he might have been laid out for burial so quiet was his repose.

I glanced about the room. Upon his desk was a litter of papers covered with the peculiar groups of figures and cabalistic signs which, I had now learned, went with his investigations of our various problems, and among them stood the shining brass tripod and slender barrel of a beautiful microscope.

My gaze came back to my friend and for the first time I noticed that some object lay upon his broad forehead as he apparently slumbered. I bent forward and stared in uncomprehending surprise. *The thing resting upon his forehead was the half-burned stub of a cigarette!*

Slowly he opened his eyes and met mine. He smiled, put up a hand, removed the cigarette and a bit of paper which had lain beneath it and sat up on the couch. "The murderer is a red-haired person of some five feet eight inches in height, with grayish-green eyes and left-handed," he remarked. "Also he is addicted to the use of cigarettes."

"Good Heavens! How do you know that?" I burst out.

Dual rose and came across to his chair at the desk. He sat down. "When you came in," he continued, "I was attempting a little psychometry, as you may have observed." He indicated the cigarette stub and the folded bit of paper which he now laid down upon the desk.

"Psychometry?" said I.

"The process of reading a person's description from some object or thing which has been about him," explained Dual. "It all comes down to vibration again, friend Glace. Those hairs which you gave me are in that folded paper. They were at one time upon the murderer's head. The cigarette was at one time in his hands, between his lips. They will partake for a time even after being separated from him of his individual key of vibration. If I can sensitize myself so as to be affected by their vibrations I may sense the sort of individual to which they belonged."

"And that was what you were doing when I came in?"

Dual nodded. "Unfortunately, however, I would not dare arrest my man on such evidence," he said with a smile. "However, it serves to put me more readily upon the trail and I can support all the facts I have learned by others which will be acceptable to the police."

"For instance—" I began.

"For instance," he took me up, still smiling, "I have said that the murderer was red-haired, and he is. The police say so, too, yet we believe that different men are the cause of Sardon's death. However, I can prove their error to the police themselves. Let me see the hairs you got from Baird!"

I handed them to him and he spread them out on the paper in which I had wrapped them up. "Material science will now assist the occult and prove my point for me in the instance I am citing. The microscope here will show a difference between the hairs from Sardon's glove and those from Baird's head. To begin with, the hairs from the genuine assassin are of a less vigorous growth, their shafts show a poor nourishment and I would be inclined to say that the man is gradually losing his hair. On the other hand, you will find Baird's hair will show a sturdy strength, good nourishment and a strong root-cap."

I sat forward in my excitement. "Then that lets Billy out," I cried.

"Billy never was in, except in the mind of Bryce," said Dual dryly. "The difficulty will not be to discover his innocence, which all my calculations affirm, but to convince the police of the fact. That is where your activities come in, Glace; in getting proof— material proof. I can tell you where to seek it, but it must be obtained by you."

"But you know—know now—who really did the thing?" Truly Dual was piling surprise upon surprise as he calmly stated his opinion of the case! "How have you learned all this? What have you done? It is all incredible!"

"Incredible is a much abused word, Gordon," said Semi Dual. "As to what I have done, I have spent some time in gaining a little evidence for the police. There were few difficulties in the case itself. All that was necessary was to reconstruct the seven minutes during which Baird was in the Merchants' Bank. Immediately after leaving you this noon I returned to the Merchants' and took a photograph of the marks of the hand made by the man whom, Baird says, he knocked down in the revolving door. Also I interviewed the cashier and obtained the wrapper of the package which Baird delivered to him and one of the folded sheets of paper as well. You may have noticed that Bryce did not consider it necessary to do that. Upon returning home, I naturally made some calculations based upon the time mentioned by Baird in his account, giving particular attention to the seven minutes during which the actual crime must have occurred. After that I examined the two hairs and the stub of the cigarette. That is all save my little experiment in psychometry which you came in upon and a telephone message to Sheldon." He crossed and again stretching himself upon the couch, closed his eyes. "Now give me your report as usual. Be careful! Omit nothing! Go on!"

I began at the beginning and ran over every incident of my work from the time I left him until my return. I told of every move, quoted every remark from the notes I had made. Times before I had done thus, while Dual lay passive and listened; so that I talked rapidly now. Not once did he interrupt me or ask a question or give a sign that he heard.

When I had finished, however, he sat up at once. "Give me the signatures and the photograph of the finger-marks on Sardon's neck," he directed.

I laid the written pages on his desk and handed him the folding camera.

Without a word, he took it and left me to sit and stare out of the window at the steadily falling snow. Dual's handling of the case was certainly more than I could understand, so I gave it up and let my thoughts go back to Billy and Connie and the little O'Niel girl and to a vague wonder as to how long they would be compelled to bear the harassment and worry of their plight.

In something like ten minutes Dual came back with my camera and handed it to me. "I have reloaded it with a fresh film," said he; "and here is a flash-light pistol which you had better take along when you go out after a bit. Your negative was a good one and I can now add the information that the murderer has a scar on his left thumb. There is a similar mark on the butt of the cigarette you found, so that we know that he was the man who dropped it in the limousine. That, Gordon, is evidence at law."

"But how does that help if we don't know where to look for him?" I asked.

Semi Dual sat down and regarded me with a somewhat quizzical expression. At length he said: "Gordon, had I wished, I might have arrested two of the chief actors concerned in this morning's tragedy within fifteen minutes after we parted this noon. Yet I did not."

I guess I stared as if I didn't believe my ears. It was a shock to have him calmly inform me that he had been within striking distance of any of the guilty parties and had held his hand. I couldn't understand a thing like that, not for the life of me!

"Why?" resumed Semi Dual, reading the unvoiced question in my mind. "Because, Gordon, I was desirous of capturing not only the accomplices, but also *the master mind.*"

I nodded. "I see. The murderer, you mean."

Dual shook his head. "No, I do not mean the murderer," he replied. "I could have had him this morning. But—he is only a tool."

"Then, whom do you mean?"

"The cause of the whole thing," replied Semi Dual. "Gordon," he leaned forward in his chair and spoke slowly; "this thing is the work of a gang. In every gang, as in every other human organization, there is an activating, thinking, planning individuality, a 'master mind.' It is that individuality I am seeking to capture; waiting until the net I am spreading shall enmesh him as well as his accomplices."

"And you think the murderer and this man are different individuals?" I questioned. "I should think the person who killed Sardon and got the money would about fill the bill."

"Certainly not," said Semi Dual. "The master mind does not work in the open. That is why such a brain, with its craft and cunning, is as dangerous to the body politic as an insidious disease. Secure in its concealment, it plans and plots and uses others to carry out its conceptions.

"If you think that the man who killed Sardon also got the fifty thousand I must tell you that you are wrong. He may have had it for a short time, but by now it is in the possession of the stronger intellect which planned the theft. Do you not see now why I am so anxious to ensnare him as well as the others who worked when he pulled the strings? He is far more dangerous than the mere assassin who openly takes his chances. But for him the assassin would not have done the deed. He is the primary cause, the germ of evil, the instigator, the chief profitor of the other's crime, which robbed your friend of his freedom and Sardon of his life.

"Not only has he inspired this murder, but others, perhaps, before it. Should he go free, he may inspire others for years to come. It was for that I held my hand when I could have closed it upon his agents, and in that I shall be justified."

"But who is he?" I cried as he ceased and lay back in his chair. "Who is he, Dual? Do you know?"

Semi shook his head. "In my own soul, yes. So as to prove his guilt to the world at large, no; not yet."

"What do you mean? That you have no material proof?"

"Exactly. I told you that I had made calculations of this affair, basing my figures of the event upon the time when it occurred. Through them all looms the figure of this master of evil, over-shadowing the figure of the calculation with his malignant spirit, like a cloud which dims the sun. Over Baird, his influence is but temporary, and even now passing away. Over others it will be a blight which will change their entire destiny."

He rose and began pacing the room. "Gordon, I must have this man. He has done evil enough. And through me, his evil course shall be brought to a close. I am the instrument of fate in this; the rock upon which this man shall break! It is written, and the stars, my friend, do not lie!"

He paused and seated himself again, with a smile. "In the end, all will be well," he said more lightly, with a return of his old control.

"And I perceive that you are still very anxious over the matter; if anything, more so than before."

"Well," I confessed, "I admit that I am rather worried lest the murderer and the others may escape while we are after this other chap."

"Do you think I would wait if that were true?" Dual said slowly. "However, you need not worry. You need not even fear that your friend Baird or his sweetheart will spend this night in jail."

I sprang to my feet. "Semi," I cried, "do you mean that?"

"Did I ever promise you anything I did not fulfil?" asked my strange friend.

"Then your calculations have shown you—"

"That the hour of retributive justice draweth nigh. Enough of this, Glace. There is yet work to be done, evidence to be gathered for—the police."

"Yet you know. Semi?"

"I know," said Dual. "I can tell you the story from the first to the last, even as it is written in the karmic records of all eternity, and mirrored by the stars—to what avail? Here!" He drew some currency from his robe, and handed it to me. "Here is money. There is need of haste. It is now after three o'clock. Use a taxicab for all you do and remember that you must be back here by six o'clock. I shall tell you what you are to do. First you will go to this florist's which Miss O'Niel mentioned and learn to whom they sold a bunch of golden nasturtiums this morning about eight o'clock. You will then leave the shop and go into the alley which runs back of the stores directly opposite the Fourth National Bank. Locate the empty storeroom across from the bank and see if there is not an unfastened window or an unlocked rear door. At any rate get into that room if you have to break a glass, and see what you will find.

"If you discover there what I expect you to, cross to the bank and ask for Assistant Cashier Sheldon, who will be waiting for you. I arranged that for you earlier in the afternoon. When you see him, you will ascertain if any one has rented a safety deposit-box or drawer in their vaults at any time since twelve o'clock to-day. Be very careful about this, Glace, and if anyone has rented a drawer or box, take a photograph of the page of the vault register upon which the signature appears.

"If you find that any such box has been rented, get Sheldon to take you into the vault, sprinkle some of your gray powder over the front of the box, and take a flash-light of it, and be sure to get the number of the box.

"After you have done this, call me up and let me know what you have found, both at the bank and at the empty room across the street. I shall then have fresh instructions to give you, governing your future course.

"While you are at the bank, you must also get Sheldon to let you have the stenographic note-books of both Miss O'Niel and Miss Golding. It is presumable that their names will be written on the pads, and you must bring them to me. Tell Sheldon that I will personally guarantee their safe return. As soon as you have the photographs of the register at the vault, and the front of the vault box, call a messenger and send the film to your paper's art department, with an order for rush work on them, and get several copies. I will see that a copy of the Sardon marks is furnished to your paper. Of course I could attend to all the development details myself, but time is essential, so I am taking this means of gaining it.

"And now, Gordon, I am going to ask you to work on this as you have never worked before, yet go carefully. Much depends upon it! Not only are we going to free Baird and the little O'Niel girl from any possible stigma, but we are going to free the world from the peril of a great mind of evil, and we must test every step of the way we go.

"Here in the civilized world of the twentieth century, it is no longer sufficient for a man to know that he is right in what he does; he must be able to prove it to his fellow men. Therefore, before we can put out our hands and make use of the knowledge which we possess to arrest the course of this man, we must have such evidence as any court of law will accept as proof of his guilt. Gordon, I am leaving the collection of that proof to you."

I rose to my feet. "I'll do the best there is in me," I promised. "The little O'Niel girl said she would sit and pray for your success. I hope she slips in a word for me as an afterthought."

Dual smiled into my eyes. "The prayers of a good woman avail much, Gordon," said he. "Women are far more subconscious in their existence than men are; hence, they can listen more closely to the voice of the spirit than their brothers can. It is easier for a woman to concentrate her mind upon some desire than it is for a man, and so she has an added force for bringing about her desire; actually creates a center of magnetic force, as it were, which attracts the thing of which she thinks. Myself I have faith in the actual assistance of the little O'Niel's prayers.

"Now one minute before you go. I see that you have been neglecting yourself in your work to-day. It is well to be zealous for a friend, but unwise both for yourself and for your end to neglect your own physical machine. Sit down and light a cigarette while I get you a stimulant!"

He rose and hurried from the room. I dropped back into my chair and made myself a smoke. Dual had himself gone to get me something. Then Henri was not anywhere in the apartments. I wondered what Dual could have done with his man; why he was not here to render his silent service.

I began to map out my assignment, the florist's, a vacant storeroom, a bank, books, photographs, a vault drawer, and a telephone back to Dual. For the life of me I could not see where it was all leading, save that I had Semi's assurance that in the end it would bring the answer to the riddle, and set free the two persons I wanted to liberate. I put it aside. I would go blindly forward, trusting in the wonderful acumen of the man who directed me, an acumen I had never known to fail.

I thought of his words, "a master mind," and I smiled. Speaking of *master minds*, what of the intellect which sat in a weirdly beautiful apartment on top of a storm assailed modern sky-scraper, and wove the meshes of an invisible net to ensnare the perpetrators of a crime; who lay upon a couch and rose from apparent stupor to pronounce the physical description of a man who had slain another man hours before, and whom the revealer admitted he had never seen?

I cast aside my half smoked cigarette. "It takes a master mind to catch a master mind," I reflected and smiled somewhat grimly as I did so. Came the question hard on the former thought, "Which was the master mind?" Surely not the misguided spirit which wrought ruin and woe to his fellows for a material gain, but rather that spirit which sensed the other's veiled presence and put an end to his course, my friend and "general"—Semi Dual.

Dual came back with a brimming glass of his wonderful preparation of fruit juices and a plate of his small, flat cakes, and set them on the corner of the desk. "Drink the liquid, and put the cakes in your pocket," he directed. "You can eat them as you go to the florist's in the cab, and you will work better for the nourishment!"

I rose again to my feet, and lifted the glass. "To the fulfilment of the little O'Niel's prayers, and the confounding of the master of evil," I toasted and drank, and set down the empty glass.

Dual nodded. "He who cometh with a pure heart, shall surely find that which he seeketh," he returned. "Now hasten, Gordon, and report to me from the bank without fail!"

I picked up my hat. "I don't profess to understand it at all," I told him, "but I'm off. I've seen you work before, but never like this. If it wouldn't be asking too much, just how do you expect to reach the murderer, if you don't know even his name?"

Dual smiled slightly as I filled my pocket with the cakes from the plate.

"The murderer will return here with Henri at about eight o'clock," he said.

CHAPTER V

UNDER THE HOLES
IN THE CURTAIN

I SUPPOSE I must have left the Urania in the usual way. Reasoning from my knowledge of such things, I am sure that I did; yet my next absolutely conscious action was telling the driver of a taxi which had drawn in to the curb as though expecting me to enter that I wanted to go to Hudson's flower shop.

The sound of the words served to rouse me to the fact that I had work to do; that there was still much to be done in order to insure Dual's success, and that he had entrusted part of the work to me. Up to that time his last words had buzzed and shrieked in my brain to the drowning of all else: "The murderer will return here with Henri, at about eight o'clock."

It wasn't possible. It wasn't even sane. What could Dual mean? How could he know that an unknown man, a person he had never even glimpsed to recognize, would come to his room, and at what time? And why with Henri? What bizarre twist in the every-day course of happening was Dual expecting to occur? What more unlikely than that the murderer should appear before the very man who should surrender him to punishment for his crime? I had seen Semi do many wonderful things, but I promised myself that if this latest prediction of his materialized I would crown it the climax of all he had done.

And all the time that my confused brain doubted, or seemed to doubt, I know there was an undercurrent of unshaken belief in the words of my peculiar friend. I couldn't logically accept it with credence, and yet I knew it was going to occur. Did you ever believe something at which your intellect scoffed, and yet still go on believing? Well, that was I—Gordon Glace, seasoned newspaperman!

At a crossing, a newsboy hopped to the running-board and shook a paper in my face. I tossed him a nickel and took the sheet. It was a *Record* extra, and I read the account, which I should have written but for the nearness with which the event had struck to myself. I recognized Davidson's handling of the story, which aside from the head-lines, was very decent indeed. I had to admit that my paper had shown a great consideration for me in the story they had put out.

And at the end was a little tail paragraph, in which I thought I detected Smithson's touch:

> Latest reports indicate new developments in the case. It is by no means certain that the police have apprehended the proper parties. The *Record,* with its usual desire to serve its readers, has one of its best men devoting his entire time to the matter, and we are led from information he has collected to look for a surprising turn in the case, with probably more arrests.

I folded the paper and tucked it away in the pocket which had held Dual's cakes. I had eaten them as I read, and felt wonderfully refreshed, although up to that time I had not realized my hunger.

The cab was slowing in front of Hudson's flower crowded windows, and I sprang out, paid the driver and sent him away. Then I turned and entered the moist, sweet-scented interior of the shop, where the varicolored stock of the florist defied the sweep of the outer storm.

A neat little saleswoman in black, with white apron and cuffs, looking very much like a lady's-maid, came forward to meet me, and I asked for the proprietor at once. The girl turned and led me to a glass-partitioned office at the rear, and ushered me into the presence of a pink-cheeked, little, old lady, who sat in a rocking-chair knitting some gaily-colored creation of silks.

"A gentleman to see you, Mrs. Hudson," said the girl.

My heart leaped. Here was luck. There would be no need to deal with some hard-headed business man who would resent my inquiries as a man of the press, and begrudge me the time necessary for his answers. If I could interest the little, old lady's curiosity I felt sure I could excite her sympathies as well. I bowed to her and accepted a chair.

"Mrs. Hudson," I began, "I am Mr. Glace. I am a newspaper-man, and I have reason to believe that you can help me in saving an innocent girl from serious trouble, if you will."

"My goodness!" said the little lady. "What has happened to her, Mr. Glace?"

"She has been arrested," I told her, "because she had some flowers—nasturtiums—which I believe were bought at your shop."

I saw by her eyes that I had touched the right chord. I had taken the tip of the matron at the jail, and was watching her eyes. "But how could that be?" she cried in sudden excitement. "We have nasturtiums, and have sold some, but how could they arrest a girl for buying a few little flowers? I'm afraid I don't understand."

I smiled in return. "I haven't time to explain it now, Mrs. Hudson," I answered. "If you'll read to-morrow's *Record* it will all be there. In the mean time, the little girl is in jail, and her friends are working to keep her from spending the night there. I want you to help me by finding out, if you can, whether you sold any golden nasturtiums, either late last night or early this morning, and if possible what sort of a person bought them, or took them away. Will you do this?"

She rose and laid her knitting aside. "Of course," said she, "if I can do anything to help any good girl from spending a night in a place like a jail, I shall be only too glad. I will ask my girls about any sale for either late last night or this morning early, I think you said?"

I bowed and she hurried out. I looked about the place. In some ways it was just an ordinary office, with a desk and ledgers and letter-files and a safe. But the corner in which I sat was different. Here was a rug and an easy chair and a rocker. There was a pair of dainty, white curtains on the rear window and flowers in pots on the sill, and a little table with a work-basket, on which lay the knitting Mrs. Hudson had laid down. I crossed and picked up the soft thing of silk, and it opened into a diminutive sock. I was fingering it in surprised admiration when Mrs. Hudson returned.

"There was only one sale made either last night or this morning of golden nasturtiums," she informed me, "and that was not to a little girl. Early this morning, just as we were opening, a large, blond woman came in and bought a bunch. I'm afraid I can't help you after all."

I laid down the little sock and faced her. "Indeed, but you have," I assured her. "You have told me what I hoped you would, I think."

Suddenly, as she spoke, I had seen all Dual was driving at at this point. One end of the snarl was straightening out. At the little, old lady's words I remembered Dual's apparently inane remark, "it might even have been a sign." Where did it lead? My next point was the storeroom. The storeroom? By Jove! I saw yet farther ahead. "I must thank you for your trouble," I told the little, old lady. "It was the large woman you see who brought trouble on the other girl. This will help us to set her victim free."

"I am very glad," she said sincerely. She crossed and took up her knitting. "I see you were looking at my work," she smiled. "It is getting near Christmas. They will be for a baby of a daughter of mine."

I left the little office with my hat in my hand and hurried out of the shop, but I took with me something of the sweet atmosphere of the place as I walked up the street toward the alley which ran behind the row of buildings which lined the side of the street opposite the bank.

I found it and crept into it out of the sweep of the storm, making my way down its length. All the old news sense, which had lain so singularly dormant to-day under the shock of the morning's happenings, now woke afresh. I had seized an end of the tangle now, and was following it toward that point where it must lead me to the heart of the snarl. Dimly I began to sense what Dual's wonderful mind must have grasped at the start; the point which had enabled him to build up, point by point, the story of the crime. I hastened my steps, scanning the backs of the buildings I passed until I came to that which I knew was next to the empty room.

I thanked Heaven for the storm. There would be no one about unless from absolute necessity, and I could move with little fear of detection. I stepped up close to the rear wall of the building and sought to peer into the room through some grimy glass panes. The blinds on the front windows were down, however, and I could make out nothing in the faint light.

I tried the door and found it fast. I tried the window and the sash moved slightly under my pressure. With a pencil I pressed up against the top frame of the lower sash. It slipped. I shoved it up until I could get my head and shoulders through, and so wriggled and crawled up and dropped down inside. I pulled the sash back into place and turned toward the front. I was inside the room.

What with the drawn blinds and the lateness of the hour at that time of year, and the storm, it was pitch black, and I stumbled forward over the bare, dusty floor toward the front, where a faint line of light outlined the drawn curtain.

I began to wonder how I was to find anything at all in all that gloom; and, even as I asked myself the question, I nearly fell over my first discovery. For a moment I thought of raising the curtain and seeing what I had scraped my shin against, but second thought told me that it was hardly safe. Instead, I felt in my pockets for a match and struck it alight. Then I saw that the thing I had struck was an ordinary packing-box, some three feet wide by, say, eighteen inches wide. It had evidently been standing in front of the street window, back of the drawn curtain, and I had not perceived it. Apparently it had been sitting with its opened-end down, for now that I had tipped it over it lay upon one side.

My match died and I sat down upon the box. Surely I thought this box could not be the discovery Dual had expected me to make, for there was nothing in the box. What then? There was something else. I reached for another match, yet even as my fingers touched it I became aware of something about the curtain which arrested my gaze. As I sat upon the box my eyes seemed to be exactly upon the level of two small holes in the heavy fabric of the blind.

Now, two holes might occur in any curtain, but these were regular in outline, symmetrical in proportion. For all they showed they might have been cut by some special design.

Without striking my match I half rose and brought my face close to the little apertures and received my second surprise. The holes were at exactly the right distance apart to accommodate my eyes. Standing as I was, and looking out of the two circles in the curtain, I could see all that was going on in the outer street.

Looking back, I know that my breath began to come fast, as I stood there squinting out. Little by little it was coming to me there in the darkness of the room. Nasturtiums, a sign, a darkened room, two holes in a blind, and back of it all two minds, one trained to the ways of evil; one equally trained to unveil that evil, playing an invisible game, in which I was a pawn.

My fingers trembled with excitement as I drew out the second match and lighted it. I waited until it was well aglow and then very carefully brought it up and inspected the curtain in the neighborhood of the little round holes. Again my heart leaped. In the smudge of the dust which had gathered upon the blinds since the room stood vacant were two smeared circles, somewhat larger than a dollar in their rimmed outlines—one drawn about each hole.

For a moment I asked myself what it meant—until my match burned down and scorched my fingers—and even as I dropped it to the floor I knew. They were the marks made by the large ends of a pair of field glasses pressed against the blind over the holes!

Suddenly the darkness of the room became peopled with fantoms of what had gone before. Mentally I could see some one sitting here in this darkened room watching the bank with glasses through the little, round holes; sitting and watching and watching until a "sign" appeared in the window of the bank which he commanded from his station, then rising and giving the signal which meant the beginning of a tragedy. And even while these thoughts ran through my brain there was something stronger which kept time to them like the basic theme of a composition—the thought that "Dual had known!"

I lighted more matches and examined the floor. There were the marks of feet in the dust. Some of them I knew for my own, but there were others. I tried to reconstruct the scene. Here was the box and the man, sitting watching. It would have to be about here, I thought. I stooped and glanced at the floor. There they were! The shuffled outlines of a pair of feet, toes pointing toward the window, and back of them, dimly marked out, the rectangle of the box where it had lain. Here he had sat and watched.

I tore off some copy-paper and picked out the clearest of the footprints and wondered how I could measure the mark. In a moment I had the solution. Very carefully I licked that whole sheet with my tongue and pressed the damp page firmly over the track. It came away smudged with dust, it is true, yet showing plainly enough the outline of the shoe the watcher had worn.

Match after match I lighted after that and went hunting for other tracks. And I found them. They led from the window where I had entered, both forward and back from the front. And they were of two kinds. Some were similar to the one I had measured. Others were larger and broader as well. And of these last there were very few and not apparently smudged in their outlines at all, as though they might have been very recently made.

Once more I resorted to my moistened paper and found it to work. With nervous haste I folded it up and put it away. Every minute that I followed the mysterious trail which Dual had set me the scent was growing stronger, and I felt the urge of time pressing me on.

I had been kneeling by the box as I measured this last track and gradually my eyes had been growing more accustomed to the gloom. Now as I rose they caught the dim outlines of something sitting in front of the open end of the box as though it might have been beneath it, and so exposed by my collision in the dark, which had tipped its concealing cover upon its side.

I groped downward and my fingers closed upon a leathern handle, traced its outlines and felt the smooth sides of what seemed to be a satchel of some sort, and stopped. For perhaps a moment I crouched there, trying to realize the truth of the wild fancy which had popped into my brain. Then I caught the leather thing up and thrust it under my long waterproof coat.

Like a thief in the night, I slipped softly upon tiptoe to the rear window and inched it up that it might make no noise. Very carefully I got to the sill and looked up and down the white line of the alley. There was no one in sight. Slowly I crawled through and let myself down, picked up the thing I had found and thrust it again under my coat.

There was a saloon of which I knew midway of the block. I made my way there and slipped in at the back and so to a private room. There I rang for a waiter, and when he came I ordered a drink and asked him to get me a piece of string.

When he came back I paid for the liquor, drained it at a gulp, and tipped him for the string. When he had departed I rose, tiptoed to the door of the box and slipped the catch on the lock. I took the copy of the *Record* I had bought and spread it out upon the table and placed the thing I had found upon it, wrapped it up and tied it with the string. When that was done I put the parcel back under my coat.

I went to the door, unlocked it, and went out through the front of the saloon to the street. Half a block down was the corner on which stood the Fourth National Bank. I bent my head to the storm and set out for the next destination, which Dual had ordered me to make.

There were few people abroad, and I met no one except one or two men, hurrying like myself, head down.

The bank was closed and its curtains drawn, but I went up and tried a door. Dual had said Sheldon would wait, and I knew that I would get in. The door swung before me and admitted me to the vestibule, through which I could see the glow of the electrics in the cages of the accountants, who were still at work. I paused and surveyed the room. I could see only the bending bookkeepers far to the rear. I pushed open the vestibule door and went in.

As I crossed the floor of the general room, I glanced toward Sheldon's railed-in space. He was not there, so I did not pause. I crossed to the entrance of the vaults, back of the place where he had his desk, and approached the custodian of the vault itself. Not until then, when I was shielded from all observation from the front, did I take my package from under my coat, and hand it to the man. "Put that in the vault and get me Mr. Sheldon," I said.

The man opened the vault grating and set my parcel inside, then told me to wait an instant, and turned to seek the cashier. But there was no need. Dick Sheldon had heard my voice, and was already coming down the passage to the vaults. "I've been expecting you, Glace," he said. "Dual asked me to wait for you. Now what can I do to help?"

"First," I responded, "come inside here and look at something I've found, and see if it's what I think it is."

Sheldon nodded to the doorman to admit us, and we passed inside the vaults. There I laid my parcel upon a table and broke the strings. As they snapped, the newspaper wrappings fell away and disclosed a *pigskin valise, fastened with two padlocks, which were still intact, but with a fresh cut in the leather of one side, extending from end to end!*

Sheldon fairly leaped forward and caught it in his hands. "My God, Glace! Where did you get this?" he cried.

"Then it *is* what I thought it was?" I asked in return.

"It's our grip, which contained the fifty thousand," said Sheldon in a husky voice. "Where—"

"I found it," I told him again. "But wait. That isn't all."

I reached in through the gaping cut in the leather, and drew out what the grip contained. *It was a suit of dark blue cloth, cut in military fashion, such as the messengers of the Fourth National were accustomed to wear!*

CHAPTER VI

CLOSING IN

SHELDON FAIRLY STAGGERED back, "The suit of the fake messenger!" he cried. "My God! Billy told the truth."

I nodded and thrust the suit back into the grip. My heart was beating madly as the realization of all this meant swept over me. "Lock this up in a safe place. It's important," I requested. "And let's get to work. We've got a lot to do here yet, and a mighty short time in which to do it."

Sheldon motioned me to a chair, several of which stood in this anteroom to the vaults proper. "Tell me just what you want," he said in a dazed tone, and sank down beside me as I seated myself.

"First," I began, "I want you to find out for me if you have rented any drawers or boxes in your vaults any time to-day, since noon."

He turned and requested the doorman to come in, and repeated my question to him.

The man nodded. "There was four," he replied.

"Can you describe the takers?" I cut in.

"Two was women, one was a young fellow from Pearsons', the brokers, an' one was a man I never saw before," he responded, after a moment's thought.

"What did they rent?" I continued.

"The women rented drawers, an' the boy did, too. The man got a box, if I remember right."

"I guess we can count the women out," I said. "Can you describe the man?"

"He was a big fellow," began the doorman, "though I didn't notice him very closely. As I remember, he was wearin' a gray coat and a cap. The thing that struck me the most about him was that he talked with a sort of drawl, an' walked sorter stiff. Oh, yes, he had a little mustache, too, with ends that looked as if they'd been twisted into points."

"Was he dark or light complected?" I prompted.

"He was light," said the man. "Anyway, his mustache was almost what I'd call yeller in speakin' of hair."

"Of course, he signed the register?"

"Of course."

"Let's look at the signature," I suggested to Sheldon; and we both crossed to a desk, where the doorman pointed to the open page and laid a finger on a certain line. "That's it," said he.

I looked at the indicated name and saw it scrawled half across the page: "A. Arthur Langdon," but in the space for the address there was not a word.

"Didn't he give you his address?" I asked.

"Said he didn't have no permanent one just now," the vault-man answered. "Said he'd let us have it in a day or two, when he got settled."

It all seemed to fit. Looking back at that day it seems to me that from the time I started from Dual's everything fell into place with the readiness of a picture puzzle after you have found the key section. Every incident followed its predecessor in so unbroken a sequence that at times I felt more like a spectator than an actual participant in the working out of the chain of events which demonstrated Dual's marvelous power of detection.

I turned to Sheldon and nodded. "I want to take a photograph of this page of your register," I resumed.

"Go ahead," he assented. "I suppose Dual is back of all this, and I would be the last man living to question an order of his."

I got out my camera, and Sheldon and the doorman propped the register under a drop-light so that its pages were fully illuminated. Then, as an afterthought, I sprinkled some of the gray powder over the edges of the page I was about to "flash." I got out the flash-light pistol, and when all was ready I focused my camera upon the register, and as Sheldon fired the pistol, I pressed the little bulb.

In a blinding flash the shutter clicked and we stood blinking and choking in the magnesium fumes which filled the air. I turned the camera over and rolled up a fresh film. "And now I want to see the box this Langdon rented," I told the doorman, who stood by wide-eyed.

He turned away and led us into the vault proper, finally pausing before one of the larger compartments, such as are called boxes, which would hold a great bulk of papers or valuables of any sort.

I glanced at the number. It was 711. I smiled. "What did he put into the thing?" I questioned. "Did you see?"

The doorman shook his head. "I dunno," he replied. "He had a big bundle of some sort—papers, I reckon. He just chucked them into the box careless like an' locked 'em up, stuck his key onto a ring, and walked out twistin' one end of his mustache."

I got down before the box on my knees, and took my packet of "gray powder" out of my pocket. Very carefully I dusted the front of the box.

"By Jove!" exclaimed Sheldon, who was watching closely, "that stuff shows up a lot of marks on the box. See—"

He was right. As the impalpable powder sifted over the metal surface, it adhered in strange lines, curved and twisted, which finally showed as the imprints of human fingers upon the front of the box.

I rose and again loaded the flash-light pistol, and handed it to the assistant cashier. Once more I focused carefully with my camera, and cried: "Now!" Again the blinding light of the flash powder filled the corridor of the vault, and died into white, stifling fumes. Yet, with the slight click of the shutter, another link had been forged in Dual's subtle chain.

That part of my work was done. We three turned back to the bank, where I at once requested Sheldon to get me a phone where I could talk without being overheard.

He led me to the same room where the investigation of the morning had been held, and seated me at Carlton's desk, with its extension instrument.

I called the office of the *Record*, and asked for Smithson himself. As soon as our switchboard girl could connect me I heard his voice.

"Hello, Smithson," I called into the mouthpiece; "this is Glace."

"What are you doin'? Did you see the extra? I run a line at the foot about you," Smithson replied.

"I saw it, and it happened to be the straight goods," I gave him back. "I've been at work all day, and something will drop pretty soon. Now listen, Smithson. I'm at the Fourth National now. I've got some awfully important photos which bear on the wind-up of this case. Send a boy up here, and tell him to ask for me. Have him take these plates back with him. Put them through rush, because I must have copies of them in one hour if I am to finish up the case to-night. If I get them, we will have the stuff for a late extra to-night. Can you do it, sure?"

"Can I do it?" yelled Smithson. "What d'yer think I'm running—a log wagon or a paper, Glace? Wait!" His voice died at the end of the wire, then faintly I heard it again. He was yelling as it seemed to me. "Boy! Hey, boy!" A faint mumble came over the wire for a moment, and then he spoke again to me. "He's gone. For the love of Mike. Glace, what have you dug up now?"

"I can't tell you; I'm too busy," I answered. "Just remember you promised to let me write the wind-up story. Good-by."

I hung up and swung back to Sheldon: "There'll be a boy here from my paper in a moment. Will you watch for him and see that he gets to me?"

He nodded, rose, and left the room. Then, and not until then, I got the operator at Central and had her ring a certain number which did not appear in the telephone book. A minute passed, and then another, and I heard the voice of Semi Dual: "Very well, Glace, go ahead."

As quickly as possible I told him all I had done and all I had learned, omitting nothing which I thought could, in the slightest, bear upon the case. He listened without interrupting, as though what I was saying were a twice-told tale. Yet, at the end, he said what meant much to me:

"You have done excellently, Gordon," he told me, "and accomplished all that I hoped you would, except getting the notebooks. Be sure and do that!"

"I hadn't forgotten," I answered; "I was going to attend to that as soon as I got the camera off to the office."

"Also," said Semi Dual, "look in the uniform for the name of the maker, and find from him where the suit was delivered and for whom made. After you have done that, try and find where the large man who rented the box is stopping. Probably you will find him at one of the more modern hotels, such as men of his type frequent. Also, before you leave the bank, ascertain whether Sheldon has a list of the serial numbers of the missing money. When you have attended to all these details, go to the police station and find Bryce. Tell him to come here with you at six o'clock, and tell him that I said that I would surrender the gang to him at any time after eight o'clock. On your way back here stop at the *Record* and get your prints of the photographs and bring them here."

I heard his receiver click back on its hook, and turned from the phone to see Sheldon coming back into the room.

"I've arranged for your messenger to be met," he said, as he sank into a chair. "Good Lord, Glace! This is a queer affair. For the life of me I can't see head or tail to it. Can't you give me a hint? The papers all talk as though Billy were guilty, and yet you and Dual seem to be on the trail of something which neither the police nor the press have been able to pick up. And you fellows must have the right of it, for you found the grip and the suit the false messenger wore. At least tell me where you found those things?"

"I found them in the empty storeroom across from the bank, there," I responded pointing out of the window across the street.

"Over there!" cried Sheldon, as though he expected some trick. "Honestly, Glace, you don't mean *that!* What would our grip be doing over there, and how did the suit get into it? Who put it there?"

"The thief, I suppose, after he took the money out," said I. "There was no reason why he should expect that I would be prying around a vacant storeroom. It probably looked like a good place to leave the things."

Sheldon shook a puzzled head. "I can't see it," he muttered. "Why, look at it, Glace: Baird goes into the Merchants' to see Grier. He is inside not more than seven minutes, and when he comes out he finds Sardon dead, and the money gone. Seven minutes! In that time, whoever did the thing had to come on the scene, assault and kill a man on guard, take the money, and make a getaway. And all in broad daylight in a busy part of town! Look at the nerve of the thing! It doesn't seem possible, and yet it occurred. I've been thinking about it all day, and it don't get any clearer. And yet I can't believe Billy would have had a hand in a thing like that. I believe he's as much a victim of circumstantial evidence as I once was myself. And still look at it, yourself. If Semi Dual exonerates the boy, it will be a wonderful piece of work."

"If you'll keep it to yourself," I told him, "I'll state that Dual promises that Billy and Miss O'Neil will sleep in their homes to-night."

"Really?" said Sheldon after a moment of utter silence.

I nodded and got up. "We've something more to do," I resumed. "Has Miss Golding left the bank?"

"While we were in the vault, I think. I left her in the cashier's office when you came in."

"Did she know I was here?" I asked, in a sudden fear that she might suspect something from my presence.

"I think not," said Sheldon. "I didn't myself until I had entered my own office, and heard your voice from the vault."

"Good!" I cried in relief. "Now, Sheldon, Dual wants you to give me the stenographic pads of both Miss Golding and Miss O'Niel. He wants them to use to-night, and will see that they are returned to you. Can you get them for me now?"

"Miss O'Niel's book should be in her desk here," said Sheldon. "I don't think she even had time to lock it before they took her away. We'll see." He rose and crossed to the desk, and tried its drawers. The top one yielded readily, and came open. He lifted the little flexible book, such as typists use to take dictation, from its depths and handed it to me.

I pocketed it and followed him into the office of the cashier, where we stopped before the desk Miss Golding used. "This is the same make of desk as the one in my section," said Sheldon. "I'll see if my key will fit the lock."

He knelt and inserted the key in the lock, while I stood anxiously by. It turned and the drawer came open. Sheldon rose and drew out another note-book and passed it over to me. I took it and glanced at its cover. Sure enough, there was the name "Marie Golding," written across the top of the book.

I tapped the words with my finger. "What do you know about her?" I asked.

"Not much," replied Sheldon, "beyond the fact that she is an expert typist. Personally, she impresses me as too experienced for a woman."

"Do you know where she lives?" I went on.

Sheldon nodded. "We require our employees' addresses, you know. She has rooms in a lodging-house at 520 Welton Street."

I placed the two books in my pocket, where they would be safe. There remained only to look at the uniform I had found, and get the maker's name, then set out as soon as the messenger had taken the camera away.

We went on back into Sheldon's section on our way to the vault. Just as we stepped into the railed enclosure, the swinging inner door from the vestibule of the bank was pushed aside and a snow-covered boy made his way into the main room.

I recognized him instantly as one of our office-boys at the *Record* and called his name. He turned and came across to me with a grin. "Hello, Glace," he began. "De old man told me to beat it up here and freeze onto somethin' you had fer de paper. Pass it over an' I'll hit it back to de office."

I gave him the camera. "Beat it back as fast as you can, Jimmy," I urged, "and tell them to have those ready by half past five."

"You goin' to hand de old man a scoop?" grinned the boy as he buttoned the camera under his coat.

"If you don't get out of here, the old man will hand you a bouncing," I told him.

He grinned and turned away. "Watch my smoke," he flung back from the door.

Sheldon and I went to the vault again, and there I got the suit out of the grip, and taking the jacket scanned it for some maker's mark. It was easy enough to find. On a little cloth tag stitched to the lining of the inside pocket was the name "Steinman, Kupp & Co.," and, as luck would have it, I knew their address. I stuffed the jacket back into the grip and again told Sheldon to lock the whole thing up.

"I suppose you have a list of the serial numbers of those bills?"

"Of course, that is routine on a heavy transfer," he replied.

My work at the bank was done. As I came out of the vault for the last time I glanced at the clock in the general room. Its hands pointed to ten minutes of five. I had a trifle over an hour in which to complete the work set me by Semi Dual; to get the address of two men, get Bryce and the prints from the *Record* office and return to the Urania on time.

I turned to Sheldon and gripped his hand. "I've got to hurry," I declared. "I've got a lot to do yet, and I have something over an hour in which to do it, so I must be getting along. You've helped us immensely, and I appreciate it. So will Baird when he knows, and the little O'Niel."

"I only hope it will all come out as you think," said Sheldon. "I know what it is to be placed as Billy and the girl are. Let me know how things go."

I left him and hurried out of the door. I glanced across the street to the taxi-stand, but there were no cabs there. I turned up the collar of my coat, pulled down my hat, and set off in the direction of Steinman, Kupp & Co. with my head down against the wind.

In some ways, that was one of the most peculiar days I ever passed. As I have said before, everything I did seemed to be due to some force, some power outside of myself, directing my steps, rather than to any real volition of my own. People may laugh and scoff at such things as luck and fate. Personally, I don't know. Yet there are times when something seems to seize us like a strong current, and sweep us along to some appointed time and place. Sometimes I have felt as though Dual, through his uncanny, telepathic ability, followed and directed my course that afternoon.

It had nearly stopped snowing by the time I had gone a block from the bank. The lights were already burning in all the stores which I passed, but the wind still howled up the street. I lifted my head and quickened my steps breasting its icy sweep.

I reached the shop of the tailors, which stood next to a popular café, and, going inside, I asked for the proprietor.

He hurried forward, a small, blandly smiling little Hebrew, inquiring what he could do for me.

"Just this, Steinman," I opened on him: "I want you to tell me if you have recently made a suit for a person representing himself as a bank-messenger—in other words, a uniform?"

Instantly his oily civility faded away. "Dot iss an odd question, young man," he responded. "Who might you pe, an' py vot right do you ask to know?"

It was no time for fooling or arguing. I had a press badge which admitted me inside fire and police lines, and I wore it on my vest. Without replying, I threw back my outer coats, so that he could catch a glimpse of the thing, and I smiled. "You'd better come over," I said.

He underwent another change. If he was suave before, he cringed now. "You are a detectif!" he gasped. "Dot is tifferent. Y'understand, we do not gif customers' names arount so careless like. But to you— Vait a minute. I shall see."

He hurried away, and I strolled to the front of the shop, and stood gazing out into the street. A taxicab was standing in front of the door of the café. My eyes noted it idly. I wondered if it were waiting or disengaged. I thought maybe I could get it for the rest of my trip.

The little proprietor came hurrying back just then. "I vill tell you, mister," he began. "Ve haf made such a suit as you mentioned. It vas made for a young man vat said he was going to vork py a bank. It vas telifered to him vun week ago. Dot is all I know."

"You know his name, don't you?" I growled.

"Yes," he admitted. "I haf looked up his name on my books."

"Well, what is it, then?"

"It iss Eugene Golding, mister detectif," said the man.

That was certainly interesting news, and I appreciated the fact. At another time I would have been profoundly interested in the development. The trouble was that something was happening outside the café, next door, which interested me still more. Still, even as I watched, I did have sense enough to ask my informant one more question, though I did not turn my head.

"And where was the suit delivered?" I inquired.

"It vas sent to 520 Velton Street," he replied slowly, pressing in beside me to see what I was looking at.

I doubt if he found it of sufficient interest to explain why I stared, but that was because he didn't understand anything about the affair. What held my interest must have appeared to him merely as a man and a woman at most.

But the woman was tall and largely modeled, with a great mass of light hair, which appeared to me to be bleached. And the man was broad-shouldered, and apparently over six feet tall. He was wearing a gray coat with a close-fitting back, and a cap. The couple were leaving the café and crossing the pavement to the waiting taxicab, and, as Steinman pressed in beside me, the man handed the woman inside.

As I have said, it had stopped snowing, and the electrics were going, so that from the front of the café a broad illumination lit up the figures of the woman and man. And as he lifted his left hand to her elbow, while holding back the cab door with his right, I *had caught the scintillant gleam of what appeared to be an immense ruby on the little finger of his left hand!*

CHAPTER VII

I CONVINCE INSPECTOR BRYCE

I CHOKED BACK a cry of amazement, and laid my hand on the door. Once more the odd, compelling sense of a directing something reached out and clutched me, urging me forward in my course. I forgot the little Hebrew who stood beside me. I am positive that I offered him no word either of thanks or explanation before I pushed open the door and stepped outside. My last recollection of him is seeing him standing in perplexed surprise as the door swung shut in his face.

Already the tall man had closed the door of the cab, and was on the curb. He had lifted his cap. Apparently he was bidding the woman good-by.

I walked out to the curb, and stood as near as possible, glancing up and down the street, as if looking for a car or cab, in reality straining my ears to hear what it was that he said.

"If you don't mind I think I'll foot it to the Kenton." That was all. He signed to the driver, and the taxi lurched away with spinning wheels. The man lifted his hand and twirled an end of his little pointed mustache. Again I saw the crimson gleam from the ring.

The same driving force impelled me to speak. "I wish you'd tell me where you got that taxi," I said with a rueful smile. "This storm has played the deuce with the service, it seems, and I'm late."

He dropped his hand and stared me full in the face. "Aw! Quite so. I had the cab waiting, you know," he remarked at the end of his stare.

"I wish I might have been so fortunate," I returned. "I presume they are all pretty busy with other fellows like us."

"Not bein' in a hurry, I rather prefer walkin', you know," said the man.

"Which way are you going?" I ventured. "I must be getting along myself."

The man actually smiled. "Really, you know. I can't see that it concerns you," he said.

"Perhaps not," I made frank response, "but I wanted to talk to you."

The fellow laughed shortly. "In that case I am going this way," he remarked and set off at a brisk walk, while I fell in at his side. "You're a refreshin' lot over here, d'ye know. Fancy a chap walkin' up to a chap an' scrapin' an acquaintance like this."

"I may as well be honest," I responded. "I had a reason for wanting to speak to you."

"Of course you had, old chap," he interrupted. "I was waitin' for that."

"Well," I explained, "the reason is your ring. It's magnificent. I saw it as you were handing the lady into the cab, and it excited my curiosity. As you may have heard, we American reporters are a very curious lot."

He raised his hand and glanced at the great ruby. "D'ye know," he observed, "you're not the first chap to be affected like that? It's a bit of old Indian stuff. Had it for a good many years. Those chaps used to turn out some very fine work, though they're a benighted lot of beggars now. I picked it up in India quite a few years ago. Chap gave it to me told me no end of rot about it. They always have a lot of superstitious nonsense tied onto their things over there. Believe in talismans and amulets and that sort of thing. So you're a newspaper chap?"

I nodded. "You're an Englishman, I take it," I said.

"Oh, yes," he replied indifferently, "though I've knocked about a good bit, more or less. Been huntin' big game for a good many years. Fact is, I was thinkin' of goin' to that part of your country you call 'out West.' They tell me there's some practically virgin territory out there. Fellow could get a bit of shootin', d'ye think?"

"I can't say from experience," I answered. "From what I have heard, there are antelope and deer and an occasional bear still to be picked up in those parts."

"Grizzlies, I think you call them," said he.

I nodded. The conversation was not going exactly to my liking, but I saw no good excuse for a subject change.

"I might have a try for one," he went on. "I've bagged tigers and elephants and lions, but I never shot a grizzly yet. About what part of the country would one go to to find his bear?"

We had reached the Kenton, and I paused. "Personally I can't tell you," I replied to his question; "but if you like, I'll have it looked up for you at the office and let you know." I drew my folder and handed him a card.

He took it, glanced at it, and smiled. "That's awfully good of you," he accepted. "I'll be here for a few days yet. Ask for Major Langdon. Glad to have met you, Glace. Good afternoon." He turned in at the door and left me wondering just how much of it all he meant, or if his keen, gray eyes had seen through my poor attempt at bluff.

I slipped around to the taxi-stand on the side of the hotel and engaged a cab. Then, satisfied that Langdon would probably be out of the lobby, I made my way cautiously inside and crossed to the desk.

Jeffrys was still clerk at the Kenton, so I anticipated little trouble in finding out all he knew about the big man with the ruby. He had a habit of observing the guests closely, and had often given me a good tip in the days when I was just beginning the newspaper game. Now he greeted me with a smile. "Hello, old scout!" he hailed as he put out a hand across the desk. "Haven't seen you around here in a coon's age! Whose trail are you cuttin' now?"

"That's what you've got to tell me," I returned with a smile. "He calls himself Major Langdon, I believe—"

"Oh," said Jeffrys, "the chap with the big red rock!"

"Then he is stopping here?"

"Sure," said Jeffrys. "Been here between two and three weeks. Got a parlor suite—No. 265. Seems an awful decent chap, barring his accent, which is something fierce, an' he'd look better if he'd shave off the wire-pointed mustache. It's my private opinion, Glace, that he wears the mustache as an excuse for showing off the ring when he's twisting the thing. Have you seen that ring? Some stone that, boy!"

I nodded. "What does he do?" I asked.

"Talks," said Jeffrys. "As near as I can dope it out, he's a sort of walking death. He acts like he has more money and time than he knows what to do with, so he goes around killing things. Says he spends his time hunting big game. Told me he got the big ruby for savin' the life of some East Indian maharaja or something like that. Walked up and took him away from a tiger that was playing with him. I sprung it on him that he'd won it 'bucking the tiger,' but the joke didn't soak in. He just stared for a minute, an' then: 'I don't think you get me, old chap,' he says. 'I shot the bloody brute, ye know.' He keeps talking about going out West to shoot the country up."

I glanced at the hotel clock and decided that I had no time to listen to any more of Jeffrys's chatter. It seemed to me that I was due at the station. Therefore, I told him I was in a hurry and rushed back to my waiting taxicab, threw myself into it, and bade the driver take me to the jail as fast as he dared. I thought the whole thing over as we skidded along in the snow.

Everything I had set out to accomplish I had succeeded in doing with what now seemed like ridiculous ease. Everything and everybody seemed to have been working to further my endeavors. Plunging blindly forward along the course set for me by Dual, I had arrived with almost unbelievable sureness at each and every point, and found what it seemed to have been preordained that I should find. I looked out at the twinkling lights of the early night, and I shivered, not because I was cold, but rather because I suddenly sensed the fact of what blind creatures we all are, after all.

So far as I could see, there were four people who had been mainly connected with the morning's tragedy. Each and every one of them were now somewhere under these same early lights, secure in their own minds, I fancied, because of the arrest of Baird and the O'Niel girl. No doubt they were smiling as they thought that already the police had picked their victims, and would seek their conviction, thus rendering the real criminals all the more safe.

I wondered what their thoughts would be if they knew of the strange presence dwelling high above their heads on the Urania's roof; sitting like destiny above mere mortals, spinning the threads of a snare which should enwrap them and bind them fast. What would they do? How would they act? Suppose, by chance, they should see my taxi speeding past. What would it mean to them? Nothing! Not once would they dream of it as an agency working for their undoing! And yet, in a sense, the throbbing motor was driving the very car of destiny itself— the car of destiny! The idea pleased me some way, and I smiled.

In a final sliding skid the taxi stopped in front of the green lights of the station. I sprang out and yelled to the driver to wait.

I crossed the pavement in a couple of running strides and threw open the door. Dan Harrington still sat at the desk. He lifted his head as I rushed in, as did several other officers who were lounging back of the rail. "Where's Bryce, Dan?" I cried.

"In the 'tecs' room," he answered after one glance at my face. "What's broke now?"

"Get him, will you?" I requested, shaking my head.

Dan pressed a button on his desk, and an instant later several of the detective force—Bryce among them—came from the detectives' room. I signed to the inspector that I wanted him.

He crossed to me with a quizzical smile. "That was a nice little joker you slipped into the *Record's* extra," he began, "after the spiel you put up this mornin' about treatin' the department right."

"I didn't write the story," I told him quickly. "That's what I want to see you about. Put on your hat and coat. I've got a taxi outside."

"What do you want me to do, son?" he asked with a sharp look.

"Quit talking and come with me," I answered. "I'll explain as we go along."

"Go along where?" said Bryce.

"To make those other arrests the *Record* spoke of," I snapped at him. "Oh, for the Lord's sake, hurry up! This is straight!"

He gave me another glance and nodded, turned away, and came back in a moment with coat and hat. "I'm going out with Glace," he threw over his shoulder at Dan. "I'll phone in after a bit."

I hustled him out and into the waiting cab, yelled to the driver to go to the *Record* office. "There's five dollars in it if you do it in five minutes," I shouted and sprang into the cab after Bryce.

"Is this straight about something new in the bank case?" began Bryce as the cab started. "No kiddin' now, son! Come across!"

"It's the best tip you ever had," I assured him, "and if we put it across I can see where you get one almighty boost."

"What's the dope?" mumbled the inspector, lighting a cigar.

"I'm going to take you where you can arrest the real murderer of the man Sardon, and a bunch of his accomplices as well."

"Meanin'," said Bryce, holding his lighted match in his fingers, "that you still claim Baird is innocent."

"Meaning," I flung back, "that I know he is innocent. Bryce, do you remember that Greenig murder case?"

"I ought to. You scored that time all right, Glace."

"I did nothing of the sort," I said, leaning forward and tapping him on the knee. "Bryce, it wasn't my work that cleared up that case."

"Then whose was it? It wasn't mine," he growled with a faint grin.

"Semi Dual's!" I cried.

"Eh?" said Bryce. "Semi Dual's? Who the dickens is he?"

"The man who helped me, or, rather, the man who really cleared up that case, the forgery case of Cashier Sheldon, and the Barstow-More murder case. Do you remember the night I called up and told you folks of the doctor's confession of murder in the Greenig case? I was in Dual's apartments at the time, and so was the doctor. You may also remember that I turned him over to your men at the door of the Urania. Dual lives on the Urania's roof. You saw him this morning at the bank."

Bryce whistled. "So that's it," he said after a moment. "How does it come, then, that his name never appeared in any of those affairs?"

"Because," I replied, "Dual is a man who works in silence, hates notoriety. Silence is the price of his services. He is the most peculiar and the most wonderful individual I have ever met. If a case interests him, he will spare no time, trouble, or expense to unravel it, provided he is permitted to work quietly and in his own way. He helped me with those cases only on condition that I would not say a word about his connection with them. He is helping me on this, and he still imposes the condition that we must say no word about what he does. He told me to promise you that, if you would come to his rooms with me at six, he would surrender the murderer of Sardon into your hands at eight o'clock. That is why I came for you. You are to make the arrests and take the credit. Unless you promise absolute silence, I am not to bring you at all."

The inspector puffed vigorously at his cigar. "It's a darned funny arrangement," he said at last. "But I'd be a fool to pass it up. If it suits Dual to act that way, why it goes with me. Mum's the word. How's he going to get this bunch up there, do you know?"

I shook my head. "I don't know any more than you do about that. But if he says he'll do it, he'll do it. I never knew him to fail to keep a promise."

"All I got to do, then, is to go there and wait two hours and he'll hand me my man? Hum!"

"You'll get the whole gang, who engineered the deal," I corrected.

"How do you know there is a gang?" growled Bryce.

"Dual says so," I retorted. "Oh, I know you think it's funny, but he's wise to the whole scheme. He even sent me to the place where I found the bank's empty grip and the sham messenger's suit of clothes."

That got Bryce. He took his cigar from his mouth with a jerk, and stared me in the face. "You found them?" he gasped. "That's straight is it, Glace?" he demanded incredulously.

"I found them this afternoon, and I've got them locked up in a safe place."

Bryce put back his cigar. "That settles it," he said. "I lay down after that. Take me to this Semi Dual. I wondered why he butted in at the bank to-day, though I didn't spot him for a 'fly.' How'd he happen to get in on the thing, anyway?"

"I called him," I said.

"Hold on there, son," the inspector objected. "Remember I was with you from the start. Say"—he sat up in his seat—"there's something darned funny about all this."

"Nevertheless I called him," I maintained.

"How?" Bryce was growing obviously suspicious.

I looked him full in the face. "Bryce," I said, "did you ever know me to tell you a deliberate lie?"

"No," he admitted; "I can't remember that you ever did, son."

"Then all I can do is to ask you to believe me," I continued. "I don't understand just how I called Dual myself—that is I can't explain it on any basis which you would accept, and yet it is true that he came to the Merchants' Bank this morning in answer to my wish."

"Is this Dual person a mind-reader?" he asked with a grin.

"You can judge for yourself pretty soon," I replied, slightly nettled at the raillery in his tone. "Here we are at the *Record*. I've got to stop here and get some things to help convince you that I am telling you the truth."

The cab stopped in front of the office, and I sprang out, raced up-stairs to the art-room, and demanded my copies of the photographs I had made.

Malley, our art man, handed them to me, and I thrust them into my pocket. "Get your plates ready from these for an extra later, this evening," I directed, as I turned to leave.

"Wait a minute," said he. "Somebody sent another print here this afternoon. It was a picture of this man Sardon, showing a lot of finger-marks on his neck. What about it?"

"It goes; I made it," I called as I moved to the door. "Make a plate of it, too, with the rest."

I seemed fated to interruption. I met Smithson as I was rushing out. "Here!" he cried, and I paused. "Who killed Sardon?" he wanted to know.

"I don't know now," I answered. "Get ready to put out an extra sometime after eight o'clock. I'll phone you the murderer's name any time after that." I turned to the stairs. I had seen the clock. It was six minutes of six.

"Here! Hold on!" yelled Smithson; but I was taking the stairs three at a jump.

I yelled the address to the driver and flung myself into the cab, which started with a jerk.

Bryce steadied me as I half fell into a seat. "What did you go after?" he questioned. "What sort of evidence have you folks got cached in the office?"

"Finger-prints of the main guy, who is responsible for the death of Sardon," I chuckled.

"Get out!" said Bryce. "You don't mean you've got the murderer's finger-prints?"

"Of course not." I felt a fool pleasure in mystifying the cocksure Bryce. "I had those by two o'clock to-day. These are the prints of the man who put the murderer up to the game."

Bryce threw his cigar out of the window. "Glace," he remarked, "I have got to admit that you and your friend have scored on us before this; but there are times when I feel like I'd like to wring your neck. First you tell me that you have found the stolen grip and the suit of the fake messenger, then you spring it that there's a gang back of the deal; next you coolly add that you've got the finger-prints of the principals and invite me to go with you to this Dual's and be presented with the whole bunch. Why the deuce can't you loosen up a bit and talk straight English for a minute? You're a pretty wise kid, but don't rub it in. Remember I'm not admittin' yet that I was wrong in the pinch I made. You hain't proved your case yet, son."

I didn't really want to get him mad. "I'll tell you the truth, Bryce," I replied. "If I had to prove my case, as you call it, I couldn't do it. I've been working all day, under the direction of the man we are going to see. I saw him this afternoon, and he sent me out to do certain things. How he knew what to tell me to do, only he knows; and yet he told me that, if he desired, he could have arrested two of the members of this gang within fifteen minutes after we left the bank. Before three o'clock he told me that he knew the entire story of the crime, and that it was instigated by some man who did not appear in the actual murder. He gave as his reason for delaying the arrest of the actual assassin that he wanted to catch the man behind it all—what he calls the 'master mind.' Now, I won't try to prove my case. That is up to Semi Dual, and he'll do it in good time; but you've got to admit that he did send me to the place where I found the empty grip."

"And where was that?" he took me up in a flash.

"In an empty storeroom across from the bank."

"The devil!" said Bryce. "And you didn't have an idea of what you was after until you got there and found it? D'ye mean that, Glace?"

"Dual told me to go to the room and see what I would find," I responded. "I went, and found the grip and the suit inside the thing."

"Sounds like magic," commented the inspector, after a pause, during which he studied me closely. "How did Dual know that, I wonder? That's about the blamedest thing I've ever listened to."

"And yet," I responded, "that is the way Dual works. I've had him do it before. Once he sent me clear out to Goldfield to find a man he wanted. That was on the Sheldon forgery case. Well, I went out there, and I found the man, and he was the real forger, too."

"Must get his dope out of a dream-book," said Bryce. "Well, we're stopping. Come on. I'm willing to be shown."

We got out of the cab, and I threw the driver a bill, rushed Bryce into a cage, and, a minute later, led him out on the twentieth floor.

We turned up the marble stairs. "Good Lord!" he exclaimed. "Is your friend a millionaire?"

I shook my head, smiling, and led him on up to the roof. When we got there, his jaw dropped in utter amaze. "Say!" he gasped, after his first glance around. "Say, Glace, just what am I up against?"

I led him across the annunciator-plate, and waited until the chimes had died away. Hard on their musical peal, there came the deep reverberation of the clock in the city hall striking six.

Not until they had sunk to silence did I answer Bryce's last surprised question. When I did, it was in just two words: "Semi Dual."

CHAPTER VIII

THE BEGINNING OF THE END

DUAL MET US at the tower door, smiled approval at me, and gave a hand to Bryce. "On time to the minute, inspector," he greeted. "That is well."

"That's Glace's fault," stammered Bryce, as he eyed Dual from head to foot. Plainly he was puzzled by the long, loose robe of white, edged in purple, which he wore. In the morning my friend had worn the conventional garb of the ordinary well-to-do citizen, and the change seemed to add to the officer's surprise.

"And the immutable orbit of destiny," replied Semi, smiling. "Will you sit down a moment, inspector, until I speak to Glace?"

We left the official sitting in the reception-room and passed into the inner room, where Dual threw himself into his chair and silently held out his hand.

I passed him the copies of the photographs and the marks of the footprints I had made; also, the two stenographic pads. Still in silence, he turned to his desk and began his examination of the various articles, while I made a cigarette and smoked and watched.

As he opened the photograph of the signature of Langdon, I saw his eyes light with momentary triumph. He stretched forth a hand and drew a sheet of paper from among the mass covering his desk, laid it beside the reproduction, and tossed it aside as though satisfied, seized upon other papers, and made some rapid calculations, and, in turn, laid these down. His face had grown stern and keen in its expression as he worked, and he moved with a greater despatch than he had ever exhibited before in my knowledge of the man.

While I watched, his reply to Bryce came flashing through my mind: "The immutable orbit of destiny," and I pondered it as I sat. To me it appeared that I was privileged to catch some glimpse of the workings of destiny; that the man before me was a sort of agent of the force, knowing how to interpret its meaning in a way veiled to us blind creatures whom it swayed in its course. He had laid down the papers and taken up the note-books, placed them side by side, and was going over them, inch by inch, with his powerful magnifying glass. Sitting there in his long, white robe, with the great crystal before him, his features thrown into bold relief by the light from the golden apple in the hand of the great, bronze Venus, he suddenly came to remind me of some strange mystic, some crystal gazer, seeing visions in the pure depths of the glass; or else the very incarnation of that destiny, that law of retributive justice, of which he spoke, applying the microscope of the spirit to the little souls of men. What would he find?

Hard on my mental question, Dual laid down the glass. "The material supports the occult," he observed, tapping the books. "Once more, Gordon, you are about to see the workings of the law proven to material eyes."

"Then you are sure of everything now—" I began.

"I was sure of everything hours ago," said Semi, smiling slightly. "I said material eyes, my friend, which do not recognize spiritual sight. But come. The sands are running low in the glass of a man's fate. Tell me all you have done, before we bring Bryce in and close the net."

"You are ready for that?" I exclaimed. "To make the arrests?"

"I am ready," Dual responded, leaning back and closing his eyes. "Time presses, Gordon. Your tale."

Again, as earlier in the day, I made my report, which Dual received in the same silence which always marked his concentration of attention. For perhaps five minutes I talked steadily, and, having finished the account, I paused.

Semi Dual roused instantly from his apparent abstraction and sat up in his chair. "You have proved a very efficient medium, Gordon; and, as I perceive that you are somewhat mystified as yet, let me say this before we call Bryce: You are wondering how I have arrived at my conclusions, because you have seen less of the action behind the scenes than before. Remember, however, that I told you that I had set up an astrological figure of this affair and was prepared to tell the story of the crime at three o'clock to-day. I have arrived at my deductions by the use of astrology, psychometry, my knowledge of chirography, and a large proportion of common sense. Now call Bryce in!"

I won't say I was surprised, because I wasn't. I had grown accustomed to having Dual read my mind. There were times when I felt as though the man could have practically dispensed with verbal speech if he had so desired. I knew that now, as before, he had sensed my unspoken lack of understanding. I made no response, however, but rose and stepped to the door of the reception-room.

Bryce was sitting stoically smoking when I beckoned him in. He rose instantly and crossed to where I stood, and I ushered him into the room where I had seen Dual work out so many mysteries.

Semi waved him to a chair, into which he sank, and swept an appraising eye about the room, until Dual's words brought him back to attention in the case in hand.

"Inspector Bryce," Semi was saying, "I asked you here, because I need your assistance in closing up this affair. Not but what I could have taken a trifle longer and terminated it myself, but because I have promised my friend Glace that his friends shall not spend this night in custody, and because the signs indicate that a certain man shall end his evil course provided I act now. To bring this ending, however, you are necessary to me."

"You're takin' a lot for granted, ain't you, Dual?" said Bryce.

Semi nodded. "In a sense," he replied. "Primarily, I am assuming that you, as a detective, are desirous of seeing only justice done, and that, if I can demonstrate to you that one person is guilty and another innocent, you will act accordingly."

"Well," admitted the inspector, "that's right enough."

"That being the case," Dual continued, "I am now going to prove to you that certain parties are guilty of the murder of Sardon and the theft of the bank's funds. After that, I shall call upon you to act. To begin with, the murderer is, as you yourself deduced, a red-haired man. He is an individual of some five feet eight inches in height, as shown by the sized boot he wore, the mark of which was plainly evident in the snow at the Merchants' Bank. He is a professional chauffeur, as indicated by the same boot-mark. He drove a gray taxicab with safety tires, from the left hind one of which the safety tread was worn or cut in an irregular circular design. This also was shown in the snow, where he stopped the cab on the far side of the limousine which Sardon drove.

"There will be a fresh scar on the right hind fender of his car, where he rubbed against the limousine in turning away after the murder, and scraped off some of the gray paint from his own car. I have a piece of that paint, by the way, which I picked up in the snow.

"He is left-handed, as shown by the photographs of the marks on Sardon's throat, which also reveal that he had a scar on his left thumb. He is a user of cigarettes and left the stub of one in the limousine, which also shows the scar of the left thumb, corresponding to the one in the marks on Sardon's neck.

"He wore a light, drab suit, and snagged a piece out of it while overpowering Sardon. It was caught on a projecting screw in the door-frame of the limousine. For the rest I shall ask you to take my word for it, that his eyes are a gray-green. You might not understand how I know that, but the rest of the matter you will admit is such as any detective might have discovered by examining the scene of the affair."

Bryce had forgotten to smoke his cigar, as he listened. Once or twice he glanced helplessly in my direction. For the most part, he kept his eyes on Semi Dual.

"By Jove!" he burst out, as Semi paused. "I got to admit that sounds convincin'. Have you got proof for all that?"

Dual smiled. "I can even show you the microscopical difference between Baird's hair and the murderer's, if you wish."

"I'll take your word for it," said Bryce. "This sounds like the work of some of them European detectives."

"One trouble with the American detectives is that they are too prone to jump to conclusions without substantiating detail," Dual resumed. "But to get on: The murderer had three associates. There was a woman, who was an inside spy at the bank. She was a large woman, with yellow eyes, who worked as a stenographer."

"Not the Golding girl?" cried Bryce in excitement. "See here, Dual, I don't get that. She was perfectly willin' to answer questions this mornin', an' never showed no signs of excitement, barrin' the time you made that crack about them flowers. What you got on her?"

"You may recall," Dual responded, "that the questions you asked were all calculated to implicate another person. Naturally, she would answer as you wished, as it could only help her own case to do so. I said what I did about the flowers for a purpose of my own, and her reception of it showed me that my suspicions were correct. Also, it was the only remark which in any way varied the program she had set for herself. Marie Golding was the confederate of the murderer of Sardon, and his sweetheart as well. You arrested the wrong pair of lovers, that is all. I have proof of what I say—I will mention this much: I have evidence to show that Miss Golding examined Miss O'Niel's note-book after the letter was written to the branch bank; also, to show that she is the sort of person who would be likely to play the part I have ascribed to her."

"How'd you get it? What is it?" demanded Bryce, who was growing rather red in the face.

"Glace got it," said Semi Dual. "As to what it is, the evidence that she examined the book consists in the print of her thumb on one of its pages, beside the shorthand transcript of the note, which print corresponds to her own on her own book. The evidence as to her character may not be so plain to you, but I will give it to you for what you consider it worth. Do you believe in chirography?"

"Dopin' out folks' characters from their handwritin'?" queried Bryce, grinning. "Naw!"

"It's a pity," Dual made comment. "One may gain valuable tips, as you call them, in that way. Now, in Miss Golding's writing on her note-book here"—he picked it up—"she has written her name. As Glace will tell you, because he has seen it twice borne out in our mutual cases, this writing exhibits the peculiarity of having breaks in the bottoms of such letters as the *a*, the *o*, and the *d*. Furthermore, the stem of the *d* is very short as compared to the loop of the *l*. The first loop of the *M* is very large, and the lower curve of the *G* does not come down to the line. Now, to a person who understands the science of handwriting, such writing would indicate an individual of a treacherous and rather cruel nature, regardless of how much superficial softness they might exhibit. In fact, their ordinary behavior is really a part of their hypocrisy. Furthermore, such persons will always be susceptible to temptation in regard to money affairs. In other words, they will steal if they think they have a safe chance."

"An' you believe that?" said Bryce in a puzzled tone. "You'd bank an arrest on stuff like that? The finger-prints are all right, but this other dope—I'm sort of leery on that, Mr. Dual."

Dual looked at me and smiled, as one who would say: "You see?"

"I have banked several arrests on similar findings," he replied in his quiet accents. "They proved to be correct, Mr. Bryce."

"Admittin' the fact," returned the inspector, "it wouldn't stand at law."

"In due time I'll produce evidence which will," said Semi Dual.

Bryce nodded. "If you can do that, all right. Go ahead."

"This woman," resumed Dual, "was assisted in a part of her work by her brother, Eugene Golding. While she worked to gain information in the bank, he acted as an outside spy and watched for her to give some signal that the transfer was about to be made. They naturally waited until a large sum was to be sent, and they arranged that the woman should show a sign on the day when it was to occur. Her brother then communicated with the fourth conspirator, and himself played the part of the messenger who stopped Baird and gave him the dummy package for Cashier Grier. Also, after the murder, the brother took the money, still in the bank's bag, and met the fourth member of the gang at an appointed place."

While Semi talked, Bryce had been chewing ruminatively at his cigar, which had gone out. Now he sat suddenly forward.

"Them nasturtiums was the signal," he suddenly interjected. "That's why your buttin' in sort of rattled that Golding girl. Honest. I reckon you've got the right hunch."

Semi Dual smiled. "I am glad you agree, inspector. We will work much better together. In support of my idea about the brother, we have a print of his footmarks, which I feel certain will agree in measurement with his own shoes, and also his finger-marks—or rather some finger-marks on the wrapper of the dummy parcel, which, I believe, will correspond to his."

"You got them, too?" exclaimed Bryce. Plainly he was growing excited at last.

"Glace got them," said Semi Dual.

Bryce shook his head. "It gets me how you fellows work," he burst forth, nervously trying to light his cigar. "You tell me you've got all this, or that Glace has done it, and he tells me the same thing, and says he don't know what it means, but that the gang will be pinched by eight o'clock. Who's goin' to pinch them?"

"You are," said Semi Dual.

"Me!" Bryce seemed unable to say more until his match burned his fingers. Then he swore.

"You," repeated Dual easily. "I shall tell you where. You will have to send for all except the murderer, who will come here himself."

The inspector shook his head. "I give it up," he said.

"We are wasting time," Dual began again. "We come now to the fourth and principal member of the gang—the instigator, what one may call the 'master mind.' As I told Glace, I could have arrested the murderer and the woman at noon. I did not because I desired to wait until I could arrest as well this prime mover in the crime. This man is a British ex-army officer, cashiered from the service for crooked dealing. He is a large man, some six feet two inches tall, and correspondingly built. He is florid of complexion, with a light mustache, which he wears pointed, and dark-gray eyes. At present he is wearing a gray overcoat and cap, and stopping at the Kenton Hotel. He wears a large ring with a red setting on his left little finger, and calls himself Major A. Arthur Langdon. He also wears a number ten boot, of which we have a print."

"Good Lord!" gasped Bryce again. "How do you know all that? Have you seen this man?"

"Not that I know of," said Semi Dual. "However, I learned the facts in various ways. Do you remember Baird's statement of the man who fell inside the revolving door? Now, it naturally occurs that only a large man would throw his hands up against the glass panel. Ordinary-sized men would have grasped the brass hand-rail. I thought of that, and made a photograph of the handmarks on the glass. That gave me my first clue, as you would say. For years, inspector, I have made a business of collecting the autographs and finger-marks of different men and women. I have a great many of what you would call police-characters. As you doubtless know, the finger-marks are a permanent method of identification. Also I may add that no matter how many aliases a man may adopt, by some subtle rule or law they always chose some one in which the letter combination will show forth the individual's character. You may doubt this, but it is true.

"After I had taken the photo of the marks on the door, I came home and went to my collection to see if I could find anything similar. Some years ago in Paris this man was arrested, but the State failed of conviction for lack of proof. They got his finger-prints and other measurements, however, and, through an acquaintanceship I have over there, I was able to add copies of them to my collection. Among my files I found a mark which corresponded to that of this *Langdon*, as he now calls himself. I was then fairly started upon his trail. Furthermore, there are marks on the blank sheets which were inside the dummy package which are identical to those on the glass door. This, I think, connects the man with the case, and shows that the package was prepared by him."

Bryce brought a hand down on the arm of his chair. "Gad! You're a wonder, Dual. We've got him with the goods all right, on that."

Semi nodded. "In the mean time," he continued, "Glace had found his signature. I compared it with the writing in the name he gave when arrested in Paris. The writing was the same. For years he has made his living by instigating theft and taking the major portion of the winnings of his tools. He is here at the Kenton, inspector. He instigated this crime, and is at least morally responsible for the death of Sardon. This is the man's history in brief, and not to bore you, every line of his written alias will bear it out. The writing is heavy, coarse, written with a heavy, ruthless pressure. The pen with which he wrote almost tore the paper; yet each word tapers slightly toward the end. The man is a selfish brute. In the letter *t* in the word Arthur, which, by the way, is his true given name, and which he has never been able to give up in his changes of name, the crossing of the letter alone serves to give us the key-note of an individual of inherent cruelty. Such a man, in other circumstances, might have been a second Nero, and have smiled at the sufferings and death of his fellow men. You will notice that the cross is remarkably heavy. Also the letters are angular, with few softening curves. The writing is that of a natural criminal with practically no 'nerves'; in other words, of a criminal machine."

Bryce reached for his hat and jammed it on. "That's enough," he declared in excitement. "You say you got the proof and that he's at the Kenton. I'm goin' over an' pinch that guy."

"He's wanted in a dozen cities in Europe," said Dual. "His arrest will be a credit to any town's detective-force. Will you let me still direct this affair, Mr. Bryce?"

Inspector Bryce paused in rising from his chair. "I reckon it's your picnic," he assented with a grin.

"First, then," Dual continued, "I shall expect your promise that no mention of my name shall occur in the matter. You shall direct the arrests, and Glace will see that due credit is given for them in the *Record's* account. Secondly, I wish you to remain here. There is a telephone in my desk here. Call up your station and send two men to 520 Welton Street with orders to arrest Marie Golding and her brother, Eugene. At the same time have two others go to the Kenton and arrest Major Langdon. Tell them to act quickly and not bungle the job! Instruct your men to bring their prisoners here as soon as they have made the arrests."

"Here!" cried Bryce. "Bring them here? What for?"

"We'll save the State the expense of a trial," said Dual with an odd smile. "Also, instruct the jail authorities to release Baird and Miss O'Niel. I don't think you want them any more."

"I reckon not," Bryce agreed somewhat ruefully. "But honest, Dual, I thought I was right."

"If I had not known that, I would not have had you here to-night," replied Semi Dual.

"All right, gimme the phone," Bryce surrendered. "Gad, this whole thing gets my goat!"

Dual opened the door of the desk where he kept the concealed phone and handed the instrument to Bryce, who planted it on the desk and squared himself off for action, as it were.

It was a tense moment; the beginning of the end, I felt. I sat watching as the inspector leaned a heavy arm on the desk and lifted the receiver off the hook. Dual, as though satisfied, was leaning back in his chair, his head resting on his hand.

Bryce spoke. "Hello! Gimme eight— Hello! Johnson there? Sure I want him— Hello! Say, Johnson, this is Bryce. Say, take a couple of men an' go to the Kenton an' grab a guy callin' himself Major Arthur Langdon. Got it? All right. Now listen. Send a couple of boys over to 520 Welton Street and get a woman by the name of Marie Golding and a feller, Eugene Golding, her brother. She's a blonde—bleached, I think—big girl with a wise look. Hurry up on this! When you got them bring the whole push up to the Urania! That's what I said! I'll be waitin' for you at the door. All right. Now let me talk to the Sarge. Say, Sarge, this is Bryce. It's all day with the Baird-O'Niel pinch. Sure, turn 'em loose, we don't want 'em any more. That's straight. Good-by."

He hung up the phone and swung back to us. "I done it," he announced. "Now I'm goin' down-stairs and wait for the bunch." He rose and went out.

I sat lost in silent wonder. Still in their fancied security the culprits lay out under the night. Yet the word which would confound them utterly had gone out from this high tower from the brooding presence of that strange agent of fate, who still sat with head in hand. Already he had given the signal which was even now causing a narrowing of the mouth of that invisible net of circumstance. Already the hand of fate hovered above them, a dreadful shadow. Soon now that hand was going to close.

"And you brought it all about," I burst out at length.

"The immutable law brought it about," said Semi. "I am but a medium of the law."

"That may all be so," I retorted; "but if it is, why don't the law work the same through other men—Bryce, for instance?"

Dual smiled slightly. "Perhaps by practice I have become a better medium of conduction than some others," he said.

"Why did you want the signatures of Baird and Miss O'Niel?" I asked. "You didn't appear to use them."

Dual looked up and I saw a light in his eyes. "You noticed it, did you, Gordon? Then I will explain. I wanted them in order to center their minds. I knew they both knew of Sheldon's trouble and that I used my knowledge of chirography to help clear that case. I had you ask for their signatures in order to turn their minds from fear to hope and trust in me; to place them *en rapport* with my efforts, Gordon. Thought forms are strong things to a sensitive spirit. I knew that while I worked to help them they, unknowingly, would help me by the hope and trust waves they sent me. You remember I told you I had faith in the assistance of the little O'Niel's prayers? Does it occur to you that her prayers are answered even now?"

"By Jove!" I cried. "So they are! She's free!"

"Suppose," said Dual, "that you call Cashier Sheldon and ask him to come here at once. Explain to him how to get here. After that, call Miss Baird and tell her the news. Ask her to get Billy to bring her and Miss O'Niel here about nine o'clock."

I looked at him in fresh wonder and he smiled broadly. "Do as I tell you," he urged.

I went to the phone. While I was speaking Semi rose and stretched himself upon the couch. He lay utterly relaxed in every muscle, his eyes closed, his chest rising and falling in great inhalations, his arms stretched wide in the shape of a cross. As I ceased speaking I became conscious that with each slow breath he was repeating over and over the one word: "Oom!"

The great clock in the corner chimed a quarter of eight. Dual rose. "The sands are running low in the glass of one man's fate," he remarked. "At eight-thirty, Gordon, the last grain will fall."

Turning to a drawer, he opened it and drew forth a number of red lamps. One by one he replaced the ordinary lights in the apartment with these others until the room was bathed in an angry ruby light.

Scarcely had he finished than the sound of the chimes broke on our ears. Dual raised his hand. "Hark!" said he. He dropped into his chair, bent, and opened another drawer. From it he lifted a snow-white turban, placed it upon his head, and sat back in his chair. So all in white and purple, he sat under the red lights save for an immense ruby which fastened his turban in front and glowed like a fiery third eye directly over the center of his brow.

CHAPTER IX

THE MASTER MIND

FOOTSTEPS CROSSED THE outer room. A tap fell on the door.

"Enter!" cried Semi Dual.

The door swung open and there came through it first, a fair-haired youth, whose wrists were circled by the steel bands of handcuffs; behind him a splendidly proportioned girl with great masses of yellow hair and yellow eyes, whose hands, though free, were clenched, her lips set into a sternly repressed line; and behind her a great bulk of a man with florid face and a needle-pointed mustache, who wore a great ruby upon the little finger of his left hand, walking with shoulders back and head boldly lifted, despite his manacled wrists; and back of him again Inspector Bryce.

Dual eyed them all in steady silence as they filed into the room. Not until Bryce had entered and closed the door did he say in a level monotone: "Good evening, Miss Golding and Mr. Eugene Golding. Please be seated, and you also, Captain Lane, take a chair."

Did I notice a slight start of the huge man or was it a shadow? To this day I do not know, yet it seemed to me that as his name fell from Dual's lips a slight spasm twitched his face.

The level monotone of Dual's speaking droned along: "It is now five minutes of eight. I shall have to ask you to wait five minutes for the fourth member of our party to arrive."

A stifled exclamation burst from the lips of the woman. Her features looked ashen even under the red light. I saw desperation look out of her eyes; the abandonment of all hope, and I realized that Dual had purposely used the word "fourth."

He swung his eyes to Bryce. "Remove the handcuffs," he said slowly. "There is no escape from this room; the door is of steel.

A movement of my finger and it is electrically charged." His hand hovered along the edge of his desk.

As one uncomprehending, yet obeying, Inspector Bryce released the wrists of his prisoners and slipped the manacles into his pocket. He glanced at me and I saw a vague, a vast questioning in his eyes. I shook my head and laid a finger on my lips.

Dual had ceased speaking. Silence filled the room. I felt rather than saw Langdon's, or Lane's, eyes fall upon me, and turned to meet his steely stare. Very slowly he nodded his head as one who perceives and accepts a fact. The clock in the corner chimed eight times. As though it were a continuation of its peal, an echo, the annunciator rang forth. Again steps came from the outer room. Once more the door swung slowly back. There appeared Henri, supporting one end of an immense hamper, and *with him, assisting him with his burden, was a redhaired man wearing the cap, coat, and puttees of a public chauffeur!*

A shrill scream rent the air. Marie Golding was leaning forward in her seat. "For Gawd's sake beat it, Jim!" she cried to the red-haired man wildly. "It's a plant!"

The hamper crashed to the floor as the man lifted his head and saw the inmates of the room. For one moment he stood rigid in amazement, then whirled to the door. But in that moment Henri had closed the door and now stood before it, barring the way.

For a moment there was silence. The red-haired man, standing half crouched like a cornered animal about to spring, Henri smiling a stiff-lipped smile before him; the rest of us sitting as though rooted to our chairs.

Then Dual's voice again broke the quiet tension: "Don't try it, Murdoch. The door is charged with electricity now." His fingers pressed a button on his desk. "See! I will show you." He picked up a small object from his desk and held it toward the door. On the instant, with a snapping crash, a myriad darting, hissing sparks sprang from the door's surface and leaped to the electrode in his hand. "To touch that door is death," said Semi, as he laid the electrode down.

He waved Murdoch to a chair next to Miss Golding, and swung to face us as we sat before him in the now silent room. His features had settled into a calm, inscrutable mask, his eyes seeming slowly to widen and become larger and brighter, as though some inward fire were flaring higher and higher in their gray depths.

For a long minute there was no sound save our subdued breathing; then there came a low, haunting murmur like the sound of voices chanting at a great distance. It floated in from apparently nowhere, yet I, who knew Dual, knew it was the voice of the wonderful instrument he had constructed to play by means of etheric vibration. Soft, illusive, haunting, the melody crept into the apartment where we sat waiting, without exactly knowing for what.

As though drawn by some strange power, my eyes sought the great ruby on Dual's brow. With a start it came to me that it was moving in time to the music very, very slowly, swinging backward and forward and from side to side; backward and forward, backward and forward, round and round. It was glowing and flashing, advancing and retreating with the slow, rhythmic motion of a throbbing heart-beat, the weird, compelling influence of the swaying head of a snake. Gradually it seemed to me that it was swelling, increasing. Its bloodlike color was tinting my whole perspective. It was no longer a ruby, but a vast red light, filling all the room.

Dimly I sensed a sigh escaping the lips of the woman next to whom I sat, but I did not turn my head. My eyes were fascinated by the vast red light of the gem, below which I could still faintly imagine rather than perceive the face of Semi Dual.

Presently I became aware, with a start of surprise, that it was snowing, and that I seemed to be back in that room at the Fourth National where we had sat with Carlton that morning. Now, however, there was no one there. Or, wait—the door of the cashier's room opened and the Golding woman came in. She advanced to the typewriter desk by the window and placed a bowl of golden nasturtiums thereon and went away.

There came a hiatus—a space of blankness—and again I was seeing. I was in the empty storeroom across from the bank. There was some one else there. It was the fair-haired youth who sat in the room with the rest of us, but in my vision he was sitting on a box, watching out of two holes in the blind of the front window. Now and then he lifted a pair of field-glasses and looked intently across the street.

Then he sprang up, unrolled a paper parcel, and drew out a suit of clothes, which he donned. It was the uniform of a messenger of the bank. He went out, carrying a paper package in his hand, ran around the block, and came down the street and slipped into an alley beside the bank.

A limousine was standing in front of the bank. A man, Baird, was coming down the steps with a vault-guard. He carried a grip locked with double padlocks in his hand. He entered the limousine.

The fair-haired youth slipped from the alley. He ran after the limousine as it started. He called. The car stopped. The youth handed the package he carried through the window. The car went on. The youth crossed the street and entered a taxicab at the stand there. The cab was gray. Its driver was red-haired. It set forth in pursuit of the limousine.

We were in front of the side door of the Merchants' Bank. The limousine was just stopping. Baird got out. The driver of the limousine, whose face was that of the dead chauffeur Sardon, left his seat and entered the car. Baird went up the steps of the bank. He carried in his hand the package the youth had given him.

Far up the street a gray taxicab appeared. It came on swiftly. It was here. It was stopping beside the limousine now. The red-haired man sprang out. He carried a thing of metal in his hands. It was a spanner. He ran around back of the limousine, and came to its door next the curb. He wrenched open the door and seized Sardon by the throat with his left hand. Sardon struggled. His gloved hands came up and clawed at the man's head. Once, twice, the red-haired chauffeur struck him with the spanner. Sardon sank back. Blood poured from his scalp.

The far door of the car opened. The youth seized the pigskin grip. He sprang back to the taxi. The chauffeur dropped his weapon and released Sardon, who sank back in a limp heap. He ran around the car and sprang into the driver's seat of the taxicab.

We were inside the bank. Baird was leaving. A large man stood beside the revolving door, looking out. He was tall and fair, and wore a pointed mustache, and a great red ring on his left hand. He was watching the two cabs outside. They were still there. Baird was at the door. The large man stepped into a section of the door. Baird threw himself into the next.

The large man stumbled and fell to his knees. He threw his hands up against the glass. He seemed trying to rise, but I knew that he was holding the door, watching the two cabs, until one should go away.

The taxi was just starting. It leaped away with a jerk suddenly. It swung in a short circle—so short that its fender struck against that of the limousine and scratched off some gray paint. I saw it fall. It struck the snow and lay there, a gray spot. The taxi sped away. The gray paint lay on the snow. It began to grow. It grew and grew until it blotted out the entire scene. It seemed to pulsate and throb, and gradually it began to change color. It grew pinkish, a delicate rose, a crimson, a deep, rich ruby tint. It began to shrink and dwindle. It was no longer a pall, but a spot—a spot of blood! No! It was the great ruby glowing on Semi Dual's brow!

A shrill scream rent the silence. It was the fair-haired youth: "My God, sis! He's killed him! He's killed him! He struck too hard. Oh, this is awful, awful! It's murder, sis!"

I opened my eyes, or seemed to. Golding was standing upon his feet and swaying drunkenly, his arm out-stretched, pointing at Murdoch. "He killed him," he muttered, and sank back into his chair.

I looked about the room. It was unchanged, unless the strange pallor on the faces of those present might be called a change. Semi Dual still sat beside his desk, the same inscrutable expression on his face. I glanced at this one and that. Murdoch was shaking as with an ague. The woman beside me was breathing in short little gasps. Her brother sat in pale collapse, his forehead beaded with sweat. Bryce's jaw was sagging, his eyes popping from a pale face. Only Lane, or Langdon—whichever he was— seemed to remain cool.

Presently Lane spoke: "Devilish clever, that! I don't know who you are or what you call yourself, but it was devilish clever. I've seen the same mass hypnotism stunt pulled in India, you know. But what does it prove?"

Semi Dual made no reply. Still in silence, he turned his eyes upon the woman by my side.

As though galvanized to action, she sprang to her feet. She turned to Langdon and threw out an arm, pointing it at his face.

"It proves what I told you!" she cried in a voice grown shrill and high and unsteady; "to beware of this man; that he was at the bank this morning; that he had spotted the sign of the flowers; that he was dangerous! Didn't I say we ought to have him watched? Didn't I come to the café this afternoon and tell you this? And you laughed at me; told me I was suffering from nerves! Well, this proves who was right!" She sank back to her seat and began to shake with sobs.

Dual turned his eyes back to Lane. "That is your answer, captain," he said.

"Quite so," replied the captain. "But since when have the utterances of hypnotic subjects been taken as evidence at law in the United States?"

"They are not," rejoined Dual promptly, "nor do they need to be. There is sufficient material evidence to serve, Captain Lane. There are your finger-marks on the bank door and duplicates of them on the paper folded to make the dummy package, and on the vault register of the Fourth National Bank. There is your signature on the same register, and a print of your boot, taken from the dust on the floor of an empty storeroom where Golding and you cut open the bag and removed the money. There is sufficient evidence. And surely you have not forgotten that you are wanted in a dozen cities whose names I could call. Besides, Miss Golding was not under hypnotic influence when she spoke just now."

Lane nodded and twirled his mustache slowly. "That's the trouble with women. They are apt to go to pieces," he said at length.

"Then you think the evidence quite sufficient, Captain Lane?" said Dual. He lifted his eyes and fixed those of the man opposite as he spoke. Like two opponents at fence, they sat and crossed glances as the swordsmen clash foils. It was the Englishman whose eyes dropped at last.

"Quite," he replied. "As I remarked before, I don't know you, never heard of you; but I will say this: I imagined that this country would be an easy place in which to operate, because they are far more superficial in their police methods than the European authorities. However, had I known of you, or that you were living in this particular city, I would have chosen some other locality for my activities. If it's a fair question, just what do you intend doing in this affair?"

"I shall let destiny take its course," said Semi Dual. "You of all men, captain, should know best what to expect—what you deserve. Inasmuch as I have acted as destiny's agent in bringing you to this point, I have performed my part of the work in hand. It is now time for me to step aside and allow other forces to take charge in bringing about an end."

Lane lifted his eyes again and looked into Dual's face. "Do you know that's rather decent of you," he said with a tired smile. "In return I don't mind telling you that years ago, when I first engaged in my present methods of life, I made a promise with myself that I would never be taken alive." Again he smiled faintly. "I seem to have been mistaken, don't I, old chap?"

"Yes?" Dual's tone made it a question. Lane's head came up again with a jerk. Once more the two men met and measured wills, looked into each other's souls, and wrestled mentally. From that encounter Lane emerged with glistening eyes, a sweat-beaded forehead, and firmly compressed lips. Dual, smiling slightly, sat apparently unmoved.

Suddenly Lane's voice rang loud and strong. "No!" he burst forth, as one who has made up his mind. He threw his hands to his mouth, held them a moment, and dropped them again. He looked at Dual and returned his smile. He glanced about the room. "I hope you folks will believe that I am sorry to leave you in such a—beastly mess," he muttered. His face was turning slowly purple. He lurched in his chair. His arms slipped down at his sides and dangled limp hands. He gasped.

Dual rose and moved to his side. He reached down and lifted the man's left hand, and held it up for us to see. *The red setting was gone from the great ring, crushed between Lane's strong teeth!*

"A glass *ampoule*, filled with a potent poison," said Semi Dual.

The clock in the corner chimed half past eight.

Dual looked at me and smiled. "The last grain of sand," said he.

Marie Golding still sobbed and shivered. Her brother sat sunken down in his chair. Murdoch stared at the dead man as if seeing visions of his own fate. Bryce stumbled to his feet. "My God!" he muttered. "The man's dead! You hadn't oughter let him do that, Dual."

"It was better for the master mind to change his plane of operations," returned Semi with perfect quiet. "You can now take your prisoners away. I don't think any of them will deny what occurred to-day."

Murdoch raised his head. "There's no use," he said. "I didn't really mean to kill Sardon, but I was excited. I struck too hard." He turned to the sobbing girl. "Can the tears, May! The jig's up! Langdon knew that or he'd never have cashed in."

There came the click of handcuffs as Bryce shackled the men. Dual glanced at the clock, crossed, and pressed the button on his desk. A moment later there came the sound of the chimes, and he nodded to Henri, who went out and returned to usher Sheldon in.

Dual laid aside his turban and met him as he entered. "Good evening, Mr. Sheldon," he greeted, putting out a hand. "We have here three of the parties responsible for the trouble at your bank. The fourth"—he waved his hand to Lane's figure—"has gone away."

Dick Sheldon started back in horror and surprise. "What does it mean, Dual?" he cried.

"Ask Bryce," replied Semi.

"That's right, Mr. Sheldon," the inspector cut in. "These are the folks who done the job. They've confessed. It was the blamedest game I ever set into, but we took all the tricks. The big feller croaked hisself when he'd played his last chip."

"That," said Dual, smiling, "is a graphic statement of the truth."

Sheldon sat down and drew off his gloves. He seemed hardly able to comprehend the turn in affairs. At length: "It is wonderful, wonderful how you do it, Dual," he remarked. "Would it be too much to ask if you have any idea where the money was put?"

Semi Dual smiled broadly now and spoke to Bryce: "Put your hand in Lane's pocket and hand me his bunch of keys."

In silence the inspector complied.

Dual took the little bunch of keys and selected one from among them, which he removed from the ring and handed to

Sheldon. "When you go to the bank to-morrow unlock vault box 711. It was a piece of daring consistent with the character of the dead man there to place your fifty thousand in the vaults of your own bank."

Sheldon turned the little flat key in his hand. "Wonderful," he finally repeated for the third time, as though the word were all that occurred to his mind.

"I think," began Semi, "that you offered a reward for the return of the money, did you hot?"

Sheldon nodded. "Two thousand," he replied.

"I have no claim on it," said Semi, and glanced at Bryce.

"I didn't do nuthin'," the inspector declared.

"In that case," Dual, suggested, "I would like to see it deposited in your bank in the names of Baird and Miss O'Niel."

Sheldon pocketed the key and glanced up. "By Jove, I'll see it done! They deserve it from the bank," he promised.

"Better take your prisoners away now," Dual suggested to Bryce. "Also I wish you'd remove the body. There can be no question of the way of his death. We all witnessed his end."

I glanced at Semi. I was crazy to be at the phone. As usual, he understood my unspoken question and nodded his head. I sprang to the desk and dragged out the instrument. I got the *Record* and Smithson, and drove him half frantic trying to tell him the story faster than he could take it down.

While I talked the prisoners left, and the body of Lane was taken away. Semi and Henri went to work, removing the red lights, replacing them with others of a delicate pink, as soft and rosy as the first hopes of spring. They pulled the little disappearing table out of the wall, dragged the hamper across to it, and from it took flowers and glass and china and food. When I was done speaking and hung up the receiver, after promising Smithson to be down in an hour to write up the story for the morning's issue, a banquet was spread in the room.

I sat and stared at the table a moment, then turned again to Dual. "Good Lord, that was all in the hamper which Murdoch helped Henri carry in!" I exclaimed, pointing.

Dual was standing beside the desk. He looked down into my eyes. "Some people might imagine an Oriental sense of humor in that, Gordon," he answered. "In reality, it was a simple method of getting him here. Henri was riding around in his cab the greater part of the afternoon."

"How did you know his name?" I asked.

"Every one who knew him thought it when he came in," said Semi, smiling. "I read it. The veriest fortune-teller knows that trick."

I nodded. "There's one other thing I don't understand even yet," I went on. "If Golding lived in the same house as his sister, why was the signal necessary at the bank? Why couldn't she have told him last night?"

"Your question is well thought of," said Semi. "But you are looking at the thing backward, Glace. The flowers were a signal—not that the money was to be sent, but that there had been no change in the bank's plans since the original plan was made. Had there been any Miss Golding would have found a means to remove the flowers before the time set for the transfer to be made."

There it was, simpleness itself, when one looked at it right.

Again the chimes sounded, and Henri hurried forth. Connie and Billy and Miss O'Niel came into the room, and were welcomed by Dual. They and Sheldon, Semi Dual, and I sat down to the table in the rosy-lighted room.

We ate and drank, talked and exclaimed until there was nothing more to be said. Sheldon even made a speech in which he told of the proposed disposal of the bank's reward, and suggested that Baird and Miss O'Niel take a holiday.

Billy shook his head. "I'll be at work to-morrow," he decided. "I'd rather come back as though nothing had happened at all."

Dual lifted his hand. Silence fell over the room. He rose, and, beckoning me, crossed to the great window at the end of the apartment. He threw it up and let the cool night wind fan in.

From far down in the white snow-clad cañon of the street rose the sound of shrill voices, piping through the night:

"Wuxtry! Wuxtry! *Record* wuxtry! All about—"

Dual turned and smiled into my eyes as he closed the window. "The requiem of the Master Mind," said he.

VI

RUBIES OF DOOM

CHAPTER I

THE INTERRUPTED CARD GAME

"SO THAT'S YOUR game, is it?"

The question was rapped rather than spoken by a young fellow, one of four men gathered about the card table.

His opposite, a dark, heavy-set person, with a black tip curled mustache overhanging his red lips, raised his thick-lidded eyes from the cards he was rapidly dealing and stared full into the flushed face of the one who had addressed him.

"What's my game?" he growled in reply.

"Slip dealing," flared the other. "You took your last card from the bottom, and—you weren't quite quick enough. I was watching you."

The dark man—it appeared afterward that his name was Swartzberg—merely smiled slightly and shook his head.

"I tell you you did!" persisted the youngster, his voice rising in excitement. "Don't shake your head at me, you card cheat!"

Swartzberg shrugged. "I hate a poor loser," he remarked to the atmosphere of the room at large.

"Pick up that card and turn it over!" demanded his accuser. "It's an ace. I'm as good a loser as any in a fair hand, but I won't stand for funny work in a gentlemen's game. A man who cheats in a friendly hand is the lowest sort of thief."

With a sudden motion Swartzberg gathered the cards before him into his hand and cast them into the center of the table in a ragged heap. "You lie," said he quite coldly.

Almost instantly the smack of a blow sounded as the younger man landed upon the side of Swartzberg's jaw.

A steward, attracted by the sounds of the altercation, entered at this point and inquired as to the cause of the disturbance, caught a glance of the scattered cards and the flushed face of the boy, now securely held in the grasp of the two other players, and grinned, as one accustomed to such scenes.

Swartzberg, secure from further aggression, felt gingerly of his jaw, grimaced at the other occupants of the room as one who would say "the impulsiveness of youth," and sauntered out.

I had noticed him before. He had a stateroom on the saloon deck midway of the port side on the same boat on which Connie, Dual, and I were running up from New Orleans to St. Louis.

I had seen him come aboard at New Orleans just before the boat was starting, and, to tell the truth, I didn't like him.

There was something about his personality which repelled, so far as I was concerned. I didn't like his dark, heavy features, his puffy eyes, his tip curled mustache, his thick, red under lip, his heavy-lobed ears, nor his self-satisfied air. In a word, there was nothing about him I did admire.

He had traveling salesman writ large all over him, and I mentally placed him in that class at the same time that I wondered what put him on a Mississippi River steamer.

The altercation which I had just witnessed occurred in the card and smoking room of the *Cairo,* from New Orleans to St. Paul, on the morning of a day in June. Perhaps I had better explain how we all came to be there ourselves, so that the things which come later will be better understood.

There had been some marked changes in my life of late. To begin with, I was no longer a reporter on the *Record,* where I had won my living for years. Instead, I was now the senior partner of the private inquiry bureau of "Glace & Bryce," with offices in the Urania Building, seventh floor.

Bryce and the sort of work I had done for the *Record* in unraveling baffling police cases were responsible for my change of endeavor. Bryce as a police inspector had been associated with me on more than one of these affairs; so that, after all, it was natural that he should make the half joking, half serious remark: "Glace, you oughter tie a can to this twenty-five-a-week an' get into a man's game. Say, kid, why don't you open a 'tec joint' of your own?"

"I might if you'd chuck the force and go hunks," I returned.

To my surprise he gave me a quick look and stuck out his hand.

After that it was a natural sequence to talk with my friend Dual, who smiled slightly and told me to go ahead. A week after, aided by Dual's backing, we opened an office and announced ourselves as ready to unravel mysteries at so much a ravel. Several things came our way, and we hired a stenographer and an office-boy. It looked as if we were going to make good.

So much for me. Now as to Connie. We were married, and this was our honeymoon trip. We had not intended taking one at the time of the wedding, and it was not until after the ceremony had been performed that we changed our minds.

I think I should say, rather, that Semi Dual changed them for us by announcing that he was about to start upon a trip to Goldfield to see his old friend and partner, John Curzon, who was managing their jointly owned mine, and inviting us to accompany him as his guests.

For the benefit of those who have not followed the events which threw Semi Dual and me together, I must say a word. Briefly, he was a student and exponent of the higher universal forces. A "Psychological Physician" was what he called himself.

Back home where he dwelt and I had worked as a reporter on the *Record* he lived in magnificent quarters which he had fitted up on the roof and in the tower of our largest sky-scraper.

Here he passed his time in the pursuit of those studies which
made him able to perform acts of sapience which I have never
seen equaled by any other living man.

These quarters of his on the roof of the Urania were reached
from the twentieth floor by a beautiful marble and bronze
staircase, leading at its head into a garden of flowers and shrubs
created by Dual about the tower, and kept green the year round
by means of a curved roof or dome of glass which arched it
during the winter months.

I first met Semi Dual on an occasion when Smithson, who
was then my city editor, sent me to interview him, and I have
never forgotten the first impression he made upon me. Tall he
was, with a splendid physique, brown-haired and gray-eyed, of
a deep olive complexion and a highly arched nose.

His physical presence mirrored the admixture of high-caste
Persian and Caucasian bloods which were his, and in his men-
tality one found the impassiveness of the Oriental, united with
the practicality of the Occidental man. On that first occasion
he had helped me to unravel a puzzling police case, and there-
after, time and again, I had called upon his peculiar powers to
reveal the truth of mysteries which baffled the police.

The abstruse sciences of chirography, telepathy, astrology,
and many others were open books to this friend of mine; yet
there was no charlatanism, no skullduggery, about either the
man or his methods.

He announced as true only what he himself had proved and
could prove. Let me quote him on his own attitude. "I will
believe anything which is capable of a scientific proof," he once
said in speaking to me.

This, then, was the man as whose guests my wife and I found
ourselves aboard a Mississippi steamer on that most magnificent
of rivers—the "Father of Waters." Dual had met Connie at a
time when he had been instrumental in freeing her brother
from a cloud of dreadful suspicion swept over him by peculiar
circumstances; and so when I mentioned our approaching mar-

riage to him he surprised and pleased me by suggesting that the ceremony be held at the Urania—in the garden, in fact.

After the ceremony, which was very simple—with only Dual, myself, and Connie, her brother Billy and his *fiancée*, Smithson (my old city editor on the *Record*), and the minister present— Dual led us into the tower and seated us at a splendid supper he had had prepared. It was then that he first mentioned his proposal of a trip, and invited us to come along.

At first Connie demurred, hesitating quite naturally to accept so much from our host; but he smilingly waved aside her objections with the affirmation that he was amply able to afford the pleasure it would give him.

Put in that light, we found it doubly hard to refuse. We accepted instead. Dual had thereupon suggested that we go by boat from New York to New Orleans, and after spending some days in the Southern metropolis continue westward. It was arranged that Bryce should run the office, and we set sail. At New Orleans one day Connie caught sight of a river steamer while we were prowling about the riverfront, with its many-colored, polyglot life, and voiced a wish that she might some day take a trip on one of the things.

Dual, in the rôle of fairy godfather, at once suggested that, instead of going West by rail, we take a boat up the river to St. Louis and catch one of the overland routes from there.

Connie accepted with the delight of a child, and I was pleased because she was. One can therefore imagine that I was feeling pretty well satisfied with the world in general on the morning when the events which held us for the next sixty odd hours began to fall into place.

I had told Connie a great deal about Dual's work on the various mysteries which I had seen him handle, and more than once after listening to me with absorbed interest she had expressed the wish that she too might see him actually engaged upon a case.

Still, as I leaned forward and listened to the turmoil of voices aroused by the dramatic interruption of the card game, I little dreamed that her wish was in a fair way to be gratified.

On the *Cairo* the men's lounge, smoking and card room was set in just off the social hall, back of the library, on the starboard side.

Coming from them, one emerged directly into the main saloon, which widened at the forward end into the library itself. At the other end was the well through which rose the companion-stairs from the main deck, and back of that was the dining saloon.

Across the social hall were two cabin *de luxe* suites which Dual had obtained for Connie and me and himself. These consisted of a small parlor, a bedroom, and a bath, and were very comfortable indeed.

On this morning, after a late breakfast, I had come to the lounge for a quiet smoke. It was perhaps ten of a cloudless day, and Connie and Dual had gone to their deck-chairs; she armed with a camera, with which she enthusiastically shot up the country and the inhabitants as we passed or stopped at small landings; Dual to lounge idly, watching the drifting landscape and think of only he knew what.

As I entered the card-room I noticed the four players seated at one of the little tables with cards, chips, and long glasses before them. They seemed to be enjoying themselves, and were apparently fixed for a day's play.

After a cursory glance I lighted a cigarette, told the white-jacketed bar steward to bring me a bottle of ale, and opened a current number of a magazine which I had brought from the library when I entered. The next thing I knew was the flare up of the light-haired young man at the card table, who now shook himself free from the restraining hands of his companions with a somewhat shamefaced grin.

Well, I had been a reporter, and there is something akin to that in the life of the detective. My instinct for getting at the heart of things has always been strong.

I got up and sauntered over to form one of the group comprising nearly every man in the room, which had by now gathered about the light-haired youth.

"I tell you I saw him slip the bottom card into his own hand," he was doggedly protesting as I came up. "He's a petty tinhorn, that's what he is; and he's been skinning us by crooked play. I thought his luck was too good to be the real thing, and I began watching him. On that last deal he—"

"Well, never mind, son," one of the other players cut in. "We're all losers to him, and there's no way to prove it now."

"We don't need to prove it!" flashed the youngster. "He as good as admitted it when he mixed his hand with the deck just before I hit him. He's a dirty cheat!

"Supposin' he is," the steward interjected. "You was playin' for stakes, wasn't you, son?"

"Well?" The young fellow turned to the petty officer and spoke more quietly than he had yet done.

"That's gamblin'," decided the official. "You fellows aren't supposed to do it on these boats; but *if* you do, why you take your chances, an' there's nobody to blame but yourself. I've seen more'n one fellow trimmed in these pick-up games. It used to be a regular trade. He called you a liar and you hit him. Let it go at that."

"He as good as stole fifty dollars of my money," said the youth more hotly.

The steward whistled softly, then grinned. "You can't prove it, son, as the gent said. Charge it up to experience. You folks was havin' quite a little game, wasn't you?"

"Hardly." The young chap swept the faces about him almost with a glance of suspicion. "It was merely a lamb-shearing contest, I guess."

"Cut that, suh!" snapped one of the other players, a dark-skinned chap with a small black mustache of the Creole type. "You saw me lose twenty to him mahself. Ef yuh keep on beefing about it, hang me, suh, ef Ah don't agree with th' sheeney that yuh air one poor losier." He shrugged his white-flannel-clad shoulders.

The steward nodded. "The gent's right," he said. "Better forget it, young feller. What's done's done, as I see it. You got one good punch to the jaw for your half century, anyway." He turned away.

So did the others; some with winks and grins, others with even less show of interest. Each returned to the spot and occupation which suited him best. Remained the light-haired youth and myself beside the table.

I sat down on one of the soft chairs and took out my case of cigarettes, offering him one and lighting another. "Sit down and tell me about it," I suggested.

Under the circumstances he complied. He was full of his troubles, ready for sympathy, and didn't care particularly with whom he talked about it. He dropped into the opposite seat, lighted the cigarette, and picked up the scattered cards from the table, bunching them in his hands. "Case of a fool and his money, I guess. Mr.—" he began with a somewhat weak grin.

"Glace," I supplied to his interrogative pause.

He nodded. "I'm John Greer, and no doubt a good deal of a fool on the face of it. I'm sorry I acted like a cub, now that it is over with. It was my hot-headed temper made me pull that cheap melodramatic stuff; but I do hate a cheat." He threw down the cards.

"The steward was right when he said that these pick-up games are apt to surprise one of the players, and that boat-gambling used to be almost a recognized profession. I'm sorry you were the fall guy," I replied.

He smiled sourly. "It isn't the money," said he. "Not that I like to lose any better than any one else, and the jolly loser is a rare bird in my experience; but if the game had been square I wouldn't have kicked. I've both won and lost more. It's just that I hate being roped in like that. I didn't particularly want to play, you see. Came up here for a smoke after breakfast, and they were trying to get some one to take a fourth hand—you know how those things go.

"They asked me to sit in. I declined, and they insisted. Finally I did come in. Everything went all right for a time, at that; and then this—Swartzberg, I think his name is—hit a winning streak and kept it up. I got suspicious after a bit and began to watch him, and he was dealing crooked. Then I got mad, and I suppose you saw the rest."

Suddenly his grin became totally unrestrained. "Anyway I bet his jaw's sore. I got in one jolly swing to the side of his map."

"It sounded sincere when it landed," I admitted.

"It was," said Greer.

Frankly, after the heat had died out of him I rather liked the young chap. He was clean-looking, well set up, with a clear, blue eye, a good breadth of forehead, and a firm jaw which gave evidence of latent strength waiting to be developed.

Furthermore, I could sympathize with him in his position. He was, after all, only a boy, sore at being treated as one. I had felt like that at times myself not far distant.

"Where did you learn to deliver the punch?" I inquired.

"At school," he replied at once, his eyes lighting. "Oh, I'm an unlicked cub out of college, and that goes double—I never was licked in the gym boxing matches. Now I'm going home for dad to lick into business, I suppose.

"Dad's in business in St. Louis, but nothing would do save I had to graduate from his own *alma mater*. I went to New Orleans with a classmate for a visit, and now I'm going home; thought it would be fun to come by boat. Still"—his grin came back again—"it seems my education wasn't finished when I dragged down my sheep-skin. What's your line, Mr. Glace?"

"I'm a detective," I returned.

"Oh, Lord!" grimaced Greer. "Worse and worse. I'm going to get home as quick as I can. I don't even know when it's safe to talk, I reckon."

"I'm on my honeymoon," I said, laughing. "Don't be alarmed."

"Congratulations on the honeymoon. I made a narrow escape," said the youngster. His finger went toward the push-button on the panel. "What'll you have?"

I shook my head. "What business is your father in?" I asked.

"Contracting—building," he answered. "I'm going in with him, now that I know how to say brick in Latin. Maybe my punch will come in handy, though, in handling the gangs."

I nodded, and for some time we smoked in silence. Presently I took out my watch. It was getting on toward eleven, and I fancied I'd hunt up Connie and see how she was making out. I sat up in my seat. Greer, too, sat up.

"Have a cigar, anyway, before you go, just to show me you don't think I'm altogether the ass these other chaps evidently consider me," he begged in a boyish appeal.

I assented, and he called the bar steward, ordering two cigars, and a drink for himself as well. "If there was any way of doing it, I'd like to go after that fellow and make him shell out my fifty," he began again in a moment; "just to show 'em that I'm not as easy as I look."

"Just who is this chap?" I rejoined.

"I don't know." The steward came back, and he paid and dismissed him. "He says he's Isaac Swartzberg, a drummer, and I imagine he is. He looks like the typical loud-mouthed con man he ought to be. One thing's sure—he thinks he is a warm number with the ladies.

"I've an idea he's one of these 'johnnies' who tries to make up to every pretty face he sees. He kept up a patter about his experiences along that line all during the game this morning. I hate that sort of man, and no doubt my swat was only one of many he deserves. Did you notice the pretty little pouting red lip he wore?"

"Particularly, my young friend," I returned. "It goes with the sort of man you appraise Swartzberg to be."

Greer laughed. "I'm glad to hear it. I suppose you ought to know. You do meet all sorts in your line of work, don't you, Mr. Glace?"

"A few," I told him. "The pendulous lower lip does not go with a high sense of moral integrity, though it is compatible with vanity."

"That's Swartzberg," agreed my acquaintance. "When he wasn't talking about girls he was bragging about other exploits of his."

"Did you know either of the others?" I inquired. "Who was the man in the white flannel suit?" Some way the chap had interested me.

Greer shook his head. "Said his name was Gaston Lefourche. I never saw him before. Rather a touchy beggar, I guess, from the way he took up my remark about the wool market."

"French Creole type?" I remarked.

Greer nodded. "Guess so." Then he reverted to Swartzberg and the subject next his heart. "Do you know, I believe that fellow uses his steady talk to distract attention while he fixes the deck. I wish I had something on him, and I'd make him disgorge his winnings of to-day."

I shook my head. "Better let him alone," I advised.

Greer grinned. "What'll you bet I can't get it out of him before he leaves this boat?" he asked.

"Not a thing," said I. "If you're contemplating any more foolishness take my advice about trying it, and *don't.*"

"But it would be fun to make him loosen," Greer persisted.

"I didn't know whether it would or not," I responded. "I've an idea he might prove a nasty customer if forced to it."

"Oh, it wouldn't be a matter of force—say persuasion, rather, Mr. Glace. What'll you bet I can't do it?"

I rose and stood facing him across the table. "If you're going to look for trouble I'll bet you find it," I said in answer. "You've kicked up some considerable fuss for one morning as it is. I think you'd better take a rest."

"All the same, I've an idea I could do it," he grinned back. "Maybe I won't, and then again—maybe I will. Just wait and see."

"Go ahead. You may succeed in raising enough excitement to give me excuse for butting in in my professional capacity," I flung back as I walked away.

I didn't know that my words would prove prophetic, but they did.

CHAPTER II

INNOCENCE ABROAD

THE BOAT HAD been swinging in toward the shore while Greer and I chatted over our cigars, and had eventually swung into a small landing with a great clanging of gongs and thrashing of paddles.

As I left the card-room and started to hunt up Dual and my wife I noticed the first slow quiver of departure. Evidently it had merely checked to allow some passenger a landing or take some one aboard.

Such incidents as this were proving a constant source of interest to Connie, who seemed never to tire of this remnant of the bygone time when many boats churned the waters of the great river.

She had spent most of the preceding day on deck, watching the odd life of the river settlements as we approached or left them, studying the ragged stevedores on the wharfs, listening to their chanting cries as they handled freight and baggage, or their more modern and less musical profanity, with an equal fascination which had not yet seemed to flag.

Passing into the social hall with the intention of gaining the deck through one of the side alleys, I first came face to face with the wheat-haired girl. That is really the only way I can think of describing the great mass of fine fibered tresses which crowned her head. It wasn't golden and it wasn't yellow. It was silvery, yellowish color, like the straw of ripened wheat.

She was one of the Southern blond types who are really at times of an almost exotic beauty. She was mounting the companion-stairs from the main deck in the wake of a colored steward burdened by her traveling-cases, and they had just reached the head of the stairs at the after-end of the social hall as I started from the door of the card-room.

As a result, I paused to allow them to pass before continuing on my way outside, whereupon one of those odd turns of fortune which occasionally happen brought us into instant and intimate contact.

The girl was wearing a shimmery gown of some light silk, held daintily in her hand as she mounted the stairs. In some way, which probably a woman will understand better than I, her foot appeared to catch somewhere among the mysteries of her skirts. She wavered and swayed and would have fallen had I not sprung forward and checked her with a hand.

For a moment she clung to me, a hand on my shoulder and one on my arm. Then, having extricated her foolishly high-heeled shoe from her ruffles or wherever it was caught, she straightened and raised a flushed face to mine.

"I thank you, suh," she said in some confusion. "You saved me a bad fall."

I took off my traveling-cap and smiled. "I am happy to have had the privilege," I told her, and saw her vanish after the steward toward her room.

"Lucky dog," said a voice not far from me, and I turned to find Swartzberg looking on with a grin. Having attracted my attention, he went on: "Some dame, that, my boy. With that good a start you ought to be solid for the rest of the trip."

I've said I didn't like the man, and I didn't like his uncalled-for comment. I turned on my heel. "I'm joining my wife," I said.

He grinned.

"So?" he remarked. "Well, no offense. Folks seem to be pretty touchy on this boat this morning. Has our young friend cooled down?" He jerked his head toward the card-room. "Think it would be safe for me to go order a drink? He's a hot-tempered cub."

"He was rapidly approaching normal when I left," I responded. "He admits he acted like a fool."

"He's a college rah-rah boy," said Swartzberg. "Daffy over these young ideas of honor, *noblesse oblige,* and that sort of thing. He'll get it knocked out of him after he's butted around a bit. I got it doped out that the Lord helps them as helps themselves. If you're married I don't suppose you're interested in the little blond you so gallantly saved from a tumble?"

I felt my gorge rise at the fellow, turned and looked down the alley along which the girl was gone. In the moment she had clung to me I had seen that her lips were soft and almost characterless in expression, and her eyes blue and wide open, with the blue of the flax and the openness of innocence, as it seemed to me.

Her face was that of an unlearned child or a woman totally shielded from experience. Because of that I resented Swartzberg's leer.

"Only that of any decent man in a woman," I said shortly, and turned my back on the man.

I went on past the companionway and gained the deck. The girl had disappeared, and the steward was just coming out of stateroom well toward the after part of the ship. I paused and looked back to the social hall.

Swartzberg had turned in his seat and was steadily watching the passage as though waiting for some one. I remembered my conversation with Greer and our appraisal of the alleged drummer. Well, here was surely a pretty face, and discipline on the boat was lax. Would he—

I turned in disgust, without finishing the question, and swung forward where Connie and Dual had their chairs. I found

Connie just turning up a fresh film in place of one she had exposed.

"Oh, Gordon," she cried as I came up, "you ought to have been out here a bit ago. You used to be so fond of local color, and I just caught a snap of some people saying good-by to the prettiest girl. They were real Southern blue-bloods, I think—big, strong, romantic-looking men, and the girl was an awfully sweet-looking little thing. She took the boat."

"I saw her," I said as I stretched out in a deck-chair. "She's just been hanging on my neck. Her stateroom's on this deck."

Connie opened her eyes. "Hanging on your neck?" she gasped. "What *do* you mean?"

"It was that or let her fall on her nose," I said, grinning. "Why will women wear high heels and a lot of loose ends to catch them in? She pretty nearly bit a hole in the top of the companionway as she came up. I caught her because I happened to be there."

"Oh!" said Connie, "is that all? For a minute I was for getting jealous. I believe I'll speak to her the first chance I get. She looked so sweet and just a little bit timid. I don't believe she's used to being away from home. There was the nicest old lady with her. I think it was her mother, and she was crying. We're going to have the loveliest lot of pictures when we get home, Gordon, if—"

"They develop all right, eh?" I laughed.

She nodded. "I'm going in now," she announced. "They'll be serving luncheon after a bit and I want to go right in as soon as I can. I've an awful appetite. I think traveling agrees with me." She arose and flitted away.

Dual and I had the platform to ourselves. He glanced across at me and smiled. "The growth of the soul is a wonderful thing to watch, Gordon. You have waked the woman in your wife with your love, yet her soul is the clean one of a child. Remember it is as little children that we enter the kingdom of heaven, and see to it that no act of yours shall change her paradise."

I opened my eyes and my lips, when he went on: "I know that of any intent, you will not, my friend; but it is, alas! so easy to err. A word, even sometimes a thought, and the mistake has been made. A spoken word, or a thought which has flown, can never be recalled. A woman gives so much into a man's keeping with herself. See that you as a man keep your trust."

Characteristically he lapsed abruptly into silence, and left me to consider the words he had spoken. He had a way of planting his words like seeds and letting them germinate thoughts in the minds they entered.

Right at that time my mind was a fertile soil to his hand, and I knew that he knew it. I don't remember that we spoke again until luncheon was announced.

We found that Connie had made good her threat of speaking to the wheat-haired girl. In fact, she was chatting with her in the library when we went in. She caught sight of us at once, and, rising, met us in the social hall. I could see by the set of her lips that something had displeased her, but it was not until we were seated at our table that she began to speak:

"I was right about that girl. This is her first long trip. She's going to visit relatives in St. Louis. After I had freshened up a bit for luncheon I went into the library, and some time later she came in and sat down and looked about. I just got up and went over and spoke to her, and she told me about her trip. And what do you think? After a bit that big, dark man came to the library door and looked in. Then he came in and began to look over the books and magazines, but that was only an excuse to keep ogling the girl. After a bit I set my eyes on him and just kept them there, and pretty soon he went out. I don't think I like that man."

"He's not a man, Mrs. Glace," said Semi quite casually, as Connie paused for breath.

"He's no gentleman, at any rate," she agreed heartily.

"And experience is a great thing, but costly," continued our host.

"Meaning the girl with the wheat-colored hair?" I asked.

"Meaning any one," said Dual, "and *particularly* the girl."

I grinned. "Now, just what *do* you mean, Dual?" I begged.

"She has had none," replied my friend. "Her face is an unwritten page. I was wondering what experience was fated to write thereon."

A waiter came just then, and so far as I remember that ended the conversation along that line for the time, yet I had a strange sensation as though Dual had sensed something which I had not. If he didn't then, he did later, as his own words were to prove.

After luncheon Connie went to our stateroom for a nap, and I went to the card-room for another smoke, leaving Dual in a deck-chair deep in the pages of a book which he had dug out of one of his suit-cases and begun to read.

I found young Greer and the man in flannels—Lafourche—sitting at a little table. Greer caught sight of me as I entered, beckoned me to come over, and called the bar-steward.

"Come on and sit down and have a cool one," he invited. "And meet Mr. Lafourche who thought me a shoe-string player this morning. Mr. Lafourche—Mr. Glace."

I shook hands with the dark-complexioned man, and took the opportunity to size him up. In appearance he might be anywhere from thirty to forty, and he was built like a steel spring, I decided. I formed the instant idea that under his loose clothing his muscles were like thin, flexible bands. For the rest he had a well-shaped head, a cool, dark eye, a small black mustache, and flexible, long-fingered hands.

"Pleased to meet yuh, Mr. Glace," he acknowledged, half rising. "Ah've just been telling Mr. Greer some of the history of the old sort of gambling which used to obtain on these rivair steamers. Fortunes were lost in a night, suh, as perhaps yuh know."

"Yes, and we were exchanging opinions on that fat hog, Swartzberg, too," grinned Greer. "What are you going to have, Mr. Glace?"

"Bring me a bottle of ale," I told the steward and dropped into a chair. "You live in New Orleans, Mr. Lafourche?"

"There and on my plantation," he responded. "Ah'm off for a vacation now, though; some frien's of mine in Sant Louis air for a trip to Wyoming, an' they invited me to accompany them, suh. Ah expect an enjoyable trip, an' perhaps some shootin'. Ah brought mah guns along on th' chance."

"Guns!" said Greer quickly. "Gee, I like a good gun! What sort do you use?"

"Perhaps yuh would care to take a look at them, suh," suggested Lafourche. "They air in their cases in mah stateroom on th' deck above. Ah only decided to come at th' last moment an' took any cabin Ah could get."

"You bet I'd like to see them," Greer accepted. "I'm some shot myself. After Glace has finished his ale let's go up."

Lafourche nodded, and soon we three rose and ascended to the promenade-deck where he had his quarters. He unlocked the door and invited us to enter, told us to sit down, and dragged out a couple of pigskin cases, which he opened to display a magnificent rifle and an equally handsome shotgun. Greer cried out in delight and began examining them with the eye of a judge, while Lafourche looked on well pleased.

"Ah pride mahself on those weapons," he said at length. "They air of French manufacture an' air a present to me from a dear frien'."

"They're peaches!" said the boy. "But if they're imported, don't you have trouble with your ammunition?"

Lafourche nodded and smiled. "Oh, yes, but Ah always save mah shells and reload them mahself. Ah carry a reloading outfit, Mr. Greer."

Greer nodded and passed the shotgun to me. I took it and turned it in my hands. It was a splendid specimen of fowling-piece, beautifully wrought and balanced. I could well imagine that Lafourche might feel pride in its possession.

Presently we gave them back and the owner strapped them up. We all rose and returned below, and I made my way outside to where Dual still sat with his book. Connie had not yet appeared, but came out presently, reaching us from the other side of the deck. She was bristling.

"I think it's a shame!" she exclaimed, as she sank into a chair, between Semi and me. "That black-mustached masher has finally succeeded in forcing himself upon that girl's attention. I came out on the far side of the deck and came around, and there he was, sitting with her against the side of the house, smirking and smiling in a way to make a person sick. Such men ought to be quarantined."

Dual smiled slightly. "Your idea is good, if not practical, Mrs. Glace," he observed. "Still it is some satisfaction to know that karmic law necessitates the causes which such people set into operation, eventually returning upon them with a cumulative effect."

Connie turned full upon him. "You are the strangest man, Mr. Dual," she said. "Don't you ever feel a desire for vengeance or anything like that?"

Semi shook his head. "I used to," he made answer, "but that was long ago. Now I have learned that justice is of the Lord, and it is sufficient to demand it and wait."

"If I wish you would teach me something of your philosophy," said Connie. "Gordon has told me about it, and it seems so wonderful and so fine and clean."

"If it is for me to do, I will do so," Dual promised, his eyes lighting. "Frankly I would like to do so. Yet we of the temple may not speak until the time is propitious. Be assured, Mrs. Glace, that when the pupil is ready the master will appear. If it is to be I, I shall be very glad. But before that time can come you must desire the knowledge for your soul, as the flower desires the rain and the sun."

"That is beautiful!" cried Connie.

"The religion of the universe is beautiful," Dual replied. "It is beautiful and easy. All one has to do is to desire—naturally— not from curiosity merely, or self-interest, but just to know; and one by one the veils rise and roll back before us and we see farther and farther into the heart of God. Faith and trust and a desire to grow in the spirit, as the flower grows with its face to God's light, because God wills it to. Man may grow like that if he will—may feel toward his God as a child to its parent. That is what the last great Messianic spirit, now called the Christ, meant when He said: 'Unless ye come as a little child ye may not enter in.' God is the father, we are His spirit children—a long way from home, yet not forgotten for one instant of eternity."

There were tears in Connie's eyes when he ceased, and she rose and went back into our stateroom. I followed after a glance from Dual.

"He is wonderful, wonderful, boy o' mine!" she said when we had reached our quarters. "God has been good to give us such a friend."

Dual joined us just after the dinner call had sounded, and we made our way to the dining saloon. I glanced about as we went in, and there was Swartzberg and the girl, chatting away in the social hall. The man's face wore a self-satisfied grin.

Our places happened to be at the captain's table, owing to our holding the *de luxe* staterooms, and I had noticed ere this that Swartzberg sat behind us at another, but facing Dual, who sat opposite Connie and me at our own. Just after we had taken our places the girl and the man came in, and Connie fairly gasped: "Will you look at that?"

"Perhaps," said I, "if you'll tell me what that is."

"Why, that man! He's had that girl's place put next to his. I know it wasn't at noon, so he must have arranged it. Did you ever hear of such nerve?"

"She must have been a party to the arrangement," I reminded her.

"She's a silly little fool," Connie declared.

"Not being married to me, she is doubtless taking what she can get," I suggested to break the tension, and Connie laughed.

"All the same, those things make me wonder how girls can be so foolish," she claimed her last word and began to talk of something else.

It was after this, however, that I first noticed a strong preoccupation in Semi Dual. His answers to my remarks became less and less ready and presently ceased. Glancing up after one unanswered sally, I found that he had laid down knife and fork and was leaning back in his chair, his eyes more than half closed, his chest rising and falling in long, slow respirations, almost as though he had fallen into a doze.

Connie, following my glance, started to speak, but I checked her. "What is it? Is he ill?" she whispered to me.

I shook my head. "Go on eating," I counseled. "Pay no attention to him. I've seen him like this before. Some day you may understand better—I can't explain now; but this much is sure. Dual is very sensitive. Something, I don't know what, has arrested his full attention and he is sensing it out. Perhaps he'll tell us after a while."

Almost as I ceased speaking Semi opened his eyes and sat up in his place, reached for his glass of water, and sipped it slowly ere he set it down, then looked into my eyes and smiled.

"What was it, Dual?" I made bold to ask.

"What was what?" he returned. "What were you looking at?" He shook his head and smiled slightly. "Not now, my friend," said he.

"He was looking at that man," Connie whispered, voicing a woman's intuition.

Dual heard her and smiled. I turned my head along our table and caught a glance of Lafourche on the other side. He was sitting so that he, too, faced the table behind me, and I fancied that he also was watching Swartzberg and the wheat-haired girl and that there was an expression almost malign on his dark, handsome face. I rather liked the young creole, and I wondered if he, too, felt disgust at the spectacle of the open flirtation of the two.

We adjourned from the dining-room to the deck to enjoy the evening, and sat there for a long time. It was a beautiful sight as the boat plowed her way up the great river, so wide that its wooded banks were beginning to appear but dim lines in the coming dusk, twisting about great bends, turning this way and that to follow the channel, breasting the current like a strong swimmer.

A young moon rose in the west and hung an amber crescent on a pale, yellow field. Now and then a mellow note of a gong clanged softly from below deck, some signal to the engine-room.

I think the soft beauty of the evening impressed us all in a similar fashion so that gradually our conversation languished and finally ceased. Nine o'clock came, and with it almost complete darkness. Connie turned her head to me.

"Run and have your good-night smoke and we'll go in," she advised.

I had been thinking of doing the same thing, so I nodded, and rising, moved off, but the spell of the night was still upon me, and some way I didn't feel like going into the smoking-room, whose lights showed through a warm, blue haze. I decided rather that I would stroll about the decks and have my smoke as I walked.

Lighting a cigarette I made my way up to the promenade-deck, and, led on by my fancy, mounted to the very top of the boat where the hurricane-deck stretched out under the star sprinkled sky.

Above my head two long trails of smoke from the funnels writhed astern, while now and then an angry red glare burst from the stacks as the stokers fed the furnaces far below. I made my way aft and stood for some time watching the broken reflection of the boat's lights on the sullen waters of the great river. Then I turned and walked slowly forward on the starboard side until I was close abaft the pilot-house. There I came to a sudden pause.

A dim light shone from the windows of the house and fell outward on the deck. Half revealed in its illumination I made out two figures, huddled on a couple of small stools, evidently at times used by the boatsmen, but now drawn close against the side wall of the house. I had hardly expected to find any one here, and naturally I gave them as close a scrutiny as was possible in the half light. Then I muttered an exclamation of disgust to myself, for I had recognized Swartzberg and the light-haired girl.

They sat there huddled under the screening wall and the dark, like a pair of moonstruck young kids rather than a woman grown and a man old enough to have been her father. I agreed with Connie that it made one sick.

I swung on an impatient heel and continued forward. I made my way to a point directly in line with the funnel and paused again, because it seemed to me that as I approached a dim shadow moved at the base of the great stack. I diverted my steps and walked directly up to the steel tube and confirmed my suspicion.

A figure was lurking in its protecting shadow, but as I came upon it it waited and I could see the flash of teeth in the dark. It came over me suddenly that he had been standing there spying on the pair by the pilot-house, and I began to wonder at the action. I could really see no cause for any one to be standing gazing at a silly girl making so public a fool of herself. Then the fellow spoke.

"Hello, Mr. Glace, Ah see that yuh too have discovered the little turtle doves."

With a start I recognized Lafourche. "Oh, it's you, is it? What are you doing here?" I said sharply.

He chuckled. "Ah was standing here watchin'," he whispered
softly. "Ah was jus' thinkin' that ef the young woman were only
our Lady Circe how easy her task to convert her present esquire
into the fabled hog." Again he chuckled. "Ah came up 'ere for
a breath of air," he continued. "Like yourself, Ah stumbled upon
the pair yonder. I drew back behin' the funnel an' watched them.
Dieu! but they are well worth watching. An' yet, 'twas a boy's
trick for a man grown, was it not?"

"What are they doing way up here by themselves?" I questioned with a jerk of the head toward the pilot-house.

"Talkin'," said Lafourche. "Talkin', Mr. Glace—in the dark—
oh, quite in the dark. Who says romance is dead? That is a
canard. Oh, yes."

"Rot," I half growled. "Let's get out of here. The man's a rascal
and the girl's a fool."

"Ah agree with you on both points, completely," Lafourche
retorted. "We can find a drink and a cigarette below."

We crossed the deck and went down. Lafourche insisted
upon having a drink, after which I hunted up Connie and Dual
and we went to our room. My mind was again full of the thing
I had witnessed on the hurricane-deck, and through association
I remembered Dual's peculiar actions at dinner. "Come on in
with us a minute," I suggested as I unlocked the parlor. "I want
to ask you a question before I forget it."

He smiled slightly, but followed us in. "Now," said I, as soon
as we were seated, "what were you looking at during dinner? I
know you saw something, and I believe it referred to this man
we have discussed before to-day. What was it, Dual?"

"The lights," said he.

"The lights!" I exclaimed.

"They were too dim, Gordon," he said. "I was speaking of
auric lights."

"Auric lights?" repeated Connie with instant interest. "Oh,
what are they, Mr. Dual?"

I remembered. Suddenly I saw again a picture of the inner room in the tower of the Urania, where a man suspected of murder had sat under the purple radiance Dual had arranged for his undoing, and I recalled what my friend had said of auric colors at that time.

For an instant I lost myself in the land of memory until Dual's voice brought me back.

"I think," he was saying, "that I may as well explain, now as another time. Science has at last proved that they exist, long after they had been recognized by other men than the scientists. Have you ever heard of the N-rays, Mrs. Glace?"

Connie shook her head.

"At least," Dual went on, "you know that light is merely etheric vibration, and that the color of each ray depends upon its vibratory character. Roentgen or X-rays are waves of so high a rate of vibration that they are invisible to the naked eye, but still capable of affecting changes in a sensitized photographic plate. The N-rays are a still higher form of light. That is all, except that some very clever French investigators have at last been able to make them affect extremely sensitive plates as well.

"Now, in order to explain more fully I must digress a bit. All life is motion and every motion produces vibration. Every cell of our bodies is in a constant state of vibration, and if that ceases the body, as we say, dies. Mental activity is no exception to this rule, for there are no exceptions to the rules of the universe. Consequently, mental activity—thought—produces vibration, corresponding to the nature of the thought produced. These thought waves radiating from the individual produce actual currents in the surrounding ether and—one step further—they can be perceived as an expression of color, varying also with the character of the thought. It is these colors which we denominate auric lights. It is at least some form of these currents which is now known and designated the N-ray.

"But long before Science announced her discovery certain men who had studied deeply and developed the ability to do so had sensed these lights, studied them; and classified them, and found that they corresponded to the lights of the physical spectrum, and that each degree or gradation formed an absolute index to the character of the individual who produced them, both mentally and physically."

The stronger the person's health the stronger the light under ordinary conditions; the purer his nature the higher up the spectrum would the predominating color be.

"You will notice that I said these men sensed these colors, and I meant just that. Each of the physical senses has its sub-conscious or soul counterpart, Mrs. Glace. We may see and hear by the objective sense or by clairvoyance or clairaudience, which are the subconscious parallels off these; we feel physically or psychometrically, and so on. That is why I closed my physical eyes just now and allowed my subconscious sense to appraise the lights I saw."

"Referring to the man Swartzberg?" I guessed.

Semi Dual smiled.

"And what color does he give off?" I asked.

"Red," said Dual. "The lowest in the spectrum. The man is a materialist—an animal."

"I could have told you that myself," I laughed.

"Doubtless," my friend responded. "However, I was considering his aura from an entirely different point of interest, my friend."

"He's certainly not a man of any high sense of principle," I replied, and went on to narrate the scene on the deck I had just witnessed, and my conversations with Lafourche and young Greer. Both Dual and Connie listened with interest. "So you see we all appraised him as you did, Semi," I made an end.

"You may add me to the list," said Connie. "There is something repellent about him to me, though it looks as if he had that poor silly girl completely hypnotized."

"He will do her no lasting harm," sard Dual.

"Quit it," I put in. "You're holding something back on us, Dual."

Semi shot me a glance. "It's a peculiar thing," said he, "about auric lights, that they often pale shortly before the individual's death. You say this man's name is Isaac Swartzberg, I believe. I think I must do a little figuring if you will excuse me."

Drawing a note-book from his pocket he laid it on the table and wrote down Swartzberg's full name, placing the letters one below the other in a vertical line. Opposite these he set a column of numerals, one to each letter of the name, and began to add their total. While Connie and I watched he plunged into still further computations, presently closing the book and putting it away. "If your young man Greer is going to recover his money he had better be about it ere long. Swartzberg is, I fear, apt to suffer a sudden demise."

"To die?" cried Connie, paling as she spoke.

"To change his form of existence at least," said Dual with a smile.

"That's what you were watching, then," I exclaimed in sudden comprehension.

Dual nodded. "His aura is far paler than it should be in a man of his apparent health," he remarked. "Further, it is growing paler as time goes by."

Connie shuddered. Myself I seemed to feel a cold breath contract the skin of my face and hands.

CHAPTER III

THE END OF SWARTZBERG

AFTER SUCH AN experience it seems but natural in looking back that Dual himself should have been the one to discover that his prediction had been verified.

If only the rank and file of us could see as clearly with our fore as with our hind sight a great many things would turn out otherwise than they do.

After Dual had left us and we had retired Connie and I talked for some time, and long after her soft breathing told me she was asleep I lay awake staring into the darkness, listening to the muffled pulse of the engines.

I was turning over the events of the day in my mind, trying to pick up a thread of meaning which now in the quiet of the night it seemed to me lay somewhere just beyond my mental grasp. I pictured Swartzberg in the card-room and Greer's sudden attack upon him. I visualized the wheat-haired girl as she came aboard and clung to me for a moment at the head of the companionway with her hand on my arm.

There had been a little gold seal ring on that hand, and now I seemed to see it plainly. Then I seemed again to see the two huddled figures beside the pilot-house, and to stumble on the figure of Lafourche behind the funnel. I turned Dual's words over and over.

Many a time I had known him to predicate some event even as now, and prove right in what he promised would occur. Time and again I had found myself shaken by an inward spasm, excited by his uncanny ability of timing the future as well as the past. Now while my mate slumbered by my side I reviewed his statements concerning the drummer, and wondered what form the verification would take.

On the face of it it seemed weirdly impossible that so well preserved a physical animal as the man looked should be approaching his end, and yet I had a strange premonitory feeling that it was true. Dual didn't make such statements as that without good reason. In some way, sometime soon then, Swartzberg's aura must pale into nothingness and go out. How?

It was a tap on the stateroom door which awakened me to the gray light of a new day upon which the sun had not yet risen. I opened my eyes and lay a moment trying to decide if I had really heard anything or not. For a space nothing came save the pulse of the engines in their dull rhythm and the sigh of a vagrant breeze through an open shutter. Then I heard the rap again.

Slipping out of the berth, taking care not to awaken my wife, I slid into a bathrobe and unlatched the parlor door.

Semi Dual was standing in the social hall, where a garish night-lamp still burned faintly in the growing light.

"Dress yourself and come out," he suggested. "We'll go on the deck and watch the sun rise. It is a beautiful day and well worth the effort and an hour's lost sleep."

I nodded and drew back. Then I smiled. If there was a man in all the world who loved nature in all her phases it was my friend Dual. Several times during the voyage down to New Orleans he had routed me out in similar fashion to accompany him and stand or sit on the deck, while the great orb of the sun set the east pink and violet blue, turning to gold, and finally to a brilliance unbearable to the eye, as it leaped out of the watery-waste. I hastened now to comply with his suggestion, fumbled my way into shirt, collar and trousers, slipped on a coat and shoes and joined him outside the door.

"We'll go outside and walk down the deck," he said, leading the way to the port alley which gave on the outside promenade. I followed, and we started back along the rows of staterooms, single file. We had progressed perhaps half the distance to the stern of the boat when Dual stopped so suddenly that I all but trod on his heels.

I raised my face in question and saw that his delicate nostrils were quivering into dilation. I would have said in that moment that he was sniffing something so subtle as to be imperceptible to me. While I watched in surprised wonder he turned directly upon me. "Do you sense it?" he inquired.

"What?" I whispered.

"The odor of death," he replied. "It has come upon us in the night. Some one lies dead inside that room behind the closed shutter in the door."

I trembled. I remembered my thoughts of the night before and this strange man's words. Suddenly it came to me that Swartzberg had a stateroom somewhere along the port row of cabins. With a catch of my breath I wondered if perhaps this might be it, and if his fate had struck down upon him while I slept.

Again I noticed Dual's nostrils quiver as we stood outside the door of the room—number fifty-seven, it was. "I will lift you up to the transom," he said calmly, "and you can look over. Come."

He reached out and raised me up until I could get my eyes above the frame of the door and apply them to the narrow transom between the casing and the top of the stateroom wall. So while he held me I fastened my eyes upon the interior of the room and felt my heart contract at what I saw.

It was the head and torso of Isaac Swartzberg lying back in his berth in the shadowy light of the room; but the eyes were wide open and staring in their position, the jaw was sagged down so that his mouth appeared to gape, as one seeking to shriek a cry for succor, and all the red was gone from his pendulous lower lip and his face, leaving it sallow and pallid like yellow wax. One hand was lying across his body, the other at his side, and upon the bosom of his night clothes, on the left side was an irregular dark spot. I realized in that moment that truly the aura had paled and flickered out. *The man was dead!*

One glance served to convince me, and I turned my face back and downward to Dual. He nodded slowly and immediately lowered me upon my own feet. "We must notify the boat's authorities at once," he declared. "Go find a steward and tell him to send some one here."

Without a word I swung on my heel and raced back along the deck, darted into the social hall, and looked about. A steward was there, working in listless fashion with a hair broom.

The man glanced up at my call, caught sight of me, standing there near the companion, and hurried in my direction. "Yassuh. Did you all call me?" he inquired.

"Yes," I told him. "Steward, go and notify the boat's officers that there is a dead man in room fifty-seven on this deck."

"A daid man!" cried the negro, his eyes starting in his dusky face. "A daid— Oh, Lordy, howcum you all know dat?"

"Never mind how I came to know it," I responded. "You get some one in authority and send him back there at once. I'll be waiting there with a friend."

"Yassuh, I'll git de purser—Mr. Keating," gasped the steward, dropping his broom and darting to the door of a room which opened onto the gallery about the companionway.

Leaving him beating a lusty tattoo on its panels, I turned and hurried back to where Dual was leaning against the rail outside of number fifty-seven.

"The steward is getting the purser," I reported. "Well, your prediction seems to have been verified. Couldn't the man have been warned?"

My friend shook his head. "It was inevitable, Gordon. My calculations of last night showed me that. Furthermore, had he had any chance for life his aura would not have paled as it did. No, Glace, my friend, the man's hour had come. Otherwise I should have warned him myself."

Footsteps were approaching the deck and we turned. A young and light-complexioned man in the dark uniform of a boat's officer was coming hurriedly toward us, with the negro steward trailing some distance behind, a mixture of curiosity and timidity upon his ebony face.

Dual greeted the officer as he came up. "Good morning, Mr. Purser. It seems that murder was done last night while we slept."

"Murder!" The purser started back a pace, colliding with the steward. "What do you mean, sir? The boy here said something about a dead man in fifty-seven, and that you had sent for me; but—"

"He didn't tell you the reason," completed Dual. "Well, we didn't tell him, but the man in this room is dead—stabbed, I think."

"Good God!" gasped the official, and swung upon the negro. "You didn't know anything about this, did you, Jake?"

"Nossuh. I ain't knowed nuthin', sah, till this gemman called me an' told me to git you all."

The man was palpably telling the truth and was trembling as he answered. The purser turned back to Dual. "And how did you gentlemen happen to find this out?" he asked with harrowing eyes.

Semi Dual smiled. "Intuition say, purser. I am an early riser. The fact that this is Sunday makes no difference in my habit. I intended going out on the deck and watching the sun rise. I got my friend Glace and invited him to come along. As we were passing this room on the outside promenade a premonition seized me that there was something amiss in this cabin. I lifted my friend up so that he could see into the room. He tells me that the man in the berth is lying there with a dark spot on his night smock, over his heart. As soon as he had seen what was within we called the steward and sent him for you. That brings us up to the present, I think."

"But, good Lord! how could he have been murdered?" exclaimed the purser. "Let's see—a man by the name of Swartzberg—a drummer, I think—had fifty-seven. Have you tried the door? Is it unlocked?"

"I haven't touched it," said Semi Dual.

The purser put out a hand and laid it on the knob, turned it, and sought to press the door inward. It was fast. He stooped and sought to squint into the keyhole, then rose and turned a puzzled face to us. "The key is sticking in the lock," he announced. "Did you notice that?"

"No." Both Dual and I shook our heads.

With a leap the purser caught the edge of the transom and drew himself up. One glance through the glass and he dropped back beside us. "Jake," he cried to the steward, "go get Captain Branning and bring him back here at once. Hurry now. Git!"

The negro scurried away down the deck and left us three standing outside the locked door. A look of unbelieving horror was upon the face of the young purser as he began speaking again. "You gentlemen seem to me right in what you have told me. The man looks like he was dead to me, but I can't imagine how his room could have been entered and yet left locked from the inside. Maybe he committed suicide."

Dual shook his head. "I do not think so," he rejoined.

"Well, as soon as the captain gets here we'll force the door and find out," said Keating, "but if it's murder I can't imagine how it was done."

Dual made no reply. Watching him I once more saw the peculiar narrowing of his lids which went with his deeper consideration of any matter. I knew that his wonderful brain was already reaching out toward some explanation of the thing which had occurred, and how a murder might have been done and the door remain locked. Keating stood frowning at the floor and fidgeting about, now and then glancing at Semi as though half in doubt as to whether to credit his tale of our discovery or not. I don't think one of us spoke further on the matter until Jake came back with the captain, a short, heavy-set, florid complexioned individual, whom we had all seen at table and found a very likable man.

"What's this about a murder in fifty-seven?" he broke forth as soon as he was near enough for ordinary conversation.

"A man has been killed in there," Dual responded. "I said murdered, because somebody killed him. I think that is the correct word."

Branning shot him a quick glance and turned to Keating. "When was this discovered, purser?" he asked.

"The gentlemen here, Mr. Dual and Mr. Glace, say they discovered it some fifteen minutes ago or thereabouts," said Keating. "They called Jake and sent him for me."

"And what, Mr. Dual, attracted your attention to the matter?" Branning asked.

"I was passing and some premonition made me think there was some thing wrong," said Dual. "I have explained to Mr. Keating."

"You didn't hear any sound or anything like that?"

"No."

"You just felt that something was wrong?"

"To tell you the truth, I smelled the man's dead essence," said Dual.

"You what?" Branning started back a step.

"I smelled the odor of death emanating from this room."

Branning shook his head. "Well, then what did you do?"

"Glace and I came and looked over the transom. The man is lying in his berth, dead."

"And the door's locked on the inside," Keating put in.

"Well, then, he committed suicide."

"I don't think so," Dual declared for the second time.

"You don't?" Branning turned directly upon him. "You were the first one to find him, weren't you? And you don't think so. Well—"

Dual lifted his eyes and met those of the captain. After an interval of silence he smiled slightly. The officer's eyes wavered and fell, and he resumed in a different tone:

"Keating, who left this boat during the night?"

"Nobody was supposed to, except an old woman about midnight. I know she did, for I saw her go. She had a room, on the promenade."

"That's right about the old woman, captain," said a voice behind us, and we all turned to see Lafourche, who had come down the passage and was now quite close to us. "I saw her get off mahself," he added as he paused at our side.

He was clothed this morning in a suit of dark gray, verging almost on black, and was wearing a soft felt hat. "Just what is the trouble?" he inquired.

"A man is supposed to have been murdered in this stateroom some time during the night," Branning told him. "If you were up until midnight, Mr. Lafourche, perhaps you may know at what time this man—Swartzberg, I think his name was—retired. He was a big, dark man—"

"Ah know him," Lafourche interrupted. "He was still in the card-room when Ah retired mahself."

"Branning turned to the purser. "Who got on last night, Keating?"

"Only a couple of men, early," said the purser. "They went right to their rooms."

"Well, if he's dead, somebody killed him, unless he *did* commit suicide," said Branning; "and if we didn't drop the murderer anywhere during the night, it looks bad for some one on board."

Dual nodded. "Regardless of that fact, I think that is the proper view of the matter," he remarked.

"Of course. Ef he isn't elsewhere he's here," said Lafourche. "Why don't you go in and see how things look from there, captain? Better find out all we can before the boat wakes up."

Branning nodded. "We'll force the door," he remarked. "By the way, you're up pretty early yourself, Mr. Lafourche."

"Ah was up and down all night," said the creole. "Ah don't know why, but for the life of me Ah couldn't sleep. Ah wandered about the deck half the night."

"Down here?" Branning flashed.

"Down heah, up theah, all around," laughed Lafourche.

"And you heard no outcry?" Branning was eagerness itself.

"Nothing," said the other. "Let's get inside."

Under Branning's direction the steward forced the lock and we entered the room. A glance showed us that it was in wild confusion. The dead man's clothing lay scattered all over the place; the bedclothing was pulled awry and lay half off the berth.

A couple of pigskin suit-cases were open upon the floor and their contents added to the litter of the little apartment. There was every evidence that the place had been thoroughly ransacked.

Keating, after a glance about, opened the shutters, admitting more light. Next he examined the inner ventilating transom. It was securely fastened. He turned back with a shake of his head.

Meanwhile, Branning had approached the berth and given a glance to the body upon it. "He's dead, all right," he announced as he rose from his inspection; "and he's sure been stabbed."

"But how the devil," stammered Keating, "with everything locked up tight?"

Dual had been poking about among the litter of clothing, shirts, collars, neckties, socks, and underwear which covered the bulk of the floor. At Keating's puzzled outburst he straightened and turned to Branning. "Have you any objection to my making an examination of the body?" he inquired. "I have assisted at more than one criminal examination in the past, and have even dabbled in detection a bit."

Gruesome as was the situation, I smiled. Dual's calling his work dabbling certainly held an element of the humorous. However, the others knew nothing of the man's real ability, and after a moment's consideration Branning nodded his head as though half in doubt.

I motioned Keating and drew the key out of the broken lock, carrying it across to near the light from the port in the end of the room. There the purser and I bent above it, and I pointed to two little scratches upon the tip, just beyond the wards.

"There," said I, "is the answer to how your assassin got in and out again. He used a steel clip, such as professional burglars carry, for nipping the keys in locked doors."

Keating whistled. "Gad!" he exclaimed. "I never thought of that!"

Dual, already, working over Swartzberg's body, heard my remark, lifted his head, and smiled. I gave the key to the purser and joined him beside the berth. He had opened the bosom of the man's night clothing, and was now pointing to the line of a cut, some half-inch long, in the flesh of the chest as I came back. It wasn't a large cut, but it had bled considerably for so small a wound.

"He was stabbed, gentlemen," said Dual.

"But what could have inspired such an act? What was the motive?" Branning began.

"There are usually but two motives for such a crime," replied Semi, bending still further over the body of the salesman; "revenge or robbery."

"Or both, perhaps!" exclaimed Keating as he paused.

Dual turned and regarded him with lifted brows.

"There was a young fellow in the card-room had a run-in with this one yesterday morning over a card game," the purser explained. "I understand he says this man cheated him out of fifty, and he offered to bet afterward that he could make him give it back. Sam, the bar steward, told me about it yesterday. Maybe the chap tried it some way and this is what happened."

"Hold on!" exclaimed Branning. "That reminds me of something else. Last night I heard voices outside the pilot-house along between nine and ten, and I looked out to see what was doing. This fellow Swartzberg and a girl with light hair were sitting there against the side wall of the house, and he was showing her something that looked like jewelry to me. I ain't a judge of such things, but he had some sort of stones, and he was letting her look at them. He heard me and shut them up quick in a case. I didn't say anything to him—at the time—just gave them a glance; but it struck me that he had brought the girl up there for a private talk."

"One minute," I interrupted. "Didn't this Swartzberg ask you to have this same girl put beside him at table, Mr. Purser?"

"Yes," said Keating; "he did. By Jove, that's so!"

Looking at Dual, I saw his eyes flash. "What color were these jewels, captain?" he asked.

"Red," said Branning promptly. "I know, because I caught a flash from them as I was looking at the fellow and the girl."

Dual nodded and turned back to his examination of the body, turning Swartzberg's head to one side, and pausing to stare at the junction of the scalp and the skin of the face. Leaning forward, we all saw the discoloration of a long, oval bruise, extending from the side of the face up into the hair.

Semi laid the head back on the pillow and straightened up. "This man was stunned by a blow, probably against the edge of the berth, before he was stabbed," he said. He paused and appeared to consider for a moment.

"Now as to motive," he went on. "If, as Captain Branning says, he was in the possession of a case of red jewels—most probably rubies, at that rate—we should search this room thorough at once."

"And while we're doing it," said Branning to Keating, "you go get that young fellow who had the row with this chap and bring him down here. We'll see what he has to say. Now come on, and let's see what we can find."

Branning, Lafourche, and I set to work ransacking the stateroom. Dual sat down on the berth while we worked.

"What sort of a case did he have the jewels in?" Lafourche inquired.

"Couldn't tell," returned Branning, running his hands through the pockets of the dead man's trousers. "It was too dark. I just happened to catch a flash of red from the things. Ah!" He drew out a handsome gold watch and held it up. "They left his timepiece, anyway."

Meanwhile, I had dug up a roll of bills from a vest-pocket, and these I now showed to the men. At a sign from Dual I handed them to Branning, who placed them with the watch. "If it was theft, the murderer didn't want money, at any rate," he remarked.

We picked up and examined all the man's belongings. We lifted the mattress and examined beneath it. We poked into every corner and crevice of the room, and we found nothing beyond the dead man's wallet, with some more currency in it, a check-book on a New York bank, and some cards and papers which seemed to establish him as a partner in the firm of "Swartzberg & Stein," importers of precious stones.

If he had been in possession of any case of gems of any sort whatever, there was no sign of them now. At last we desisted in the search, and admitted that we had covered the entire list of places possible and impossible where the jewels might have lain. Save for Branning's assertion, the things might never have existed. There was simply no sign.

Dual waited until we had finished and then nodded slightly. "Gentlemen, the motive of this crime appears to have been robbery, either actual or attempted," said he.

CHAPTER IV

FINDING THE RING

"**BUT WHO COULD** have done it?" stammered Branning dazedly. "We have nothing to go on—not a thing. There isn't any clue."

"There is a clue, perhaps—that is, what the average detective would consider as one," said Semi Dual quite calmly. "I haven't examined it closely as yet."

"What do you mean, sir?" Branning hastily inquired. "We haven't found anything that I know of. What is this clue?"

"Something which I found before you began looking," said Dual. "Wait until Keating gets back with this young man and we see how he acts—not that I believe that you will find anything there."

Footsteps came down the deck, and the door opened to admit the purser and young Greer. The boy was wearing a puzzled expression, and as soon as he was inside his eyes swept our faces and darted to the bed. He recognized Swartzberg and started slightly.

"Why, what's the matter?" he began.

"Somebody killed Swartzberg in the night," Branning informed him. "They stabbed him and took a lot of jewels—rubies, we think—which he had on him. We know you had a run-in with him yesterday and offered to bet you could make him shell out."

"My Lord!" Greer turned pale. His eyes sought mine half accusingly, and I knew he was asking himself if I had told Branning and the others of the row in the card-room. "Who told you I made such a bet?" he inquired.

"The bar steward told Keating," said Branning. "We got it straight."

Greer nodded and again glanced at me, this time with an expression of relief. "Is it really murder, Glace?" I nodded my head. "Where were you last night?" asked Branning.

"In the card-room till midnight; asleep after that," said Greer.

"Did you see Swartzberg there?"

"Yes."

"Speak to him?"

"No. He was drinking steadily, and I had no reason to accost him."

"What do you know about him?"

"Nothing. I never saw him until the card game which started the row. I know he was playing crooked, but that's all."

"Ah don't think there is any reason for drawing Mr. Greer into this, captain," Lafourche put in. "Ah was one of the players, and Ah know that he came into our game at my invitation, as we wanted a fourth hand. Ah also believe that his accusation of this man Swartzberg was correct. Ah had been watching his play mahself."

"Did you," said Branning, "speak to Swartzberg after the row?"

"No."

"All right," the captain decided; "you can go back now. I may want to ask you some more questions, but this is all now. Go out quietly, and don't talk about this. It will be discovered soon enough, and we want to do all we can before the passengers grow excited."

"If I can do anything to help—" began Greer.

Branning shook his head. "I'll let you know if you can. Not now."

Greer turned on his heel, gave a last glance to the dead man in the berth, and passed out.

"And now," resumed the captain, "about that clue, Mr. Dual."

Semi was still sitting on the edge of the berth. Now he thrust a hand into his pocket and brought it out closed.

"It may or may not prove important," he began slowly, "but I fancy it may give us a start on discovering the location of the rubies at present. I found it almost at once after we came into the room. It was lying on the floor close by the edge of the berth.

"Looking at the matter calmly, it seems rather odd that it should have been left behind if it really belonged to the one responsible for the murder, because had he lost it during a struggle he would probably have been conscious of so doing, and have made a search for it before he left; but at any rate here it is."

He opened his hand and displayed a *small gold seal-ring!*

For as much as a minute nobody said a word then.

"A woman's ring!" cried Keating and Branning with one voice.

"Manifestly," said Semi Dual. "Maybe it was a part of his jewelry," Branning suggested.

"I hardly think so," returned Semi, "for it is already cut with a monogram—C.I.E."

"That's right," nodded Keating. "But a woman! Do you think a woman would be guilty of this?" He gestured, to the dead man.

"I think a woman may have the rubies at present," said Semi Dual.

"Who is there on the boat with a name to fit those letters?" Branning turned to the purser.

"Wait a moment," I broke in. "What was the name of the girl with wheat-colored hair who got on yesterday between ten and eleven?"

Keating started. "Elwood," he said, after a moment. "Why?"

"Elwood begins with an 'E,' and she wore a seal-ring which looked like this. I noticed it," I explained.

"And Swartzberg had a light-haired woman with him on the hurricane last night."

Branning leaped to his feet. "That settles it. We've got to see this girl and find out what she knows."

"Maybe Swartzberg gave her the rubies last night. Good Lord! Maybe they were accomplices in some deal," exclaimed Lafourche of a sudden.

"Then why the murder?" snapped Branning. "The murderer left everything else."

"One moment, gentlemen," said Semi Dual. "Captain, I believe that you desire to conduct this matter as quietly as possible. We can gain nothing by causing excitement among the boat's company, of course, and the more we can learn before the knowledge of what has happened becomes general the better. Suppose then that we drop this matter until after breakfast, and then if you wish we will go into the matter as affecting this young woman. The boat is just waking up, and to cause any disturbance at this time would bring the whole company about our ears."

Branning considered a moment, and then nodded. "That is a good suggestion," he accepted. "After the breakfast hour we'll interview this girl, and if the ring is hers it's a safe bet that she is mixed up in this crime."

"That would be the obvious conclusion," said Semi Dual, "and now, that being decided, I think Glace had better get his wife and we'll have a bite to eat." He rose. "Come along, Gordon, and we'll join Mrs. Glace."

I saw Keating and Branning glance curiously at him as I rose and prepared to follow, and I smiled. Dual was palpably on their nerves by his nonchalant air. On that Sunday morning of tragedy he was the coolest person of us all. Having just displayed a bit of apparent evidence, warranted to connect a woman with a ghastly crime, he advised delay in following it up and began in the next breath to speak of refreshment in an every-day voice.

He puzzled them as he had puzzled better trained minds than theirs before now, and yet I, who knew him, knew well that his interest in the case was greater than ever.

As I followed him back toward our stateroom I pondered his remarks and wondered what purpose they held. Presently my curiosity found expression in words. "What did you mean by 'obvious conclusion,' Dual?"

"Obvious—plain—on the surface—clearly appearing—apparently the correct conclusion," he flung me as he swung along the deck. "Ordinarily correct unless—too plain, Gordon."

"Then you think—" I began.

"Wait. Time will tell. Get Mrs. Glace and we'll have breakfast," he said.

I went in and found Connie dressing. "Where have you been?" she cried.

I sat down, and while she finished putting on a morning dress I told her briefly all that had transpired. She was, of course, deeply interested and no little excited.

"And they're going to question the girl after breakfast?" she inquired.

I nodded.

"They're going to try and see if she knows anything about this affair," I replied. "I am sure the ring is hers. I saw it on her finger when she clung to my arm at the companionway head yesterday."

"I don't believe she did it, just the same," flared Connie. "That girl never went into that man's room and knocked him unconscious and stabbed and robbed him. Why don't you use your wits, Gordon, instead of trying to implicate a poor child like that?"

"I'm not trying to," I expostulated. "No one has accused her of murder as yet, Connie. We're just following up clues, or rather the only clue we have."

"I'm surprised at Mr. Dual for allowing such a thing," sniffed my wife. "Well, let's get breakfast, and then I'm going to be ready to take care of the child after you men have tortured her."

We went out, joined Semi, and made our way to the dining saloon. The breakfast crowd was there, and Captain Branning was presiding at the head of the table.

But it seemed to me that, despite his attempts to appear affable, there was a suppressed subcurrent of excitement among the passengers already. Branning had told Greer to keep a tight mouth, and from my knowledge of the boy I felt that he had. The steward might have babbled, but surely not to many.

And yet, as we came in and took our places, it seemed to me that I felt the eyes of those already at table pick us up. I didn't like it, either. I'd been in the limelight all along as the husband of my wife—people always spot the bride and groom—and this added focus of eyes did not please me at all.

As for Dual, he might have been at home in the Urania with myself and Henri, for any sign he gave of the exciting events of the morning.

He quietly opened his *serviette,* ordered some fruit and a jug of milk, and began a conversation on the scenery, the industries of the country, and the history of river travels in the past.

I let my eyes wander to the table behind me for the wheat-haired girl. She was not yet in. Then she came, and I studied her face with interest. It was calm, undisturbed, smiling as she walked gracefully to her place.

Certain it was that if she had any guilty knowledge of the past night's horror she was amply able to mask it under her appearance of fresh young innocence.

I even saw her glance at the place beside her as she sat down, as though she expected the dead man to appear at her side.

I glanced back at the head of our table and saw that Branning was watching her every move. Then as a matter of prudence I gave my attention to my food and to Connie, who, I perceived, had been watching the girl as well.

"Well, what do you think now?" she whispered.

"The time for thinking hasn't come yet," I told her.

She set her lips and refused to make any reply to anything else I said.

The breakfast crowd began to thin out. I caught Branning's eye and his almost imperceptible nod. I glanced at Semi, and he also nodded slightly.

Connie was waiting, anyway, and we all rose and went back to the social hall, where Lafourche joined us a few minutes later.

Connie went into the library, saying she would get a book and read for a time, and Greer came up to us men.

"What have you found, out?" he wanted to know.

"Not much, Mr. Greer," said Lafourche. "Mr. Dual here found a ring—a woman's seal ring—which we have reason to think belongs to a young woman this Swartzberg was talking to last night. We are waiting for Mr. Branning, who intends to question her."

"Who was the girl?" asked Greer.

"The blonde with the strikingly light hair. You may have seen her yesterday," I replied.

"What! You don't think she did it?" Greer grinned.

Keating came up just then with Branning in his wake.

Lafourche shook his head. "Swartzberg was a big brute," he remarked. "Ah don't see how a woman could have done him up. She would have to have a lot of nerve and strength."

"Swartzberg was unconscious when stabbed," began Keating.

"Well, he had to be knocked that way, didn't he?" flared Greer.

"But there is the ring," said Branning. "How about that?"

"That is what we are to find out, is it not?" observed Dual, with a smile.

Branning nodded. "If we're going to talk let's get into a more private place than this. We're attracting attention, and there is something I want to tell you before we start. Come into Keating's room."

Followed by the curious eyes of the after breakfast loungers, who had begun to observe the apparent conclave of passengers and ship's officers in the hall, we turned and followed the purser to his room.

He opened the door and we filed in, Greer coming along without any objection being raised by Branning.

We found such seats as we could, and the captain immediately began to speak.

"While we were at breakfast and Miss Elwood was out of her stateroom I ordered Keating to have a stewardess make a careful search of her quarters to see if she might find any sign of the missing rubies. As soon as I came from the table Mr. Keating met me and reported the results. It seems that the stewardess found absolutely no trace of the jewels, but she did find this—"

He reached into a pocket and brought out a scrap of paper which resembled a page torn from an ordinary note-book. This he handed to Semi Dual.

Dual gave it a glance and passed it to me.

It contained what appeared to be a pencil written address and that was all. At the same time I scanned it with a great deal of interest because the address inscribed lengthwise of the page was that of

ABRAHAM SWARTZBERG
Hotel ——, West 27th St.

New York City, N.Y.

I passed it to Lafourche and Greer. "Where did the steward-ess find this?" inquired Dual.

"In the purse of the young woman," Branning replied.

"Some relative of Swartzberg's, it looks like. His name was Isaac," said Greer.

"Anyway, this proves that she knew him," the captain resumed as he took back the piece of paper. "I don't think we can doubt longer that there was something between them or that this Miss Elwood is the woman who was sitting against the pilot-house with him last night when I saw the rubies for the first time. This would also make it appear more certain that the ring you found, Mr. Dual, is really hers."

Lafourche frowned. "Do you suppose that she could have been a confederate of his, captain?"

"Confederate?" repeated Branning. "Why would the man need a confederate, Mr. Lafourche?"

The Creole shrugged. "Ah was thinking of the scene on the hurricane-deck you described," he replied. "Ah, too, saw them sitting there, and so did Glace. Ah watched them for a time, till Glace stumbled on my point of vantage and routed me out."

"Then you, too, saw the rubies?" Branning was somewhat excited.

"Yes. Ah saw him show her something just before Glace strolled up. That was what made me watch them. They seemed to me to be actin' mighty funny, runnin' way up thar to talk about somethin' in almos' a whisper. Ah was yieldin' to a natural love of mystery when Glace came upon me an' spotted me spyin' an' so Ah didn't get to see the end of theah *tête-à-tête*."

"Did you see the jewels, too, Mr. Glace?" Branning inquired.

"No," I told him. "I just saw who the two people were, and I was disgusted at the way the girl had let the man pick up with her."

"But if they knew each other," suggested Keating, "that would put a different light on that."

Branning frowned. "We'll talk to this girl herself and see what she has to say," he remarked. "If she knows anything about the thing we'll try and get at it, and if we can't get on the trail of these infernal stones through her I'll ransack this old scow of a steamer from one end to the other. They can't pull this sort of stuff on my boat and get away with it. If I have to I'll lock the people on board in their rooms and make them submit to a search. The longer I think about it the nastier it seems to me, and if the girl was a pal of this fellow's she's got to come across with anything she knows. We'll get her up to my cabin, where there's more room, and see what we can find out, and the sooner we do it the better, I guess. Keating, you get her and bring her up there quietly."

"Just a minute, captain," interposed Dual. "This is necessarily going to be a very unpleasant ordeal for the young woman, and under the circumstances I wish, unless you would consider it presumption, that you would allow me to suggest a change in your plans."

"Well?" Branning waited.

"Suppose that you have Mr. Keating bring the young lady to the stateroom of my friend Glace. We will have plenty of room there and will be free from all disturbance. Furthermore, I am sure Mrs. Glace will recognize the claim of a fellow member of her own sex upon her sympathies and will be able to make things easier for the other woman during our investigation."

I wondered what Connie would say if she could hear that. She had expressed surprise at Dual's passivity in the girl's behalf, and here was proof of his considering it. I felt sure she would be sorry for having misjudged my friend.

Branning accepted at once. "I'll be glad to accept the suggestion, if Mr. Glace is willing," he replied.

I nodded and rose. "My wife is in the library. I'll go and bring her back do the stateroom," I said, as I turned toward the door.

"Then we'll do that," decided Branning. "Keating, bring Miss Elwood, to suite 'A.'"

Keating departed and I followed him out. I found Connie staring out of a window in the library rather than reading, and she turned as I stopped at her side.

"How is the inquisition going?" she wanted to know.

"The inquisition hasn't started," I retorted, "and you'll see where you were wrong in a minute or two. Dual has just asked that you return with me to our suite. They are going to bring the girl in there, so that she may have the support of another woman's presence during their questioning. That was Semi's own proposal, when the others were for having her up to the captain's cabin."

"Really," said Connie, rising. "Well, I'm awfully glad I misjudged him. He's always seemed so kind and considerate before. I was sitting here wondering what you men were doing to the poor girl. Come on, boy, let's go back."

We went back and entered our stateroom. On the way I noticed Greer and Lafourche entering the door of the cardroom. Evidently we were not to have them at the investigation. Dual came in a moment later with Branning.

Dual glanced at Connie and smiled. "There are times when one is compelled for good reasons to allow events to take their natural course, Mrs. Glace," he remarked. "The most we can do, or ought to do, in fact, is to mitigate the situation without interfering with major issues."

Connie flushed. "I feel sorry for this girl," she began.

Dual smiled his understanding and Branning broke in.

"You understand that as the captain of this boat I have to investigate this crime, an' that I've got to use every clue I can get. I don't want to make trouble for any one, least of all a woman, but I have to do my duty."

"Of course," said Connie. "Maybe I've let my sympathy run away with my judgment. I sometimes do."

Dual turned directly to the captain. "Mr. Branning, will you let me talk to Miss Elwood when she comes in?" he requested.

Branning nodded acquiescence. "I don't mind," he said.

There was a tap on the door and I swung it open. The wheat-haired girl was standing outside. Her face lighted slightly as she saw me. "You are Mr. Glace, aren't you?" she began. "The purser said that the captain was in your room and wished to see me."

"Come in, Miss Elwood," I invited. Semi Dual offered her a seat and she thanked him as she sank into it and looked about the room.

After giving her a moment to settle herself, Dual began to speak. "Miss Elwood, we have asked you here to see if you can help us in clearing up a mystery involving one of the passengers on this boat—"

"A mystery—about a passenger?" repeated the girl. "My, mercy—what do you mean?"

"We will explain," said Semi Dual. "It will be necessary to ask you several questions. First, did you or did you not, when you came aboard this boat, wear a small gold signet ring?"

If anything the girl's wide eyes seemed to widen. As without voluntary thought I saw them glance momentarily toward her left hand, now devoid of any ornamentation whatever. "Why— why do you ask me that?" she stammered.

"Because one was found on this deck this morning," said Semi Dual. "It was thought that it might possibly be yours."

"What was it lak'?" she questioned in turn.

Semi smiled. "You had best answer that," he told her. "One proves ownership by describing the property correctly."

"But why did you think it was my ring?" It seemed to me that a frightened look had crept into her eyes.

"Because," said Semi, "some one saw you wearing it yesterday, and when it was found this morning he recognized it. Did you lose it or give it away?"

"Give it away!" cried Miss Elwood. "Ah don't think I know what yuh mean, suh. Why should Ah give it away?"

"That," said Dual, "is what we are trying to find out. Now another question besides. Did you last night see some jewels, rubies, which a man named Swartzberg had in his possession?"

There was no doubt now about the frightened expression of the woman's eyes. The glance she threw about the parlor was suddenly that of a trapped animal seeking a means of escape.

"Ah—Ah cain't answer that question, suh," she stammered at last.

"Miss Elwood—you must answer that question." Dual's voice had all at once lost its suave note and grown stern, cold, commanding. His eyes, those strangely compelling gray eyes which I had seen arrest the rising hand of a desperate man armed with a revolver, fastened themselves upon the girl's face.

She sat there and gazed back at him, while every drop of blood seemed to drain from her face and lips, leaving her pale and trembling. "Why," she said, in little better than a whisper—"why must Ah answer yuh—why?"

Dual rose and stood before her and put out his hand, took hers, and raised her to her feet. Then while we watched he took the little ring found beside the berth of the man in fifty-seven and slipped it upon her finger, where a reddened groove in the flesh received it as though made for it.

"Because," he said, speaking slowly, "this ring of yours was found this morning in the room of this Swartzberg, where during the night some one had entered. Mr. Swartzberg was found murdered and the rubies were gone."

"Murdered!" The girl wrested her hand from his grasp and started back, gazing with wild terror into his eyes.

"Murdered," said Semi Dual.

"And yuh found mah ring there? No! No! Oh, my God, no!"

With a piercing scream the wheat-haired girl sank fainting into the outstretched grasp of Semi Dual.

CHAPTER V

THE THIRD DEGREE

LIKE A BABY he lifted her up in his strong arms and held her, her head rolling across his arm and her body against his chest.

Then, while we all sat silent, he carried her to the leather-padded divan built into the wall of the parlor and laid her at full length upon its tufted surface.

"And now, Mrs. Glace, if you will examine her clothing while she is still unconscious, it will spare her that added unpleasantness when she rallies. Gordon and the captain and I will turn our backs."

"You want me to search her?" cried Connie. "Really, Mr. Dual."

"If you will be so kind—to her," said Semi. "It is a woman's task."

"Very well." Connie rose and approached the girl's motionless form. "What am I expected to find?"

"A small leather case, I imagine," Dual told her, and walked over to Branning and me.

We turned away from the divan and silence followed. I had seen Connie drop on her knees beside the girl, and I knew that she was at work. None of us spoke as we waited the outcome of the search.

Presently I thought I heard a sound. It was faint, suddenly checked, a mere catching of the breath, from the direction of the divan behind us. Followed another interval of silence and then the voice of my wife, strained, choked, well nigh unrecognizable to me.

"You may turn around now. I have done what you asked, and I suspect that I have found what you wished. Oh, the poor foolish girl!"

She was holding out toward us a flat black case of morocco, which fastened with a clasp. Dual took it as she ceased speaking and fairly tore it open as it seemed to me. Without any words he held it forth so that we could see its contents—a shimmering, flashing, twinkling mass of deep red stones.

He closed the case upon them and handed it to Branning. "There are the ill-fated stones, captain," he said as he did so. "If you will permit me to advise you, guard them well while they are in your possession."

He swung to me. "Gordon, go to the smoking-room and get some brandy. Quickly now, we must break Miss Elwood's shock at once."

I made my way to the lounge as quickly as possible and, getting the bar-steward, ordered a glass of brandy.

As I entered the room I noticed Lafourche and Greer at a little table, the latter smoking a cigar and the former his seemingly perpetual cigarette. While I waited for the steward to get my order I approached and halted beside their table. Greer glanced up at once.

"What did you find out?" he wanted to know.

"The ring was hers," I told him.

"And what did she say?"

"When we told her about Swartzberg's murder she cried out that she didn't do it and fainted. That's why I'm up here after brandy."

"The poor kid," said Greer.

"After she fainted we found the rubies on her," I went on.

"Mon Dieu!" gasped Lafourche. "Really? Well, just the same, Mr. Glace, Ah don't believe that woman ever did for that pig. There's some other explanation."

"It looks bad for her just now, however," I rejoined.

"I don't believe it," said Greer, setting his jaw. "I don't believe that girl would do anything like that. She isn't that kind. She's soft and fluffy like a kitten. She's no adventuress. She'd have to tell me she did it herself before I'd believe it."

"She seems to have two champions at any rate," said I. "I'm afraid the captain will take an opposite view."

Greer sneered. "Yes, and he'd have tried to lay it onto me if the ring hadn't turned up and steered him on another trail. I suppose he's the party who scared her into fainting."

"No," I told him, "that was Dual."

Lafourche nodded. "All the same, it is not only monstrous to suspect a woman of committing that murder, it is foolish as well. So your friend conducted the examination. Odd-looking chap, that fellow. Ah've an idea he doesn't always tell all he knows."

"He's a wonder, in his way. As for telling what he knows, he speaks when he is ready," I returned.

"Well, isn't there something we can do to help the girl?" Greer suggested. "It's a rotten fix for her."

"If any one can help her, my friend Dual will," I told him.

Back in the stateroom the girl still lay, utterly relaxed with closed eyes, upon the divan. Connie was bending over her, loosening her clothing. Dual sat in a chair, but rose as I came in, took the brandy and approached the girl. Raising her head with one hand slightly, he forced the edge of the glass between her teeth.

Very slowly he tilted the glass until a trickle of the contents found its way into her mouth and down her throat. After a moment she choked slightly, struggled and opened her eyes. Dual laid her down, extending the glass backward to me.

"Lie still a moment," he said in the tones of command. "You'll be all right in a minute or two."

She fastened her eyes on his face and held them there for a moment. "What does it mean?" she said with an effort. "Is Mr. Swartzberg dead—who killed him?" She shuddered.

"That," said Dual, "is what I want to talk to you about, when you are strong enough."

"Yes—yes," she murmured. "I will be strong. We must talk—find out. Do you suppose they killed him for the rubies? But, of course, they did. He said"—with an effort she lifted herself up on an arm—"he said they were the heart's blood of a nation. And they were red—red like blood."

"Everything is red in this affair," said Semi Dual. "It has a red aura. Glace, get a pillow or two."

I went into our bedroom and took the pillows out of the berth, returning with them to the parlor. Dual took them from me and speedily arranged them at the girl's back, until she was in a half reclining position.

"Comfortable?" he asked.

She nodded slightly—"Yes."

Dual seated himself on the end of the divan, next her feet, so as to face her. "Now, we must go into this matter, if you are able. I want to ask you some questions, and you must try and answer them. First, I must tell you that we know you had the rubies—"

The girl's hand darted to her body. "You took them!" she cried. "Oh, yuh took them. What did yuh do with them? Oh, please!"

"Captain Branning has them," Dual told her. "Now, don't worry."

"But Ah mustn't lose them," said the woman. "They were a trust. Yuh must give them back. They aren't yours."

"No, they aren't ours, and we want to find out whose they are," said Dual. "You must tell us that."

"Yuh must give them back," she insisted. "They air wuth thousands—a fortune. They represent the hopes of thousands. Yuh had no right to take them. Oh, what shall Ah do!"

"Miss Elwood," said Dual slowly, "the first thing you do must be to regain your control. No one intends taking anything from you unjustly, but whoever killed this man Swartzberg, did so in order to obtain those rubies. We must find out the truth of the affair. Try and trust me to handle the matter and give me what help you can. First, now, what is your given name?" He drew a note-book and prepared to write.

"Catherine," said the girl.

"Spelled with a 'C,' Miss Elwood?"

"Yes."

"Do you know the date of your birth, Miss Elwood?"

I saw an expression of surprise sweep the woman's face. I didn't really wonder, either. It did seem a rather odd way to begin the investigation of the circumstances which involved her. The question seemed almost trivial, viewed in that light. Yet I knew, as she did not, that Dual was gathering the material for one of those abstruse astrological calculations which would show the outcome of this affair, and I felt a sensation of admiration and wonder for the man before me. After a moment the girl replied:

"I was born on the 25th of July, 1893."

Dual wrote this down. "Do you know the hour of the day?"

"I have been told that it was about 3.15 A.M."

"Excellent," said Semi Dual.

I glanced at Branning. He was looking at Dual in amazed incomprehension. I doubt if he had ever even heard of such methods as my peculiar friend used in his efforts at crime detection, and to him all this talk of birthdays and hours must have seemed strangely lacking in bearing upon the case in hand. I knew that before we were done with the matter he would see results if he couldn't understand the methods used.

Then I allowed my eyes to wander to my wife, and I remembered that she had often said she wanted to see Dual engaged upon a case. I wondered how she was enjoying her present opportunity, or if she understood. Her sweet face, however, held nothing it seemed to me save sympathy for the wheat-haired girl who was lying back pale and troubled among the pillows piled behind her. I dropped my introspection and came back to the voice of Dual.

"Did you ever meet this Mr. Swartzberg before yesterday, Miss Elwood?" he was asking.

"No, sir," the girl replied. "I never saw him in my life, until after I came aboard the *Cairo* yesterday morning."

"Didn't even know his name, until he told you?"

"No, sir."

"Then how did you come to engage in conversation with him—to have your chair at table placed beside him—to have his rubies in your possession, Miss Elwood?"

Miss Elwood flushed. "Ah suppose it was not the thing to do," she said slowly, "but yuh see Ah did not know a soul on board, except Mrs. Glace, here, who had spoken to me before luncheon, and she was lying down in the afternoon. This Mr. Swartzberg came into the library where Ah was sitting after luncheon and sat down with a magazine. After a while every one else went out and he asked me if Ah had read a certain article in the magazine he had been reading. He was very polite and courteous in his mannah and Ah answered him. That led to other things, and the first thing Ah knew we were chatting along like old acquaintances, so that after a while, when he suggested that we go outside, Ah said Ah didn't mind, and we went out and sat on the deck. It was then that he suggested that he get my place at the table changed next to his, and just before dinner he told me he had had it arranged. Ah asked him what his occupation was, and he said he was a jeweler and imported a great many diamonds and rubies, and—"

"You told him you loved rubies," Semi remarked.

"How did you know that?"

"They are your talismanic stone, according to ancient belief," explained Semi. "They keep you from harm."

"Ah'm afraid they haven't brought me any luck, nor poor Mr. Swartzberg, either," said Miss Elwood, "although yuh are right about my having said that Ah loved them."

"Don't worry about the explanation," Dual suggested. "Your remark was natural in a person born at the time you were."

Miss Elwood opened her eyes wider. "Yuh are the oddest person," she rejoined. "Ah suppose that Ah ought to be afraid of yuh, but instead Ah feel perfectly safe. Ah feel Ah can trust yuh, and yet yuh seem to be making me do what Ah said I wouldn't."

"Be content to trust me, then, Miss Elwood," said Semi Dual. "And then what happened next?"

"After Ah'd said that about lovin' the rubies he told me the most romantic story Ah've ever heard," resumed Miss Elwood. "It was just lak one reads in books of romance and adventure. He told me that he had a lot of rubies with him an' that he feared that he was in great danger because of them."

"Ah asked him jus' what he meant an' he told me how he came to get th' rubies. He said that there was a very old family in northern Mexico who had had them in their possession evah since the' days of the Spanish settlin' of that country, handin' them down from one generation to another, an' that now this family was a very prominent one in a rebellion against the tyranny of the present government.

"They needed a great deal of money to help them in their desire to throw off the yoke of oppression. So after a gatherin' of the whole family it was decided that they should sell this collection of rubies, and devote the money to buying weapons to arm their soldiers. After they had decided to do this they looked about to find some one who would buy the rubies, an' they finally sent word to Mr. Swartzberg, who was in business with his brother and another man, askin' them if they would buy them.

"Mr. Swartzberg said that he agreed to go to El Paso and meet one of the men of the family an' inspect the jewels, an' he did. He said that he found them to be very fine, and so he told the man he would take them back to New York and sell them for him, and he started to do so. He said he knew it was a rather risky business, and that after he left El Paso he thought he saw a man following him, so he thought that when he got to New Orleans he'd take a steamer and throw them off the track.

"That's how he came to be on the *Cairo*. But just as the boat was leavin' he saw a man on the dock, and he was the same man who had followed him from El Paso, so he feared they had trailed him and put a man he didn't know on the boat to try and steal the rubies from him.

"He said he thought they were agents of the government against which this family was starting a revolution. So he said he was afraid they might get the rubies or kill him, an' then all at once he asked me if Ah wouldn't take them and keep them for him, because if any one got into his room and didn't find them they would think he didn't have them, and it would be all right. He asked me to keep them till we got to St. Louis, and he said if Ah would he'd give me one for mahself. Then we fixed it that Ah should give him mah ring, and if he couldn't come for them he would send that by a messenger to show it was all right, an' if anything happened to him Ah was to send them to an address he wrote down for me on a piece of paper, where he said his brother would get them and sell them the same as he would.

"So after dinner he took me up on the top of the boat where we could be alone. He gave me the rubies, and we came back down here—and that's all."

Dual held out his hand to Branning for the case of rubies, and showed it to the girl. It was a rectangular affair, about six or seven inches long by perhaps three or four inches wide, with some sort of design stamped upon it in tarnished gilt. It was made of soft black leather and fastened by a clasp.

"Is this the case he gave you, Miss Elwood?" Dual asked.

"Yes. At least it looks like the same."

"When did you last see Mr. Swartzberg alive, Miss Elwood?"

"Just after we came down from the deck. He said good night and went into the card-room, and Ah went to my own room and to bed."

"And you knew nothing about anything happening to him this morning?"

"Not until Ah came in here and you told me that he was dead—murdered, you said, and that the rubies were gone. That frightened me dreadfully, though of course Ah knew I had the jewels, but it seemed so awful that they should have killed him, and so—Ah guess—Ah fainted. Ah thought it was so awfully romantic and was going to be such an adventure to tell about when Ah got home, and now—Ah reckon—that—" Suddenly she began to sob convulsively.

Glancing at Semi, I surprised an expression of compassion on his face. To my mind, that look of pity meant that he saw the seeming flimsiness of the girl's story and was grieved that the blow must fall upon her.

I pieced out in my own mind what he had said of the rubies— that they were the woman's talismanic stone. She had said that she loved them. How deep, how primitive, I asked myself, was that love? Was it possible that while she slept her subconscious self had taken possession of her, and that she had risen and sought to possess herself of the rubies? People had killed before this for the possession of jewels, as witnessed by the tragic histories of some of the world's magnificent gems.

Yet the girl was young and beautiful. No wonder that Semi's face fell into lines of sadness as he regarded her sob-shaken form. I glanced at Connie and read the unspoken sympathy in her eyes.

She had risen and gone to the side of the girl, seeking to check her outburst of nervous grief and terror. Gradually under her low-voiced urging Miss Elwood controlled herself, and again sat upon the divan. Not until then did Dual address her again.

"You have friends to whom you are going in St. Louis, Miss Elwood?"

She nodded in mute reply.

"That being the case," Semi said to Branning, "how would it do, captain, to leave the young lady remain in this suite in charge of Mrs. Glace until we can decide what is best? She will be far more comfortable with another woman, and Glace here can bunk on the divan in this room. He has slept in worse places, as I know."

Miss Elwood sat up at the words. "You mean that Ah am to be kept here—that you don't believe me—that you think Ah could have killed him—that Ah'm under arrest!"

"We mean, my dear young lady, that you must not try to leave this steamer until we have found out about this matter, or until we reach St. Louis," Dual told her. "However, I predict that long before we arrive there this matter will be past. Captain Branning, what do you think of my plan?"

"I'd a whole lot rather fix it that way than to keep her in her own room," said Branning. "But it's rather hard on Mrs. Glace."

"I'll be glad to do it," Connie told him quickly. "This little girl needs a friend now if she ever did."

"That's very good of you," said Branning. "We'll let it go like that to-day, then, and to-night."

"That being settled," Dual said, "I suggest that Gordon and I go to luncheon. With your permission, Mrs. Glace, I'll send a waiter to take your orders here."

I felt small appetite at luncheon time. Dual, however, disposed of a cantaloup, some wheaten cakes, a pot of coffee, and some ice-cream. I watched him in utter amazement as he devoured the mixture. He was more of a puzzle to me to-day than ever before, and all the time he seemed strangely preoccupied, as though thinking of two things at once, which was unusual for him. Presently, without having said a half-dozen words, he glanced at me and rose.

We stopped at the stateroom and inquired if any service was needed, and upon being assured that there was nothing we could do Semi drew me to a seat on a divan in the social hall.

Immediately after he began to speak: "It's red, Gordon. The whole thing is red—Swartzberg's aura last night, the spot on his night smock, the rubies themselves, the astral gem of the girl. All red, my friend—the color of violence and tragic intent. Now, where does that lead?"

"I hate to think about the apparent answer," I responded.

Dual raised his eyebrows, then smiled. "She needs the lesson rather badly," he remarked, as though fully apprehending my inmost thoughts. "Still, that is not answering the question. The red color gives the key-note to the whole occurrence, Gordon; and in the ending the affair must come back to its basic theme. It will end red. Doesn't that mean anything to you?"

"Less than nothing, if that be possible," I confessed.

For a moment I thought Dual was inclined to smile at my density. "You have evidently forgotten, then, or failed to apply my sermon on auric light of last evening," he said. "See here! If the key-note is red, the one who killed Swartzberg is either a person with a red aura or one whose aura may easily become so preponderated."

"Admitting that is true, what of it?" I asked.

"The events of to-day, you must admit also, have certainly tended to keep that person's mind fully concentrated upon his act. His thoughts will still be of the murder, necessarily, and of the rubies he didn't get as the price of his crime. His thought-waves and, consequently, his present aura, at least, will be red. Now do you see?"

"I understand what you say," I assented; "but look here! Now that the murder is generally known and talked of, won't practically every person on this boat be thinking more or less of the murder? If the thought of murder gives a red thought-wave, how are you going to pick your assassin out of the rest?"

This time Dual did smile. "Very good, indeed," he rejoined. "But your argument holds the germ of its answer in itself. Are you aware that we think of the act of another with far less concentration than of an act of our own; and that the dynamic strength of a thought-wave depends upon the energy given out as its initial impulse, and, consequently, upon the degree of concentration with which it is generated?"

"That sounds all right," I agreed.

"That *is* all right," said Dual, his smile growing. "Now, if one were able to compare the auras of, say, some dozen people who were thinking of this crime, one with the other, could he or could he not decide which man was the murderer?"

"He could, if he were endowed with the power of sensing auræ at all, I suppose," I replied.

"Or"—Dual offered a counter proposition—"supposing that one had had an opportunity of sensing a certain aura before the murder became generally known, how about it then?"

I leaned forward. "What are you talking about?" I cried.

"The red aura," he said and smiled again.

"Dual," I whispered on edge, my hand gripping his knee—"Dual, what are you concealing from us all in that brain of mystery?"

He shook his head and, reaching into his pocket, drew out his note-book and a pencil. "I have yet some calculations which I wish to make in this matter," he remarked. "They will take me less than an hour if I am not disturbed."

But ere I left him Greer and Lafourche came out of the library and paused beside where we had been sitting.

"We're threading a rather bad channel here," said the creole, "with a lot of bars; and there's any amount of waterfowl about. Greer and I are going to get my fowling-piece, and he's goin' to show me how to shoot. Want to come along?"

"I don't, but Glace does," said Dual without looking up. He bore down hard on his pencil and there came a tiny snap. "There!" he exclaimed in annoyance. "I've broken the point of my pencil. As you were the disturbing element, Mr. Lafourche, lend me your knife."

The creole laughed and complied.

With complete deliberation Semi repointed the lead and handed the knife back. "Thank you," he said. "Now, take Glace away with you and keep him. I have work to do."

Together, we three turned up the stairs to the promenade-deck and left him leading the figures of his abstruse calculations over page after page.

CHAPTER VI

SEMI DUAL'S METHODS

WE GOT LAFOURCHE'S shotgun and made our way up onto the hurricane-deck alongside the pilot-house, from whence we could command a view of the great river.

Branning himself was at the wheel, taking the boat along the uncertain channel with watchful care. The river was spread out over shallow flats and bars, where the waterfowl gathered, and it was these which had caused Greer to suggest the expedition to the top of the boat. He slipped a couple of shells into the breech and let drive at an immense heron which rose slowly and flapped awkwardly away from our course. At the second barrel the bird crumpled up in mid air and dropped slowly back into the brown flood, to be swept away.

"Good shot!" approved Lafourche.

To me it seemed a cruel and useless waste of a harmless life. I used to enjoy trap-shooting, and was fairly good at the clay pigeons. I liked the exhibition of marksmanship, the union of hand and eye involved; but I have never seen the sport in the taking of innocent life.

Greer grinned. "She's a dandy smoke wagon," he remarked, reloading the piece. "Here, Glace; try a shot."

I shook my head. "Thanks," I replied. "Without intending offense, I regard that sort of work as petit murder."

"By Jove," said the youngster, growing serious, "I never thought of that!" Lafourche laughed with a flash of teeth and a very Latin shrug. Branning glanced from the open window of the house. "I feel the same way about it as you do, Mr. Glace," he chipped in. "If the good Lord put them birds here, let 'em live, says I. I warrant your friend Dual feels the same way."

"Of course." I nodded and lighted a cigarette. To tell the truth, I felt that I had spoken with rather poor consideration, even though I felt as I did.

Branning wagged his head. "We're through the worst of this strip," he resumed speaking. "You boys come up here and let's talk. I want to ask you about this friend of yours, Mr. Glace. He impresses both Keating and me as a rather peculiar man."

I smiled as we three went up the few short steps and entered the pilot-house; of the *Cairo*, where Keating was sitting, while Branning stood at the wheel. It was not because of what the captain had said, but because it simply included both him and the purser in the number who had sensed my friend's unusual personality of power, regulated and controlled.

"In what way?" I asked.

Branning shook his head and Keating laughed slightly. "It's rather hard to define," he made reply. "Did you ever hear of the iron hand in the velvet glove, Mr. Glace?"

I smiled more broadly, and he went on:

"That's, in a measure at least, how your friend impresses me. He is courtesy itself, and yet one has the feeling that if he wished to exercise the power he could carry all opposition before him and gain any end he desired. Branning and I have been talking about him. We both have the feeling that he knows more of this matter than he is saying, and far more than either of us or even yourself. Naturally, we are anxious to know just what it is."

I took out my cigarette-case and handed it around, took one myself, and lighted it before I replied: "In a measure, Mr. Keating, both Branning and yourself are correct. I have known Semi Dual for some time, and I have seen him handle more than one puzzling case. More than that, I have never seen him fail to get his man when once he started after him. His methods are peculiar, and he talks only when he is ready; but for your mental ease let me add that I have reason to say he has started after the murderer of Swartzberg, and I fully expect to see him clear the affair up."

"Really?" said Lafourche, puffing out smoke in a cloud. "Barring the girl, Ah don't see that there is th'slightest evidence against any one, an'equally Ah don't believe she ever killed that fellow. As Ah've said all along, it isn't a woman's job. Ah don't know how she got the rubies, but Ah'll risk a bet Swartzberg gave 'em to her."

"That's what she says," I admitted.

"Then thar yuh air," said the Creole, waving his cigarette. "That bein' the case, where does your friend have anything to go on? Ah don't know him lak yuh do, Mr. Glace; but Ah'll lay yuh ten to one yuh see him fail in this."

"You're on," I told him on the instant. "Dollars or cents?"

He grinned, showing his teeth under his short mustache. "Dollahs of co'se, Mr. Glace," he replied.

I produced a ten-dollar bill and handed it to Greer. "Hold the stakes," I requested. "I can use a hundred of Lafourche's money on my wedding-trip."

Lafourche counted out a hundred from a plethoric roll and tossed it to Greer. "Just what does your friend think, now that the money is up?" he inquired.

"He hasn't expressed a definite opinion as yet," I returned.

"He thinks the girl's guilty," declared Branning. "Look at what he did! He practically left her under the guard of Mrs. Glace till we reach St. Louis. He thinks she stole the rubies. That's what I think."

"Is he a detective or an amateur dabbler?" said Keating.

I grinned. "He's both," I answered; "that is, in the sense you mean. He is not a regularly constituted detective, and yet to call him an amateur would seem rather a joke to me. At the risk of exciting your incredulity, gentlemen, I may say that Dual is a modern metaphysician—a student of what are commonly called the 'occult forces.' Back home Smithson, city editor of the paper I used to work on, called him the 'occult detector.'"

Young Greer, who had been busily stowing away the stakes in our wager, glanced up in surprise at my words. "D'ye mean that he goes in for this 'new-thought' business—mind-reading, crystal gazing, and that sort of stuff, Mr. Glace?"

"If you really want an answer, I'll try and explain it as best I can," I returned.

Keating nodded and Branning's face showed interest. La-fourche smiled as one greatly amused, and Greer frowned. "I've got an idea there's something in it," he said.

"To begin with," I commenced, "my friend does not exactly 'go in,' as you put it, for any theory or fad. He is a man who has studied deeply, both the forces of life or nature if you prefer, and men as well. He has conducted his studies along strictly scientific lines, accepting a fact as true only after he has demonstrated its proof. He has proven and convinced me at least of the truth of a great many things commonly regarded as superstitious. The crux of the whole matter is the old proposition of the fourth dimension in natural philosophy. A person perceives only what he can sense. A creature with an eye fixed on an immovable level would recognize only length. If the eye turned side-wise it would sense width as well; if up and down, also length, breadth, and thickness. Men in the concrete perceive only what their development has given them the ability to recognize. Yet there are higher planes of perception, and a man by training himself can develop to a degree where he can recognize the higher laws, which other men of a lesser evolution term supernatural forces. Having reached that point, he finds the supernatural becomes the natural instead."

"Are we to understan' that your frien' is a superman?" said Lafourche.

"I don't know," I told him. "At any rate, he uses these higher laws as naturally as we do the lower ones. What would you say if I told you that at present he is using them in this case?"

"Ah'd be inclined to ask Greer fo' your ten right away," he laughed.

"Maybe, if he can do what you say, that is how he sensed that Swartzberg was dead this morning," Keating cut in. "I thought at first that he was handing me something when he pulled that about intuition, and then all at once I found myself believing him. I've been thinking about that all day."

"That's exactly how he did it, Mr. Keating," I said.

"But he told me he *smelled* it. He called it the essence of death!" Branning exclaimed from beside the wheel.

"He told you the truth, too," I replied. "When a man has developed to Dual's plane he can sense things subjectively as well as objectively, captain, and every objective sense has its counterpart in the subjective plane. When he told me myself that Swartzberg was dead I noticed that he was sniffing the air as though he got something I couldn't find."

"Hound dawgs do that, too," smiled Lafourche. "Is your friend a dawg?"

"Shut up, you skeptic!" laughed Greer. "Say, Glace, does he believe in astrology, too? I've always been interested in that. I don't see why the magnetic waves of the other planets shouldn't affect life on the earth."

I nodded. "Dual says they do," I answered. "I've seen him do some wonderful bits of forecasting from astrological calculations."

"G'wan!" Branning turned, his face broadening into a grin.

Greer took him up at once. "That isn't superstition any longer, you know, captain," he declared. "Science has proved that there is an interchange of magnetic waves between the various planets of the solar universe. I'll bet those old Chaldeans and Egyptians knew a bit more of the truth about some things than we do nowadays, with all our modern wisdom—things we are just beginning to rediscover. Why, Flammarion has shown that there is reason to believe that the whole ether is a sort of photographic plate and that it records every action which anybody performs, and that if we were able to sense them we could review every act ever committed since time began."

"Thank Gawd, we are blind in a sensory way!" grinned Lafourche as Greer finished. "Fo' my part, I can see enough by reviewin' my own misdeeds, without seekin' a world full of ethereal pictures."

Keating nodded slowly. "I don't know about the picture gallery," he began. "This is the first time it's come my way; but as for the effect of the planets, I don't really see why not. Maybe it was the observation of something like that which was responsible for the old custom of planting things in different phases of the moon."

"Exactly," I answered. "I have seen Dual set up a figure concerning a crime many a time."

"What for?" asked Branning.

"To learn the truth," said Semi Dual.

We all turned to face him where he was standing on the top step, just outside the door. He had come up and approached the pilot-house while we were talking, yet so interested had we become in our discussion that we had not noticed until he spoke.

"Come in—come in, Mr. Dual," invited Branning.

Semi nodded and stepped inside the door. "I perceive that my friend Glace has been retailing things of the past," he remarked; "but it is the present and the future which must hold us now."

"Speakin' of the future," began Lafourche, "Glace has been regalin' us with the information that yuh can do a trick of calculatin', usin' the stars as indicators for various qualities, an' get an answer as to what's goin' to happen. Ef that were so, Ah can't see but yuh could put the detectives all out of business. Glace's talk was interestin', but Ah don't subscribe to his faith in it mahself. Sta' gazin' is all right fo' girls an' lovers, but Ah reckon th' man who gets what he goes aftah is the man who acts."

"As a man thinketh, so he is," said Semi Dual.

"That's hardly an answer to mah question," said Lafourche. "Do yuh claim that that sort of thing can be done?"

"You made an assertion as to your beliefs, if I am correct," Dual said slowly. "To answer your last remark: Yes."

"Then why don't yuh do it, an' tell us how this thing is comin' out," challenged the creole. "So fah, all we've accomplished is to cast suspicion on a pore gurl, who never did what it looks like she did, to mah mind. Ef th' stars show how a thing's goin' to end, and who did a certain thing, why don't yuh wait till to-night an' find out?"

For the second time that day Dual turned and stared a man in the eye, in that level, brain-penetrating, soul-searching stare I knew from my first experience with him. "And what if I have already done so, Mr. Lafourche?" he asked.

Lafourche sought to brazen it out, but his dark eyes wavered. "But how could yuh when there are none of th' little stars shinin'?" he laughed in a simulated ease.

"If one knows the planetary positions, one can calculate from that knowledge," Dual said calmly. "It is not necessary to scrutinize the heavens in the majority of instances to-day. Therefore, it is not heedful to wait for to-night, for to-night will have its own toll of events, I predict, though of less serious import than those of the one before."

"And what," persisted the creole, "of the ending of the affair?"

"In the ending," Dual said slowly, "the jewels will return to their rightful owners, and full justice shall be satisfied in an unexpected way."

"Good!" Lafourche began rolling a cigarette. "I suppose yuh have the fateful baubles now, captain, eh?"

"Yes." Branning nodded his head. "I shall turn them over to the authorities when we reach St. Louis, and report the case."

"An' you're goin' to turn th' gurl over too?"

"I have no other course to follow, Mr. Lafourche."

"Unless her innocence were proven, captain."

Greer laughed shortly. "She don't need to prove it with me," he threw in. "Lafourche and I don't agree on astrology, but we are together on the matter of the girl's innocence."

"But gentlemen, one must admit that her story of how she came by the rubies is, to say the least, flimsy," said Branning.

"Just what was it?" Lafourche inquired. "Greer and I haven't heard it yet."

"That's so," said Branning. He began and gave a rapid résumé of the girl's story.

Lafourche and Greer listened with eager interest and a frown gradually grew upon the creole's face. When Branning had finished he gravely considered the tip of his cigarette for some moments and then began to speak.

"Ah don't know as I'd exactly call that flimsy, captain. As Ah judge the matter this Swartzberg was a shrewd sort of coward, an' the story the gurl says he told her was just the sort of tale to impress a romantic creature such as Ah would judge her to be. Fo' my part Ah am inclined to take her story at its face value an' continue to believe in her innocence. Mr. Dual, Ah'll lay you even money the gurl is cleared of suspicion before she leaves the boat."

Greer laughed. "What are you trying to do, Lafourche," he chuckled, "hedge? You just bet Glace that Dual wouldn't clear up the case."

Lafourche shook his head. "That stands too," he answered. "It's mah money talkin'. What do yuh say, Mr. Dual?"

"I never wager," said Dual.

"Against your principles?" Lafourche laughed.

"Against my knowledge, rather," replied Semi. "Nothing happens from chance in this life. Everything is but cause and effect. Mr. Greer, did you get many birds?"

"I got one, and then Glace accused me of petit murder and I desisted," said Greer.

Lafourche picked up his gun. "Well, what are we going to do now?" he queried. "Greer, Ah'll take yuh on at 'coon-can' if you have nothing bettah to do."

"Gotcha," laughed the youth. "I need some of that roll of yours myself."

Lafourche nodded. "Come on and watch mah dealin' closely," he said, grinning.

We four passengers left the pilot-house and went below.

That evening at dinner, by Dual's suggestion, Branning arranged a place at our table for the wheat-haired girl, and we took her in with us. It was well for her that we did so, for aside from our support she was already an outcast among the passengers of the *Cairo*. The details of the murder, which had now leaked out, had become common property, and the fact that the girl was under detention served to cause most of the travelers to regard the woman as already convicted of a heinous crime.

Cold glances of suspicion or curiosity were her portion from most of those at the tables. Some of them, mostly women, even went so far as to make comments in voices which were purposely pitched to reach the girl's ears. More than once as she struggled to eat her dinner I saw tears in the blue eyes which she kept fastened upon her plate.

As soon as we had returned to the social hall, Dual found a steward and had him carry chairs back to the extreme end of the saloon deck, where the rail ended above the great paddle-wheel of the *Cairo*, and place them there in the little square corner where they offered complete seclusion from the annoyance of the passengers.

Thither he led Connie and the girl, and it was then that I noticed for the first time that the steward had placed five chairs. I glanced at Semi as Connie and Miss Elwood took seats and he smiled.

"Suppose you find young Greer and suggest that he make one of our party," he told me. "I fancy Miss Elwood and he will enjoy an hour's conversation."

I grinned and turned back to the card-room, where I found the light-haired youth still chatting with Lafourche. I beckoned him to me and he came at once. "How would you like to meet Miss Elwood?" I asked.

"Bully," said he. "She is a nice little girl, and so far I've been languishing at a distance. What is the answer, Glace?"

"Dual told me to ask you if you'd like to spend an hour with us and the girl on deck," I replied. "He's got chairs back by the wheel, where she can get an hour's air without being stared at by the groups on this boat, and he thought she might enjoy a chat with you."

"Your friend is a man of most wonderful perception," grinned Greer. "I think he's a mind-reader. Come on and take me to the lady fair. I shall try my worst to cheer her up. I am an artist at slinging the optimistic lingo. I shall endeavor to divert her mind from herself to me, which should please us both."

"Come on," I said, laughing; and taking him by the arm I led him back to where the three sat. There I presented him to Miss Elwood, and without hesitation he took the chair next to her and began to chatter of all the inconsequential things in the world. Presently Miss Elwood laughed. That was after about fifteen minutes, by which time the conversation had become practically a dialogue between the two. In ten minutes more I fancy they had completely forgotten that Dual, Connie, or I were among the living, or were but dimly conscious of it.

Connie glanced at me, with her eyes dancing in the twilight. I nodded in answer and looked at Dual. He smiled. " 'Two shall be born the whole wide world apart—' You know the rest of it, my friend, perhaps. It is a beautiful thought, and the best of it is it is true. More; when those two meet let no man seek to in any way interfere with the working of the—law."

I shook with an inward quiver of emotion and let my eyes wander back to the boy and girl. They were sitting very close together, he talking eagerly; she with downcast eyes, a soft color in her cheeks, her hands clasped in her lap. I swung back to Dual. "You knew," I said softly. "Dual, you knew."

He smiled upon me. "He who seeks to read may ofttimes find an answer," he replied.

Night fell, and presently we went in and sought our beds. Greer and the girl came last and parted only at our door. Connie took the girl to our berth and I removed my coat and vest, shoes and collar, and threw myself upon the divan.

Little by little the sounds of the boat died down; but still I lay awake, turning the events of the day in my mind. Some way I was keyed to a tension which defied sleep.

I turned, and tossed, and puzzled over the matter and as much as anything I puzzled over Dual's action in throwing the two young creatures together this evening and then pulling that quotation about twin souls on me.

Suddenly I sat up with a gasp and grinned in self ridicule. There was the answer I was seeking. I was a great detective, I was. With my knowledge of Semi I could not for an instant believe he would have allowed that meeting if he even dreamed that the girl was guilty.

I looked at my watch. It was twelve o'clock. I laid down again and thought it all over. Was it possible, I asked myself, that Swartzberg had really tried to use the girl, as her story would indicate and Lafourche had suggested before he heard her story?

Yet if she were guiltless who in Heaven's name had entered the stateroom of the man during the night before and slain him and left him lying dead behind a locked door? Some one who had sought to rob him of the rubies he carried and had probably discovered too late that they were no longer in his possession—some one who had killed and yet failed to gain what he sought.

One o'clock came while I turned and twisted the facts which I knew, and after a while two. In disgust at my inability to sleep, I arose, slipped on my shoes and coat and went out into the social hall, crossed its deserted floor and made my way to the forward part of the saloon deck, where I leaned against a stanchion and gazed out over the night-shrouded river.

A soft, damp coolness rose to me as the boat forged her way up the river, and I stood and let it play on my brow. Then suddenly a something darted past me, with a soft-sighing flutter like the beat of invisible wings.

I started back in an instinctive movement, paused, and waited a moment, then laughed.

Probably I thought it was only the whir of some night-bird which had almost dashed itself against the front of the boat and fled onward in the dark. It was not until hours later that I knew I had made a mistake.

CHAPTER VII

THE RUBIES VANISH AGAIN

I TURNED BACK to my stateroom and glanced again at my watch. It was two-thirty-five. However, my stroll on deck seemed to have freshened me a bit, and I threw myself back on the divan and fell asleep. It was only an uneasy slumber, however, broken by occasional wakenings, and I rose and again consulted my watch. It now lacked about ten minutes of five.

Utterly disgusted now at my inability to sleep, like a sensible man I gave up the endeavor and dressed myself. Then quite softly I opened the door of the suite and again slipped out into the social hall.

As before, it was totally deserted. Not even the stewards were yet at their cleaning. I passed through it to the library and took a seat where I could see the river, now plainly visible in the rising day. I sat there for some time and then got up.

I was still strangely restless, and I concluded to walk about. I walked back into the hall, and then fate or some such prompting took hold of my wandering feet and guided them down the sweep of the companion-stairs to the main deck.

I passed out to the side, turned, and presently found myself standing at the foot of the swing gangplank on the port side. How long I stood there I really do not know. I know that I watched the water ripple away from the prow of the boat, and after a bit I started and walked to the tip of the deck.

Then, instead of retracing my steps, I continued my course so as to make a complete circuit of the forward deck and return down the starboard rather than the port side.

I had progressed almost to the forward wall of the super-structure, and had decided that I would go back and rouse Semi Dual to keep me company, when I suddenly stopped as though rooted to the deck. My roving eye had caught sight of something which drove every particle of boredom and purposeless straying out of my mind. It lay almost at my feet, close to the wall which rose from the main to the saloon deck above.

In fact, I had almost trodden upon it before I saw it. When I sensed it, after the first momentary pause, I flung myself upon it like a terrier onto a mouse.

In one grasping swoop my hand seized upon it and lifted it for my inspection, and I am sure I gasped. For the thing I had so inadvertently discovered *was a black leather case, somewhat scuffed and soiled, bearing upon one side an armorial design in tarnished gilt, and fastened with a clasp!*

It fell open in my hand as I raised it, and showed an interior lined in age-yellowed white satin, and nothing else. It was empty, and yet I was sure it was the same case I had seen but yesterday filled to overflowing with a scintillating mass of deep-red jewels.

Well, the jewels were gone. That fact was certainly patent to any one, let alone myself, who stood there in stupid amazement, the looted case dangling in my hand.

And then reason and the instincts of the detective reasserted themselves. How had the case come there was the question. Suddenly I remembered the fluttering rush of something before my face hours before. I glanced upward along the side of the decks rising above me and sought to locate the place where I had stood. As near as I could figure, I was almost directly below it now. The case, then, had dropped straight past me and landed on the deck to await later discovery. So much was plain.

But, said my brain, the case was in the hands of the captain last night, and it held the rubies at that time. In that instant curiosity gave place in my mind to fear. I saw several things. First I had stood on the forward part of the saloon-deck. Almost above me in that location was the captain's cabin on the forward starboard side of the promenade.

And the captain had had the rubies last night. Merciful Heavens, had the tragedy of the night before been repeated? Had the captain met the same fate as Swartzberg?

Had the murderer of the Jew, failing to gain what he sought the night before, returned to the quest during the one just past and wrested them from Branning at last?

Having done so, had he sought to toss the case into the river, and had it by some chance struck a stanchion or been deflected by a gust of wind, so that it fell inward and landed upon the deck?

My breath clogged in my chest.

Thrusting the empty case into my pocket, I leaped into action, darting to the companionway and up it two steps at a time, until I stood panting outside the door of the purser's room.

My knuckles fell upon it with a crash and I kept hammering until Keating poked out a scowling face, which changed to surprised question as he saw me standing there.

"Let me in," I told him, and pushed into the room.

"Dress yourself quickly," I went on as he closed the door.

"What—" he began in startled question.

I pulled out the case and held it toward him.

"Do you recognize this?" I burst out. "Do you know where I found it? On the main deck close to the house.

"There's something wrong here, Keating. Branning had this last night, and it was full of rubies. It's empty now."

"My God!"

The purser grew pale and sprang to his clothing, dragging and jerking it over his body in purposeful haste.

"How did you come to find it?" he asked.

I told him.

"Branning had 'em all right last night," he said as I finished. "Do you suppose— Oh, for God's sake, come with me, till we see!"

He flung himself at the door and tore it open. We sprang out and took the stairs to the promenade-deck on the jump, turned and ran along the deck to the captain's cabin, and paused. For an instant Keating looked about, as though nerving himself for what he would see, and laid his hand upon the door.

Like that of Swartzberg twenty-four hours before, it was fast—locked from the inside, its shutter closed.

Keating nodded, as though verifying a suspicion, and dashed his fist against the door in an imperative rapping, paused, and stood while I held my breath.

From within it seemed to me there arose a muffled grunting and whining more like the complaint of an imprisoned animal than any human noise.

Once it came, and again while we stood, then Keating drew back and leaned forward, hurling his shoulder against the door.

It creaked under the blow, then swung inward with a slam as the lock snapped and precipitated the purser into the room. Crowding after, I was on his heels as he staggered to a balance, and we both turned our eyes to the berth.

Captain Branning lay there securely trussed both hand and foot, and apparently without a head. The latter detail, however, proved to be due to the fact that a pillow-case had been drawn over his ruddy features and tied under his chin.

The whining and grunting redoubled upon our entrance, and the figure began contorting itself in a vain effort to rise in the berth. Keating reached his superior and tore the pillow-case from his head so that its staring eyes and cloth-gagged mouth protruded from a ragged collar ripped from the tied edge of the case.

"Captain," he mouthed as he worked to free the night's victim, "my God, but I'm glad to find you living. What happened here, anyway?"

Branning, untied, sat up on the edge of the berth and began wiggling his numbed fingers as if in some doubt of his ability to do so. Keating unfastened the cloth which gagged him and uncorked a torrent of bottled-up rage and explanation.

"It was all mixed up with them damned rubies!" exclaimed the captain. "Them condemned stones are makin' more trouble than I ever had on a run in my life.

"Just let me lay hands on the joker who come after them last night an' I'll make him walk on air by his thumbs, s'welp me! Things are getting to one darn fine state when a captain ain't safe on his own boat, an' locked in his room.

"Here I been lying here for hours, yellin' my head off an' tryin' to kick the back out of the berth, an' not a deaf mute, wooden-headed hand could I raise. Is the *Cairo* a young woman's seminary where every one goes to bed with the chicks, or a river packet? Where you all been? Did he dope the rest of you, or what?"

"Who?" gasped Keating.

"Who?" mimicked Branning, red in the face. "How do you suppose I know who? If I knew, do you suppose I'd be sitting here now? But if he hasn't left the boat I'll know who before I'm a day older, and you can lay to that! Who got off this boat last night?"

"Nobody," said the purser.

"How do you know?" exclaimed Branning with a sneer. "Maybe there was, and maybe there wasn't. You was asleep."

"I can find out, anyway, Mr. Branning," said Keating, almost as though apologizing to the irascible spirit he had set free.

"Later," snapped the captain, and turned to me.

"Hullo, Mr. Glace!" he remarked. "What brought you up here?"

"It was Glace found the empty case on the main deck," Keating explained before I could answer. "He brought it to me, and I was afraid that you might have been—"

"Empty," interrupted Branning, frowning. "Of course it would be empty. The murdering thief who was after them won't take any chances at letting the case lay around; he'll hide them somewhere else. Now we *will* have to turn this old scow inside out. Say, Glace, is Mr. Dual or Lafourche awake?"

"I don't know," I responded. "I've an idea Dual is up. Shall I go get them for you?"

"Yes, if you will. This is all mixed up with them cussed gem stones, so they may as well be in on the deal. Tied me up in my own cabin, darn his hide!"

I made my way to Lafourche's stateroom and rapped on the door. I had to repeat my summons before he replied:

"Hey, thar! What yuh want?"

"Lafourche," I called softly, "get up. Somebody broke into Branning's cabin last night, tied him up, and grabbed the jewels."

"Eh? The devil!" exclaimed the creole. "Wait a minute!"

I heard his feet hit the floor, and a moment later the key grated in the look. He thrust out a tousled head.

"Hello, Glace!" he said, rubbing an eye. "Is that straight— really?"

"Yes," I answered. "He sent me for you. Go up there, will you? I'm after Dual."

He nodded.

"In a jiffy," he assured me.

I found Dual up and dressed, and told him briefly what had happened.

He smiled slightly.

"And you found the case?" he remarked.

"Yes. I think the thief meant to throw it into the river, but it chanced to drop onto the deck instead."

"That," said Semi, "is another obvious conclusion, and I fancy correct. Well, suppose we go up."

We mounted the stairs, and met Lafourche just making his way forward. Together, we three continued and entered the captain's room. Branning had risen from the berth and was vigorously stamping his feet.

"Good morning, gentlemen," he greeted. "I suppose Glace has told you all about it. If anybody had told me it could happen I'd have laughed in his face. Tied up in my own cabin. I'd like to tar and feather the cussed devil who done it before he's hung."

"What happened?" said Semi Dual.

Branning grinned slightly. "I reckon I don't know exactly, but I'm going to find out."

"At least," said Dual, "tell us what you do know. When did the thing happen?"

"I don't just know that, either," growled the captain. "I didn't get a chance to look at my watch."

"I think I can help out on that," I volunteered. As quickly as possible I ran over the incident of my standing on the deck in the night and sensing the case as it dropped in front of my face. "It was just two-thirty-five when I got back to the parlor of our suite."

"Then," judged Dual, "allowing for the time it took the captain's assailant to tie him up, search for and find the jewels, remove them from the case, and decide to throw the latter away, we may judge that the attack was committed certainly between one and two."

"That's about right, too," agreed Branning. "I know it was about that time, anyway, for it seemed to me I'd been asleep a long time when I woke up and found the fellow at my throat."

"That being settled, then, tell us all you remember," prompted Dual.

"All right," said Branning. He sat down on the berth. "I went to bed last night about midnight and fell asleep almost at once, as I always do. Before turning in I took the rubies an' put them into that locker, which, you can see, has been busted open to git them.

"I'm a pretty sound sleeper, an' so I suppose I never heard the thief when he got into the cabin."

"Let's see," grinned Lafourche as he put out a hand and withdrew the key from the lock. "Ah believe the key to Swartz-berg's room showed the marks of a burglar's nipper, didn't it? Well"—he raised the key and scrutinized it closely—"here they air on this one, too!" He held it out.

I took it, and Keating and I bent above it. Sure enough, it showed the tiny scratches where the instrument had gripped its end beyond the ward.

"That's how he got in, then, dodgast him," continued Branning. "As I said, I didn't hear him at all, and the first thing I knew I was dreamin' that I was bein' strangled by a devil-fish. I woke up then and found my dream wasn't all imagination by a long shot. Something had me by the gullet, but I couldn't see what it was because the yaller houn' had pulled a blanket over my face an' was chokin' me through that. I tried to yell, but I couldn't seem to get wind enough to raise so much as a whisper."

"And yet yuh don't look lak a chap it would be easy to stran-gle, cap'n," said Lafourche. "Thet neck of yours ain't exactly what one would call a slendah pillah."

Branning grunted. "When I come to again," he continued, "I couldn't quite figure out what had happened to me. I tried to yell and I found that devil had gagged me. I tried to see and I got next to the fact that he'd tied my head up in a pillow-case. I tried to get my hands up, an' they was fast; ditto my feet.

"Of course, I knew he was after the red stones, and you bet I cussed them, too. Then I begun kickin' the side of the berth and gruntin' in hopes somebody would come to find out what was the matter; but everybody was sleepin' sweetly, an' nobody come.

"After while I reckon I went to sleep again. I know I remember thinkin' I might as well, seein' as I couldn't get nobody to untie me. The next thing I knew, was Keating rappin' on the door an' then bustin' it in."

"At that rate," said Keating, "some one was prowling about the boat from one o'clock till two-thirty last night. Funny nobody saw him—"

"Everybody was sleepin'," growled Branning, and Lafourche laughed.

"You didn't notice anybody when you were up, did you, Glace?" Keating went on.

"Not a soul," I assured him. "Anyway, this lets th' gurl out," Lafourche declared, smiling. "With huh in Glace's berth with Glace's wife, an' Glace on the parloh divan, Ah reckon she didn't find an opportunity for takin' any stroll about the boat nor chokin' ouh wo'thy cap'n."

"You can lay to that!" burst out Branning. "It wasn't no fluffy-headed kid with baby-sized fingers shut off my air!"

Lafourche's smile widened into a grin. Ah'd 'a' won mah bet about th' gurl bein' cleared, Ah reckon, Mr. Dual."

Semi smiled. "You will recall that I refused to take the other end of it, Mr. Lafourche," he replied.

The Creole nodded and shook some tobacco into a paper. "Right," he said. "Ah reckon what yuh said of your knowledge was correct. We were both right. Well, Ah'm glad."

"So am I," declared Branning. "She was a pretty little thing, an' I hated like sin to even think she might have done it."

"Hold on!" interrupted Keating. "Could she have slipped out while Glace was on deck last night? Do you know if she's still in your suite or not, Mr. Glace?"

I shot him a glance. "No, I don't," I retorted. "I didn't disturb the ladies when I got up this morning; but if you think that girl could get out of bed and pull off a stunt like this with my wife on the job you're way off. I left the suite after two, and I was back at two thirty-five.

"Do you suppose that girl could get up, dress, leave the suite, come up here, get into Branning's room, choke him insensible, get the rubies, hide them, and attempt to throw the case away in any half-hour at most? Remember, I didn't sleep until I went back. I was awake all night till then, so she didn't get out while I was there."

"Thar yuh air, Keating," said Lafourche, grinning over his cigarette. "Don't be a blitherin' ass."

"There ain't no question," Branning spoke shortly. "I tell you the girl's out of it, because it was a man. He had fingers like a steel trap, and I hit him. I know the feel of a man's ribs from experience.

"It wasn't no soft bit of a girl that lit on my neck last night. An' if she didn't do this, she didn't do the other. This fellow pulled it the same way he did the night before, only he killed the drummer."

"Then what are we going to do?" inquired Keating. "There's somebody on this boat who has those rubies and goes wandering over the place at night whenever he darned pleases. What gets me is why he don't try to make a sneak now he's got them."

"How do you know he hasn't?" snarled Branning. "Glace had to pound you up."

"I can soon find out," the purser declared with some heat. "I wasn't expectin' the man with the stones to lay down and let somebody—"

"Shut up!" Branning got to his feet. "I'll take charge of this here now. You go find out if any one *did* get off, an' do somethin' 'stead of talkin'. When you find out, tell it to me, an' if he's still aboard I'll get him if I have to tie up to a snag, lock every mother's son aboard in his room, an' go through them one by one."

"Grand," laughed Lafourche, puffing smoke. "Ah'll go order the steward to send something up to mah room to help out mah imprisonment. Also Ah would suggest that while we air settin' heah talkin' we air bein' very un-gallant. Ef we no longer believe that the gurl is guilty we should in all kindness inforhm huh of th' fac'."

"That's right, too, Mr. Lafourche," said Branning. "But I think we will allow Mr. Dual or Mr. Glace to handle that."

"Mr. Lafourche has shown the chivalric impulse in his suggestion," Dual began speaking, for the first time since he had addressed the creole before, "and I am glad that things have so shaped themselves as to remove all shadow from the young woman. In view of what he has said, I shall ask your tolerance for a moment. Yesterday he asked me why I had not set up an astrological figure of this event, and now I will tell him that I did, and that I learned a number of things, important among them being that the girl was devoid of all complicity in the affair. In proof of which I will again recall to his mind the fact that I said I had knowledge."

"Yuh was right," Lafourche noddled; "but ef you knew that, why did yuh let thet pore gurl suffer under an' unjust suspicion?"

"For her *own* good," replied Dual. "Mr. Lafourche and gentlemen, that little woman, as shown by my calculations, reached a great turning-point in her life some forty-eight hours ago.

"Up to now she has led a passive existence. From now on it will be fuller. She needed this lesson in order to teach her some of the dangers which lie along the road of life. She will never forget, and she will be stronger for the experience, painful though it was. It was through this very ordeal that she has met one who will from now on find his destiny linked with hers, through the rest of their mutual lives, so that nothing but a great good shall come to them both from the episode.

"Therefore, having learned all this from my calculations, I stood aside and let her learn her lesson, while at the same time she met that one who will from now on guard her path of life."

Lafourche shook his head. "Greer, Ah suppose," said he. "Your talk of astrology is all too deep for me, though I reckon yuh know what you're talkin' about. Did yuh perhaps learn anythin' about the real perpetrator of the deed?"

Dual paused before he made any reply to the question. To me it seemed that he was plunged into a serious consideration of some detail in the affair. "There is so much good in the worst of us," he said at length, "that at times it grieves one to find it shadowed by an unrevocable and justice-demanding evil."

Lafourche knocked the ashes from his cigarette with a finger. "Meanin'," said he, "that you ar' keepin' your own counsel, which is your privilege, suh. However, barrin' my ignorance of astrology Ah fancy yuh an' Ah agree on a lot of things. For instance, as to that quotation yuh jus' started: 'There is so much good in the worst of us, an' so much bad in th' bes' of us, that it ill behooves any of us to criticize th' res' of us.' That, suh, is largely my philosophy of life."

"In the general sense it is a good one," returned Semi. "However, I will state that I have not as yet completed my investigation, though I will predict that the man who entered Captain Branning's room last night and extracted the jewels from his locker furnished us with the final clue necessary to clearing up the affair."

"You mean that he left something which will tell us who he is?" exclaimed Branning with manifest excitement.

"I think so," said Semi. "Glace, let me see the case you found on the deck."

I took it out of my pocket and handed it to him. He opened it and scanned its lining closely. Presently he drew the magnifying glass he always carried from his pocket and went over the entire inside of the case with its aid. When he had finished he put away the glass, folded up the case and laid it on his knee.

"I was right," he told us calmly. "After a further trifling examination I am positive that I shall be in a position to terminate the entire affair.

CHAPTER VIII

DUAL GOES INTO ACTION

"**YOU MEAN GET** the murderer and find the rubies?" questioned Branning, coming to his feet.

"Exactly, Mr. Branning," said Dual.

"Then you found the clue you was expecting?"

"Yes, of course."

"An' what was it? We all want to know, I reckon."

"That," said Dual, "is what I am going to investigate further. If my examination confirms my belief I shall then be ready to act. In the mean time I will ask you, captain, to take no further steps in the matter until I shall have had another talk with you. I will probably call you all into a final conversation before the matter is settled. For the present I think Glace and I may as well go below." He rose and slipped the case into his pocket.

I got to my feet. "I'm going to tell Greer to get ready to pay me that hundred," I remarked to Lafourche.

He shrugged slightly. "*Ef* Ah lose Ah shall pay, Mr. Glace," he replied, tossing his cigarette out of the door.

By now it was full day and we made our way to the saloon deck at once. Just outside of our suite Dual paused a moment and smiled. "When you see Mrs. Glace and Miss Elwood bid them a very good morning for me," he requested, "and tell your wife that Miss Elwood is freed from all suspicion. She will, in my estimation, be the proper person to break the good news to the younger woman."

I nodded and passed into the parlor. As usual Dual's tact had found the solution of the way to relieve the girl's embarrassment and bring the glad light back to her eyes.

"That you, Gordon?" called Connie as I came in.

"Yes," I returned.

"We've been wondering where you'd gone," she went on, appearing at the door of the parlor. "I'm hungry, and I'm sure Miss Elwood must be, too."

I beckoned her to me. "Come here, little one," I said. She approached and I told her quickly of what had happened in the night and its effect upon Miss Elwood's position. While I talked her eyes lightened and her lips grew into a delighted smile. At the end she turned and fairly bounced back into the bedroom. "Catherine! Catherine dear!" I heard her voice full of glad excitement. "Such good news! Captain Branning was tied up and robbed of those hateful rubies last night and—" The closing door broke off the rest.

I laughed. I wondered if Branning would agree with the exact phase of the matter Connie had expressed, though I knew well enough what she meant. Quite shamelessly I got up and crept across to the bedroom door and listened. The sobs of a woman came to my ear, and I turned away again and sat down as I realized that the wheat-haired girl's terror and grief were being washed away in a flood of tears.

And then the door opened and the two girls, or women if you prefer, came out. If I hadn't heard those sobs I wouldn't have believed Miss Elwood had ever shed a tear in her life. She was radiant. She came across and gave me her hand. "Ah want to thank you for all your kindness, Mr. Glace," said she. "But fo' you and your deah wife, an' Mr. Dual, Ah don't know what I should have done." Then in a very casual voice she went on. "Does Mr. Greer know?"

"Not unless Lafourche has found him and informed him," I told her, and watched her flush a rosy pink.

"He's a deah boy," she said quickly, "and he was awfully nice last night. Actually he made me forget for a time."

Dual came in just then and we went in to breakfast. It was during the meal that Lafourche produced a dramatic episode which I suppose one must ascribe to his Latin blood.

Rising in his place he addressed the assembled passengers: "Ladies and gentlemen, it is with regret that Ah have to declare that a great injustice has been done to one of our numbah, and it is with a pleasure equaling that regret that Ah am able to inform yuh that all cause fo' any suspicion has been removed during the past night. The innocent victim of circumstances who has suffered for a day and a night is now proven beyond all doubt to be what she appears—an honah to the name of pure womanhood." As suddenly as he had risen he sat down.

Catherine Elwood flushed scarlet and dropped her eyes. There followed an outburst of handclapping from the people at the tables who turned toward the girl. Yet a moment later this gave way to a nervous chatter as each turned eyes on his neighbor as though asking where suspicion must next alight.

After breakfast Semi sought the cabin of the purser, and Greer came up with a beaming face to buttonhole me. "What happened?" he asked in an excited whisper. "What was it Lafourche was talking about?"

"Come into the card-room and I'll tell you," I said, smiling, and led him across the social hall to the men's lounge.

We found a little table and sat down, while I rapidly brought his knowledge of the matter up to date. He listened with twinkling eyes as I told my story, leaning forward to catch every word. "I knew it," he said eagerly as I finished. "I was dead sure your friend Dual was with me in believing her innocent when he called me back to talk to her last night."

Lafourche strolled up and caught the last few words of his speech. "Dual, eh?" he remarked as he drew up a seat. "That chap's one of the oddest individuals Ah ever met. Ah'm beginnin' to agree with Glace that he knows more than the average man. Lak' Branning yesterday, Ah'm beginnin' to wondah just what he does know and how he really finds it out."

"You can be sure of this much," I told him; "if Dual says he knows a thing, he does. My friend is not given to idle speech."

"Ah reckon," responded Lafourche "Ah reckon—"

He sat up in his seat and snapped his fingers to the bar steward. "Yuh gentlemen will join me in a glass?"

"I'll try some of Glace's ale," Greer accepted.

"Make it a double," said I.

"Bring me a little Bourbon," directed Lafourche.

He leaned forward upon the table, smiling. "Dual certainly was right in what he said about the girl. Mr. Greer, what would you say ef I told you that he predicted this mornin' that yuh'd mahrry her after while?"

Greer flushed like a girl of sixteen.

"It's scarcely a topic for public conversation, Mr. Lafourche," he said quickly. "That little girl's name has been bandied about sufficiently on this boat. At the same time, between us, I don't mind telling you that personally I would be willing to have that prediction come true."

Lafourche smiled frankly upon him.

"Mr. Greer," he rejoined, "Ah accept your correction without offense. In broaching such a matter in such a place Ah was guilty of a lapse." He extended his hand across the table. "Will you, suh, accept my hand. Yuh are a gentleman, suh. Ah desire to apologize."

The two men clasped hands just as the steward returned with our drinks. "At the same time," resumed Lafourche, "before we finally drop the subject, allow me to say that should the event prove the prophecy, Ah wish to most heartily congratulate yuh an' express my certainty that yuh will make huh happy. Ah drink to th' health of yuh both." He lifted his glass and we three drank the toast.

"Speaking of prophecies," I remarked, "what would you say, Lafourche, if I were to tell you that night before last my friend Dual predicted Swartzberg's death?"

"Eh!" Lafourche, who had been holding the empty whisky glass in his hand, set it down on the table with a crash. "What's that? How do yuh mean predicted his death?"

"He simply stated that Mr. Swartzberg was about to meet his end," I replied.

"*Dieu!*" exclaimed Lafourche. "An' the next mawnin' he subjectively sensed his death. Just how, Mr. Glace, ef you don't mind, did he arrive at his fo'cast of the man's death?"

"There is no reason that I know of," I responded, "why I should not answer that question, Mr. Lafourche. Did you ever hear of auric light?"

"I have," put in Greer.

Lafourche shook his head.

"That is the answer," I continued. "By way of explanation let me say that you have both at times heard the expression, 'personal magnetism,' yet do you know what it really is? Briefly, it is the effect produced upon you by the atmosphere thrown off by a person with whom you happen to come in contact. Not only does each and every person throw off such a personal atmosphere or personal currents, but these emanations may be truly said to be an index to his character as expressed in acts and thoughts. Also these currents have been found to be possessed of various degrees of luminance. It is these lights given off by the personal currents which we mean when we refer to auric lights.

"Various thoughts and acts give different colors to these currents. A man sufficiently sensitive can sense these emanations and perceive their colors. From them he can give a true statement as to the character or health of the person under consideration. Night before last Dual told my wife and myself that because this Swartzberg's aura was pale beyond all proportion to his appearance of health the man must inevitably die."

"Inevitably?" Lafourche questioned, frowning. "Mr. Glace, do yuh think your frien' can really sense these heah lights?"

"Of course he can," exclaimed Greer. "Lots of folks know how to do that, Lafourche."

The creole looked somewhat surprised at this voluntary substantiation of my statement, but made the best of it. Greer's interest in the occult seemed to be sincere.

"Then," said Lafourche, "if a man knew the colors of various thoughts he could literally arrive at an opinion of what a man was thinking about?"

"Most certainly," I concurred. "In fact, Dual told me yesterday that one could pick out the murderer of Swartzberg by observing the color of his auric waves."

"An' that coloah, Mr. Glace, would be what?"

"Red, Mr. Lafourche."

"And would your frien' really risk an accusation on evidence of that sort?"

"Personally he would," I assured him; "but he, as a rule, seeks to support his subjective findings by objective evidence."

Lafourche shuddered slightly. "It's uncanny," he declared with utter seriousness. "Reminds mah of voodoo yarns Ah've heard my nigger mammy tell. Ah think Ah'd better have another drink. Ah am not naturally superstitious, Mr. Glace; but Ah confess your words have given me a distinct shock." Again he snapped his fingers at the steward. "Yuh gentlemen will do me th' honah?"

"A little more ale?" said Greer. I nodded. Lafourche merely waved his hand toward his empty glass.

He rolled a cigarette and lighted it, smoking in a contemplative silence while waiting for the drinks to be brought. Once or twice I thought he was going to resume the conversation, but each time he closed his lips about his cigarette as though having changed his mind. Presently Greer laughed.

"Gad, Lafourche!" he remarked, "what's got into you? You act as though Glace's voodoo yarn had given you the colly wobbles. Buck up!"

"Ah was jus' thinkin'," replied the creole. "Mr. Glace's remarks hold a deep interest fo' me."

"He's not quite so sure he's going to win my ten-spot as he was yesterday," I said lightly.

Lafourche shrugged. "Supposin' that youah frien' does pick his man correctly, as yuh fancy he will, he has yet to find th' rubies' in ordah to finish clearin' up th' case."

"And he'll do it," I predicted. "Why, man, I've seen him take a hair from an unknown murderer's head and the stub of a cigarette which the man had smoked, lie down and place them on his forehead, and rise with a description of the man on his tongue; and later I've seen his description proved correct."

"How could he?" queried Lafourche quickly. "How could any one do a think lak that?"

"By psychometry," I explained. "He subjectively senses the personal vibrations fastened on an object by the person who has possessed it. In a way, it is akin to what Greer said yesterday about the ethereal pictures of past deeds. Nothing is hidden from a man like Dual. I'll warrant you he could take that case which I found this morning and tell you the entire scene through which it last passed. Put Dual in a room where those rubies were hidden and he'd sense them out."

"Really?" There was a subnote of something like grudging credence in the Creole's voice.

"Furthermore," I went on, carried away with my subject, "since the color of thoughts of violence, tragedy, murder, and the like is red, the task of finding the rubies should be easier still, because they themselves harmonize with the basal color scheme of the entire affair. They, too, are red."

"*Dieu!*" The steward came back and served us. Lafourche lifted his glass and drained it at a gulp. "Mr. Glace," he said thickly, "ar' yuh tellin' me true?"

"Absolutely," I assured.

He put down the empty glass, holding it by its brim with a finger and thumb, and began tapping the top of the table with its thickened bottom as he spoke. "Grantin', fo' the sake of argument, that a man's thoughts ar' of varicolored waves, each standin' fo' some mental quality or motive, then Ah reckon Mr.

Dual was merely statin' what he considered a fac' when he said to mah yesterday: 'As a man thinketh, so he is?'"

"Not what he considered a truth," I retorted, "but what is a literal fact. A man who can sense and segregate those luminous waves, as my friend does, can tell exactly *what* a man is. That statement was made a good many hundreds of years ago by One who died a martyr to His love for His fellow man."

Lafourche nodded slowly. "Th' same One who said also: 'Greatah love hath no man than this: that he lay down his life fo' his frien'.'" He paused, and an expression of deep speculation grew upon his features before he went on: "Ah wondah—Ah wondah—how much could be forgiven to a man who, though guilty of some misdeeds in his time, should lose all—even to his life—in seekin' to save some one else?"

His words, his tone, affected me strangely. It seemed an odd sort of question for the handsome, debonair, Southern gentleman to make. Yet I tried to answer it as I some way felt it was asked. "A great deal, I imagine," I told him. "I think, however, that I can better answer your question in the words of my friend than in my own: 'When the lesson of this life shall have been learned, and the soul freed by our so-called death, that station and place in a different plane of existence which it shall occupy is determined by the total balance between the debits and credits, for and against it, on the karmic scroll.'"

The man's dark eyes widened as I was speaking, and he breathed deeply. His lips parted slightly, and as I finished I saw the muscles of his neck contract in a spasmodic gulp. "Ah reckon," he said slowly, relinquishing his hold on the empty glass—"Ah reckon that Ah have failed to properly appreciate Mistah Semi Dual. Ah reckon that pairhaps Ah was speakin' more truly than Ah fancied yesterday aftahnoon when Ah suggested that he might be a supahman. Ah have never given much thought to religion or a futah life. Ah've jus' gone mah own way an' let othahs do th' same. Ah wondah—*is* theah a futah life?"

"I believe so," I said quickly. "Why, Lafourche, do you think any man can learn enough in one life to fulfil the divine purpose of his creation?"

"How about Dual?" he asked.

"He is a very old man," I told him quickly. "Would you believe me if I told you he is several times our age?"

He smiled slightly in a whimsical, quizzical fashion.

"He has learned how to keep himself young," I declared.

"Mah Gawd!" the creole exclaimed of a sudden. "Stop it, Mr. Glace! Yuh ar' fillin' mah mind with th' most remarkable lot of notions. Let us return to ouh other subject. Does your frien' know who the real murderer is?"

"He told me as long ago as yesterday that he did. That is, he gave me to understand as much."

"Yesterday! Then why has he delayed in actin'?" queried Lafourche in visible surprise.

I shook my head. "Dual's actions are apt to be as obscure as the laws he uses in seeking his reason for acting," I answered.

Lafourche forced a smile and sat up to the table. "Come, come!" he remarked. "Heah we ar' sittin' an' talkin' lak a lot of children, scarin' ouahselves with ghos' stories, instead of grown men. Ah for one will believe youah frien' has solved th' mystery when Ah see them rubies produced."

"At least," said I, "you must admit that Dual was right about the girl."

"So were Ah an' Greer," said the Creole, laughing. "Any one who was a judge of human nature would have believed in that li'l' woman. No, Mr. Glace, Ah fancy yuh have not yet proved your case. Ah won't deny that there may be somethin' in these so-called 'occult forces.' Ah don't know enough to criticize, but Ah do not believe that one can reach definitely correct results in a mattah by their use alone. Jus' what is your friend' doin' in this affair now? He spoke of a consultation we were to have latah."

"I don't know what he's doing," I confessed.

"Neither do Ah," said Lafourche and laughed again.

It was then that the figure of Semi Dual appeared in the door of the card-room. He loomed there for a minute, glancing about the room, caught sight of us three at the table, and crossed to our side. "I think," he began as soon as he reached us, "that we are now ready to begin the final closing up of the ruby matter. If you are quite at leisure I wish that you gentlemen would accompany me. I have just sent word to Captain Branning to meet us in ten minutes in the cabin of Mr. Lafourche."

"In my cabin?" questioned the Creole as he turned toward Semi.

"Exactly," returned Dual. "Do you, perhaps, object?"

"Oh, not at all, suh! Certainly not." Lafourche rose.

Greer and I also got to our feet and prepared to follow Dual's lead. The four of us passed out of the card-room and entered the social hall. Connie and Miss Elwood were sitting upon a divan and glanced up as we appeared.

Instantly Lafourche left us and approached the two women, pausing in front of the wheat-haired girl, and began to speak: "Miss Elwood, Ah have not had th' honah of an introduction, but Ah fancy yuh know mah name. Permit me, as a gentleman, to offer mah sincere congratulations upon th' happy outcome of your association in this mos' unpleasant mattah."

Miss Elwood smiled, rose, and put out her hand. "Ah thank you, Mr. Lafourche." She accepted his felicitations. "Ah understan' that you were one of those who refused to believe in mah guilt from th' first. Yuh have a gurl's heartfelt gratitude fo' that."

Lafourche took the little hand, bent, and touched it with his lips. "Ah was determined from th' first that yuh would come to no ha'm," he said softly. "Once more, accept mah congratulations. *Au revoir.*"

The four of us mounted to the promenade-deck and made our way to Lafourche's stateroom. There we sat down and prepared to wait the arrival of the captain. In the mean time we kept up a desultory conversation, in which Semi presently took a part.

"Mr. Lafourche," said he, "when we were on the hurricane-deck last evening I noticed the fowling-piece you brought down. It struck me at the time as being a rather beautiful weapon. I wonder if I might look at it while we wait?"

Lafourche seemed slightly surprised at the request, to judge from his face, but his native courtesy came to the fore.

"Of co'se," he assented, and began to unfasten the leather case which held the gun.

Dual took it in his hands, and turned it this way and that, as though admiring the beauty of workmanship expended upon it, ending quite naturally by breaking the breech and inspecting the twin barrels. A box of shells—so far as I could judge, the same from which Greer and Lafourche had taken ammunition to the upper deck on the previous afternoon—stood in the corner beside the other case containing the Creole's rifle. Suddenly, as though moved by an impulse incited by the black circles of the barrels, Dual leaned down and, selecting two of the cartridges, slid them into the breach of the gun and closed it. For a moment he balanced the weapon upon one hand. "A truly beautiful weapon, Mr. Lafourche," he said. "A French arm, as I surmise?"

"Yes. A present to muh from a frien' of mine ovah thar," Lafourche replied.

"Yet I judge it is hard to get ammunition for it in this country," Dual suggested. "Or do you perhaps reload your own shells?"

Lafourche nodded. "Always," said he.

Dual nodded, still holding the gun lightly balanced. Then, without warning, he threw it to his shoulder, pointed it out of the open door of the stateroom toward the outer sunshine, and pressed his finger to the triggers.

We all awaited the report. Myself, I was utterly surprised at my friend's action. Whatever wonder I may have felt, however, was succeeded by the surprise of the next second. For, instead of the crashing report of both barrels fired at once, there came nothing more than a faint snapping as the hammers went home on the shells.

At that moment Branning came in and glanced about in surprise.

Dual lowered the weapon and again broke the breech. He extracted one of the shells and, holding it in his fingers, turned to Lafourche.

"One would imagine," he remarked quite calmly, "that you have made an error in reloading this particular cartridge, Mr. Lafourche. Apparent you forgot to put in the powder. Suppose we see."

Quite naturally he drew out a penknife and prepared to extract the wad from the shell.

CHAPTER IX

THE HIGHEST COURT

"STOP!"

With the lithe leap of a panther, Lafourche sprang to the door of the stateroom, flung it shut, and turned to face us.

His hand darted under the left breast of his coat and reappeared holding a glistening pearl-mounted revolver, which he trained upon us.

"Stop!" he repeated, all the soft drawl gone from his voice, leaving it hard, cold, and full of menace, like the blue-black barrel of the weapon in his hand. "Don't make a move, any of yuh. Sit still where yuh ar'; an', Mr. Dual, yuh let thet shell alone."

If the boilers of the *Cairo* had suddenly let go I do not believe we would have been more surprised. Branning's face went deadly white, and then as quickly a purple red. Greer's jaw dropped in amazement and then closed with a snap. "What the devil!" he began, and the blue muzzle swung upon him.

"Yuh keep still now, Mr. Greer," commanded Lafourche.

As for myself, I looked into the man's eyes along the barrel of the weapon, and someway I became imbued with the conviction that we were all utterly safe—that he did not intend—did not desire to injure one among us. I turned my head to Semi Dual. He was standing with the cartridge still in his hand, gazing straight at the creole and smiling into his face. A second later he began to speak:

"A very futile action, Mr. Lafourche, though a natural one. Do you imagine, sir, that it will avail you anything to add other lives to your score? Is it not clear to you now that I really meant what I said when I told you I would clear up this affair of the jewels? Cannot you see that I spoke from knowledge rather than supposition? Put up your weapon, Mr. Lafourche."

Lafourche shook his head. "No one can leave this room till Ah am willin'," he declared.

"Remain by the door, then," said Semi Dual.

The creole dropped his hand and rested it upon his hip, still holding the revolver pointed so that it appeared to cover now one, now another, now all. "Yuh ar' quite right, Mr. Dual," he replied, "that Ah do not wish to injure any one of yuh, fo' yuh have all acted lak the gentlemen yuh ar' in this unfortunate affair. At th' same time, a man mus' preserve himself as he may. Ah wish circumstances might have made it possible fo' us to part as frien's, an' Ah certainly regret th' necessity fo' mah swashbucklerin' methods of th' moment."

Dual met his eyes fully as he ceased speaking. "Mr. Lafourche," he returned, "I think you will believe me when I tell you that I know perfectly what I hold in my hand. At the same time let me assure you that I am sure each one of us will carry into our future lives a sincere admiration linked with a profound regret for one who had within him the true instincts of a chivalrous gentleman."

The creole smiled with a lighting of the eyes, a flash of teeth in pleasure. "Ah thank yuh, suh," he said quickly. Then, as if from sudden determination, he continued: "Open that shell, Mr. Dual."

Semi slid the blade of his knife about the wad, lifted it out and tossed it aside, closed his penknife, and put it in his pocket. While we all watched he tipped the cartridge and held it above his hand. *In a glistening, tinkling, scintillating gush of red a stream of rubies fell into his palm!*

Again Lafourche's teeth flashed in a smile. He nodded. "Yes," he remarked as though in answer to a question. "Ah am th' man. Ah killed Swartzberg night befo' last. Ah over-powahed Cap'n Branning las' night an' got the rubies out of his lockah. Ah threw the case into the rivair, as Ah thought. Ah very clevaherly, as Ah imagined, loaded mah cartridges with the stones. Ah should hav' escaped after that, but Ah thought mahself safe."

"You stayed on to be sure that your act had cleared the woman," said Semi.

Lafourche nodded again. "Ah am glad yuh said that, Mr. Dual," he replied. "Ah see yuh understan'. It was mah act placed her undah suspicion in th' firs' place. Ah felt in honah boun' to undo that part of mah work, of co'se."

Semi nodded.

"Ah took a gamblah's chance on makin' mah escape aftah freein' huh, an' now Ah'm merely tryin' to look out for mahself. Ah hope yuh gentlemen uhderstan'. Ah merely intend to keep yuh heah in this room until th' nex' stop, an' then Ah shall leave th' boat. Ah won't do anythin' unpleasant unless some one really insists or forces mah to."

"You will not need the gun," Dual told him. "As to your escaping, I fear you will fail; but I shall ask you to take our pledges that none of us will precipitate any trouble by trying to leave this stateroom until such time as it can no longer interfere with your plans."

Lafourche's eyes lighted and he leaned slightly forward. *"Parole d'honneur?"* he cried.

"Parole d'honneur," returned Semi Dual. "Gentlemen, you agree?"

We nodded our several heads.

"Again Ah thank yuh," said the creole. He slipped his revolver into the holster he wore under his left arm, drew tobacco and papers from his pocket, and began to roll a cigarette.

"And now," continued Dual, "suppose I tell you something about this affair before we part."

"Ah would be delighted," smiled Lafourche.

"To begin with," Semi went on at once, "from the very inception of the matter there was really no reason to think that Miss Elwood was the slayer of Swartzberg. Her ring, however, became a valuable clue in locating the jewels at first. Knowing how the fact of her having them must impress the passengers, I deliberately arranged that she should be taken care of by my friend's wife, Mrs. Glace, until such time as circumstances should clear her of all suspicion. Personally I knew she was not guilty from the first.

"Now as to the crime itself. Yesterday we discussed briefly my means of learning the truth of such matters. I will tell you again that I set up a figure of this affair and sought to learn the truth. One of the first things I learned was that Swartzberg did not come rightfully by the jewels."

Lafourche nodded his head vigorously. "That's right," he said.

"Another thing was that the jewels were not the property of any one in this country. And I will ask you to recall that I predicted that they would be returned to their rightful owners, Mr. Lafourche. I also learned at the same time that you were the murderer, but that you did not originally intend to commit murder. Now let me draw a picture of the affair.

"You watched Swartzberg on the hurricane-deck night before last, and you saw that he had these jewels. But for my friend Glace's stumbling upon you, you would have seen him give them to Miss Elwood, which you did not. Therefore, believing that the man still had them, you went to his stateroom and entered by means of a small instrument commonly used by burglars for the purpose, so constructed that it will seize and turn a key in the lock. You had come on the boat prepared for the act you attempted to perform, and, as I know you are no burglar, I deduce that you were sent to recover the rubies Swartzberg stole.

"You sought for the rubies in the room. Swartzberg awoke. You struggled. You rendered him unconscious and continued your search. You failed to find what you sought. Then, and not until then, did you think of killing the man. But you realized that, having failed and having been seen by him, your mission was a failure unless he was silenced. Therefore, you took your knife and deliberately stabbed him through the heart. Such was the story my calculations showed me, but I found material proof as well. Yesterday you will remember that I borrowed your knife to sharpen my pencil. I did so from purpose, and while I whittled the wood to a point I examined the knife. Mr. Lafourche, you thought you had cleaned the weapon thoroughly, no doubt; but, despite your precautions, deep in the socket, where the blade fits into the haft, *you overlooked a shred of blood!*"

"Mon Dieu!" The Creole's teeth gritted between his back curled lips. With an effort he controlled himself and shrugged. "The criminal's usual slip," he said. "So that was how yuh spotted me, suh?"

"That was not how I spotted you," Dual responded. "As I have told you, I selected you from the others by my own means. The knife was only material evidence which corroborated my own findings."

"Jus' how did you selec' mah?" asked Lafourche.

"By your aura at first," said Semi Dual.

The creole nodded. "Glace said so, but I wouldn't believe him," he admitted. "Ah didn't want to, Ah guess."

"Yet that was the way," Dual affirmed. "One who can sense them finds thoughts a valuable aid to detection. Each thought has its color. The thought of murder is red. After you had committed your unpremeditated crime you thought and thought about it and of the rubies, which are red as well. Yesterday morning, when you forced yourself to return to the scene of your action and pose as one mystified, you were thinking deeply of your position and your action. At that time, Mr. Lafourche, your aura—was red."

"Gawd knows it ought to hav' been," said the Creole—"red as blood an' black as despair. Ah killed because Ah thought Ah had to, Mr. Dual."

"Yet you killed," Semi repeated. "That is irrevocable, despite both your and my regret. Now as to the finding of the jewels. You will recall that this morning I told you the one who took them from the captain's cabin last night had left the final clue. In that I was right. Inside the empty case, against the white lining, I found a blackened smudge, as though a soot-stained finger had smeared the satin. Only the spot was not of soot, but of the *fine dust of powder!*

"Mr. Lafourche, I knew you had slain the man in stateroom 57. I knew you carried firearms with you. I knew from my friend Glace that you had said you reloaded your shells, a thing you yourself admitted to me a short time ago. Was it not easy then, to perceive that one of a clever mind might think of unloading the cartridges and refilling them with a fortune in rubies? But for the chance which deflected the case you meant to throw into the river I might not have found them so soon. And yet, as I told you yesterday afternoon, nothing happens from chance, so that in reality it was the working out of influences few of us understand which made the case fall on the deck, and point the way to your hiding-place for the jewels."

Lafourche eyed his cigarette for a full minute after Dual paused, then: "Yuh ar' right in every particular, Mr. Dual," he declared. "Ah don't want to bore yuh folks, but Ah'd lak to tell mah side of th' story while we ar' waitin' to say good-by," he smiled.

"Ah ain't a common, moral degenerate killah," he went on, "an' Ah want yuh all to know why Ah am guilty of takin' life. Th' story goes back a good ways. Firs' Ah must tell yuh that Ah am a secret agent fo' a group of people in a nation to th' south of us. These people ar' what ar' known as revolutionists, Ah suppose.

"Sometime ago they desired to raise funds to buy ahrms an' ammunition fo' their followers. They decided to sell a collection of famous stones, sacrificed to their cause by one of their numbah. In ordah to do this they entered into correspondence with agents in New York, who arranged with the firm of this Swartzberg to send a representative to El Paso to meet a delegation of the revolutionary party an', if as represented, buy these jewels.

"That was how it was done. The delegation crossed th' Rio Grande to El Paso, and with them they brought the rubies. They met this Mr. Swartzberg, an' he declared the gems to be all he desired. The money was jus' about to pass when a rap came on th' door an' a demand was made to open to representatives of the United States government. The newcomahs claimed to be customs men, an' promptly confiscated the rubies and smuggled goods, tellin' the membahs of the delegation that they mus' come to the custom-house to redeem them by payin' the duty. The delegation lef' after Swartzberg had promised to wait their return. At the custom-house, howevah, they learned that nothin' was known of the stones. They rushed back to the hotel where Swartzberg was stoppin'. He was gone. They learned further that a train had just lef' fo' the East. They then realized that they were victims of the old fake police-raid game, worked with phoney customs men. They could not pursue at once on a train, so they wired to me at New Orleans.

"Ah went to the depot, identified Swartzberg, and shadowed him. A few hours later one of the delegation arrived. We both kept Swartzberg under surveillance till he took the boat, an' as he didn't know me Ah was th' one who came with him to get back th' jewels.

"So that yuh see th' story he told the li'l' gurl was really ouh side of the case, an' excited her love of the romantic an' adventure. When Ah had searched his room an' could not find the rubies, as Mr. Dual says, Ah realized that Swartzberg had seen me an' that mah mission would fail unless Ah killed the cold-blooded thief. Ah did it, though it was mighty unpleasant. The rest of the affair, Ah reckon, yuh know."

He paused, and then suddenly he smiled again. "Swartzberg promised the li'l' gurl a ruby," he remarked. "Mr. Dual, pick out one of those in your hand an' give it to huh with mah compliments."

A rap fell crashing upon the door. With an oath Lafourche came instantly alert. His eyes swept the room in sudden suspicion. "What's that?" he rasped.

I glanced at Dual in that moment of tension, and I knew that it was the end. He was gazing at the startled creole with a face full of a vain regret. "That, Mr. Lafourche," he said in answer, "is Mr. Keating and some of the deck-hands. I instructed him to come here at this time if we had not yet come down."

For a moment Lafourche seemed to stagger. He paled slightly and his hands clenched. Yet it was for only a second that he wavered. By a superb effort he regained his control. "*Kismet!*" he said, shrugging. "You are right again, Mr. Dual. Tell 'em to wait."

"Wait a minute, Keating!" called Branning before Dual could speak.

Lafourche nodded to the captain. "Thank yuh," he said.

He drew himself up very straight and slender and gazed about the little room, and he smiled. "Mr. Greer," he began, "the othah day Ah had occasion to criticize your ability as a losah. Ah fancy that now th' tables ar' turned an' yuh can judge of mine. Ef I remember rightly Ah owe Mr. Glace one hundred dollahs. Will you kindly pay it to him?"

His hand darted to his coat. There was a muffled report. Lafourche's face twitched, yet he still stood tall and slender and very straight. "Gentle—men, *au revoir*," he gasped of a sudden, folded together, and sank prone upon his face.

In a leap Greer and I reached him, but Dual shook his head, even as we turned him over. "Too late!" he said.

He crossed and unlocked the door, upon which Keating was beating a frantic tattoo, and set it wide so that the light streamed in upon the still, upturned face.

"Come in, Keating," he directed. "Mr. Lafourche has taken his case to a higher court than any made by man."

ABOUT THE AUTHOR: DR. J.U. GIESY

BORN NEAR CHILLICOTHE, Ohio, August 6, 1877. That makes me a Buckeye, and some people have suggested that I was a nut. Of my actual birth I have no recollection. So this is mere hearsay evidence. When I was eight months of age my parents removed to southeastern Kansas and took me with them, as I was still unable to shift for myself.

When I was thirteen we again removed to Utah, where I received my common school education in common with other youngsters of a similar age. In 1805, I entered the Starling Medical College, Columbus, Ohio, and received my medical degree from that institution in 1898.

Returning to Salt Lake I served an interneship in a local hospital and have practiced medicine in that city ever since, with the exception of the time I spent in the United States service during the World War as a captain in the Medical Corps. As regards the Army I am still a major in the Reserve, attached to the Division Surgeon's Office of the 104th Division. In 1916 I was instrumental in organizing the first Plattsburg camp ever held in the State, starting the movement and acting as secretary of the general committee which put it over.

I began to write in 1910. Unlike many well known writers, I have had rejections since. At the same time I've found a lot of editors who liked my work. I have written as an avocation ever since. At present I am associate editor for Utah on the staff of *California and Western Medicine*, and the staff of the *Archives of Physical Therapy X-Ray and Radium.* Because of the latter fact I am a member of the American Medical Editors Association.

I am also a member of the Salt Lake Chamber of Commerce, and a life member of the American College of Physical Therapy, which I have served as an officer for several years. My ancestors made me a Son of the American Revolution, and I have made myself more or less of a nuisance to a lot of people all by myself.

J.U. Giesy

I was married in San Francisco, to Juliet Galena Conwell, in December, 1904, and the marriage took. Personally I think they did better work along those lines, that long ago. Anyway we're still living in the same apartment, with no intentions of divorce.

Just why the editor should want to print this confession I really can't imagine. But that's his business. He's asked for it and here it is!

ABOUT THE AUTHOR:
JUNIUS B. SMITH

I WAS BORN at Salt Lake City, Utah, September 29, 1883, at approximately 3:55:27 P.M., right ascension of the mid-heaven (for the benefit of my astrological readers) 16 hrs. 27 min. 57 sec., or 246° 59' 15"; position of planets, Neptune 20° 45' ret. Taurus, Saturn 10° 6' ret. Gemini, Mars 22° 10' Cancer, Jupiter 0° 26' Leo, Moon 22° 24' Virgo, Uranus 24° 34' Virgo, Sun 6° 27' 23" Libra, Venus 8° 52' Libra, Mercury 20° 31' ret. Libra. Declinations: Sun 2° 34' south, Moon 0° 7' south, Neptune 16° 13' north, Uranus 2° 50' north, Saturn 20° 2' north, Jupiter 20° 18' north, Mars 22° 25' north, Venus 2° 20' south, Mercury 11° 17' south.

With this meager astronomical data, the astrologians will know more about me than I could write in a volume.

For the benefit of you other readers:

I am an attorney at law and practiced for many years, paying my office expenses in the lean years by writing. I never had the bitter experience of having to write years before anything sold. At the beginning of my writing career, Dr. J.U. Giesy and I joined intellectual forces, and our first joint effort was submitted to *Argosy* way back in 1911. It sold, first time out. Rapidly we "dashed" off more and they sold also. We each write separately as well as jointly, at such times as we cannot get together.

Early in life I took up astrology as a hobby and lived to see it recognized in judicial decisions as a science. That I have

helped, in some measure, to
brush away the misconcep-
tions in the minds of many
people regarding this much
maligned subject is perhaps
testified to by my election
to Fellowship in the American Academy of Astrolo-
gians, an organization that
one can't get into for the
asking.

I've wasted enough time
playing checkers to have
built one of the Egyptian
pyramids single-handed.
Another hobby is short-
hand, which has fascinated
me for thirty years. I understand several systems. I can
sling a wicked toe on the

Junius B. Smith

dance floor, but only dance when my weight crowds two
hundred. One year I spent the summer on the desert drying
out, where my own cooking, plus the heat, effected a material
reduction. But I come honestly by it: my father weighed two
hundred and sixty in athletic condition—three hundred when
not.

And speaking of ancestors: My grandfather was a brother
of Joseph Smith, who founded the Mormon Church, which
probably explains why I was born in Utah.